Keep This _____ _____ting

- FRANK Tol

THE ANGRY
BUDDHIST

Seth Greenland

THE ANGRY BUDDHIST

Europa
editions

Europa Editions
214 West 29th Street
New York, N.Y. 10001
www.europaeditions.com
info@europaeditions.com

Library of Congress Cataloging in Publication Data is available
ISBN 978-1-60945-068-7

Greenland, Seth
The Angry Buddhist

Book design by Emanuele Ragnisco
www.mekkanografici.com

Prepress by Grafica Punto Print – Rome

Printed in the USA

To the memory of my father

CONTENTS

THE ANGRY
BUDDHIST

PROLOGUE

Everyone knows that when a certain kind of single American female on a Mexican holiday drinks too much tequila she will get a tattoo. And when she is in a sybaritic seaside town like Puerto Vallarta with a girlfriend, they will get matching ones. The women in question were an attractive pair. They had fallen into the sensual thrall of Mexico for nearly a week and into the sensual thrall of each other's arms whenever the door closed behind them in their cliff top hotel just north of a curving, white sand beach ringed by gentle green hills. They were visiting from the dry precincts of the Mojave Desert in Southern California and the aromatic salt breezes wafting in off the Pacific Ocean released the gossamer ribbons binding all of their *gringa* inhibitions.

The single woman, lithe, alluring and in her early twenties, and her married lover, two decades older but no less attractive, had spent the warm early December days playing tennis, tanning beneath deferential palms, splashing in the turquoise waters, and chasing the flavorful local seafood with endless pitchers of margaritas, each night at a different local bar that catered to the crowds of well-to-do tourists who flocked to these shores each winter. And every evening, pleasantly buzzed, they would stroll back to their hotel, past Tango Tattoo, a raffish place nestled between a florist and a souvenir shop, which displayed a sign in English that read *Your Design or Ours*. The drawings offered by the artisans at Tango drew inspiration from the locale and featured a variety of mythological, architectural, and religious motifs borrowed from indigenous culture. Mayan, Incan and Aztec creatures vied for space on the tattoo parlor walls with, skulls, serpents and saints, Day of the Dead-inspired designs proliferated alongside popular cartoon characters and flowers of such vivid reds and yellows, they seemed to emit a scent.

Intoxicated by the combination of anonymity and alcohol, the women would dare each other to step inside and each time they would laugh and keep walking. But this was their last night before they would take the plane back to Los Angeles, the connecting flight to Palm Springs, and car rides back to their separate lives. The holiday had been a lark, taken at the behest of the single woman and paid for by the married one, whose husband thought she was deserving of a break with a girlfriend and remained unaware of his wife's Sapphic proclivities. Their revels now were ending and this finality lent a sense of portent not evident in the course of the previous week. The married woman was not happily married and this splash of freedom had been mitigated by her knowledge of its impermanence. She was going to be returning to her family the next day; running off with another woman, making the kind of drastic change that most people never even contemplate, was simply not in her character. But the thought of commemorating this week of liberty with nothing more than some photographs to be stared at forlornly, accompanied by the sounds of her husband's snoring, nearly made the wedded woman weep.

For the unmarried, a tattoo acquired on a Mexican holiday requires no explanation. A married person vacationing without their spouse has no such luxury. Upon the return home, there will be an unavoidable moment of reckoning when the human canvas can only hope that the body art will find favor. So credit her for crossing the threshold of the tattoo parlor, where she hesitated, second-guessing her impulse until her lover suggested that they get matching tattoos. If I get one, the younger woman had asked, will you? If I pull up my white linen skirt and let this tattoo artist do his magic, won't you? Whether it was the week of sunlight and salt air, the aroma of tanning butter mixed with Chanel No.5, or the sense memory of her companion's dexterously probing tongue as they lay naked and entwined, she could never be certain, but when the needle whirred and the point pressed against her skin with just enough pressure to delicately break the surface the married woman knew that whatever happened between the two, for better or worse, they would be forever linked.

The wife and mother chose a manga design of a kitten. Because who, really, would object to that? And not on her supple bicep, the top of her breast, the base of her spine or any of the other places popular for the flaunting of body art but, rather, because she was nothing if not discreet, on her left buttock where no one save her spouse would ever see it.

Later that night, in the aftermath of having their bottoms painfully and repeatedly pierced and stained, the lovemaking was a little more physically uncomfortable than usual and they both woke up sore, with terrific hangovers and varying degrees of remorse. If the youthful instigator of the tattoo caper had hoped the inking would bond the two women, this supposition was quickly deflated by the emotional distance of her companion who was out of bed, showered, packed and waiting in the lobby within half an hour of waking. The older woman didn't want to talk about what they'd done and when the younger woman tried to joke about it, suggesting they come back next year to get matching ones on their opposite cheeks, her friend didn't smile.

They rode in silence to the airport and on the flight to Los Angeles the older woman compulsively scrolled through digital editions of newspapers and magazines on an electronic reading device, unable to settle on anything for more than a few minutes, while the younger one listened to personal affirmations on an iPod.

They made awkward conversation in the departure lounge at LAX and on the short flight to Palm Springs, the older woman pretended to sleep. On the sidewalk in front of the terminal the younger woman tried to kiss her lover lightly on the lips but the older one, still slightly hung over and in residual pain from the needle, turned her head and they managed only a desultory brushing of ears and hair. Then they took separate taxis home, one to a complicated marriage, an oft-absent husband, and a child who gave her little comfort; the other to an empty house.

Their reunion would not be a happy one.

MONDAY, OCTOBER 29

CHAPTER ONE

I n the desert the sun is an anarchist. Molecules madly dance beneath the relentless glare. Unity gives way to chaos. And every day, people lose their minds.

But you wouldn't know this in Palm Springs, California. A hundred years ago a wasteland, home of the Cahuilla Indian tribe and a handful of white settlers who had relocated to this desolate outpost from points east. Today a golden oasis drawing privileged tourists from cooler climates in search of sunshine, clean air, and a place apart from the rest of the world. In air-conditioned cars they cruise exclusive neighborhoods gaping at perfectly restored mid-century modern homes that cling to the inhospitable land. The verdant lawns are neat as graves. The streets are quiet as Heaven. You would think nothing ever happens here.

You would be wrong.

On a heat-blasted afternoon in late October Jimmy Ray Duke positions himself to the side of a political rally in the Save-Mart parking lot just off the Sonny Bono Memorial Highway. Average build, dressed down in a loose black tee shirt, green cargo pants, and running shoes. Behind dark sunglasses his bloodshot eyes regard Harding Marvin, Police Chief of nearby Desert Hot Springs, who stands gun barrel straight on a riser that makes his six-foot four, two hundred and forty pound frame appear even more imposing. Shaved head looming over a dress blue uniform, Marvin, known to one and all as Hard, is energized as he steps to the microphone in front of nearly a hundred people. Jimmy has listened to Hard speak innumerable times because he used to work for him.

"Election Day is one week from tomorrow," Hard booms, perspiration running in rivulets down the side of his broad face. "And on that day we're going send some new blood to the United States House of Representatives. We're going to send a message to the elites that the same old same old doesn't cut it any more. We got the other side running scared now. Well, they can run . . . " He waits a moment for the expected cheer that materializes on cue. Jimmy watches as Hard lets it caress him like the supple hands of a Thai masseuse. The Chief concludes with the inevitable words about the opposition's inability to conceal their whereabouts. The appetite for recycled hokum at political rallies being bottomless, the cheer momentarily reignites, before Hard proclaims, "This is someone who supports a strong defense, supports a strong dollar— and as a law enforcement officer this is particularly important to me—she is a supporter of the death penalty." The crowd loves this and another cheer blooms then subsides back into percolating anticipation. "It's a great pleasure to introduce a gal who is gonna kick butt from here to the other side of this great country. Ladies and gentlemen, she's hell in high heels"—more shouts and whoops. This is an image they love, hell, fancy shoes, the cloak of religion pierced with stilettos neatly summing up the exploitable duality. Then: "Give it up for Mary Swain." Hard steps back with a flourish and leads the applause.

She glides to the microphone and Jimmy notes the burnished skin, the blinding smile, the five hundred dollars worth of blond highlights, fitted red blouse set off against the matching white linen skirt and jacket that wrap her like cellophane. Then he envisions her without any of it. Which he knows is the whole idea.

Mary Swain thanks Chief Marvin then turns to the crowd and says, "What a great day in the American desert."

Signs wave adorned with her name, cell phones are held skyward, people taking pictures. Jimmy wonders how any sane person could come out to hear a politician talk on this scorching afternoon. Breathes deeply, tries to relax. He has been attempting to meditate lately and to this end has been struggling through books about Buddhism. Exhausted from another bad night's sleep, he's here for a reason: to practice seeing life clearly without an emotional charge on his way to liberation from suffering.

Jimmy watches the show for the next twenty minutes as Mary Swain performs with a mixture of stories, jokes, and fire, pulling, tweaking, and working the crowd into a supine mass of quivering optimism. Her voice is friendly, homespun. It invites you in, asks you to sit down and pours you a cup of coffee. It confides in you, says you and I are friends. It says you, the voter, have an ally as beautiful and shapely as I and together we will share the bounty with which God has gifted us. She learned this flimflam from her husband, a master of the high-end grift. Shad Swain became rich selling sub prime mortgages to bad loan risks then bailed before the con imploded. They met ten years ago when Mary was working as a stewardess on his Gulfstream 6 and now have four photogenic children.

My opponent went to Washington and forgot about you, the people who sent him. After I win, we can all forget him, but I won't forget you, the real Americans!

The real Americans? What is that supposed to mean? Jimmy doesn't care for Mary Swain's brand of sexed-up palaver and he's as real as any American. But the crowd devours the red meat, communes with Mary, and then in lieu of a cigarette they rhythmically chant: ma-RY, ma-RY, ma-RY while her gleaming smile widens. The candidate, lustrous chestnut mane tumbling over broad shoulders, downshifts to a crinkly grin, satisfied and sure. She's saying "We will take this fight to the heart of the beast" and they're devouring it, the *we*, the *fight*, the *beast*, each element of the rhetoric bringing them along with this avatar and her promise of power and release.

Jimmy sees Mary Swain gazing out over the undulating mass of citizens; the white faces, the brown ones, all of them full-throated despite the afternoon heat thrusting from the blacktop like a death ray, and hears the call for renewal, prosperity, and faith. Mary Swain is magnetic, a natural performer and Jimmy catches himself enjoying her act. He knows she is just a politician selling the usual swill, but it's hard to take your eyes off this woman. He marvels at the cool appearance. His armpits are moist with perspiration but Mary Swain looks dry as the desert air. Her bearing is a runner's, erect, shoulders back, chin pointed toward the future. And her legs. Jimmy has never seen legs like that on a politician. Her hemline stops several inches above her knees, the better to highlight supple calves that curve into a pair of red pumps. Jimmy figures Mary Swain's a little younger than he, late thirties, but spas, trainers, and botox lop ten years off. She looks more like a character in a video game than a candidate for the United States House of Representatives.

Jimmy observes Arnaldo Escovedo, slicked back black hair and reflector sunglasses, walking toward him. A middleweight Golden Gloves fighter twenty years ago and now a police detective on the Desert Hot Springs force, the man still moves lightly on the balls of his feet. They exchange a collegial nod. "You like her?" Jimmy says. Arnaldo raises an eyebrow, lets Jimmy know, yeah, he likes her. Jimmy chuckles, asks if he's on duty and Arnaldo nods. The job: mingle with the voters, look for suspicious behavior, mixed nuts that might want to blast their way into the news—make sure nothing untoward happens. Before he resigned from the force, Jimmy would have pulled this detail, watching the crowd, on the lookout for the overly excitable or mentally defective. He's still on alert out of habit. But the crowd is raucous, not unruly.

Arnaldo asks Jimmy what he's doing here. No challenge in his tone, only wants to know.

"Just an interested citizen," Jimmy says.

"Trying to spook the Chief?"

"Not on purpose," Jimmy says.

"Better not let him see me talking to you," Arnaldo says. He grins at Jimmy and continues his circumnavigation.

"Just can't get enough of Hard Marvin, can you?" Jimmy looks over and sees Cali Pasco standing next to him. Tight jeans and a white tee shirt hug her slender figure and she wears a pearl gray lightweight blazer over it to hide the shoulder holster and the Beretta it contains. The cowboy boots give her another inch of height. Thick brown hair pulled back in a ponytail that falls through the back of a blue baseball cap makes her look younger than her thirty-two years.

"Sergeant Pasco," Jimmy says, grinning.

"Detective Sergeant," she says. "You want to fight about it?" Playing, a gleam in her brown eyes.

"I don't want to get my ass kicked so early in the day." They always liked each other when they were colleagues and Cali appreciated that Jimmy never tried to sleep with her when he was married. "So you got promoted?"

"Hard forced some guy out, I think Jimmy Duke was his name." Probing with the joke, and he doesn't walk away. "So there was an opening."

"They'll make anyone a detective these days."

"Helps if you're a girl." Cali gives him a smile, keeps ambling along the perimeter of the crowd. He likes how she carries herself, the ease with which she moves, that she can sling it and take it and come back for more.

I was talking to my oldest daughter about what it means to be an American, and you know what she said to me? It's about freedom!

Jimmy glances to where Hard Marvin is standing, behind

the candidate. Sees the man looking at Mary Swain with the combination of awe and lust that seems to be the effect she has on males predisposed to her philosophy of a muscular military and no taxes. Notices Hard is fiddling with his wedding ring like he wants to take it off. Imagines the Chief is visualizing going tantric on Mary Swain and the thought nearly makes him laugh.

Jimmy is immune to the candidate's charms. Mary Swain reminds him of the popular girls back in high school, batting eyelashes and sweet poison tongues. It's not that he dislikes her actively, other than in the way he dislikes all politicians, the hurly-burly of government not something to which he pays much attention. Whenever he bothers to listen to a politician, it all runs together. *America's Future, God, My Opponent is against what you love.* And Mary Swain seems a little angry, which is something to which Jimmy does not respond well. He notices the crowd today has become angry, too, and Mary Swain feeds off them as she launches into her closing, draws herself up to her full height—five foot nine in heels—and exhorts them to take back the government from the socialists and atheists and all the un-patriotic operators who have betrayed their sacred trust because our best days are in front of us and if they vote for her it will be morning in America again and our nation will reclaim it's destiny as a beacon in a darkening world.

God bless you, God bless our troops, and God bless the U.S.A!

Jimmy remains in his position near the riser as the rally breaks up. He has nowhere to go, figures he'll see if Hard spots him and wonders whether Hard will say anything if he does. Mary Swain shaking hands with the sweaty crowd, people taking her picture, shouting encouragement. Jimmy watching Hard at her side, the sun glinting off his shiny head, shaking hands, too, smiling, backslapping; working it like someone with something to prove, someone who wants to *matter*. A few minutes go by, Jimmy standing his ground, Mary and Hard still pumping hands. Most of the throng has drifted back to their cars, but there's still a scrum of diehards near the front who need a personal shot of 90 proof charisma.

Jimmy's waited long enough, pushes in, elbows through. Hard spots him and his smile freezes in a rictus of alarm. The Chief's right hand drops to his sidearm, a Glock 9, Jimmy realizing *the man thinks I might be a shooter*. And he's a little disappointed, his feelings hurt, because Hard, who knows him for godsakes, believes the slightest possibility exists that he could go Lee Harvey Oswald on Mary Swain. Jimmy wondering if Hard is actually going to make a move toward him but the big Chief holds his position. Mary Swain gripping the hand of a retiree in a Hawaiian shirt and a tan baseball cap with gold stitching that reads U.S.S. Ronald Reagan, the man trembling with excitement and gratitude. Then Jimmy thrusts his right hand out and the candidate takes it in hers.

"Good luck, Mary," Jimmy says, holding his left hand away from his body where his ex-boss can see there's no weapon in it.

"I hope I have your vote," she says, her white teeth blinding.

"Oh, sure," Jimmy says. He notices the slim hand with the French manicure, smells her cocoanut sunscreen. Up close, the visceral Mary Swain Experience ignites. Jimmy lets go and just breathes her in for a brief moment, the lustrous hair, the perfect skin, and that infinite smile.

Then *blink* she moves down the line and Jimmy snaps out of it. Now he and Hard are face to face for a moment full to bursting and he thinks, yes, people these days are gun-toxicated and ready to rock and he knows Hard knows it, sees him twitch, the man already wound tight as a blasting cap, ready to explode, and Jimmy, with the inborn mischief of a guy who doesn't know how to stay out of trouble, can't help himself. So he winks. In that moment he senses the other man's discomfort and revels in his own enjoyment at having caused it. Jimmy cares how Hard reacts. Wishes he didn't but, yes, he cares. He is still a prisoner of the idea that any of this matters. He understands this kind of delusion is not the way of the dharma. By his reaction to Hard Marvin, Jimmy knows that freedom from suffering is not imminent. Yet he yearns for freedom. And what is more American than that?

Walking toward his pickup truck, he hears "Uncle Jimmy!" and turns to see Brittany, the seventeen-year old daughter of his brother Randall. Skinny and vibrant, with an appealing grin, Jimmy thinks she'd look better without the streak of magenta dye in her mop of brown hair. In her uniform of Converse sneakers, a plaid skirt with ripped fishnets and a baggy tee shirt with the name of some band he doesn't recognize emblazoned across the chest, she is indistinguishable from the average teenage girl save for the oblong spiral notebook in her hand. Brittany asks him what he's doing at the rally and he tells her it's his duty as a citizen to hear every candidate's line of blather. She gazes at him intently when he says this, staring right into his eyes as if she is not only taking in this information but also parsing it, extrapolating, and contemplating how it can be used to her advantage. To her uncle, she does not seem like an ordinary teenager but something more purposeful. It's slightly unsettling. When he asks her why she isn't in class since it's a Monday morning and the law of the State of California requires she be there, Brittany informs him that she's doing a school assignment. She accepts his offer of a lift back to Palm Springs Academy.

Jimmy drives a blue 2002 Ford pickup with a dented front fender and a busted taillight he's been meaning to repair for weeks. Brittany settles into the passenger seat and on the ride she talks to him about politics ("What kind of freak goes into that line of work?"), her parents ("kind of annoying") and the colleges she's thinking about applying to. Most of the schools are on the east coast and have fancy pedigrees. But maybe she won't go to college at all, she tells him. Her grades are excellent and her board scores, too, but doesn't the world belong to the entrepreneurs, the self-starters, new gods of the wild and relentlessly entertaining American pageant who bend reality to their implacable will? And they don't teach those skills in college, do they? Jimmy listens and nods, impressed with his niece. He drops her off and watches as she walks across the lawn and into the glass and steel building of the Upper School. Brittany almost makes Jimmy wish he were a father. Of course, that would mean he'd be yoked to his ex-wife Darleen for the rest of his life. He knows the kid who's worth that hasn't been born.

http://WWW.DESERT-MACHIAVELLI.COM
10.29 – 8:43 P.M.

Did it bother anyone besides the Machiavelli that Chief Marvin introduced the feisty former flight attendant otherwise known as Mary Swain at her rally today? Yes, Blogheads, I know that he looked like he was delivering a strip-o-gram at an all girl birthday party, but the Machiavelli did not enjoy the symbolism. Is there something slightly South American or even, dare I say, German, about a guy in policeman mufti, with a gun at his hip, introducing a political candidate in the Land of the Free Giveaway? Aren't the police supposed to be neutral when they're in uniform? What kind of message does this send to the hoi polloi when cops in uniform are backing candidates? It's a little fascist, frankly. I don't mean to imply that Mary Swain understands fascism, it's not like they teach it at flight attendant school, but there's a direct line from uniforms shilling for candidates to someone knocking on your door at 3:00 A.M. and dragging you off to where they hold you without trial until they feel like letting you go, unless they want to push you out a window and tell everyone you jumped. And was it me or did the Chief look a little turned on by the whole spectacle? Is Marvin hard for the flight attendant? Let us not forget, Blogheads: Mary Swain's danger lies in her cheerful erotic charge. When fascism arrives it will not be in jackboots but, rather, wrapped in an American flag, carrying a cross and wearing fuck-me pumps.

TUESDAY, OCTOBER 30

Fifty miles south of Palm Springs and three miles east of the Salton Sea, Calipatria State Penitentiary squats baking in the morning sun. Across the street from the prison is a television news van. A young reporter who looks like she studied at the Victoria's Secret School of Journalism has taken a position outside the gates. Her cameraman is ready to swing into action at the first sign of human emotion.

In the passenger seat of a Lincoln Town Car, Randall Duke checks his smile in a pocket mirror to make sure there's nothing left from the fruit plate he ate at breakfast. Satisfied his teeth are bright and television ready, he slides the mirror into the breast pocket of his cream colored suit. He is trim and broad-shouldered and his erect carriage suggests a height he does not possess. A couple of inches under six feet, with his helmet of perfect hair and glossy face, he looks like a successful Oldsmobile salesman, a quality he shares with many of his male colleagues in the United States House of Representatives, where he has served three terms.

The Lincoln's motor is running and the air conditioner on. The idling car isn't shrinking his carbon footprint but Randall is less concerned about the environment than he is about the possibility that the television camera might catch him perspiring. No one likes a sweaty politician.

He checks his watch. Jabs a number into his BlackBerry. Exasperation clouds his face when after three rings it goes to voice mail.

"Jimmy Ray, it's your brother again. We're down at Calipatria and it would have been nice if you were here like you said you'd be."

Randall runs a finger along his smooth jaw line. He's getting impatient. There are hands to shake today, votes to wheedle. He's thinking about Mary Swain and the rally she staged yesterday. It's unheard of for a challenger to pull a crowd like that. Randall doubts he could get a hundred people to a rally that wasn't tied to a specific group that needs his help. Mary Swain herself was the draw. Randall hasn't faced a problem like this before, a magnetic opponent that could actually win. She has—a word he hates—"buzz." Mostly, he hates the word because he doesn't have it. But Mary Swain? People are already talking about her in Washington. *Rolling Stone* did a story and that was bad enough, a major national publication covering a local race. But the headline! That sent Randall right over the edge: "Desert Fox". Why was no one coming up with a sexy nickname for him? Randall had enlisted in the Army after high school to earn money for college and had served in a bomb disposal unit where he attained the rank of corporal. He never actually diffused a bomb in combat conditions because it was the 1980s and there were no wars going on at the time, but that shouldn't matter. Right now he knows he needs to stop thinking about the threat of the Mary Swain candidacy. His campaign has an answer for her and it's about to emerge from that prison.

The cameraman, Angels tee shirt and a backwards baseball cap, swings his lens to the prison gates. The reporter rouses herself. A thickset guard appears and then a young man in a sturdy, motorized wheelchair. The guard steps aside and the man rolls out on the blacktop. He's wearing jeans, a short-sleeved pale blue button front work shirt and a caved-in grin.

This is Randall's cue. The Town Car door flies open and he bounds out, walks briskly toward the wheelchair. Randall reaches down and embraces the seated man, pats him on the back, feels the television camera on them like sunlight.

"What's up, Wheels?" Randall says.

"Sure could use some pussy," says the man in the chair.

Randall's smile curdles for a moment but he quickly shifts it back to grin-and-win. Turns to the reporter, Lacey Pall, who holds a microphone. She's two years out of college, her first on-air job.

"You're in a hard fought re-election campaign, Congressman. Why are you here at the prison?"

They both know why he's at the prison. The news truck would not be here otherwise. But playing along, Randall says, "I'm here to welcome my brother Dale back because family is the most important thing to me," *family* the code word that tests consistently well in focus groups. Who doesn't love family? Along with baseball and Jesus, it comprises the American Tri-fecta. Backwards Cap widens his lens to take in the scene.

"Even if I can't vote," Dale says. Clearly energized by his release, he'd be bouncing if a motorcycle accident nearly twenty years earlier hadn't robbed him of the ability to walk. Dale Duke started out handsome but the desert sun lit a hard knock life and the combination of the two took care of his looks. Now his leathery cheeks are a wallet for his dwindling, discolored teeth.

Randall marvels that his brother just served a three-year stretch for burglary and he's smiling like he won the California State Lottery. "We're proud of Dale," Randall informs the home viewers. "No one is above the law but everyone deserves a second chance. He's going to live right this time."

"I like my tequila with lime," Dale chimes in. Randall's eyes slide to his brother. He couldn't be drunk, could he, at nine in the morning? Randall's smile tightens. Lacey looks confused.

"Today I'm here to welcome my brother back."

Lacey turns to the camera, flashes her perfect dentition.

"Randall Duke, in a tight Congressional race, takes the morning off to welcome his brother out of jail and shows that family is more important than politics." She runs her forefinger across her throat and asks her cameraman if that was good. He nods.

"Get everything you need?" Randall asks.

"Thank-you Congressman," she says.

"Call me Randall."

"Randall." Smiles.

He squeezes her hand and tells her in a jocular way he hopes he has her vote. This is a running gag between them. Randall's face is like a promise and he believes that Lacey, despite her professional reserve, finds him harder to resist than she'd like. Lacey moves off and Randall eyes the curve of her hips.

Observing this from a discrete distance is a man in his thirties squeezing a tennis ball. A class ring with a blue stone accents the ring finger of his left hand and he wears a simple wristwatch with a black leather band. A dark suit hangs loosely on his lean form. He wears a starched white shirt and a red tie and his shoes are polished. Behind wire-rimmed sunglasses his eyes are closely set and blue. They hang over a thin nose, small mouth, and a chin that has seen the enemy and is now in retreat. Thinning blondish hair adds to his boiled potato pallor. This is Maxon Brae: campaign manager, aide de camp, and general factotum to the glory that is Randall Duke. It was Maxon's idea to make Dale's release a media event. His research has shown an unusually high number of families in the district have some experience in the world of addiction. Dale is meant to be Randall's ticket to their hearts and votes.

Briskly motoring himself to the car, Dale stops, looks at Randall. "Open the door, bro." Randall opens the back door of the sedan and waits. Dale tells his brother he could use some help.

Randall wraps his arms around his brother and as Dale

pushes off the chair, hoists him into the backseat. He notices that Dale smells of industrial soap. Maxon steps up and places the motorized chair in the trunk. Randall asks if Dale is comfortable.

"I need a car with hand controls."

"Maybe we can figure out a way for you to earn one."

They drive north toward Palm Springs, Maxon at the wheel, Randall riding shotgun. The Town Car doing eighty but the desolate landscape is so vast it barely feels like they're moving. Dale gazing out the window at an endless freight train heading south toward the Mexican border.

"*I like my tequila with lime?*" Randall's tone is incredulous. "What the heck was that?"

"Knew a Compton brother, played wheelchair ball, each day we'd scrawl pretty words large and small, pages and pages of song and poem, about life in a our new home, we doing hard time, busting hard rhyme." The words flow out of Dale, the rhythm of the language relaxing him. Neither Randall nor Maxon react to the poetic burst, but this does not seem to bother him. "Was a human beat-box, too. Do the crime, do the time, tequila with lime? What's the problem?"

"If you're on camera with me, Dale, I'd appreciate it if you'd keep your mouth shut. Are we clear? Things aren't the way they used to be."

"They got newspapers in the joint, Randall. I know you're King Shit."

"You can't be screwing up now, little brother, hear me? You'd have done two more years in the can if I hadn't worked that parole board. Stay clean, I'll put you on the payroll."

"That'd be fine." Dale offers a snaggletooth smile in anticipation of a star-bright future with the Randall Duke political juggernaut. After three years spent in the company of murderous Crips and Bloods, Aryan Brotherhood mutants, assorted sociopaths, psychopaths and generally bad actors, he can hardly wait to roll into his new life. Then, unable to resist: "Just like cherry wine."

"Don't embarrass me."

Maxon turns around to face Dale, says "At least wait til after the election." Randall laughs, and then Dale does, too. The tension dissipates slightly. Dale removes a little notebook and a pen from his pants pocket and scribbles something down.

"What are you writing there, Dale?" Maxon asks.

"Can't remember shit I say, got to write it every day." He finishes jotting, folds the notebook and places it back in his pocket. The brain injury that causes the memory lapses—another unfortunate result of his motorcycle accident—also left Dale prone to seizures. To control these he takes 200mgs of an anti-seizure medication three times a day. "How do you boys feel about making a pit stop at the Medjool Date Oasis?"

"The Date Oasis?" Randall says. "Heck, I'd like to take you bass fishing up at Lake Havasu with cooler full of beer and sandwiches, or treat you to a weekend in Las Vegas, wheel you up to a roulette table and stuff your pockets with chips. Take you to see Cirque de Soleil. Get you drunk. Pay a shady lady to do whatever it is they do."

"That's what I'm talking about!"

"But I'm in the middle of a campaign, remember?"

"We'll do it after," Dale says.

"Sure will," Randall says.

"I'd like a date shake right now just the same," Dale says. "Been dreaming about a date shake, every night I'd lie awake."

"Good to have something to look forward to."

"Remember that time Dad took us to the Medjool Date Oasis, you, me and Jimmy?

"You like that new hot-rod chair I got you?" Randall says, done with Memory Lane. Dale tells him it's a hell of a chair. "Got you the Ferrari of wheelchairs, Dale. You can't help family, what's the point?" Finished with his brother for the moment, Randall turns around and faces forward. The Town Car speeds through the desert waste, the only sound the rushing of the tires.

Scrolling through his emails, Randall turns to Maxon and says, "You get any new numbers?" He's referring to the daily tracking polls, the lifeblood of the modern campaign, the ever-shifting northern star by which they navigate.

"It's a toss up right now," Maxon says.

"I'll tell you what, it's a bitch running against somebody Joe Sixpack wants to leave his wife for," Randall says.

"Mary Swain, high octane," Dale says. He takes the notebook out again and jots down this bon mot.

"That's pretty good, Dale," Maxon says. "Don't let the other side hear it, they might start using it themselves."

"That's all I need," Randall says.

"We're lucky she's not campaigning in a bikini," Maxon says.

This is a conversation Randall and Maxon have been having since Mary Swain emerged victorious from the other party's primary election last June. Four months of frustration and confusion. Randall may not have a high profile in Congress but he's been re-elected easily twice. Now along comes this pulchritudinous charm dripper with a sunlight smile, a rich husband, and a tongue that is slicing Randall Duke like Swiss cheese. Mary Swain hasn't heard the truism that states in a Congressional race the incumbent always wins. Randall can't be seen to be patronizing or he'll lose female voters who become resentful if they perceive one of their sisters is unfairly taking fire. The women stick together like snakes in winter, take care of their own. Randall has to be a gallant when it comes to Mary Swain or he can depend on endless grief from the *XX* chromosome cohort whose support he needs like oxygen.

The modern world is pounding Randall today.

But it's working for Dale.

If Mary Swain weren't running even in the polls, Dale would still be playing wheelchair prison ball. She shot out of her primary with such a powerful tail wind Randall and Maxon immediately began thinking about how to enhance Randall's chances. What they came up with: play up the family angle and humanize him. Dysfunction is something a politician used to run from. Today family meltdowns have replaced married with children as the new normal. Infidelity? Check. Substance abuse? Check. Teen pregnancy? It's a boon! And why should this previously impossible thought have become the new truth? Because people in America want leaders to whom they can "relate," people who *feel* like them, who suffer their pains and are conversant with their woes on a visceral level, a level beyond thinking, because who wants to think? This preverbal emotional level is where they hope Dale will help. Randall has a contact on the state parole board and after some deft arm-twisting, it was concluded that Dale's rehabilitation was ahead of schedule. The California Department of Prisons wanted to hold him longer, but Randall made it clear that his vote on a bill to federally subsidize the pay of California prison guards was contingent on Dale no longer being within their purview.

Randall turns to Maxon, says "Check the contributors list, find a dentist. Get little brother there this week." To Dale: "We're going to buy you some new choppers."

"I want to pay for them myself," Dale says.

"That is an honorable thing. We'll find a way for you to do that."

"Black cat."

"What?"

"Black cat rhymes with 'that.' I'm just working stuff in my head is all."

"You have to say it out loud?"

"You need to loosen up, Buttercup."

Randall considers responding, but realizes there is not

much upside. If Dale can confine his anti-social tendencies to compulsive poeticizing, they will all be lucky.

Dale is slumped in the backseat, eyes closed, counting the minutes to Palm Springs, when he feels the car turning. They cross over the railroad tracks and into the town of Mecca. When Dale opens his eyes he sees a gas station just across the tracks and a *groceria*. Beyond that an auto parts shop and combination billiard hall/video arcade. Laid out on a grid, the town of Mecca evokes the other side of the solar system, as far from the well-irrigated green belt that runs from Palm Springs to Rancho Mirage to Indio as the Earth is from Saturn's Rings. Everyone on the streets, a woman in front of her house, a girl waiting for a bus, a man standing by the open hood of a beat-up Toyota pickup, looks Mexican.

"What are we doing here?" Dale asks.

"Got you a place," Randall says. "Friend of mine built some units down here. Clean, new, got the wheelchair access."

"In Mecca?" Dale does not sound pleased.

"You can't afford Palm Springs yet, little brother."

"You want to tell me what I'm supposed to do when I'm down in Mecca Town? Wanna mess around . . . bring my peoples down . . . "

"Stay out of trouble, that's what."

Dale slumps deeper into the backseat, his poetic verve evaporating. Randall looks up from his BlackBerry. "Who's this Desert Machiavelli guy, you think?"

"The blogger?" Maxon asks. "Damned if I know."

CHAPTER THREE

S unlight fires from under a drawn plastic shade and lights the interior of a mountainside mobile home. Tropical fish drift past swimming east and west in a variegated palette of hues. They are on Jimmy's plasma screen television, a continuous silent loop that he plays when whatever is available for his viewing pleasure annoys him. This is most of the time. What he had enjoyed most about the fish when he purchased the DVD on which they swim was that he didn't need to feed them or clean their tank. It was right after his wife had left and the video fish were all the companionship he wanted. But he has come to appreciate the sense of meditative calm with which they move. Looks at his watch. Is it already nearly ten o'clock? That means he actually fell asleep at some point last night, which provides him with a fleeting moment of happiness.

Rising from the couch, Jimmy steps over a maze of Chinese takeout containers and Mountain Dew empties and pads over the fraying Navajo rug into the bathroom. No one's around, so he leaves the door open behind him. He's achy this morning, his muscles sore. Insomnia has plagued him his whole life and right now he feels as if he hasn't slept in a month.

The trailer is a two bedroom with a kitchenette. Nothing on the white walls, a maroon couch—the color selected for its ability to conceal stains—a table, and two chairs. *Two* chairs. That day at Ikea, Jimmy was optimistic. Figured why decorate? He's going to be renting for only a month. That was a year ago.

Darlene had told him the marriage was over. He stayed drunk for a week.

Here he is in the mirror. Sick of looking like a mug shot. Runs warm water, lathers his face, shaves. There. That's good. No, it's not. But it's a start. Today, he thinks, is going to be a good day.

"Right, Bruno?" he says to the German shepherd sleepily eyeing him. Bruno stirs himself from his mottled plaid bed, gets to his feet and performs a downward facing dog. Jimmy opens the door of the trailer and lets him out.

After he measures out the coffee, a dark Sumatra that buzzes him at one and a half cups, Jimmy sits at his kitchen table and waits for it to brew. In front of him is a photo album. His anger management counselor, an overweight guy with ginger hair, a bald spot, and a wispy voice that made Jimmy want to wring his neck, had suggested that as part of his work-mandated therapy, he focus on something he loves. They bantered back and forth about it and after Jimmy had said beer and pizza, and the other members who were taking it more seriously got on his case, he admitted a soft spot for dogs. Not little yappy ones, but big Labs and Ridgebacks, St. Bernards and Akitas. Stan, a black guy with the body of a weightlifter, suggested he cut out pictures of dogs from magazines and make a scrapbook. "Calm your shit right down," Stan assured him as he described the one he was doing with a sailboat theme. The idea struck Jimmy as hopelessly insipid but the next day he went to a crafts store and purchased a forest green faux-leather photo binder. Jimmy didn't want to cut pictures out with a scissor and glue them into some scrapbook. What he would do: photograph the dogs he encounters with the camera in his cell phone, feed the pictures into his laptop, print them and place them in his book. It would serve not only as a means of calming himself, but also as a record of his various days. Jimmy had taken a strip of duct tape and placed it across the cover of the book. With a sharpie he had scrawled *BOOK OF DOGS*. He would stop anywhere he saw one—an arthritic Lhasa Apso on a Palm Springs sidewalk, a matted Collie in a tourist's station wagon, a chained pit bull in a fenced desert yard—and ask the owner if he could take the dog's picture for his book. Usually they didn't mind. The project has been extant for little more than a month and Jimmy already has pictures of nearly two-dozen breeds.

He's on his second cup of the Sumatra looking at a photograph of a Jack Russell terrier that belongs to a robbery victim he had questioned the week before he was busted from the force when his cell phone chirps. He's not happy to hear it. He wants to crush it under his heel. The anger. Still working on it. Maybe he should buy a ringtone. Something by Willie Nelson. Can't be pissed off when you hear that voice.

"Why didn't you show the flag this morning, Jimmy Ray?" Randall asks. "Don't you remember our brother?"

"Overslept." Jimmy used to wish he had different siblings. He eventually amended that to wishing he was an only child. He appreciated Randall intervening when he had some trouble at work, but whenever he saw him, and recently it hasn't been often, he always found the man too concerned about the family "brand." And when he thought about Dale, well, that was pleasant like an aneurism.

"Would have been good to get a picture of the three of us. He's out now, remember?" Randall still with an edge. Jimmy tells him he remembers, in a tone that adds: and perhaps the state is making a big mistake, without actually saying the words. What he says is: "Thank god he'll be home for Christmas," and assumes Randall will recognize the joke.

But if Randall wants to parse the nuance contained in Jimmy's inflection, he gives no indication of that. "Can you do me a favor and look in on him? You got that key I sent you, right? The one to the condo I got him?" Jimmy grunts an affirmative reply, then overcome by an atavistic need to discomfit his brother, says "So, Randall, I was at that Mary Swain rally yesterday."

"Yeah, why?"

Jimmy can sense his brother's annoyance crackling through the phone. "She is Szechuan hot."

Randall says, "Just be sure come Election Day you vote for the family business," and clicks off. It amuses Jimmy that his brother doesn't remember he moved out of the district when his marriage broke up.

After the second cup of coffee he places his meditation cushion on the living room floor, sets a timer, then sits cross-legged and for the next twenty minutes observes his increasingly bothersome thoughts. How can anyone sit on a cushion, he wonders, and not have their heads explode from the overwhelming nature of their inner phantasmagoria?

Rises and stretches his legs. It's torture for him to sit and do nothing but he's learning there is something to be said for observing what arises and then doing absolutely nothing other than watching it pass. Lets Bruno back in the trailer, refills his dog bowl with water. Maybe he'll actually follow through on Randall's suggestion and sprinkle some sunshine on Dale's life.

http://WWW.DESERT-MACHIAVELLI.COM
10.30 – 11:15 A.M.

The Machiavelli had the cockles of his cynical heart warmed when he turned on the TV and saw coverage of Randall Duke greeting his brother when he was released from prison. It was like some kind of bizarro Hallmark hallucination, the slick pol with the gimpy jailbird. Randall obviously thinks this is going to get him some votes since he hasn't done anything out of the goodness of his heart his entire life. And Dale is a serious piece of damaged work, a scumsucker who wasn't due to be paroled for another year. Nice to know the law treats us all equally. Of course, you Blogheads are aware the Machiavelli has occasionally been known to side with the criminal element—especially where crimes of vice are concerned—but he does not like the cut of Dale Duke's jib. The Machiavelli has not made up his mind about this election yet. Under normal circumstances, he would never vote for an empty suit like Randall Duke—he voted for the Vegan Party candidate in the last election an hour after eating a cheeseburger, rather than pull the lever for that vacuous twit—but his opponent the Stewardess is more suited to model on the cover of *Gun Nut* than to be a Representative in the United States Congress. Not to be an elitist snob and taking nothing away from her pretty legs, but did the Stewardess even graduate from college?

CHAPTER FOUR

I n a slim cut black wool blazer—consciously chosen for its length which covers her burgeoning backside yet still hangs in a way that does not invite comparisons to a table top—a loose white button-front blouse, maroon leggings and knee high soft black leather boots with a low heel, her layered, expensively dyed blond hair covered by a faded raspberry golf cap with the logo *Life Is Good*, Kendra Duke is a picture of slightly overweight chic. In most of America she would be a bikini model but she knows the standards in Palm Springs are not those of the great white flour and sugar consuming non-coastal areas of the republic.

A shopping expedition has delivered her to Couture Canyon Apparel where the wide, well-organized racks of designer clothes are arranged in pleasure-inducing geometry. This store is the bargain basement province of Kendra's favorite designers whose overpriced creations command considerably more in the gilded precincts ninety miles to the west. On weekends the place is crammed with breathless Los Angeles bargain seekers rendered weak-kneed by the site of Versace reduced by a third, and the frenzied yanking of dresses and jackets off racks, the impatient lines outside the changing rooms, turn the place into Cairo at rush hour, but on this weekday morning it is as quiet as a chapel.

She notices one other shopper, a trim older man with a full head of steel gray hair wearing a well-cut white linen suit as he examines a display of Prada shirts.

This morning Kendra's brief is a specific one: to shop for something to wear on Election Day, Day of Days, Judgment Day in Duke World, one week from today, when she will be photographed and videotaped, recorded for posterity yet again as a human corsage, an appendage of Congressman Randall Duke. An appendage! That was definitely not the plan back in her twenties when she was ten pounds lighter and considerably more dewy when it came to the machinations of the universe.

Against the wall opposite the entrance is an enticing rack of Dolce and Gabbana and Kendra zeroes in. Scoping the selection with a practiced eye, she pulls two outfits off the rack—a green double-breasted skirt suit with a half-sleeved blouse and a silver lurex quilted Jacquard dress—and finds a changing room. Even with outlet mall pricing, both selections are over two thousand dollars, but Kendra believes she deserves a treat and does not think Randall will take exception to this. Assuming he wins the election. The way he has been talking about Mary Swain the past few weeks has her worried.

Strutting out of the dressing room barefoot, Kendra heads for a full-length mirror. The suit is flattering. Probably because it's a size 10, and so what if its only worn once. She pivots from the mirror and glances over her shoulder at her reflection. Not bad for a forty-two year old woman, she thinks. Despite the suet in her sway, she is not lacking in confidence. Kendra was a drum majorette with the marching band at the University of Southern California—where she graduated *cum laude* in communications—and still comports herself like someone accustomed to twirling a baton in front of eighty thousand football fans at the Rose Bowl. Whenever Kendra looks at herself in a full-length mirror, which is several times a day, she strikes a subtle performance pose. Sometimes it is entirely subconscious and she catches herself doing it, but it does not embarrass her. A former professional singer and lover of the bright lights, she is haunted in small ways by their absence from her life. This is the signal element in the difficulty she has with her marriage. Any successful politician is a performer, a hoarder of whatever oxygen is in the immediate environment, and this leaves Kendra the songbird gasping for air. Her singing career, though never particularly successful, supplied enough of this attention to afford her an independent identity. Since it's eclipse by her role as Mrs. Randall Duke, there has been nothing to replace it: not her husband, who is permanently distracted in the manner of anyone who is perpetually running for office, and not her teenaged daughter who is far more interested in separating from the family then giving her mother the slightest bit of attention.

Back in the dressing room, Kendra slips out of the skirt suit and tries on the quilted Jacquard dress. She tilts her head down and smiles, then looks at her face: adorable. Feeling exhilarated she twirls around and hikes the back of the dress revealing a well-formed if slightly-too-large ass bisected by a white silk thong, and a four-inch high manga kitten tattooed on her left buttock. She had regretted getting the tattoo a day after having it done, but right now she loves the sass it provides and almost wishes someone were watching her.

Out on the floor of the cavernous store, Kendra pirouettes in front of the mirror. She adores the dress. It is less conservative than the skirt suit, does not scream politician's wife, but she worries Randall will find it too flash. The downside of these kinds of outlet stores, these massive retailing barns that traffic in manufacturing miscalculations, is the absence of doting salespeople. Kendra would appreciate some doting right now. This is a woman who sang for thousands of people in her career— although, to be clear, not at the same time—and now the only noise is the low drone of the straining air conditioning.

There was a time she believed she would remain a performer for the rest of her life. What had changed? While appearing with a Seventies revival band at a county fair outside of Fresno Kendra had met a law student named Randall Duke. Spotting her eating a candy apple in the food tent, he told her he loved the way she sang *Mandy*. As pickup lines went, she had heard far better but Randall was persistent, and not without charm. That day he purchased five copies of *Disco Lady*, her self-released CD—the cover of which featured Kendra at the wheel of a Ford Pinto—for gifts, and when they married a year later Kendra reluctantly gave up her career, with the understanding that it would resume when the children they intended to have were no longer young.

"What do you think?" Kendra looks to her left and sees the speaker, a beautiful woman in a pale yellow Valentino suit. The hemline stops just above her knee and her calves are spectacular. A Panama hat pulled low. Large dark sunglasses. Her presentation is that of a glamorous spy in a Hollywood movie and she looks vaguely familiar to Kendra. The woman smiles at her, showing a set of perfect porcelain teeth. "My husband is over there, but I'd rather get a girl's opinion."

Kendra glances toward the older man in the white linen suit on the other side of the store. He's looking at a rack of summer-weight bespoke jackets. "That outfit looks totally great on you," Kendra says.

"Don't you love shopping here in the morning before everything is picked through?" Her tone is friendly, confiding, the voice warm. If the woman were not with her husband Kendra would consider asking if she wants to get coffee.

Kendra strikes a pose with her dress. "Be honest," she tells her new friend with the stylish hat and big sunglasses.

The woman puts her right hand to her chin, supporting her elbow with her opposite hand—perfect manicure!—and considers Kendra's presentation.

"Your husband's gonna love it." Kendra wonders how the woman knows she's married. Looks at her ring finger, sees the diamond, oh . . . right, that. "You look familiar," the woman says, and Kendra's heart does a two-step. A fan?

"I used to be a singer."

"Really? What's your name?"

"Kendra Kerry. I sang all over the west coast with a seventies revival band. Maybe you saw me somewhere."

The woman studies her for a moment. "No, no, somewhere else. Well, I've got to get going. Thanks for giving me your opinion. Us girls have to stick together, right?"

"Definitely," Kendra says.

"If you don't mind, I'd like to introduce myself," the woman says. "I'm Mary Swain and I'm running for Congress. I'd love to have your vote."

Oh, no, no, no. The hat, the large sunglasses, the whole incognito posture. If Kendra had been less distracted she would have noticed And now Mary Swain has made this ridiculous request. Mary Swain had to have seen her somewhere with Randall. Did she create so little of an impression? "Sure," Kendra says, in that instant when thinking would ordinarily take place.

"It was great meeting you, Kendra," Mary Swain says. As she walks away, her taut, well-exercised form in recession is a ringing coda to the impression of perfection she leaves in her wake.

Kendra feels like she's been smacked in the face. The sensation is not sharp, but dull and resonant. She sees Mary Swain and her husband at the cash register now. Mary Swain *has* to know who she is. Has she been playing with her? Had she come over simply to enact some kind of sadistic spider and fly routine? Surely, whether or not she had seen Kendra sing at the Kern County State Fair is immaterial. The woman has to know she was talking to Randall Duke's wife. Surely, she has to have at least recognized her from pictures taken with Randall. There are some on the Randall Duke website, aren't there?

She'll have to check later. She knows there haven't been any pictures of her in the newspapers lately, not that anyone reads them anyway, but still. Mary Swain had to have recognized Kendra somehow. *Had* to have. How utterly and resonantly humiliating! That she could present herself to Kendra as just a civilian shopper is appalling. Who does this plucked and toned shot of estro-power think she is? Kendra considers herself a force with which to be reckoned. For someone like Mary Swain to feel no compunction about standing in the middle of an outlet store and toying with her in this cat-with-a-clueless-mouse manner is unconscionable.

When she retreats to the dressing room, Kendra is distracted from these malign thoughts by her phone. The caller ID: Palm Springs Academy, the school her daughter Brittany attends. The female voice on the other end asks if this is Mrs. Duke. When Kendra answers in the affirmative, the caller identifies herself as Mrs. Halstead, the head of the Upper School, and informs her that her daughter Brittany has been caught sending nude pictures of herself over the Internet to a boyfriend which has resulted in a two day suspension effective immediately and would you mind terribly picking her up right now?

CHAPTER FIVE

T he bullet kicks up a shower of dirt six inches from a surprised rattlesnake. Hard Marvin holds his police issue Glock 9 away from his body, braces his right wrist with his left hand. He wishes he had hit the snake. Doesn't want to be out here in the Mojave on his day off, guns and a sun that can break you, killing rattlers. But Nadine Never wants to learn how to shoot, the girl a live wire, a rocket powered fun bundle with needs in central nervous system stimulation significantly above those of a normal person. Hard's dog, a Rottweiler named Bane watches calmly as his master squeezes off another round, bullets ricocheting off rocks, boom echoing off the distant hills, but the snake has already slithered under a boulder. Bane takes this opportunity to lie down. Hard glances at Nadine but she doesn't seem to mind that he hasn't killed the snake. That's a good thing about these young ones, Hard reflects. They aren't as demanding.

"Shit," he says, squinting behind his aviator sunglasses. In his experience, women like to see deadly snakes get their brains blown out by big strong guys. He figures it must tap in to some genetic need they have to be protected. Hard doesn't claim to know a lot about women, but it would have been better if he'd killed the damn snake. "All right. You try."

He slides behind Nadine, savors her slim blondeness. About half a foot shorter than Hard, she wears jeans and a sleeveless white belly shirt that shows off a flat stomach sliced by an inch of thin gold chain dangling from her navel. Her toned shoulders and arms are dusted with freckles. Her hair falls a few inches below her neck, bangs swept to the side, and a pair of inexpensive beaded turquoise earrings ceases their gentle swing as she stills herself to aim. She extends her arm away from her body and Hard eases the Glock into her right hand. Then he places his hand softly on hers and subtly grinds his pelvis into her denim-sheathed bottom. This is the best part of teaching a girl to shoot, he reflects: spoon position warrior version. He feels himself getting an erection.

"It's gonna kick, so be ready."

"Aren't we gonna wait for a snake?"

He doesn't want her to kill a snake now. It won't be good if she kills one and he doesn't. Never mind he's tired of her already, regretting promises made. "Could take all day," he says.

Hard has been at his police job nineteen years, coming up on a pension. Been working since he left the Marine Corps, the highlight of his hitch the Grenada invasion of 1983. Hard would have preferred to say he'd seen action in WW II or Korea or Vietnam but if it was Grenada then what the hell, at least he'd seen combat. Married a tae kwon do teacher when he got his discharge, smart businesswoman, owns her own dojo, Mojave Martial Arts. Two boys in the Army, both stationed overseas.

One night last year Hard was draining a can of Buck Rhino energy drink at the AM/PM on Twentynine Palms Highway when he saw a girl emerging from the snack aisle holding a bag of salted sunflower seeds. Before he could say anything, she asked if he was Hard Marvin. The best introduction he could have hoped for. A beautiful woman had made him for Hard Marvin and she was smiling when she said it. He'd been confronted by enough citizens in public places and it wasn't always pleasant, so he was already ahead in the encounter. He told her that yes it most certainly was the Police Chief of

Desert Hot Springs in the flesh right next to the snack aisle and asked what he could do for her. Nadine said she could think of a few things and Hard started wondering if cameras from some television show were trained on the two of them. He asked if she was from around here and she told him no. Hard was a lot older, but a few graying chest hairs did nothing to diminish his confidence. They conversed for a while and she said she worked at Fake 'N' Bake, a local tanning salon. He should come by some time.

"Aren't I tan enough?"

"I could spray you a few shades darker, make you look more mysterious," she said, and told him she worked the evening shift three nights a week. Hard took the hint and stopped in two nights later, bought her a drink in a bar one town over and glanced at her drivers license when the bartender carded her. Twenty-two years old? That had caught him by surprise. She seemed older, tougher than twenty-two. He listened to the hopes, the dreams; registered the general emotional weather report: partly cloudy. Hard told her he was married—standard operating procedure—but apparently she didn't mind since they were having sex in the desert later than evening on a camp blanket Hard kept in the bed of his Dodge Ram truck.

"You're the kind of girl I could leave my wife for," he lied, as she laid her head on his muscular shoulder. Two weeks later he was telling her the same thing only then he thought he might be serious.

That first night under the stars was when she asked him to teach her to shoot. And she took the Taser off his belt, ran her finger over it, said, "I want to learn how to use this, too." Like she's planning to be a one-woman SWAT team. Hard said forget about the Taser, but I'll teach you how to use a gun.

Hard and Nadine would meet at the Sandy Hills Motel where the owner has some potential issues with *los illegals* he employs as maids. The Police Department looks the other way, something the owner appreciates. So the lovers burn the sheets gratis for a few hours once, maybe twice a week. Hard brings a bottle of tequila.

In the hotel room the first time: Nadine lying on the bed in a thong that Hard pulls off with his teeth. Inhaling her scent he takes a knife out the pocket of the pants he's thrown over a chair. With the knife he cuts a lemon. Takes a lemon quarter and squeezes it on her left breast, watches the cool juice running over her areola. Her nipple hardens. With his other hand he grabs a box of salt and leaves a snowy trail across her other breast. He pushes her knees up. She giggles as he pours the tequila on to her belly a little at a time, and he watches as it sluices downward over her pelvic bone. Hard tried that one time with his wife and she nearly punched him, made him get out of bed and wash the tequila-moist sheets. But Nadine! She arches her back as Hard sucks the liquor out, the sharp taste of the tequila mixing with the pungent flavor of Nadine, licks the salt off her right breast, the lemon juice off her left, and as they move their hips, roll and thrust, his perfervid mind reels with the usual delusions: let's get married, go to Mexico, sunny dreams. Kind of thing anyone paying attention knows will end in tears. But no one's ever paying attention. Besides, Hard doesn't really want to go to Mexico. He's got other things on his mind since he's spent time with Mary Swain, gorgeous, compelling, no, that doesn't do her justice—*inspirational* Mary Swain. He's getting ambitious. Not the kind of thing he feels the need to discuss with his girlfriend. Hard is still lost in his exhilarating thoughts, drunk on possibility and the boundless future when *BAAANNNGGG* the gun discharges next to his ear. He sees Bane's four paws lift off the desert floor.

"Goddamn, Nadine!" The blast ricochets off the rock formations, Hard's ears ringing. "You nearly shot Bane!"

"I thought I saw something move over there." She had piv-

oted ninety degrees to the right and squeezed one off, catching
Hard by surprise. This girl, he thinks, is dangerous. Not dan-
gerous sexy, either. She looks at him with a lopsided grin.
"This is fun."

"Anything happens to that dog . . . "

"You love him more than me?"

"You're damn right I do. I love that dog more than any
human." Trying to keep the stress out of his voice, Hard looks
over at Bane, standing in a semi-crouch and shaking. "Point is,
you can't be shooting every which way."

"I swear something moved."

"Didn't nothing move. Now aim where I told you."

Nadine swings the Glock back around and fires again. Hard
can't tell if she even aimed the weapon. It was turning him on,
though. Now Hard is having second thoughts about breaking
up with her. He would at least wait until after the election.

Nadine pulls out her cell phone. Hands him the weapon
and throws an arm around his shoulder. "Now point that thing
and me, but don't pull the trigger, okay?"

Hard thinks she's crazy, but everyone's got quirks. Still, a
picture? "Nadine, I'm not sure that's such a great idea."

"Why?"

"*Why?* Because I'm a damn police chief. And I'm *married*,
remember?"

"I know, I know, but I won't show it to your wife, I swear."

"Nadine, sweet thing . . . "

"Don't you trust me?"

"Sure I trust you. It's not *you* I'm worried about. What if
someone else gets their hands on a picture like that?"

"Okay. You want to know the truth?"

"Sure I do."

"It kind of gets me going. I might like it on those cold
nights you're not there." She smiles at him, blue eyes wide.

"Sorry, darlin. Can't do it."

Nadine puts the safety on and places the barrel against her own cheek and laughs.

"Fraidy cat."

Hard is unable to fathom why the girl likes a gun tickling her cheekbone, but wonders why all women can't be like this. In Hardville, they would. Guns and tits and Hard's checking his sanity at the door. He would have liked to take the picture but he's not crazy. What's to stop her sending it to his wife? Would Mary Swain ever let him point a gun at her? While he was fucking her? That was another thing he had tried with his wife. She wouldn't talk to him for a week. He has to control these kinds of thoughts—they aren't going to lead to peace on Earth. But it sends a tingle from his lumbar region to his loins.

Nadine holds the cell phone at arm's length, points it at herself and snaps the picture.

"If you were in the picture, it could have been our wedding announcement."

Hard hopes she's joking but doesn't say anything. When they're walking back to his truck, Bane trailing behind them, Nadine says, "You ever kill anyone when you were in the service?"

"No, but I've killed guys." Hard gives her a little smile to show her how unaffected he is in the aftermath of dealing out the ultimate punishment.

"As a cop?"

"That's right."

"Tell me one."

"This time I was working with the INS south of here, we got a roadblock set up, we're looking for illegals, right? So we stop this truck, Mexican plates, and it's hauling tomatoes north. Well, you always got to wonder about a Mexican truck, no matter what's in it. So the boys and I, we stick a couple of pitchforks in the tomatoes and we hear this scream, well." He hesitates here. Hard has told this story countless times and he is in performance mode, each pause and breath perfected. Nadine is enthralled. "Then all of a sudden three Mexicans fly out of the tomatoes in three different directions and we start chasing them. I catch my guy, and he's a little guy, but he's strong so when I try to get the cuffs on he coldcocks me. I was trying to be a good cop, do it by the book but that's when I kind of lost it and when I caught up I put him in a choke hold and that's all she wrote."

"You killed him?"

"Didn't mean to." When Hard sees the look on Nadine's face, not condemnatory exactly, but not accepting either— hasn't she just asked to hear the story?—he adjusts his swagger level down a notch. "Little *hombre* gave me no choice."

"Did anything happen to you?"

"What do you mean? Did I get punished?" Nadine nods, looking at Hard with new eyes now, the man an actual killer. "There was a hearing. They always have one of those when someone gets killed but, no, nothing happened. Got promoted a year later."

"You think there's retribution?"

"What, like from God?"

"Do you?"

"Death gets everyone in the end," Hard says, feeling very much the Philosopher King despite not having killed a snake. He figures the tale of the dead Mexican will shore up his macho bona fides with Nadine. He's thinking about having sex with her right now when she says: "I really wish you took that picture with me."

There goes the mood. Hard doesn't reply. A roadrunner zips past them fifty feet away. Hard briefly thinks about shooting at it, but he's already failed to hit the snake and doesn't want to compromise the newly minted respect he believes he just earned from Nadine by missing.

"Hard?"

"Yeah?"

"You didn't say anything when I said 'wedding announcement'."

He doesn't say anything the second time either.

"Hey, Hard," she says. "Smile." He turns around and she snaps his annoyed expression.

"Dammit, Nadine."

"You're no fun."

When Hard doesn't respond, Nadine trots a couple of steps in front of him, yanks her jeans down to the tops of her taut thighs, bends over and moons him. The manga kitten tattoo on her tight ass never fails to make him smile. She looks over her shoulder at Hard, her saucy expression shot through with a barely discernible vein of gravity. Hard marches past, slaps her on the butt and tells her he needs to get going. If he bothered to look he would have seen her bright young features sag toward the dry desert floor.

CHAPTER SIX

J immy Duke is rolling south on Highway 111 through Palm Springs in the blue pickup truck. One hand on the wheel, his elbow resting on the open window, he ponders how fate could have served him a sibling like Dale. It was one of the subjects Jimmy talked about in the anger management sessions. What he was doing in anger management: a gang member wanted for murder cut him with a switchblade and when the criminal was finally subdued Jimmy broke his jaw. And his nose. Only two punches. He thought that showed a certain degree of self-control but it was the second time he had engaged in violent retribution when a lowlife he was trying to arrest had failed to obey orders and Hard Marvin insisted he get professional help.

The group therapy experience was something Jimmy failed to embrace so the leader suggested that Jimmy might benefit from the study of Buddhist meditation techniques. Intrigued, he had signed up for an on-line class being taught by Bodhi Colletti, a woman in Tacoma, Washington. He has spent the last four Sunday mornings sitting with his laptop at the kitchen table listening to Bodhi talk about the dharma. Jimmy aggravated the other students by repeatedly interrupting and asking what, exactly, was *the dharma*. Although she had given him a long and complicated answer as far as he could tell it boiled down to what Buddhists call the Four Noble Truths.

1. Life is suffering.
2. There is a cause for that suffering.

3. There is an end to it.

4. There is a means to that end.

Instructing her on-line novitiates, Bodhi Colletti talked about how to process the negative thoughts that inevitably arise in the course of sitting on the meditation cushion and remain in the mind's eye like bad weather. She talked about watching a thought rise, resisting the temptation to label it good or bad, then placing the thought in a pink bubble and watching it float away. She pointed out that the pink bubble, while not originating in Buddhist texts, was something her students often found helpful.

At first Jimmy thought the whole thing ridiculous, particularly the part about the pink bubble. How did people come up with this shit? But when he actually tried to do it he was astonished by the efficacy of the technique. The next time a thought about his ex-wife Darleen arose—he was remembering the time at the end of their marriage when she drunkenly told him about an affair with her colleague at the hotel restaurant where she worked as a hostess—he conjured the pink bubble. Following Bodhi Colletti's instructions, Jimmy imagined his ex-wife Darleen encased in it. Then the pink bubble began to float away. Jimmy resisted the urge to imagine dousing the pink bubble with gasoline and lighting it on fire. That first time, however, he did manage to wish Darleen well as she soared skyward and disappeared into the clouds. The method worked a little better the next time a thought about his former spouse occurred to him, and still better the time after that. He knows he can never tell anyone about this technique—*You put your ex-wife in a pink bubble and wish her well?* Anyone would laugh—but he does not argue with the way it eases his vexation.

There is a palpable awareness in him that this easing of vexation will involve more effort than Jimmy wants to exert. But he knows he will to have to find some motivation if he's going to meet new people. Cali Pasco, newly minted Desert Hot Springs

P.D. distaff detective, isn't exactly new *per se*, but she was off limits as long as they were on the force together. Now, though, he's got nothing to lose. She answers on the third ring, sounds happy to hear from him. Hi, Jimmy, how you doing? Fine, you? I'm good, what's up? Well, I was wondering . . . and they make what neither calls a date but involves them having dinner together tonight.

The apartment is an improvement over the cell in which Dale has spent the previous three years even if it's in Mecca. A bright one bedroom with handicapped access on the first floor of a building with walls and a roof, as a place to resume a free life Dale knows he could do a lot worse. The building is not due to open for another month and Dale is the only tenant. He spends his first hour alone watching a TV show about cars, plotting how he might get his life back on track, and not the one where he's hustling recreational vehicles to retirees. Yes, Randall has bought him a new wheelchair, arranged for a place to live, and got him a job, but it wasn't like Dale Duke could ever go completely straight. Whatever he does this time, he vows it will be better planned than the scheme that resulted in the three-year stretch at Calipatria. That was a home invasion in Rancho Mirage. Being paraplegic limited his utility if not his desire in the home invasion field. So Dale was the lookout and the wheelman. A lot of Los Angelenos own weekend houses in the desert. Dale and his partner Gorman, a guy he knew from high school, were working the second home circuit and doing good business. They'd steal appliances mostly and sell to a fence in Hemet who ran his operation out of a secondhand furniture store. Gorman would go into the house with his cell phone on vibrate and Dale, seated behind the wheel of his hand-controlled van, would keep him abreast of what was occurring on the street. They'd done nearly twenty jobs together and other than an unexpected run-in with a pit bull that Gorman nearly blinded with pepper spray, they had never had any surprises. On the night they were pinched a freak winter storm had knocked out a cell phone tower and the two of them weren't able to communicate when Gorman went into the house that belonged to a couple from Los Feliz, a high-class neighborhood on the east side of the Los Angeles. A Sheriff's Deputy in a patrol car had noticed Dale parked outside this particular house and had pulled alongside the van. The uniform was engaged in a conversation with him when Gorman emerged carrying a thirty-two inch flat screen television. Gorman quickly ascertained the situation, dropped the television and ran off into the desert. The officer persuaded Dale to stay put by pointing a gun in his face. When he told Dale to get out of the car, the man was nonplussed to learn he was dealing with a paraplegic. Gorman got picked up the next day and the two of them went down. It was a front-page story in the local paper because Dale's brother was serving his second term in Congress. Randall had cursed whoever it was who said there was no such thing as bad publicity. Dale Duke was certified bad publicity, having been in and out of jail most of the last two decades, drug possession, check kiting, now breaking and entering. Gorman: still in prison, his brother a pipefitter not a Congressman. Dale: ready to rock with ten thousand dollars cash parked in a safe deposit box in Borrego Springs.

Being the bad boy is something Dale embraces more from a paucity of choices than an inner conviction. With only a high school education and no marketable skills breaks have never come winging through his window. It would be a pleasure unbound to show Randall that he is possessed of innate worth. But where is the opportunity? Selling recreational vehicles does not satisfy his craving for larger meaning on a bigger stage.

Stripped to his boxers and tee shirt, Dale lies face down on the floor doing one-armed pushups, withered legs behind him, crudely tattooed arm thrusting up and down. In prison he lifted weights and played wheelchair basketball with the five other inmates in chairs. The scarring in his brain that causes the seizures also resulted in a weakened left arm that is immune to weightlifting. On his upper right side, Dale looks a gymnast. But his left arm and legs, they look like a bad science experiment.

On his twenty-fifth pushup the door opens and he hears a familiar voice: "You're not gonna get up and lay me out, are you?"

"Jimmy Ray motherfuckin Duke," Dale says. "You want to arm wrestle?"

Jimmy drops the bag of takeout food he's holding on the table and says sure.

They line up opposite each other on the floor and grab hands. Jimmy counts off and they begin. Both are powerful men and neither has an advantage at first, but the superior leverage Jimmy has as a result of all of his limbs working, combines with Dale's push-up induced fatigue and allows him to finally get the back of Dale's hand to touch the floor.

"You get stronger in prison?"

"I want a rematch and next time I won't do any pushups before."

"You're not getting a rematch, Slick. You might win."

"Forget *might*, dude."

Jimmy flops on the couch and looks around. He tries not to look as Dale crawls along the floor and hoists himself on to a chair like a seal. Feeling sorry for Dale is not in Jimmy's repertoire. And how do you feel sorry for someone as badass as Dale anyway? He'd just laugh at you. "Why are we in Mecca?"

"Randall wants to put me where I won't be seen, Jellybean."

"You just call me Jellybean?"

"I'm rhyming is all. Got to rhyme to pass the time. Fuck that anyway. Randall's hiding me."

"You blame him?"

When Dale doesn't respond immediately, Jimmy wonders for a moment if he wasn't a little too blunt. Jimmy announces he's brought lunch and asks if Dale is hungry. Although he never once visited his brother in prison, it's as if they talked a day earlier. He takes out a sandwich and tosses it to Dale. "I remember you like tuna, but I hear there's too much mercury in it now."

"I can't eat tuna no more?"

"I got you roast beef. They're shooting the cattle full of hormones, but what the hell, right? And I got you some beer." Jimmy flourishes a six-pack of beer. "All for you. I quit drinking."

"Bullshit."

"Swear to God."

Dale laughs. Unlike his charged relationship with Randall, he and Jimmy have an easier rapport, one that comes from each knowing the other will never ask for anything. The brothers chew their sandwiches in silence. Dale considers asking Jimmy why he never came to see him the three years he was in prison. But he decides nothing good could come from that line of inquiry.

Jimmy cracks open a can of soda. Takes a swig, says: "The Congressman did pretty well by you."

"You see this wheelchair he got me," Dale says, pointing to the contraption now parked several feet from the chair in which he is currently seated. "Motor vehicle is what it is, engine painted red and shit. And he hooked me up selling RVs."

"Who's buying RVs now? Price of gas and all."

"Alls I know is I'm getting paid, likes to be getting laid."

"Big brother told me to keep an eye on you, check in. Gave me a key to your place. Hope you don't mind."

It bothers Dale that Jimmy has been presented with a key, doesn't care that a paraplegic might need emergency help, chooses to resent the lack of trust he believes it reflects. But on the surface he is determined to keep it light. "Give me lectures on the straight and narrow, bow and arrow?"

"No lectures from me. You go right ahead and do what you want. And stop the damn rhyming, please. You're getting on my nerves."

"And if you catch me, you'll throw my ass in jail?" Dale pauses, then says: "Then forward all my mail."

Jimmy smiles. Can't help it. He says, "I'm leaving law enforcement in a couple of years, Dale. So if you're gonna be a fuck-up, I'd appreciate if you'd wait until I was out of the catching fuck-ups business."

"It's a new day, Jimmy Ray."

"Well, that's swell." The word *swell* an ironic hint that he's not buying what Dale's selling. Dale misses it. "You want a lift somewhere?"

"Lets take a ride to Bombay Beach."

This is a speck of a town on the shores of the Salton Sea about twenty-five miles south of Mecca. It is not a place anyone generally asks to be taken. Where Dale would really like to go is Borrego Springs so he can pick up the cash he has stowed, but he doesn't want to explain to Jimmy what he's doing in the Wells Fargo bank. He can take a cab.

"Why you want to go there?"

"To touch the water."

"Just roll your ass into the kitchen turn on the tap you want to touch water." Dale laughs. At least that's how Jimmy chooses to interpret the soft guttural bark that issues from his throat.

"You remember the time Dad took us fishing down there?"

"Yeah, I must've been about twelve. We rowed around in some piece of crap rental boat and I nearly got heat stroke."

"I used to think about that day while I was in prison. Think it was maybe the only thing I could remember the three of us ever did with him."

"What'd he take us, like, once?"

"Yeah, once. I caught a fish, but he wouldn't let me cook it because he said I'd get sick." There is a silence that hangs between them for a moment as they each recall that day more than thirty years earlier. "We got date shakes at the Medjool Date Oasis."

"How do you remember that?"

"Just do. Tried to get Randall to stop off and get one today but he's too damn important now." Looks for backup on this sentiment but Jimmy gives him nothing. "You won't take your poor cripple-ass brother down there today?"

"Tell you what. You got a rain check for next week. Get a date shake at the Medjool Date Oasis, head down to Bombay Beach, how's that sound?"

"Profound."

Jimmy spends another ten minutes there. He tells Dale about his new job he's about to start and Dale talks about what it was like being inside for three years. He'd never done a stretch that long before but he tells his brother he handled it well. Jimmy makes Dale nervous. Not because of anything he's doing, though. But his presence, his work in law enforcement, and their history together are a rebuke to Dale's entire life. Dale has felt this way about both of his brothers for a long time. Although grateful for the visit, when Jimmy says goodbye and closes the door behind him, Dale is relieved. The day is starting to stress him and stress can bring on a seizure. He reaches into his pocket for his meds and takes his second dose of the day.

CHAPTER SEVEN

A fter a ten-to-five shift at Fake and Bake, Nadine returns to her house in Cathedral City, just east of Palm Springs. Her place is a small, two bedroom bungalow, fourteen hundred square feet, built with cheap materials during the nineties real estate boom. The house had been foreclosed on six months earlier but Nadine is not the owner. A client from Fake 'N' Bake is a loan company representative and he surreptitiously arranged for her to move in. The water was still running and Nadine found someone on Craig's List who knew how to hook up a generator so although she is technically a squatter, the place feels like a home, the Foreclosed sign in the front yard notwithstanding. An easy mixture of whites and Latinos, the low-key town is desert-on-a-budget and Nadine blends right in.

She puts a Lean Cuisine teryaki chicken dinner in the microwave and lets Diablo the Chihuahua out for a run in the fenced yard. Nadine straightens up while her food cooks. The place is sparsely furnished with a white velour couch, two upholstered chairs and a coffee table, all purchased at local garage sales. She removes the dish from the microwave and while it cools on the kitchen counter, she takes a shower. Hard called earlier and asked if he could come over. She had hoped he would ask her out to dinner but that wasn't on his agenda. She told him not to expect to be fed and he had said that was fine with him.

Nadine towels off and gets dressed. Her slim legs taper into delicate ankles, one of which is sporting a gold anklet Hard had given her. Examines herself in the mirror. She's wearing a pair of low-slung Capri pants from which a hot pink thong peeks in the space below a sleeveless white cotton blouse. She has been dieting and exercising at a hotel where she pretends to be a guest and her already attractive form is in fine shape.

Nadine fishes in the medicine cabinet, locates a bottle of Valium. She had taken one about three hours earlier, as far as she can remember, and wonders if it's too soon for another. But she was feeling on edge today, figures she can start cutting back tomorrow. Down it goes, chased with a Diet Coke. Sitting in a chair with a magazine, she wonders when her life is going to change. Nadine did not have a lollipop childhood, and hoped that the dark clouds that shadowed her early years would finally dissipate. She thinks about her mother, who ran off with a friend's husband when she was little and her father, a Navy veteran who raised her and an older sister on a restaurant manager's salary, bringing the girls to free tennis clinics in the city parks. The sister didn't take to the game, but Nadine loved it, playing for her high school team and earning a spot on the varsity at San Diego State. Her father had been a heavy smoker and was sipping a whiskey sour in a Tijuana bar when he went into cardiac arrest. Nadine took it hard and dropped out of college a year short of graduation. San Diego was starting to feel old and she found a job as a tennis instructor at a desert resort. But a month after she arrived, the property was sold and the new owners wanted to give it a facelift so she found herself filing her nails on the unemployment line. To her chagrin, Nadine discovered there were not a lot of tennis instructor jobs to be had. She saw an ad in the paper one day and so began her career as a tanning technician. The job is a stopgap; something to do while she tries to determine her future. Now she has been assisting people with their tanning needs for more than a year and is getting antsy. The Valium's taking the edge off that feeling. At least that's the idea. When Hard is an hour late, she wonders if she should take another. How many has she taken today? Recently she's been losing count. The bottle advises no more than one every six hours, Nadine leaving that suggestion to the amateurs. Figures the chemical palliative is easier on her internal organs than the four tequila shots it takes to get the same effect. She calls Hard, but it goes straight to the message.

Now she's tap-tap-tapping on her beat-up iBook, filling out an on-line application for a popular reality show. A professional football player from the depths of the eighties is allegedly in search of a wife. He made a couple of bad action movies, had a DUI arrest, then declared bankruptcy. In his picture on the web site for the show he has a mane of hair blown dry from here to Las Vegas and full lips that have been god-knows-where. Wrapped in fake endangered species skins, his entire mien screams STDs but Nadine doesn't care. She's not planning to marry the guy, and since twenty women are going to be chosen as contestants she probably won't have to anyway, assuming she is even selected. But she likes the idea of being brought to Los Angeles for a few weeks, installed at the mansion where the show is taped, given free food, a shopping spree at a mall, and the other seductive perks made available to those women lucky enough to be chosen.

Now her attention is drifting from the application. Is that the Valium? Wonders whether or not taking too much Valium can cause some kind of hyper-activation in the brain. She's heard it can put a girl on the crazy train. But if you take too much Valium, you'd die, right? Or would you go crazy and then die? And if she were to go crazy, would she be aware of it? Did crazy people know they were crazy? It was a conundrum. She'd have to get on the Internet and do a little research.

If her social life were better she's certain her tranquilizer intake would drop precipitously. Lately it's been an utter disaster. From the time Nadine was in high school she displayed an unerring lack of discernment when it came to men, which she mistakenly attributed to her occasional bi-sexuality. She has gone back and forth between men and women with a pendulum-like regularity and occasionally wonders if this fluidity has hindered her deeper understanding of either gender. But she has listened to straight girlfriends with their endless complaints about the inscrutability of boyfriends, and to straight men that cannot fathom their incomprehensible girlfriends. She is comforted by what seems to be an endemic ignorance on the entire subject.

Before Hard there was the fling with the married woman with a successful husband and a kid. The woman claimed it was the first time for her, the cheating part and the same-sex angle. Nadine was sad when her lover ended it, and in a place of genuine vulnerability. That was the week she had met Hard. She wishes she could transplant her Chihuahua's personality into Hard. She gazes at her dog, lying on the rug at her feet, chewing a golf ball. Diablo looks at her with large brown eyes that bespeak a world of understanding, sympathy and love.

She suspects Hard no longer loves her, if he ever did. Their relationship had begun in a burst of optimism, Nadine hoping her streak of bad luck had come to an end and was extremely disappointed when she discovered he was married and seemed ambivalent about leaving his wife. And this was five minutes after meeting him. She wonders whether her life is on some kind of frantic loop, an endlessly repeating catastrophe? Are there any men who are not incorrigible liars or manipulative cheats? If there are, they must exist in a shining realm to which Nadine has not gleaned the access code. And she is sick of it. It isn't like Nadine to raise hell, particularly when it comes to men, but she has reached a point where she is feeling like the universe has painted a target on her back and the gods are hurling darts.

Her cell phone rings and she checks the caller. Chief Harding Marvin. He's more than an hour late so she debates for a moment whether or not she should answer.

"What?" Hoping her tone will instantly convey her level of displeasure.

"Sorry, I didn't call sooner." Nadine listens in chilly silence. "I was doing some work for Mary Swain. I'm a precinct captain for the campaign. Didn't I tell you that?"

"Yeah, Hard, you told me. Like, ten times."

"You still want me to come over?"

"You can do what you want."

He tells her he'll be there in half an hour.

Nadine mixes a pitcher of margaritas. Decides if Hard so much as looks at her cross-eyed, she'll empty it on his head. She reapplies her makeup and evaluates her reflection in the bathroom mirror. Other than the dark circles under her eyes, she likes what she sees. When the doorbell rings, Nadine waits a full second before getting up to answer it. Hard is holding a dozen roses and a paperback book that he thrusts toward her.

"*The Collected Poems of Robert Service?*"

"Best American poet in history." He walks past her into the house. "M. V. goddamn P., Nadine. Most Valuable Poet."

Nadine fills a vase with water. While she is arranging the flowers, he reads her *The Shooting of Dan McGrew*, a manly poem about a fellow who gets into a scrape in the Yukon and pays for it with his life. There is a catch in Hard's throat when he gets to the end. Nadine is touched by this, Hard not one to display his emotions anywhere they can be seen. When he kisses her neck, she elbows him away, wanting to punish him for his tardiness, his insensitivity, and what she worries is the general pointlessness of their arrangement, but he persists and when he tries again she lets him. Then they are in the bedroom having sex, Hard on top of her, Nadine staring at the ceiling thinking about whether or not she'd even run off with him were he to ask her, and she briefly wonders if she would even be letting him fuck her had she not overdone it with the Valium.

After sex the two of them quickly dressed. It was as if they didn't want to face the intimacy their nakedness suggested. Now her legs are crossed, accenting the fuscia paint on her toenails. Nadine and Hard are seated on the sofa drinking margaritas. Diablo is watching them from his perch on the chair across the room. She finishes her drink and asks Hard if he wants another. When he says no, she gets up and pours one for herself.

She returns to the sofa and sips the drink. She crosses her legs again, lets her sandal dangle. A while ago Hard had talked about taking her down to Cabo for a weekend to go deep sea fishing and she is hoping he'll mention it again so they can firm it up. He had told her he had to get home in an hour and she wanted some sense of a plan before he departs. This is when he mentions perhaps they should not see each other any longer. Nadine's sandal drops to the floor.

"Why?"

"It's not like I don't want to but my life's complicated enough. I'd love to keep doing *this*."

"You mean you want to keep fucking me?"

"Come on, girl. That's not fair. I don't give *The Collected Poems of Robert Service* to everyone."

Nadine takes a moment to register the absurdity of the words Hard has just spoken. As if she cares a dust mote for Robert Service, or any other poet for that matter. Hard could have recited *Purgatorio* from memory and it would not have made a difference. Synapses firing wildly, her only concern is survival. Her hold on a stable life is slipping and the poems of Robert Service are, in this context, a provocation.

"I can't stand Robert Service! I don't care about the friggin Yukon!" He has no response for that. A man's taste in poetry is a sensitive place in which to strike. Trash his personality, but hands off *The Shooting of Dan McGrew.* Nadine senses his goal is to get out of there without a scene. Something in her does not want that to happen.

"What am I supposed to say?"

"Why can't you leave her?"

"This is tougher than I thought, telling you. You're my gal."

She thinks he might actually mean it. He sounds sincere. But to her ears, they always do. She can't judge anymore, has no faith in her ability to discern the slim reeds of truth in the limitless swamp of prevarication. When she'd been confronted with similar situations in the past, she had had cried but she does not want to do that now.

"I thought we were gonna get married."

She wants him to take her hand and tell her what he said was a mistake and he can't live without her anymore but she's still sober enough to realize that is ridiculous. This won't be the moment he confesses his love but the one where he tries to weasel out of every cheap word he's ever served her.

"I think that's probably not gonna happen."

The margaritas are strong and hers have travelled directly to her impulse inhibitors. This becomes clear when she realizes the words coming out of her mouth are: "What would you think if I told your wife about us?"

He takes another sip of his drink and regards her with what she views as a certain degree of detachment. She doesn't like it. "What would I *think*? I'd think it was not the best course of action."

"Not the best course of action." Nadine is mocking him and, further, she understands the price he has to pay for the sex is the acceptance of her mocking—at least temporarily. She knows he considers himself a gentleman and will at least hear her out before departing. "Why not?" It is a ridiculous follow-up, but she can't think of anything else to say.

"Now, look," he says, as if to a child, "I'm not gonna leave Vonda Jean and she's not gonna leave me."

"How do you know?" Nadine senses she is starting to sound desperate and pitiable and that makes her angrier than she already is. She wishes she hadn't consumed the second margarita. And all that Valium.

"I've done this kind of thing before. And she knows."

"She does?"

"And she hasn't left."

"If she lets you fool around, then why can't we go to Cabo? It's an open marriage, right?" This is reflexive, and the desperate pathetic feeling already pulsing through her intensifies. Why can't she just dump her margarita on his thick-skulled head? Because she has already drained it. There is the remainder of the pitcher, resting in the pass-through window of her kitchen. But does she want that kind of melodrama? "You said it was open, Hard. The marriage."

"That was kind of an exaggeration, maybe. Nadine, look. A lot of people depend on me, not just my wife. They don't need to know about this. We had a good time and I do care about you."

"What about that job in your office we talked about?" She's already retreating from the marriage fantasy, trying to tamp her pique into the manageable form of a job request.

"If you call in a month or so, we'll see if we can't get that set up. I've got to help Mary Swain get elected first. She's an important woman." This assessment pierces Nadine, who looks away and thinks about Hard's implication.

Nadine has suffered through enough similar situations to recognize a blow off. What will happen if she calls police headquarters: polite runaround and no job. It wasn't like there was a quid pro quo when they started sleeping together, but the highhandedness, the dismissal, galls her.

She rises and walks to the kitchen a little unsteadily, carrying her empty glass with her. There, she fills it with water from the tap and chugs it down. Despite her admonition that he should not expect to be fed, Nadine had prepared a bowl of melon balls before Hard's arrival, taking the time to scoop out the cantaloupe and honeydew and arrange them artfully in a State of New Mexico commemorative bowl she had purchased on a trip to a tennis clinic in Albuquerque. The melon balls were going to be served with the margaritas but what was the point now? She looks at her recalcitrant soon-to-be-ex-lover and inhales through her nostrils trying to steady her nerves. The post-coital relaxation she was experiencing earlier has vanished. The emptiness she usually feels—the accrual of bad memories, wrong choices and rotten luck—tiptoes back in, and gets comfortable. Taking a salad fork, Nadine spears a melon ball and places it in her mouth. She chews and lets the cool juice wash down her throat. Her stomach gurgles and she remembers she forgot to eat dinner. Glances over and sees the Lean Cuisine teriyaki chicken congealed on a plate next to the microwave.

Through the pass-through window she can observe Hard facing away from her, sipping his drink. Nadine thinks about the Mexican he claims to have killed while working with Immigration. How he seemed to take on a new persona, Hard Plus, just like the Hard she knew, only stronger, more formidable. And how men like Hard never seem to pay a price for their actions but are allowed to repeat them again and again.

Taking the bowl of melon balls, Nadine steps out of the kitchen. She regards Hard from the rear, an Indian peeking out from behind a rock at a settler encampment. Sees the bullet head set on broad shoulders. She can discern the outline of the muscles in his back against the tightness of his khaki shirt. Hard seriously Alpha. She can see why he is a leader, a man with a future and not just in law enforcement but to hear him tell it, in politics, too.

When Nadine stabs him in the neck with the salad fork she misses the jugular vein by less than an inch. Still, there is a lot of blood. He doesn't scream but leaps from the chair, grabs her wrist and wrestles the weapon from her, cursing. Then he roughly shoves her away. When she staggers back, her heel catches on the cheap knit rug and she falls to the floor where she watches Hard press his palm to his neck for a moment, then hold it in front of him, dripping with blood. Hard walks toward the bathroom as Diablo bounds from the other side of the room and barks like someone has fastened an electroshock ring to his little scrotum and turned the dial to ten. Astonished at her own audacity, Nadine remains on the floor as Hard emerges from the bathroom, a bloody towel now pressed to his neck, keeping a wary eye on his tormentors. Top volume shrieking pours from the dog. When Hard makes for the door, the animal bolts across the floor and leaps at him. Still holding the towel to his wounded neck, he kicks the Chihuahua away but this only further animates Diablo, who clamps his jaws on the man's left ankle. It takes a well-placed kick to dislodge him and the Desert Hot Springs Police Chief wisely uses this gap in the action to slide through the door.

There's an advantage in stabbing a married guy, Nadine thinks. He doesn't have much in the way of recourse.

After Hard leaves, she lies down on her bed cradling Diablo and looks at the Taser she had surreptitiously liberated from his belt when he had gone to the bathroom after sex. Why had she stabbed him with a fork when she had had the Taser at her disposal? It certainly would have conveyed her feelings more forcefully. Jam it under his armpit and the man would have thought the Devil had stuck him with a pitchfork. Why did she always do things in half measures? In considering the efficacy of Tasers versus forks, she finds herself reflecting that perhaps she should stop dating for a while since it is obviously causing more stress than she had realized.

As Nadine strokes Diablo's head, she reflects on the threat she has made. What could possibly be gained by calling his wife? As a mostly rational person, she knew the answer: not much. Nonetheless, she is still irate at what she perceives to be the arrogant way in which she has been treated and deeply resents how powerless it makes her feel, how inconsequential. And that only makes her more irate. Although she has already stabbed him in the neck, she wants to hurt him in a more lasting way, a way that goes far beyond insulting his taste in poetry. And then she wants to go to Mexico with him, drink cocktails festooned with umbrellas, and at sunset have sex on the beach while fishermen unload their nets in the dimming distance. Nadine can hardly begin to understand herself. At least she had the foresight to purloin the Taser. It will probably come in handy.

CHAPTER EIGHT

T he hillside home of the Duke family is nestled in the Little Tuscany section on the northwest side of Palm Springs. In the long shadow of the rust-colored San Jacinto Mountains, the house is a perfectly restored exemplar of the mid-century modern style. Relatively modest, especially in contrast to nearby architectural showplaces once owned by such luminaries of yesteryear as Dinah Shore and Bob Hope, the wood post and beam L-shaped one story structure has a pleasing flow. The living room comprises one wing and is walled on two sides entirely in glass through which the garden, the pool and the mountains provide a magnificent panorama. The kitchen is at the fulcrum and the three bedrooms lie at the other, longer end of the house. Built in 1955, it is furnished in a style that quotes from the era, without replicating it. Randall had no interest in mid-century modernism and neither, initially, did Kendra. It was Maxon Brae, a member of the Palm Springs Architectural Conservancy, who prevailed on her to purchase this home when it came on the market. Maxon had informed Kendra that it would only help the family business if they had a house on the local preservationist tour. Insecure about her own non-musical aesthetic sense she signed on to Maxon's vision. As for Randall, he would have been happy to buy a house on a golf course but acquiesced to his spouse and advisor.

Kendra sits on a kitchen stool eating chocolate ice cream from a glass mug with the words *Gerald Ford Invitational Golf Tournament* embossed on it and trying to forget the reason the

Palm Springs Academy had called earlier. She can't figure out her daughter. The girl is unusually intelligent, a straight A student taking Advanced Placement courses who writes superbly and until recently played the violin in the school orchestra before deciding it no longer comported with her image of herself, whatever *that* was. And why she would be sending naked pictures of herself to her boyfriend Scott, a weedy high school senior with a vacant quality that Kendra correctly ascribed to excessive dope smoking, was impossible to understand. Brittany claimed he was some kind of computer genius but if that were true, why did the picture scandal erupt? Did he not know the word *encryption*? In the car ride back from school, she had barked at her daughter for a few minutes about the shame she had brought on herself and her family but her intensity drained when the girl offered no defense. They entered the house in strained silence. Brittany headed to her room and Kendra to a calming glass of Zinfandel. The girl is now writing a school-mandated essay on why this kind of moral turpitude, if not held in check, will lead to the disintegration of Western Civilization.

A laptop lies open in front of Kendra and she is reading the latest posting on a blog written by some supercilious jerk calling himself Desert Machiavelli. She has no idea who this person is but she hates him. Desert Machiavelli is brutal toward everyone but it's Randall he's taking aim at today so Kendra is already tense when she hears the word "Mom!" discharged from behind her like a weapon. Turning, she faces an annoyed Brittany. "Why did you write 'please start your essay' on my Facebook wall?"

"Because it's the only way I know you'll pay attention."

Brittany makes a sound involving both snorting and coughing distributed in equal measure and intended to convey extreme displeasure. The teenager twirls a lock of magenta-streaked hair. A tight white spaghetti strap shirt is stretched over her nearly flat chest and a black miniskirt rides high on pipe cleaner thighs. In her hand is a paperback copy of *Slouching Toward Bethlehem,* the pages overflowing with post-it notes.

"Do I have to go to that lame party with Daddy tomorrow?"

"The Purity Ball?"

"I have a paper on Joan Didion due at the end of the week and I'd like it to be good."

"Well, you'd better get cracking because you're going to that event with Daddy." Brittany's spirit deflates at this news, a phenomenon to which Kendra pays no attention since it happens on a daily basis. "In the meantime, you have to eat something. There's lasagna in the oven."

"I had some raisins, okay?"

"How many?"

"Three."

"Boxes?"

"Raisins."

"Is that supposed to be a joke?"

"No!"

Kendra regards her daughter helplessly. The two of them have been engaged in a variation of this conversation for the past several years and she is justifiably concerned that the girl has an eating disorder. But Brittany's energy level is high and that stare of hers bores right into you! It has a spooky power, the kind exhibited by certain religious leaders. There are times Kendra can feel her daughter looking through her, past her eyes and into her brain, as if the kid could understand not only what her mother was thinking but what she would be thinking a minute from now. She has discussed this with Randall but he claimed to have no idea what she was talking about. It's not as if Brittany has superpowers or something; there's nothing paranormal happening, Randall said. She's just a little intense sometimes.

But the girl sees everything going on around her. There are times Kendra just has to look away. Through the kitchen windows the ragged mountains are visible in the distance, bronze in the afternoon light.

"You are going to sit at that table and eat lasagna."

"That's child abuse," Brittany says. "What if I have, like, ten raisins?"

"You're going to starve to death, Brit." The hum of a vacuum cleaner drifts in from the living room where the Salvadoran cleaning lady is working. The woman, a grandmother, does not understand anorexia. It is not something they have in El Salvador.

"I won't starve," Brittany assures her. "I'm just not hungry right now." The girl runs her hand through her hair. It does not escape Kendra that her daughter did not appear that different from runway models she had seen on television. But in her view, their haunted, emaciated look does not belong on a high school senior.

"You're going to the Purity Ball with Daddy tomorrow, and you have to eat something at the dinner. Don't make Daddy tell you to eat. Everyone's going to be watching him."

"Did you tell him about what happened at school?"

"He's campaigning today, so, no. And I'll make a deal with you. I won't mention it to him if you eat some of that lasagna."

"You swear?" Kendra nods. "Whatever." Brittany grunts in displeasure as she departs.

Kendra takes another can of the chocolate drink out of the refrigerator. Wonders for a moment if drinking several diet drinks defeats the purpose but Brittany vexes her and that justifies it in her mind. Better diet drinks than vodka, she concludes.

Kendra's cell phone rings and she looks at the caller ID: Private Caller. She doesn't like to pick up the phone not knowing who it is, but Randall has taught her that you never know when it might be a donor so she dutifully presses the Talk button and says hello.

"Kendra?" She doesn't recognize the caller, a woman.

"Who is this?"

"Remember me?" Flirtatious, tense.

Kendra doesn't bother lowering her voice since the only adult in the house is the cleaning lady whose grasp of English is, at best, vague. Then it comes roaring back. Nadine! Oh, god, why is this person calling? What could she possibly want?

"I need to see you." The air conditioning is frosting the house, but Kendra feels her body temperature leap two degrees. "Please.

"I asked you not to call here."

The voice says "Meet me for a drink at Melvyn's at 6:00. There's something I want to show you."

"I can't come."

There is a long pause on the other end, during which Kendra debates whether to just hang up. This is someone she has no desire to ever see again.

"It can help your husband."

Kendra hands the parking valet her keys and enters Melvyn's. The place is old school, venerable by Palm Springs standards, which means it evokes the Technicolor era of big-finned cars and unfiltered cigarettes. Framed black and white photographs of dapper Melvyn the desert dandy line the walls, smiling with his famous customers, images of deeply tanned men in suits with thin lapels, women wearing ermine and lots of makeup, everyone looking Rat Pack. A long, tiled bar trimmed with mahogany runs along the left side of the room. The white tablecloths are starched. It's just shy of the dinner hour and the place is nearly empty. Kendra and Randall come here occasionally. If anyone sees her they'll think she's just having a drink with a friend.

Nadine waves from her seat at the end of the otherwise empty bar. She wears a clingy yellow sweater with a scooped front, a blue cotton skirt and tan flats. A small gold tennis racquet dangles from a thin chain around her neck. Kendra sits next to her on an upholstered bar stool.

Nadine's tan masks a tired face. Kendra thinks she looks as if she hasn't had much rest lately. But she smells good. Like lemons. Nadine thanks her for coming. Kendra offers a tight smile, then looks around again, making sure she hasn't missed anyone who might know her. Not that sitting with Nadine is suspicious behavior. She just doesn't want to be blindsided in the middle of their conversation. Two matronly women are getting a head start on a bottle of Riesling in the dining room. They wear expensive dresses, lots of jewelry, and bored expressions.

The bartender approaches, an older guy with a red face and a full head of dyed-black hair. "I'll have another," Nadine says, holding her glass. "Seven and seven." The bartender nods and looks at Kendra. She hopes he won't recognize her. His expression says he doesn't.

Kendra orders a Mel-tini, a concoction of raspberry vodka, peach schnapps and cranberry juice. The bartender nods and turns around to mix the drink. "What's this about?"

"You can't be friendly? It's been almost a year."

"I'm a little stressed out."

"The campaign?"

"Yes, and other things."

The bartender places Kendra's drink in front of her on top of a cocktail napkin with a pencil drawing of James Dean printed on it. She takes a sip, then another.

"How's Brittany? Is she still playing?"

"Oh for heaven's sake, Nadine, I shouldn't even be here. But now that I am, I want to be honest with you. This encounter is not really appropriate, so . . . "

"You're hurting my feelings."

"I don't want to do that. But I have limited time. There's an event tonight."

"She has so much potential as a tennis player."

"She hasn't played much lately," Kendra says, draining most of her Mel-tini. She's barely eaten today and the drink sneaks up on her. It's a pleasant sensation, one that takes some of the edge off being sucked back into Nadine's orbit, so she signals for another.

"Are you all right?"

"I'm fine." Then, considerably more relaxed than she was a moment ago, "Brittany was suspended from school for two days." She has no idea why she's telling Nadine this other than she is overcome with the compulsion to share the information with someone who knows the girl and will be supportive. Kendra finishes the remainder of her drink. She daubs her lipstick with James Dean's face, crushes the napkin and places it in the glass.

Nadine leans forward conspiratorially. "I have a Valium in my purse."

"I'm okay, really. Do you know what sexting is?"

"Sure."

Kendra thinking *Of course you do.* "That's why Brittany was sent home today."

"She wasn't doing it with a teacher or anything?"

"No, thank god."

"I sent pictures of myself to Chief Marvin."

"Chief Marvin? Is he an Indian?"

"The police chief. You know, in Desert Hot Springs? Hard Marvin?" Kendra looks baffled. Is she supposed to know the person Nadine just referenced? Or care that she sent him pictures? "We were intimate."

This revelation arrives like a giant metal object from outer space, one that is puzzling when glimpsed on radar and whose meaning is not inherently apparent when viewed with the naked eye, and Kendra cannot imagine what Nadine means by telling her. In the catalogue of possibilities reviewed by Kendra during the drive to the restaurant, reasons Nadine might have wanted to meet, this one had not occurred to her. Further, what interest could she have possibly had in the sexual peccadilloes of Chief Marvin? Kendra assumes Nadine has had multiple sex partners. That Chief Marvin was among them means nothing. Still, she feels impelled to say something so out comes: "Intimate?"

"We had an affair."

"Why are you telling me?"

"I have emails he sent me."

The bartender chooses this moment to return. Kendra hopes he has not heard any of the conversation. He serves the drinks and silently slips away. Nadine withdraws a neatly folded piece of paper from her black leather purse and hands it to Kendra.

"Read it."

Kendra unfolds the paper:

From: Harding Marvin < hardmarv1@gmail.com
Subject: Sexy You
To: "Nadine Never" < love40@yahoo.com
Date: Tuesday October 2 1:23 P.M.

You are a glorious sexy girl and I hope you understand that, my sweet Nadine. Can you comprehend how beautiful your smile is? Have you been informed lately how warm your blue eyes are and how they glow with the special nature of your soul? I mentioned to you that when I married I did not need love, but as the battle scars of life have worn on me this is something I don't mind telling you now I want. I love your gentle kisses and your tan lines and your magnificent twin peaks . . .

When Kendra arrives at the phrase twin peaks she folds the piece of paper in two and demurely hands it back to Nadine.

"Is that his real name?"

"It's Harding. But everyone calls him Hard."

Kendra looks down the bar where the bartender is reading a newspaper. The ladies in the dining room are now eating their dinner. "I'm a little confused. Where do I fit into this?"

Nadine looks away impatiently, her manner conveying slight annoyance at having to now impart such an obvious piece of information. Kendra waits for her to continue. Lowering her voice to a whisper, Nadine says, "He's close to Mary Swain's campaign and he's married. She's all family values and come to Jesus, right? So if this gets out about Hard, it's not gonna help her."

Kendra knows the American version of politics is played with everything from pointed elbows to pointed knives but she has never been confronted with anything this contemptible. The campaign has been rough, charges and counter-charges flying, and the election is now a week away. Any advantage is gold. But erotic emails from Hard Marvin to Nadine? This is not traffic in which Kendra wants to play. Because, really, what could it do? Marvin might have problems with his own job, but how, exactly, is it supposed to damage Mary Swain? The buffed and ruthless candidate would flush him like a crushed bug.

Kendra's sense of decorum restrains her from just getting up and walking out and she dutifully pushes the conversation forward.

"What do you want me to do, Nadine?"

"I'm moving to Seattle. I need money."

Kendra takes a gulp of her second Mel-tini, wonders how far Nadine is prepared to take this.

"Do you want to ask your husband?"

"I don't think he wants to go there. It's not like it's you and Mary Swain." Kendra says this half-joking, wanting to relieve the tension she is feeling. It doesn't work. Her shoulders creep toward her ears. Breathing is shallow. Although she manages to remain cool on the surface, Kendra wildly calculates the possible ramifications of Nadine's startling arrival back in her life. The idea of slipping sexually charged emails to some slavering journalist in order to torpedo an opposing candidate is repulsive to her, although in the annals of campaign tactics it is hardly unheard of and even, in certain circles, admired.

"I'm looking for fifteen thousand dollars."

Nadine is clearly a little more of an untethered trunk on a pitching deck than Kendra had realized and this is a situation she will need to handle with the delicacy of an art forger. Nadine has nearly finished her second drink—at least it's the second one she has seen her consume—and Kendra does not want there to be even the slightest possibility of a scene. She knocks back the Mel-tini, and says "Look, Nadine, I wanted to give you the courtesy of a face to face meeting which is why I'm here, but I can tell you this is not something Randall's going to go for." Her tone is quiet, calm, and tinged with disingenuous regret. She has wrestled her panic into temporary submission. Political wives are masters of the crsatz, trained to systematically annihilate any genuine emotion or thought. As Randall's wife, Kendra dissembles as naturally as she smears butter substitute on a non-fat corn muffin.

Nadine appears momentarily deflated. Kendra watches her face for signs of storm clouds, hopes the reaction will be subdued and not lead to public histrionics. "Are you sure?"

"I think I know Randall pretty well."

"You don't even want to ask him?"

An impulse arises in Kendra to reach across the table and slap Nadine hard across the face. She knows a swift physical strike can be emotionally satisfying but that kind of behavior will not only fail to create the desired long-term result, it will surely exacerbate the present state of affairs. "Nadine, this isn't a good idea. It's the kind of thing that can come back to bite you. You're better than that," Kendra lies.

Nadine tilts her head and smiles crookedly. Kendra thinks she is trying for impish, but it reads more like a tic.

"Its not just Hard." She waits for Kendra's reaction, but none is forthcoming.

"Nadine, I'm not following you."

"I could tell them about us which I don't want to do but I could. The matching tattoos we got down in Mexico are pretty neat."

Pretty neat? Kendra can think of a few words to describe what Nadine has just said but "pretty" and "neat" are not among them.

"You're blackmailing us?" How can something like this be occurring, she wonders, a turn of events so cheap and tawdry. Is it not enough that she has sacrificed (temporarily, please God) her own career to perform as the smiling mannequin at Randall Duke's side, that she, a professional entertainer, articulate, ambitious, and determined, has been relegated to serving as caretaker to a moody teenager? And why did she allow herself a fling with this tanning technician who is threatening to smash her carefully constructed future like a house of toothpicks.

"That is definitely the wrong word. It's blackmail when you pay me. No one's blackmailing anybody. I would never do that. But I'd like to see you try to explain the matching kitty tattoos we got on our butts." Nadine smiles, as if this is amusing.

"Don't do this," Kendra says, in a tone she hopes is equal parts threatening and advisory. Kendra doesn't know Nadine well. They had become acquainted at a tennis clinic where Nadine was one of the coaches and the two of them met for coffee at Nadine's suggestion. She had told Kendra she wanted career advice and Kendra, always looking for an advantage, had assumed Nadine was better positioned in life than she actually was. Still, the vivacious instructor was energetic and fun, and when she volunteered to coach her daughter Kendra couldn't see why not. After their third lesson, when Randall was in Washington, Kendra had asked Nadine if she wanted to come over for a drink. Later she wondered what could possibly have motivated her. Boredom? Curiosity? Or simply the opportunity to explore an aspect of herself she had yet to acknowledge. They had drunk wine, watched TV for a while and waited until Brittany had gone to bed. When Nadine ran the tip of her forefinger down Kendra's neck Kendra shivered but she didn't object.

Since Kendra was concerned that her daughter might see them, their subsequent encounters occurred at Nadine's place. When Nadine suggested they go on a tennis holiday to Mexico, just the two of them, Kendra viewed it as a satisfying way to get back at Randall for his myriad transgressions.

Kendra had never had sex with a woman before but after getting over her initial trepidation, she found it to be not dissimilar to being with a man: the sex became dull and soon ennui spread like the wild orange flowers that bloom in the high desert every April. When Nadine lost her job, finding work was all she talked about. Kendra was sympathetic but this was beginning to feel too much like being in an actual relationship so she ended it as gracefully as possible.

What the two women shared was more a series of trysts and Kendra's view of Nadine is not predicated on a deep well of experience with her. This lack of information suggests that the woman's behavior might now be highly unpredictable. That she is trying to peddle compromising emails is already beyond the pale. Clearly, Kendra has misread her. She had made Nadine for a party girl, not a criminal.

"Are you sure you don't want to at least ask him?" Nadine says.

Kendra looks directly at her and whispers: "This is an extremely bad plan."

"People really like Mary Swain," Nadine says. "They think she's sexy. Your husband is gonna need all the help he can get."

Kendra considers this for a moment. She knows Nadine is correct on both counts. But this scheme reeks of desperate and foolish. Not every journalist would devour a tidbit like this, but what if Nadine tipped off the Machiavelli blogger?

"Bad things happen to people who do what you're doing, Nadine. Really bad things."

"What do you mean?" Nadine says, like they're just two friends chatting.

"Use your imagination," Kendra says. Her eyes are pitiless and Nadine seems startled by this response.

Kendra drops some money on the bar and leaves the restaurant. She almost expects Nadine to follow her out and continue their conversation in full view of the parking valet and is surprised to find herself out there alone. Her foot keeps time to the mad beat in her head as she waits for her Chinese lantern-red Mustang and when it arrives she dives in as if she is fleeing a bank robbery.

http://WWW.DESERT-MACHIAVELLI.COM

10.30 – 7:32 P.M.

As we hurtle toward the Apocalypse—sorry, I mean the election—lets take a moment and reflect on the Randall Duke career. He's an Army veteran and a graduate of the University of Santa Clara Law School. Randall is running for his fourth term in the United States House of Representatives. He's a member of the House Rules Committee. He's a member of the Homeland Security Committee and the Sub-committee on Border, Maritime, and Global Terrorism. And, finally, he's a member of the Judiciary Committee. But what, exactly, has he done in Congress during his time as your representative? He would tell you he has brought federal dollars and jobs to the district. He would tell you he has fought for veterans' benefits. He would tell you he has sponsored a hate crimes bill. But has his name been attached to any major piece of legislation? No, my friends, it has not.

Now lets look at Mary Swain. She's a former flight attendant on a private jet with a sketchy educational background and the mother of four young kids. We know she likes church and sports and making babies. But do we really know her? She claims to have been born in the Upper Peninsula of Michigan, close to Canada, but where are the records? Mary Swain has never produced a birth certificate. I think you Blogheads will agree there is a case to be made that she is a closet Canadian and is not even eligible to run for this office. Whatever you want to say about Randall Duke, the man served in an Army bomb disposal unit under combat conditions. He is an American hero. Mary Swain, on the other hand, has excellent legs.

CHAPTER NINE

W hen the sun drops behind the mountains but there is still light in the western sky, Jimmy leashes Bruno and takes him for a walk. Surveying the Yucca Valley spread below, he considers his older brother's latest maneuver. He knows Dale would not have been released without Randall's intercession and he also knows this wouldn't have happened if it weren't going to benefit Randall. Growing up in Palm Desert, the two oldest Duke boys had always been competitive with each other. Both were athletes and because Jimmy was the physical equal of his older brother, they were always scrapping for dominion. It was an ongoing conflict, never settled. Dale had liked Jimmy well enough, but he idolized Randall. Whether because Randall was the oldest, or the better-looking one, or just because he was less ornery than Jimmy—a boy who never backed down from a fight and wasn't above picking them—it was his oldest brother that Dale tried to emulate. Throw in that Randall did well in school, always had fine looking girlfriends, and worked two jobs in the summer so he could afford an orange 1975 Camaro with racing stripes, mag wheels, dual overhead cams, and a V-8 engine, he was the one that was easy for a kid brother to admire.

School was always a struggle for Dale and while his older brothers played varsity football and baseball, he had never made it off the J.V. Their mother was a sickly woman who read the Bible every day and despite tubercular lungs, smoked Camel non-filters. She loved all three of her sons, but she felt particularly protective of her youngest. A southern woman, Jimmy could remember the way she called his younger brother Mama's little possum. The nickname was designed to cause problems for any boy cursed with it. Dale hated the handle, resented that he needed to be looked out for. When he was around thirteen, one of his friends overheard Mrs. Duke calling Dale her little possum and next day at school teased him unmercifully. Dale went after the kid and both boys got suspended for fighting. The suspension was face-saving for Dale because his friend had kicked his ass all over the playground. That night at supper, Mrs. Duke had suggested that either Jimmy or Randall avenge their baby brother but this did not fly with their father, the Reverend Donnie Duke, who pointed out that vengeance is mine alone, saith the Lord.

All three Duke boys wanted to please their father. He and Mrs. Duke had met and married in Huntsville, Alabama and moved to the desert in the late 1960s for her delicate health. With a gift for words that he passed on to Randall, Reverend Donnie's balletic tongue made him a natural in the pulpit of the Desert Redeemer, an Assembly of God church in Borrego Springs. Everyone knew him to be a good man, not some hell-fire agent of a punishing God who used the Gospels to put the fear in people, but a gentle soul who tried to teach his sons to do right. He was bereft when his wife died of cancer at forty-nine. Randall was a senior in high school. Jimmy was a sophomore then and Dale in the eighth grade and the Reverend did his best as a single parent for the next five years until a stroke claimed him at sixty-two. Dale had come home and found his father dead on the kitchen floor, two Hungry Man TV dinners burnt in the oven.

Randall was in his third year of law school at Santa Clara when the Reverend Duke went to his reward. Jimmy was at University of Redlands and Dale a high school senior. The new role as family patriarch came naturally to Randall and he got a judge to grant him custody of his youngest brother. He was renting a house with three law school friends and Dale moved in with them. At the time Jimmy was glad Randall had stepped up, but later he wondered if Dale's life might have turned out better if he had been the one to get custody. He knew it wasn't realistic; only nineteen, what judge would have placed his younger sibling with him?

Randall enrolled Dale in a local high school in Santa Clara but the change of venue did not inspire the youngest Duke to care more about his education. Mostly he hung around with Randall and his buddies. With Randall's tacit approval, the guys treated Dale like an errand boy. To pick up spending money he would do their food shopping, clean the house, and perform odd jobs like car washing or yard work. He didn't have his own bed so he slept on the dirty living room couch. He went to school when he felt like it, and his brother was too busy with his studies to supervise him.

It was around this time that Randall developed a fondness for cocaine. The first year of law school is a well-known killing floor and those who can't keep up are ground to dust and discarded. Randall was spending late nights buried in books and the coke kept him marching.

The oldest and youngest Duke brothers and their housemates lived in a quiet residential area of single-family homes and they blended in with the teachers, accountants, and storeowners who were their neighbors. Young mothers pushed baby-laden prams past children riding bikes in the shadows of old growth trees and Girl Scouts sold cookies door- to-door. It was a placid, family neighborhood. So Randall was surprised one spring night when a wild party erupted at the house next door. This was the home of a middle-aged couple, the husband a pilot for a regional airline and the wife a guidance counselor, and he assumed they were away and their college age sons had commandeered the place for a blowout. He was seated on the concrete floor of the garage with Dale while engaged in this speculation. It was after eleven o'clock at night and Randall had a test in tort law the following morning. They were on the floor of the garage because Randall was snorting lines of cocaine off an REO Speedwagon CD and didn't want to do this in the house since his roommates might ask for a line. The stuff was expensive and he couldn't afford to be generous.

It was a hot night and they had left the garage door open. The house had a driveway shaped like the letter J and the garage faced the dark backyard. The bay they were sitting in was usually occupied by a yellow '67 Cadillac but its owner was out on a date. *Sussidio* by Phil Collins was blaring at them from the party next door. Dale later told Jimmy that he liked that song, maybe that's why he was distracted when it happened.

Two headlights washed over them, a car pulling into the curved driveway. Randall was bent over the coke, taking his second hit. He looked up from the powdery tin foil in time to see that it was not his housemate's old Caddy, but a black and white being driven by a Santa Clara police officer. They later learned that another housemate had been studying for the same tort exam and had called the police to complain about the noise coming from their neighbor's place. The officer was stopping to check with the complainant before rousting the party. When Randall realized it was the police, he flew out of the garage like he had springs in his feet and was down the street before the cop figured out what was going on but Dale didn't think to run. Instead, he gathered up the tin foil and crammed it in his pocket ignoring the headlights flaring on him like a camera flash.

When Randall came to visit him in the juvenile lock-up the next day he said Dale, if I go down for this I'll never be a lawyer. My life will be over. I can do way more good for you down the line, and I mean way more, if you just take the bullet. He all but begged and then pointed out that he had never asked his youngest brother to do anything for him before this. And he never would again.

Dale loved Randall, who had taken him in when their father had died, so what could he do but his brother's bidding? There was no money to bail him out and he remained incarcerated until his court appearance.

It was while visiting him in the lock-up that Jimmy learned exactly what had happened. Dale was already skinny but he had lost weight in the four days he'd been inside. He laid it out for Jimmy how their brother had asked him to take one for the family and that he was willing to do it. Jimmy recognized the toughness his little brother was selling for the posture it was, that he was still the kid who had gotten his ass kicked all over the schoolyard. Jimmy had tried to talk him out of it, to tell him that Randall needed to clean up his own problems, but Dale was proud that he was finally in a position to provide something of worth.

The day Dale was sentenced Randall had a final exam in contract law and couldn't be there. But Jimmy was in the courtroom when Dale stood and nodded as the judge told him he hoped he would use the next phase of his life to reflect on his behavior and sentenced him to serve in the N.A. Chaderjian Youth Correctional Facility until his eighteenth birthday. Jimmy remembers watching his brother try not to cry.

Dale had used that time to become acquainted with tough rednecks from Stockton, wannabe rappers from Oakland, junior division criminals from all over northern California in for B and E, robbery, drug dealing, assault and manslaughter. He was released with a working knowledge of how to fashion a weapon out of a bedspring, with his first crude tattoo—the letters T-H-U-G on his stomach—and with a sense that life was not going to work out for him in a traditional way.

This is what Jimmy thinks about as he takes Bruno off the

leash and lets him run. It's what he thinks about when he takes a shower and gets ready to go out. And it's what he thinks about when he climbs back in his pickup and heads out to meet his former associate, Cali Pasco. Randall is for Randall. That will never change.

CHAPTER TEN

Piloting the Mustang down the palm-lined streets in the starlit early evening, Kendra's mind is a storm of vexation. The cool of the air conditioning on her supple skin does nothing to tamp her distress. Her heart thuds against her chest wall and she has to concentrate to breathe evenly. The intersection of North Indian Canyon Drive and East Vista Chino comes on her like a curtain rising and when she realizes she is going to run a red light she hit the brakes so hard the Mustang skids and she pitches forward. Checks the rearview mirror to make sure no one is behind her, puts the car in reverse and backs up to avoid getting clipped by someone equally distracted.

Kendra cannot hold her liquor and after a single drink will experience the heightening of whatever emotion she is currently feeling. So the despair coursing through her is amplified by the combination of vodka and schnapps contained in the pair of Mel-tinis she drained. This encounter with Nadine is a fitting capstone to a series of emotional setbacks. For several years she has occasionally thought that her marriage to Randall is one of convenience. Her choice to remain in it is not the easiest thing for her to deal with since it eats away at her sense of self-esteem, the particularly American creed to which Kendra adheres. You must "reach for the sky," "dare to dream," "believe in yourself." If the mechanism that regulates self-generated optimism is faltering, it feels like the ground might open and swallow you.

Then there is her daughter: meant to be a joy, she has become a stranger. And now what was a little innocent diversion, a lubricious sidebar to her anodyne daily life, a small reward for the quiet depredations she suffered as a political spouse, is looming as a disaster that could end Randall's political career and with it their future.

Driving past a sprawling golf course she considers her equally unappetizing options. She could do nothing, although that carries a high risk. Perhaps Nadine is bluffing. Being involved in a scandal will not help in her quest to escape the confines of the tanning business and propel herself back into the more expansive world of resort tennis. If Nadine has her own interests at heart, this will not advance them. But Kendra cannot count on Nadine being rational.

She can always pay the money to have her sit on the compromising material. But perhaps Nadine isn't telling her everything. Perhaps there is further evidence of their affair that she is withholding until a more strategically propitious time. Nadine said she had no intention of blackmailing her but how could she be certain? And once Kendra allows herself to be blackmailed, there is no way to know when it will stop. What if she had pictures? Nadine could continue to bleed her for money, or she could release the images for sport. There is no way of knowing. And since pictures hardly exist as physical photographs anymore but rather as indolent pixels brought to life at the stroke of a key, there would be no negatives to destroy. They would always remain, like free radicals in a human body, waiting for just the right moment to coalesce into something fatal.

The next option is to summon her courage, tell Randall and see what he advises. After absorbing the shock, she assumes he will act in his own interest and that strategic selfishness will require a degree of cool calculation on his part from which they both might benefit. While this gambit involves admitting a lesbian affair to her husband the week before an election, given Randall's record of serially mangling their marital vows he can hardly object to her doing the same. Although she suspects he will be upset with the timing.

Kendra had caught Randall cheating on her early in their marriage when they were taking a spa weekend at a resort in Arizona. Her mud wrap had been rescheduled due to over-booking and she returned to their suite to find him bending a chambermaid over the credenza. She had torn a lamp from its moorings and thrown it at him, and then flew home a day early.

Back then Jimmy was single and upon her return Kendra sought him out. The two of them had always liked one another. At her wedding Jimmy had been the best man and the general theme of his toast was Randall's utter unworthiness of a grade A premium bride like Kendra Kerry. He had had a few drinks that afternoon but only enough to heighten the poetry of the moment and his words were heartfelt and kind. The truth: Jimmy had been a little jealous of his brother. Kendra was beautiful and talented, and her years around football players both in high school and college had given her the ability to swear and tell a joke, something Jimmy found captivating. So when she turned up at his condo the night she got back early from her spa weekend, he had not been displeased.

It was early summer and the clothes she wore were sheer and revealing. Whether this was by design or by accident, Jimmy never knew. Aware her brother-in-law did not keep a stock of Chardonnay in the refrigerator, she arrived with a bottle and a corkscrew. He filled a couple of highball glasses— stem glasses not part of his *modus operandi* either—and they sat side by side on the living room sofa. She was edgy, but her makeup was perfect. Kendra confessed what had happened in Arizona, told him how mortified she had been, and Jimmy pretended to be shocked. But he knew Randall had been sexually profligate prior to his marriage and had suspected that the nuptial state would do nothing to change his habits. He took no joy in being right as he observed his sister-in-law's sadness and Chardonnay-fuelled distress. Kendra cried a little and asked his advice. Divorce was a definite possibility, she was certain. She sipped another glass of wine, then poured a third. The phone rang—it was work-related—and when Jimmy came back from answering it, she slid closer to him. In what had truly been intended as a gesture of comfort, he put his arm around her shoulder and was slightly taken aback when she tilted her face up and kissed him gently on the lips. Although he would have loved to take her to bed, he couldn't let this happen, so he defused the situation by channeling the Reverend Donnie Duke and gassing about the importance of marriage and how she had to pray for the strength to forgive his brother and heal their union. This tactic served to chill her ardor considerably.

It was not something she had appreciated at the time.

When the bottle was empty Jimmy realized he was still working on his first glass. Energy spent, passion vitiated, Kendra curled up on the sofa. Jimmy brought her a pillow, arranged a spare blanket over her and went to bed. The following morning she was gone. They never spoke of that encounter again. By the time it became clear she was not going to leave Randall, the closeness that had existed between them that evening evaporated.

Upon Randall's solo return from the spa weekend, Kendra had made it clear to him that, whatever he was going to do in the way of philandering, he needed to be less cavalier in his approach. Randall had been so grateful for her forbearance he didn't commit adultery again for several weeks. And he had made sure to do it while he was travelling. But for all of her husband's cheating since that time in Arizona, he has managed to keep it from fouling the nest. This has been their arrangement, their quid pro quo. In return for her tolerance of his sexual peccadilloes and not divorcing him, it is understood that, should his career continue its ascent she will remain at his side.

A thought takes shape like the outlines of a cavalry appearing on a ridge: What if Nadine does not have any evidence save for the matching tattoos? Perhaps this whole encounter is some kind of attempt to get her to offer money without Nadine actually extorting her in a technical sense, but rather by a masterful use of nothing more than innuendo. Perhaps the whole thing is a bluff.

But it's not. Kendra quickly dismisses that hopeful notion as the sort of weak thinking that has put her in this situation in the first place. No, there must be real, incontrovertible evidence of her bad judgment and, by extrapolation, her husband's lack of moral fitness for public office.

Kendra's cell phone is ringing when she pulls into her driveway. A message from Nadine. She feels her heart thudding and takes a deep breath before checking it. There is no text, only an attachment. She opens the attachment and waits for it to load. In a moment she is looking at two-inch high video of Nadine's naked ass, the manga kitten tattoo staring at her like a hangman. There is a piece of music with the attachment that Kendra slowly discerns through her panic, Michael Jackson singing *Beat It.* Tiny Video Nadine shakes her booty side to side in time to the music and Kendra's head seems like it's going to fly off her shoulders. But then her emotions abate and she begins to feel a little quiver because however horrifying Nadine's return to her life might be, the time they spent together did have its enjoyable moments. The memories of the clandestine assignations that this video calls forth, stripped of the context in which they had occurred and rendered purely pornographically, are kind of a turn on.

A tapping on the car window snaps her out of the near-trance she is in. Brittany stands there in jeans and a band tee shirt that reads *The Violent Mood Swings.* Kendra slams the phone into her lap hard enough to send sparks to her face. She rolls down the window. If the girl has seen anything, she isn't letting on.

"Do I really have to go to this retarded Purity Ball with Dad?"

"Yes," she tells her daughter. "It's going to be an important night for your father and purity is a very important thing. Particularly now."

"I'm not a virgin, you know."

In an instant the weather pattern on Kendra's face shifts from cloudy to storms as she climbs out of her car and grabs Brittany's forearm. "What did you say?"

"I'm joking! God, I just texted pictures, which you already know since you're like Kim Jong Il."

Entirely too thrown to engage any further in this conversation, Kendra releases her daughter's arm and proceeds into the house without looking back. Inside, she quickly deletes Nadine's email. But she is haunted by the idea that some ghostly hint of it will remain in the device so she slips into the garage where Randall keeps a tool kit. Wielding a hammer she smashes the phone to bits and tosses the wreckage into the garbage.

CHAPTER ELEVEN

Twentynine Palms is home to the Air Ground Combat Center, the largest Marine base in the world. Fourteen miles east of the town of Joshua Tree on Route 62, it's the last outpost of civilization for nearly seventy miles. The quiet high desert streets and modest houses are home to a mixture of military dependents, ex-military, retirees looking for cheap housing, people who hate cities, and lovers of the vast emptiness. Winter nights the temperature drops to near freezing. Summers can get up to a hundred and twenty degrees. It's a tough, hardscrabble place where the residents earn their flinty outlooks because they're hardy enough to live there. If you're passing through on your way to Arizona and want to stop at a bar for a cold beer, know it's the kind of town where the drunken Marine seated to your left might pull a gun.

The Marvin's house is a tidy bungalow painted a deep red at 21 Desert View, on a small rise on the west side facing east over the rooftops. Three wooden steps lead to the front door and the sound of a neighbor's wind chimes floats in the early evening breeze. Mounted above the lintel is a hand-carved sign Hard made in his garage workshop. It reads *Casa Contenta*.

Vonda Jean Marvin likes dinner to be over in time to watch her game show at 7:30 so the Marvin family dined for years at 7:00 every evening. The serving, the conversation, and the dishes invariably done in less than twenty minutes. Now that only Hard and Vonda Jean are at home every evening, it's just the two of them at the kitchen table. Bane lies snoring on the linoleum floor. There is a bandage on Hard's neck covering the wound Nadine inflicted. To his relief, Vonda Jean hasn't asked about it. In her early forties, she is in superb physical condition and rivals Bane in fearsome. Her body is slim and tight in the black tracksuit she's wearing. Her attractive features are permanently set in an expression that suggests someone is trying to hustle her. She teaches various Asian hand-to-hand combat techniques five days a week at Mojave Martial Arts and while the constant pounding has taken a toll on her knees, at a distance, with her silky blonde bob and cinched waist, she could be mistaken for twenty-six.

Although Vonda Jean is not a big woman, especially when glimpsed near her hulking husband, Hard is afraid of her. Her wrath is mighty and Hard is loath to provoke it. He has been tempted to smack her after a few of her more excoriating outbursts, but what stays his hand is the knowledge that, while he could never actually kill her, he believes she is perfectly capable of shooting him in his sleep.

They are eating fried chicken Vonda Jean picked up at KFC since she didn't feel like cooking tonight and Hard never feels like it. There was a time she would have prepared a hot meal for him as a matter of course, but those days have gone the way of the muscle cars he used to favor and the cheap gasoline on which they ran. Vonda Jean doesn't believe in divorce, if she did she would be eating take out chicken with someone else right now. The two of them have reached a sour equilibrium. Vonda Jean is in the early days of the life's next stage and not in a good mood about it. It isn't something she'll discuss with Hard, things she can discuss with him being an evershrinking category. So she chews her chicken and tries to imagine she is somewhere else with someone else and assumes he is doing the same. The only sounds come from the television in the living room. She always leaves it on so she'll have something else to listen to in the event Hard starts talking.

Vonda Jean on her third beer, Hard working to catch up.

They don't get a lot of visitors at night so it is something of a surprise when the doorbell rings. Bane barks energetically. He charges to the door and waits, hind legs tense, anticipates the tearing of a human thorax. Vonda Jean rises and shushes the dog. Bane ignores her and keeps up the racket. A young woman is standing at the door. Tanned and athletic, she gives a half grin when Vonda Jean asks over the din of barking what it is she wants.

"Chief Marvin," is the reply.

"Harding," Vonda Jean calls over her shoulder, the only one in his life who calls him by his birth name. "Someone at the door for you."

Bane determines the threat level will not require his skills and wanders away.

In a moment Hard rumbles out of the kitchen. "Can I help you?" His attitude suggests nothing other than a desire to be of service. There is no sense he has ever seen her before.

"I think you can," Nadine says. She is confident, standing there in the doorway, backlit by the streetlight in front of the Marvin home. Vonda Jean takes another look in the girl's direction. Is there something in her tone that begs notice? Difficult to tell. Maybe she's just flirty. Hard has played himself out of contention anyway so what's she worried about?

"Do you two know each other?" This from Vonda Jean.

"I'm a civilian volunteer at the Desert Hot Springs Police Department."

"Good for you," Vonda Jean says. The theme music from the game show drifts in from the living room and she excuses herself. Hard beckons Nadine inside with a friendly wave. She follows him to the kitchen, the dog trailing. Hard watching Nadine's non-reaction to the dog. Contrary to nature, she does not appear at all frightened of the animal. It figures. Compared to her demented Chihuahua, Bane has the manners of an English butler.

In the kitchen Hard looks at Nadine and quietly growls, "I thought we were done after you stuck a fork in my neck. What the Sam Hill you doing here?" Bane settles into his corner bed, ignoring them.

"Someone threatened to kill me," Nadine hisses, as if the intensity with which she expresses this information might motivate Hard to do something about it.

But what he says is: "I don't blame them, Nadine. You're a righteous pain in the ass."

"Did you hear what I told you?"

"Have you been drinking?"

"So?"

"I oughtta arrest you for driving over here."

A voice from the other room: "Harding, do we have any avocadoes?" Nadine starts at the sound. It is as if she has forgotten there is another person in the house, someone who is more than an adjunct to her hazy plan. Hard half expects Nadine to respond on cue and go marching into the living room for a sit down with his wife. He is relieved that she remains rooted in the kitchen. Hard glances toward the counter and sees three avocadoes in a plastic bowl. He shouts to his wife that tonight is her lucky night. From her perch in front of the television in the living room Vonda Jean, voice like a bullhorn, asks how he feels about making her some guacamole. Keeping his eyes on Nadine, he tells Vonda Jean he'll be pleased to.

Nadine says, "I could take that guacamole in there and tell your nice wife everything."

"You're seriously misreading the situation if you think that woman's nice, Nadine. She's nice like a wolverine."

"I'm just saying."

"Maybe she'd shoot you."

"You want to kill me, you better do it yourself."

Nadine is certainly assertive. It is a quality of hers that Hard greatly enjoys in another context, but right now it is more problematic. Removing a bowl from the cabinet, he pretends to turn his attention to the avocadoes. He knows what Nadine is capable of and is in no mood for a repeat performance. Had she hit a carotid artery with the salad fork, his blood would have painted her kitchen wall. Is there a link between a desire for the unhinged, swing-from-the-rafters sex Nadine practices and mental instability? And if there is, what does it say about him? Hard likes to think he has a crazy side, too, but not like Nadine who Hard thinks might be crazy in the way of heavy medication and locked wards.

"How's your neck?"

"You lifted my Taser, didn't you?"

"I have no idea what you're talking about."

Does she have it on her? He could grab her and find out, but she might scream and that would bring Vonda Jean running. Instead, he takes a paring knife out of the drawer, keeping a wary eye on Nadine. Did she wince when she saw the blade? Maybe it was a twitch. Twitching is not an encouraging sign.

Hard is dexterous with a knife, can bone a fish or skin a rattler with his eyes closed. How easy would it be to stick Nadine? Good payback, too. Being an officer of the law, Hard doesn't like where his mind is going, and upbraids himself silently for not thinking like one. The man can go black. He resolves to try and pray on it. Hard's not religious but if he's going to get into politics that will have to change.

Now he cuts the avocados in half, dislodges the pits and scrapes the fruit from the stippled skin. He places the pieces in the bowl where he mashes them to a pulp with a spoon all the while remaining acutely aware of every muscle tic from Nadine. He gets a lemon and a jar of salsa from the refrigerator. Slicing the lemon in two, he squeezes both halves into the bowl. Feels the astringent juice running over his fingers. Then he pours some salsa on top and stirs the viscous glop together.

Nadine watches in silence. The knife, covered with a film of green, lies on the counter. It occurs to Hard she could reach for it. Thinks about the Taser again. He knows the damage she can inflict with a salad fork. A Taser in her hands would be a nuclear weapon. He hopes Nadine will behave. Should he warn her about the dog?

"You're a regular Chef Boyardee, Hard. How come you never cooked for me?"

"Nadine, I'm gonna bring my wife this guacamole." Indicates the bowl with his hand. His delicacy of tone is intended to have a calming effect but just barely offsets the murderous aspect behind it. "Right now I want you to wait in here. When I get back to the kitchen we're gonna call you a cab because I don't want you driving home. If you do anything, and I mean anything, that deviates from that plan . . . " Before Nadine can react, Hard grabs her right arm, swings it behind her back, twists her around and clamps his hand over her mouth. The move is so swift and violent Nadine goes limp from fear, her eyes swinging wildly around the kitchen. Bane lifts his head but otherwise remains still. For a moment Hard thinks Nadine might have fainted. He quickly pats her down with his free hand, determines she has no weapons. When he sees her eyeballs bugging he places his lips next to her left ear and says, "I could snap your neck right now." His breathing quick, her skin warm. Hard notices the pulse in her artery and her lemony scent. "Nadine, understand. I mean you no harm but don't try and put one over on me because that won't work. I'll let you go but you stay calm now. Nod your head if you're willing to do that." He eases his grip and Nadine, beaten, nods meekly. Hard lowers his hand, disappointed. It appeared he had half a mind to kill her just then. He didn't feel anything with that Mexican. Wonders if he'd feel anything if he killed Nadine. Probably not, he concludes.

"You okay?" Nadine nods again. "Now wait right here. Don't want you picked up for a DUI." Taking the bowl of guacamole, Hard opens the pantry, grabs a bag of corn chips and leaves the kitchen. Vonda Jean doesn't look up from the TV when he hands her the bowl of guacamole.

"What's she doing here?"

"Gal's got some personal problems."

"You're her shrink?"

"It's not like that. I'm calling her a cab."

"Is she your girlfriend, Harding?" Still not looking away from the TV screen.

"I don't have a girlfriend, all right? Someone threatened her, she wanted to tell me."

"You're the knight in shining armor."

Hard wants to take the bag of chips, crumble them up and dump the contents on Vonda Jean's head. But instead he hands it to her. Then he gets down on his knee.

"I swear to you, I barely know her. I'm a public figure, Vonda Jean. All kinds of kooky people come up and tell me things."

"At our house?"

"She's not coming back."

"I like you on your knee. You look good down there."

How does she know he is on his knee? She hasn't so much as glanced in his direction since he entered the room. He looks at his wife desperately wishing he were no longer married to her. But that will have to wait until after the election.

"Why don't you ask her to come in here so we can chat," Vonda Jean says.

"What about?"

"Just being social. Tell her to come in."

"She's shy." Hard back on his feet now.

"She's shy? I thought you said you didn't know her."

"Gal had a rough day. I told you, someone threatened her."

Before Hard can do anything, Vonda Jean is walking into the kitchen. Hard follows her.

In the kitchen, Bane is devouring his dinner. Hard can't

remember; has he fed him? The door leading to the backyard is open, a warm breeze blowing the gingham curtains over the sink. Nadine is not there. Vonda Jean looks at Hard like this is his fault.

"Where's your friend?"

"First of all, she's not my friend. I thought we already made that clear."

"You're awful sensitive about it, aren't you?"

Hard chooses to ignore this riposte. "And second, I have no idea where the hell she is. Far as I can tell, she left. Now go on back in there and watch your TV show."

The couple has exchanged more words than they have in the entire previous week and it is enough for Vonda Jean. She turns and marches out of the kitchen. Hard goes to the refrigerator for a bottle of beer. He unscrews the top and settles into a chair where he watches Bane contentedly finish his dinner. Hard's week had been going so well. There was the face time campaigning with Mary Swain and the introduction he provided that day was one of the highlights of his entire career. Hard had never spoken in front of so many people before and he likes the way it feels, the love they give Mary Swain an inspiration to him. Hard likes to stir things up. He has opinions and doesn't mind sharing them. To go off like that in front of a crowd and have them respond the way they did, the shouts, the vibrating energy, that was something he could get used to. Hard doesn't want to be a Police Chief forever. He is looking at the larger world now. Perhaps he'll run for Mayor of Twentynine Palms and if Mary Swain ascends to loftier heights he can follow her to Congress. Representative Harding Marvin. But with Nadine on the loose, the woman predictable as a cobra, Hard is worried. The trouble she stirs up could derail any hopes of advancing his station in life.

Hard considers Mary Swain and Nadine, one so self-possessed, the other so desperate. Why had he misread Nadine?

It would have been easy to resist her convenience store come on. But whom was he kidding? Hard isn't wired to resist the hormonal blandishments of anyone who looks like Nadine. Still, he would prefer to be having sex with Mary Swain. There's a woman he can respect—and that would be new for Hard, extramarital sex with someone he esteems. Mary Swain can do that, get people thinking in different ways. Clever and gorgeous, she probably could show him a thing or two naked. Hard is in awe of her ability to work that sex-kitten quality, American female politicians generally skewing in the schoolmarm direction. He wonders if he could massage that angle himself. He makes the baldness work for him, something not all white men can do. But he doesn't know if he can take his sex appeal as far as Mary Swain. Hard is going to spend the evening of the election watching the returns in her hotel suite. And it'll be the first time in forever he's in a hotel room not thinking about the mini-bar or porn-on-demand.

The canned laughter of a sitcom seeps in from the living room. Another evening at home with Vonda Jean, Nadine wandering God knows where. Hard needs a concrete plan. He needs to get divorced, and he needs to make sure Nadine doesn't cause problems. Takes a deep swig from the beer bottle and finishes the contents. Then he returns to the fridge and helps himself to another. Bane is mopping up his kibble. Hard realizes it isn't a good sign that he envies the dog. When you're envying your dog, he knows, something must have gone seriously wrong with your life. And where was Nadine? Maybe the coyotes will take care of the problem.

In the living room Hard sits in his brown naugahyde recliner and watches an hour of mind-numbing television with his wife. Figures its penance for the unwanted visitor. When he can take it no more, he grabs another beer from the refrigerator and heads for the back yard. Bane follows him out there and lies at his feet. Sitting beneath the stars, he takes out his phone and thumb-types the following message:

I meant what I said tonight. Keep it up and something bad will happen to you.

Then he hits Send. Nadine might be a little unbalanced, but he knows she isn't dense. He suspects she won't be contacting him again.

CHAPTER TWELVE

Although Randall has owned this architectural show-place of a home for five years he has never danced in the living room; or any of the other rooms, for that matter. Tonight he stares into his daughter's eyes. Barefoot and impossibly bored, Brittany is wearing a tight tee shirt and loose sweats. Randall is dressed in a golf shirt, pressed blue slacks and wingtips.

"Don't step on my feet," Brittany says.

Randall tells her he'll be careful. "You know your dad's in charge tomorrow, right?"

"What does that mean?"

"I'm the M.C. So it's kind of our party, you and me. I'd like you to have a good time, or at least fake it." Randall trying with the girl. Smiles to let her know he's attempting to have fun.

He takes her hand and when he twirls her a little too quickly Brittany stumbles. She recovers and says, "Things fall apart, the center cannot hold."

Randall has no time for his daughter's Delphic pronounce-ments. He points the remote control at the stereo and presses a button. When the strains of bland pop kick in he takes Brittany's right hand in his left, places his other hand on her flat hip and proceeds to guide her clumsily around the room. Past the Eames chair, beneath the faux-Warhol lithograph of Randall, around the glass topped, teardrop table they glide. Randall moving lightly, heel to toe, heel to toe, the girl show-ing all the enthusiasm of a hostage. Maxon had told Randall to practice dancing with his daughter before the Purity Ball so they could get some video that might make the evening news. Failing that, it would look good on the campaign website. So Randall views this tripping of the light fantastic as campaign-related activity. Brittany is, in Randall's view, Kendra's project. When she was young and cute he took more of an interest, but the advent of adolescence has stripped her of what little charm she possessed and now his goal is to exist in some kind of uneasy truce. He enacts the role of doting father and hopes that his example will motivate the girl to act the role of loving daughter.

They are on their third self-conscious circumnavigation of the room when Kendra enters from the kitchen. Randall smiles at her, thinking she will be heartened to see this bit of family fun, however forced and uncomfortable it might actually be to the participants. He is surprised when his wife does not return his smile but instead informs him she would like to confer outside. Right now. Randall asks her where she's been.

"I had to get a new phone," Kendra says. "Mine broke."

As he follows his wife toward the backyard Randall looks over his shoulder and sees Brittany watching them with catscan eyes. He marvels at his daughter's ability to go from appearing bored to focusing with the intensity of a doctor preparing for surgery. The moment she sees her father has noticed her watching, she flits away.

Kendra stands in the backyard, her face lit by the gauzy light emanating from the swimming pool. Expensive reproductions of vintage 1950s steel and vinyl patio furniture are arrayed on the flagstone deck. The barely discernible silhouette of the dark San Jacinto Mountains looms like a reproach in the western distance. She briefly considers informing him of their daughter's "sexting" incident in the hope that this will reduce the impact of the Nadine fiasco, but she had given

Brittany her word she wouldn't say anything. So she gathers her courage and launches into an account of the ill-considered fling, the trip to Mexico and the story of the matching tattoos before concluding with an aria of apologies.

How would Randall process all of this? What would he do? Should she expect a flash of anger, a wild-eyed lashing out, or a heartfelt mea culpa about how his behavior must have led her to this and could she ever forgive him? Whatever she was anticipating, it was not the sight now in front of her: Randall seated on a chaise longue with his head in his hands, muttering no, no, dang it, no.

The reflection of the pool lights play delicately on his exposed neck while Kendra's mind drifts back to their honeymoon cabin on the California coast, the surf pounding the rocks below, Randall holding her in his arms and promising he would always take care of her. Looking at him doubled over, she is not so sure he will be able to deliver.

Emitting a low moan, Randall lifts his head and stares out over the desert, as if an answer lies somewhere in the parched darkness. The election is close and might be decided by just a few votes, the votes of people who will be put off by Kendra being at the center of a particularly lubricious scandal.

"You got matching tattoos?" he says, as if repeating the simple fact would somehow allow his bruised psyche to gain purchase long enough to halt its plunge into the abyss.

"I told you I was sorry."

"When you think about what's going on right now? I don't know that sorry cuts it."

"You want to talk about that chambermaid in Arizona, Randall? Because I'll talk about her if you want." Randall does not respond to this. What would be the point? The moral high ground has no empty parking spaces. For all of his serial pulping of marital vows it had never occurred to him that his wife could do the same, much less with a woman, and the shock to his system is profound. His mouth is dry, his stomach rising. The backyard surroundings are familiar yet everything looks slightly different as if animated by a heretofore-undetectable vibration. Randall is seized by a desire to make the movement cease, to return his world to a state of rest. And he can avoid the sense of betrayal by dealing with logistics.

"Are you gay?"

"Not that it matters, but no."

"It matters if we're going stay married."

"Do you want to?" A challenge.

Randall considers this a moment before responding, "Heck, yeah. Of course I want to stay married. Look, I've made mistakes and all. And I can't even say I don't deserve this. I probably do. But dang it, a *lesbian* affair?"

"Maybe part of me was trying to get back at you."

He thinks about this a moment. It is a sentiment that is impossible to disagree with. Although he has no interest in using this as an opportunity to end his marriage, he's justifiably concerned that the condition of his marriage could have a deleterious effect on his career. Who wants to be known as the Congressman whose wife became a lesbian, even temporarily? Let him try to explain that to his colleagues on the Homeland Security Committee. "Your timing, darlin, is impeccable."

"Does it at least help that it was over a year ago?"

"You think anyone ever forgot Chappaquiddick?"

"Ted Kennedy kept getting re-elected."

"That was Massachusetts!"

Kendra considers Randall's point. The Kennedys are a dynasty well known and beloved, sufferers of tragedies great and small. Sympathy could be called upon in the case of Teddy, the car and the bridge. In the unforgiving Mojave, there is no reserve of good will upon which Randall can draw.

"I was thinking about leaving," she says. "If you want to know the truth."

Randall looks up, genuinely surprised. The wages of his behavior are not something he has ever bothered to calculate. So prevalent is his approach to marriage in the political class, he has assumed discretion would deliver him from divorce. It isn't like he has ever fallen in love with anyone else. He loves Kendra. As much as he can love anyone. At least he believes he does.

"You were thinking about leaving?"

She nods her head, exasperated that he could be so obtuse as to not consider this possibility. "Randall, your life's a permanent campaign. Your daughter barely knows you. You keep this up and what's going to be left?"

Randall lifts his head from his hands, straightens his back. What she said is true, there is no doubt. Since being elected to Congress he has flown home for the weekend every two weeks and his time in the desert is devoted to fundraising. Brittany has become entirely Kendra's responsibility, the family little more than a photo op for his campaign literature. But Randall is ambitious and this is the price. He talks to his colleagues in Washington and he knows his choices are not exceptional. Contemporary American politics fetishizes the family while decimating it. This is how things are. As marriages go, theirs isn't worse than a lot of others. Kendra has been a superb political spouse. He doesn't want to leave her and he doesn't want her to leave him. But the lesbian disclosure is troubling. He is not the sort of male who finds it titillating. Did she have to so utterly un-man him? Has his behavior been deserving of such abasement? Unfortunately, it is done. He has no choice but to take his medicine.

"Well, if you had to fool around, I'm glad it was with a woman," he lies. He can't even envision her with another man. Right now Randall is amazed he can even produce a coherent sentence. Kendra places a comforting hand on his shoulder and he puts his hand on hers. They remain silent for a few moments.

She says: "So should we just pay her?"

Rising from the chaise longue, Randall walks toward the
pool and stands at the edge. A light breeze causes a barely discernible ripple. He peers to the bottom willing the answer to
bubble up and burst through the surface. "I thought she didn't
ask for money."

"She didn't. At least not directly."

"Then paying her now? That's irresponsible and we're not
going to do it." The energy that seemed to have drained out as
he processed Kendra's information slowly surges back. The
internal math has been done, the sums rendered. Randall says
things others have said thousands of times before, but he says
them with a sense of ownership, as if he had been the one to
think of them. He's quiet for another few moments but Kendra
thinks they will be all right. A desert hawk wheels overhead, its
wings backlit by the rising crescent moon. "What do you think
she's going to do, best guess?"

"Can't say."

"I'll take care of it."

He has regained his footing and is calculating how this
obstacle can best be dealt with in a mode that will address the
short-term needs and minimize the long-term ramifications.

"I figured you'd know what to do."

"Mind if I ask you a personal question?" He takes her
silence for assent. "All the bull we've gone through, we still
love each other, right?"

Her relief at the manner in which Randall is now handling
the remarkably inconvenient revelation is overwhelming.
Despite this, Kendra starts to laugh.

"I'm sorry," she says, regaining control.

"You think it's funny?"

"If this is love . . . I don't know, maybe it is." Her hands are
on her hips and she is shaking her head in bewilderment. "Do
we love each other?"

"Do we?"

"I'm not sure that's relevant right now."

And a deep place in her is touched by the softness of his voice when he says, "I know what you mean."

"Do you want to stay married?"

"Kendy, we're good together," he says, taking her hand in his.

Kendy, she thinks. *Kendy!* He hasn't called her that in a decade. The plangent tone and the disquietude of his manner tell her how deeply he is unnerved by the situation. She was in no way certain he would react like this. Kendra Kerry Duke knows she stands at the most critical juncture in her married life. Were she to tell him now is the time for their union to end her timing could not be more auspicious. The campaign will soon be over and they will be able to separate quietly. She will be able to move on to the next phase, get an apartment, perhaps resume her singing career. She could remarry if she wants. There will certainly be a willing suitor eager to have the still-youthful ex-wife of Randall Duke on his arm. So she knows what she says now will resonate for years to come. And what she says is:

"I think we're good together, too."

When they walk back in the house it is with the tacit agreement that they will do whatever they must, no regrets.

http://WWW.DESERT-MACHIAVELLI.COM

10.30 – 11:49 P.M.

While you Blogheads have been sleeping the Machiavelli has been rooting around the foul rag and bone shop of Mary Swain's past. What do we really know about this woman? Did she even graduate from college? She served drinks on her husband's jet while he was still married to his first wife, that much we know. That she says she goes to church a lot, we know that, too. Mary Swain says she loves Jesus the way most of us say pass the salt. But Jesus loves mankind, does he not? And that includes gay people. Did Mary Swain tune that part of the universal love message out? Whatever you might say about Randall Duke, his wife Kendra is a friend to you gays out there. A gay birdie whispered in my ear that her appearance at the Palm Springs Charity Drag Ball last year had people saying she looked like a female impersonator, which was meant as a compliment, I think. So while her husband is a little wishy-washy in the area of gay rights, his wife is a friend of the Friends of Dorothy. As for the Stewardess, although she claims to have gay friends, she has said she thinks homosexuality is a choice. Think of this on Election Day, my Desert Queens! The American Hero, or the Closet Canadian?

CHAPTER THIRTEEN

It's after midnight and Jimmy and his former police force colleague Cali Pasco are seated on the sofa in his trailer listening to Waylon Jennings on the stereo. Cali drinking a beer, Jimmy sipping herbal tea. Their relationship has always been within respectful professional boundaries so, although neither will acknowledge what has taken place this evening as anything more than two former co-workers spending some time together, the hours have passed with the ease of a marble rolling down a chute. At Pappy and Harriet's, a barbecue joint deep in the hills north of the Morongo Valley, they had danced to a country band and ate and danced and drank, or, Cali drank and Jimmy wanted to, but didn't, then they danced some more before Jimmy started telling Cali about the *Book of Dogs* and Cali asked when he was going to show it to her. After stopping at a market to get one last beer, Cali followed him home in her Green Volkswagon Jetta. Now the book is on her lap and she's flipping through the pages.

"Tell me about this one," she says, pointing to a picture of what looks like a Chow-Shepherd mix. A strand of hair falls over Cali's eyes and she delicately places it behind her ear. Jimmy notices her graceful fingers for the first time, the unblemished skin, clear polish on the nails, a thin band of silver on her thumb.

"Owner's house had been robbed."

"How about this one," pointing to an old beagle.

"Two guys have an antique store downtown. Dog's name is Oscar."

"Why'd you start doing this, making the book?"

"Something to do after I left the force, help chill me out."
Keeping the book on her lap like she doesn't want to let go
of it Cali takes her boots off, first one than the other, places
them next to each other on the floor. "What was it that happened with you and Hard, exactly?"

Jimmy exhales, thinks about whether he wants to get into it,
such a pleasant night so far. He takes a sip of tea, leans back and
considers. This is a barometer. The way Cali reacts will tell
whether they're going out together again. Bruno wanders over
and puts his head on Cali's thigh. She scratches behind his ears.

"I was doing a search and seizure in a joint operation with the
Sherriff's Department at a meth lab in a trailer east of town and
we got two dogs with us. One of the suspects, this wiry tweaker
is cuffed. He's standing there all agitated and for no reason he
kicks one of the dogs. Well the dog doesn't like that and he bites
the guy's ankle, draws some blood. Just a flesh wound."

"I remember when this happened. Didn't realize you were
involved."

"He was a citizen in custody and he claims the dog attacked
him. Now Mr. Meth Dealer's suing the town and the lawyer for
the city council is all over Chief Marvin telling him he needs to
show he values the lives of everyone in his jurisdiction, and
that means criminals, too. So word comes down from Hard
that the dog is headed for death row. This didn't go over well
cause I worked with the animal and I liked him, but I kept my
opinions to myself. Some whiny please-sir-don't-kill-the-dog-
gie speech wasn't gonna fly. Kind of surprised by Hard's attitude about this dog, though. The man has a Rotty he loves. So
I tell him I'll take the dog on his last ride, bring him down to
the animal control station for the trip to Dog Heaven. I pull
into the Animal Control parking lot and park but I leave the
motor running and I don't move. I'm thinking the only way to
do this is do it fast.

"My wife left me, I'm living in a trailer, I got this dog and now I'm supposed to kill him? Before I know it I'm crying. Then I feel this cold wetness on my neck and I look over and see the dog's face right next to mine. So I take out my cell phone and lean back in the car seat to get a better angle. I snap the dog's picture before I slip the choke chain over his head and lead him across the parking lot and into the building. They got the walls decorated with framed posters of kittens and puppies if you can believe it. Lady named Coral works there and I hand her the choke chain.

"I could tell Hard was pleased when I put this cardboard box with the dog's ashes on his desk. He showed the box to everyone who came into his office, even took a picture of it and sent it to the Mayor and the Town Supervisor to show them Chief Marvin was on top of the situation. So it kind of bites Hard in the ass a few weeks later when he's going over some routine reports from Animal Control and he doesn't see the dog's name listed. I'm staking out another meth lab with the Sherriff's Department when Hard calls me, wants to know what the hell's going on, was the dog dead or alive? And he had better be dead, Hard says. I knew lying was pointless so I say I couldn't kill that dog, Chief. And Hard says What'd you do with him? I tell him I took the dog down to Anza-Borrego and set him free in the desert. You set that dog free? And I say In the desert, Chief. He's got to be dead by now.

"He's waiting for me back at headquarters, curses me out, says I'm suspended pending further investigation. That's when I tell Hard I'm gonna throw him out the window." He pauses. "Here's something I read in this Asian philosophy book: wait long enough on the river bank and you'll see the body of your enemy float by."

Cali nods, takes this bit of ancient wisdom in. Jimmy hopes to convey a sense of newfound depth, to make Cali understand he is no longer the guy she knew on the force but has morphed into someone more sensitive, someone with whom she could have sex and possibly not regret it in the morning. He's actually trying to become deeper, and it's a tricky transformation to convey. It wasn't something you could brag about without sounding like a fool. But to his relief, Cali doesn't pursue it. She wants to know: "What happened to the dog?"

"That's his head you're scratching."

When Cali smiles he knows telling her every detail was the right decision. She gives a little laugh, looks at Bruno, then back at Jimmy.

"I'd like to think I would've done the same thing," she says. "No way I could put down this handsome guy." She rubs Bruno's head, nuzzles him. The dog licks her cheek, her nose, her eyelids.

Jimmy looks around the trailer, grateful that he straightened up before going out to meet Cali. The CD ends and he gets up and puts on Johnny Cash. When he sits back down he takes her hand and holds it. The stress and strain of his day-to-day are gone. To remain suspended in the night quiet of the trailer listening to the old school honkytonk music just looking into Cali's brown eyes.

"You're staring at me," she says.

"Let's make a mistake."

He kisses her and she kisses him back and then he gets up and they dance a little to Johnny Cash, Jimmy's hand on her waist, her palm on his shoulder, neither one of them saying anything, cheeks touching, sensing each other's warm breath. They kiss again and Cali's hands drift up and she slowly unbuttons the front of his shirt, one button, then another and Jimmy reaches under her blouse and unhooks her bra. He runs his fingers up the small of her back and around the soft curve of her hip and over her breast and she unzips him and takes him in her hand and then she says You got clean sheets? He tells her yes he does and keeping her hand where it is she leads him into the bedroom.

WEDNESDAY, OCTOBER 31

Before he gets to work in the morning Hard has to do some campaign business so he is out of bed earlier than usual. In the bathroom he locks the door. Dressed in cotton pajama bottoms, he turns toward the mirror. Twists his head to the side and delicately removes the bandage from his neck. Probes the distinctive tine marks of the still fresh wound with two fingers. Cursing Nadine once more under his breath, he shaves, taking extra care around the perforations. Then he showers and applies a fresh bandage.

He has distributed lawn signs to constituents around the district and has been disappointed by how few he has seen. This morning he intends to spend an hour knocking on doors and asking people whether they'd mind if he places Mary Swain signs in their yards. Vonda Jean is still pretending to be asleep when he walks into the kitchen.

Bane lays curled on his bed. Usually he is up scratching the door to go out but Hard assumes the unseasonable heat has tired him out. He pours himself a bowl of corn flakes, drowns them in milk and sits down at the kitchen table to read the morning paper. Out of habit, he scans the front page for some mention of himself. Nothing today. That will change on Election Day, he thinks with satisfaction.

At 7:30, the sun is already blaring. Halfway through his cereal, he looks over at Bane. The dog hasn't moved. He can sleep all day. Right now Hard wants some company. He calls the dog's name. Bane does not stir. Again, he calls, "Bane!" Louder this time.

Hard places the newspaper on the table and kneels by the dog. He rests his palm on the dog's chest. Instead of the steady rhythm of breathing, Hard feels a lifeless mass. Bane does not appear to have a pulse. He shakes the sleek body but the dog does not move. Places his ear to the ribcage. Nothing. Hard quickly gathers the dog up, a hundred and twenty pounds of flesh, sinew and bone, throws him over his shoulder, carries him out of the house and places him gently in the bed of his truck, jumps in the drivers seat, puts the cherry on top, and drives a hundred miles an hour to the animal hospital, dialing the vet's home number on his cell phone and telling the sleeping woman to meet him at her office right now, Bane Marvin does not appear to be breathing.

It takes nearly twenty coronary-inducing minutes to get to the Yucca Valley office of Dr. Amber Foyle, an attractive young woman with whom Hard would have been happy to replace Vonda Jean. But that is not on his mind this morning. Bane is his favorite member of the household and the dog's life must be saved at all costs.

Dr. Foyle has already unlocked the door and is waiting for their arrival. Hard comes dashing in like he's running an Olympic event, the large dog limp in his gentle arms. The vet tells him to place Bane on the examination table and he instantly obliges. The stethoscope is pressed to the dog's chest. Hard waits, his breath shallow and agitated. He cannot conceive of what could have happened. Bane is six years old and, at least until this morning, in perfect health. Hard has heard of puppies dropping dead but never an adult dog. They had taken a brief walk before dinner but nothing unusual had occurred.

Increasingly nervous, Hard watches as Dr. Foyle examines the inert animal. After nearly five minutes, she tells him Bane is dead. He has to sit down when he hears this. Although rough and insensate with humans, Hard genuinely loves his dog. Other than cheating on his wife, one of his few pleasures is taking

Bane on long walks in the twilight, after the heat has died down, or in the dawn before the sun has lit the horizon. He doesn't need a leash, the dog walking along with him easy as water.

After a respectful pause, the vet asks Hard if he wants her to run some tests on Bane to learn what exactly has transpired, and he readily accedes. Hard is so downhearted by the morning's events, he neglects his plan for the lawn signs and instead drives straight to headquarters.

Every morning during the campaign, Randall and Maxon have breakfast at Rick's Restaurant and Bakery on North Palm Canyon Drive, a see-and-be-seen biscuits and eggs place popular with tourists and locals. Someone they know is always dining at a nearby table and the atmosphere is friendly and convivial. They review the day's schedule, share man gossip, and make plans to take over the world. It was during a conversation at Rick's seven years ago that Randall looked up from his breakfast *fajita* and told Maxon he was going to run for Congress. On the way out the door there are always hands to shake, backs to slap, and a day's worth of good feelings to be shared. These are all the reasons they are not there this Wednesday morning but have gone instead to the Viceroy, an elegant small hotel a block north of downtown.

They are the only two diners eating breakfast in the pool area adjacent to the dining room. Randall is seated on a white leather banquette, Maxon opposite him. The pool deck is lined with yellow and white striped chaise longues, each with a rolled white towel at its foot. White flowers spill out of Roman urns mounted on plinths. Ornamental birdcages hang from trees. The Hispanic waiter arrives with their food—fruit salad for Randall, *huevos rancheros* for Maxon—and departs with a murmur and a nod. Maxon shakes a bottle of hot sauce over his plate.

"What did you tell her?"

132 - SETH GREENLAND

"I told her I'd take care of it," Randall says.

His fruit plate remains untouched. Randall has not had much of an appetite since his wife's revelation the previous evening. He didn't sleep well and spent the dark hours envisioning different iterations of his career's end. Right now he's hoping the coffee will kick start his jangled system. Maxon glances around to make sure no one is within earshot. They're still on the early side of the breakfast rush.

Quietly, Maxon asks, "Is Kendra gay?"

"Hell, I don't know, and I don't really care." This is expressed with a bravado that belies Randall's true attitude since no man so insouciantly accepts a wife's adulterous behavior unless it is for his personal delectation. Randall hopes Maxon does not see through his facade.

"Hey, brother, I'm just asking. Are we going to be dealing with a divorce?"

"No one's getting divorced."

"Well, that's good. But you might want to think about leaving her after the campaign. No one gives a rat's ass about divorce. We just don't want it going on when you're running for re-election. It can get messy."

"This flippin tennis teacher implies she has eyeball evidence of some kind of lesbo love session and I don't care how gay this town is, there's enough retirees and ex-military going to be freaked out that their Congressman's wife's gone to the dark side to cost me the motherflippin election." Randall looks both ways, his features pinched in distress. Then he locks eyes with Maxon, says, "I mean, how's it going to look if one minute I'm hosting the Purity Ball and the next minute I'm married to a gay?"

This is not the kind of conversation Maxon was expecting to have when he left his perfectly restored mid-century modern rental in the Twin Palms neighborhood twenty minutes ago. A development like this right before Election Day is seriously bad juju. Not that it would have been better had the indiscretion come to light earlier. But he does not want it fresh in a constituent's mind as she reaches for the lever.

As a young buck Maxon had harbored his own ambitions as a candidate, but his inadequate hair, squint, and pasty Scandinavian complexion are a hard sell in an era when the visual aspect of campaigning makes an attractive physical presentation a pre-requisite for high office. Voters don't want any leader. They want leaders who look like they play leaders on television, leaders like Randall. Maxon gazes in the mirror and sees a guy who sells menswear at Nordstrom's.

He was working as a political consultant in Sacramento when State Senator Randall Duke let it be known that he was looking for someone to run his first Congressional campaign. Maxon leapt at the chance. He had studied the masters of electoral hardball, those bare-knuckled, meretricious practitioners of evil for hire, and was keen to put the lessons to use on a broader playing field.

Six years ago, when Randall first ran for the United States House of Representatives, the seat was open because the incumbent had died in office. His opponent was a woman named Karen Niles. An attorney at a public interest firm who had successfully sued Riverside County to force them to provide better housing for the homeless, she was married with a young son. Her husband was a surgeon. Any political party would have been hard pressed to find a better candidate and she was viewed as a sure thing against Randall Duke who was thought to be callow and a little dim. But Maxon was able to turn a spotlight on a vacation to Egypt she'd taken with a woman friend ten years earlier and spin it into an Islamic-sympathizing fantasia that most observers believe caused her to lose the election.

"I do everything an incumbent's supposed to do. The Latino outreach, the domestic violence march, I'm leading the Desert AIDS walk for Pete's sake. And if anybody takes that the wrong way, I'm hosting a dang Purity Ball. I'm working on saving the Salton Sea, I'm a friend to the veterans, I visit every senior center in a hundred mile radius. And I don't just visit the seniors, Maxon, I visit the flippin gay seniors! Who else in Congress gives a crap about the gay seniors?"

"The gay seniors have great affection for you."

The two men are silent for a moment. A party of four young male golfers wanders in and sits at a nearby table. Oblivious to Randall and Maxon, they're talking loudly of tee times and stock picks.

"Point is, I've been delivering the goods to my constituents for three motherflippin terms. I fly back from Washington every other week to listen to their problems. I do everything right and now I'm in this situation? With Mary Swain gaining on me and a lesbian snake lying in the tall grass waiting to sink her teeth into my foot?" Randall spears a pineapple cube and shoves it into his mouth.

"Somebody comes at you like this, you give them some money and they're right back with their hand out again," Maxon says. He notices one of the golfers is looking their way. The man says something to his tablemates and they laugh.

"There aren't a lot of clean options," Randall says.

"There aren't any clean ones. You want me to talk to her?"

"What's that going to do?" Randall asks, a streak of helplessness in his voice. Perhaps this really is the end. All political lives have an arc. Randall has always assumed his would be a long one, but it's an unpredictable business.

"Who is she?"

Randall takes a small spiral notepad and a cheap ballpoint pen out of his pocket, flips the pad open and jots something down. He tears the page out and slides it across the table. Maxon glances at the paper, the name written on it. There's also a place of business, a tanning salon. He's invested years of his career, prime years, in the Randall Duke brand and he won't see the brand damaged. No more House seat means no run for the Senate, no run for the Governorship. No good options. Play this wrong and Randall Duke winds up operating a couple of Baskin-Robbins franchises in Arizona, Maxon making sundaes. Maxon's not going to let this happen.

"I'll talk to her," he says, folding the paper and sliding it into his shirt pocket.

"How're your *huevos*?" Randall asks.

"They're all right. Probably should have got the fruit salad, though. Don't need the carbs." Then he gets the joke, smirks. "Don't worry about my *huevos*," Maxon says. He digs into his pocket and removes his wallet.

"I'll get breakfast," Randall says.

"I know," Maxon says. He opens his wallet and shows Randall a gold law enforcement badge.

"What the flip is that?"

"Remember when you spoke to the California Law Enforcement Association? I got them to make me an honorary deputy."

"You son of a gun." Randall is still laughing about it when the waiter brings the check.

Chapter Fifteen

C ali drove home to her apartment in Yucaipa at three in the morning and caught a few hours of sleep. Then she got up, showered and headed to work thinking about whether she'd ask Hard to be reassigned today. He had her working on crimes against property cases: residential and commercial burglaries, all types of theft, check crimes, credit card forgery, embezzlement, scams and vandalism. She was interested in crimes against persons: robbery, rape, adult and child sex offences, child abuse, runaways, missing persons, mental cases and, of course, homicide.

Especially homicide.

Something had happened between Cali and Hard shortly after she had joined the force, and it factored into how she dealt with him. What it was: Coming off a patrol shift, getting a drink at the water fountain in the hallway outside the squad room she felt a hand on her back rubbing in a north south motion then running a finger along her bra strap. She turned around ready to swing at whoever it was until she found herself looking into Hard's face. He cocked his head and told her what fine things he was hearing from her superior officers. He said he'd like it if the two of them had a drink after work one evening and being a young officer she was flattered if a little wary. More than a few drinks were consumed and Hard got Cali into his truck where he tried to have sex. She thought she could get him to calm down with a handjob but when he still insisted on fucking her Cali smashed a forearm into his chin causing Hard to nearly bite his tongue off and drool blood for half an hour.

Why didn't this talented and attractive young woman, this paragon of law enforcement not file a sexual harassment claim against her brutish superior when the sad facts were so clearly on her side? Although she would have been awarded a pile of money, her career would have been over. Not over as in *ended* but over in the sense that she never would have been granted admission to the male-controlled club whose members don't look kindly on women who leave their colleagues twisting in litigious winds. She was looking at a future of bad assignments, marginalization and frustration. Being a deeply practical woman, Cali made a clear-eyed assessment of the situation. Her conclusion: Boo-hoo, lets move on.

After realizing that she was not going to file a sexual harassment claim Hard has kept a cautious distance.

Cali stopped at Dunkin' Donuts and bought a dozen glazed. The box is open on Hard Marvin's desk, Cali not above working the pastry angle, whatever it takes. Shameless. She doesn't care, sips takeout coffee. Hard's container—milk and two sugars, she checked with his secretary—is untouched, the cover still on. The office is large and the chief sits behind his clean oak desk, the only decoration a mass-produced Frederick Remington sculpture of a cowboy riding a bucking bronco. On the wall behind the desk is a framed oil portrait of General George S. Patton. Cali sits across from Hard in a high-backed stained wood chair.

"You want to catch a homicide?"

"I'm ready."

"After being a detective less than two months."

Hard doesn't want to deal with this woman right now. His dog just died, after all, and this is a mourning period. All he wants to do is stare out the window and feel the pain wash over him as he cogitates on the unsatisfactory nature of human relationships and the superiority of dogs. And here's this woman sitting across from him whining about how she's not getting the kind of assignments she likes. He never would have promoted her if the Town Supervisor hadn't informed him that the detective squad could no longer be run as a boys' club and there wouldn't have been an opening if Jimmy Duke hadn't fucked up the way he had.

Cali makes sure she maintains eye contact with her boss. She thinks of him as an old guy, nearly fifty, and no feminist. Senses he likes her well enough but would prefer it if she were the department secretary. His big feet are up on his desk and he chews a golf tee, which he takes out of his mouth to sip from a can of Buck Rhino energy drink. Probably not touching the coffee she brought just to spite her. Hard sticks the tee back between his teeth after he swallows.

"You're doing decent work, Cali. You and Arnaldo made a good bust the other day."

"I don't want to keep doing the undercover stuff."

"You getting nervous?"

"Hell, no. I'm not nervous. I want a change is all."

"Get a new hairdo."

He smiles to let her know he's kidding around, as if that makes it all right. She has to act like it's funny, show she can take a joke when all she wants is to lay him out. It's a girl's life. Then she says: "I want to catch a homicide. Like I said."

He looks at her like she just tickled his chin, sort of a half grin, an expression that says what the hell are you doing and why don't you quit it? Now he's diddling with the laptop on his desk, staring at a list of names.

"Rojas, Torres, Reyes, Jimenez." Looks up at Cali.

She says, "Yeah?" Like what are you getting at?

"Those are the first four names on the wanted suspects list for homicide."

"Okay." Neutral.

"You notice anything about them?" She already knows the answer but isn't going to take a quiz so she waits for Hard to connect the dots. He gives her a look—didn't she want to answer him? She keeps quiet. "Cali, I'm not saying this to be racist, which I'm not. But nearly all the homicides in the county are committed by people of Hispanic descent."

"What of it?"

"If you catch my drift."

"Not sure I do."

"I don't believe their race is predisposed to killing folks, but that's the way it is in the desert. Statistically, I'm talking about. You could look it up."

"Your point?"

"Do you *hablo Espagnol?*"

"Do all the detectives on the force speak Spanish?"

"That's not what I'm asking. They were hired before that skill became a necessity. What with the shifting demographics and all."

"Chief, all due respect, but I don't think that's the reason. I'm the only female detective, which isn't something I should have to point out. I'm saying, respectfully, if a homicide occurs, I want a shot. I'm not asking to be the lead detective." Hard bores into her with eyes that want to turn her to stone. Only thing Cali's wondering is why she didn't do this before. The boys club is on the run these days, pressure, lawsuits—the whole P.C. approach that she is not above exploiting. This bringer of morning donuts can also bring the pain of legal recourse. The sex incident rumbles like distant thunder so when he exhales through his nose it occurs to her that she has his big shoulders pinned to the floor. But she doesn't want to press the point in a too obvious way. "I've been listening to language tapes," she says, like a good girl. Allowing the man some dignity. No need to lord over him when she already has his balls in a vice.

"It's good to have hobbies."

"What I'm telling you, sir,"—the word *sir* served with a little vinegar—"is I'm learning how."

"There's never been a woman work a homicide on this force before."

It sticks in Cali's craw when people state a fact when they're implying that the fact will continue to exist as a fact because it always has existed as a fact. She isn't in the mood for Hard Marvin's lack of imagination. "So you're telling me if I spoke Spanish and had a penis I'd be in like Flynn?"

He had once again removed the golf tee from between his teeth and was halfway through swallowing another mouthful of Buck Rhino. Now he pulls out a pocket-handkerchief and wipes the dribble off his chin. Then he stares at her. "Put in a request and I'll take it under advisement."

"I've been on the force almost eight years."

"And a detective for two goddamn months."

"My evaluations have always been good."

"I know that, too."

A buzzer on Hard's desk sounds. It's his secretary letting him know the veterinarian is on the phone. Hard dismisses Cali with a curt wave of his hand. She grabs the donuts and retreats from the office. Cali knows this battle will be won and Hard doesn't deserve any more of her donuts.

Dr. Foyle reports that while Bane's heart and lungs appear perfectly normal the dog has apparently ingested some kind of sedative. The final results from the lab will be available later today. Before he places the phone back on the cradle he feels a murderous rage welling within his breast, impelling him to the door of his office and out of the building, on a mission to avenge the death of his dog. Hard longs for payback, short and brutal. But he remains in his seat. With the election coming up, he will need to act in a circumspect manner.

It is one thing to strike at him—that is something he can understand. It speaks to his warrior instinct. But to attack an innocent animal, albeit one that would have ripped you to bloody shreds should you have so much as arched an eyebrow the wrong way? That is entirely beyond the realm of acceptable human behavior and someone will be made to pay.

When Hard's rage descends from homicidal heights to a more manageable level of distress he picks up the phone and calls Nadine. After one ring it goes to the answering message. Her cheery voice raises his aggravation level several notches, but he controls himself long enough to tell her to contact him immediately.

For the remainder of the day fury runs through Hard Marvin like a flash flood down a desert culvert, waxing and waning but never straying far from a base level of deep and abiding rancor. He reads reports, gives assignments, and eats a steak burrito at his desk but its impossible for him to concentrate for more than a couple of minutes on any task. Hard plots the kind of elaborate revenge fantasies that would land him in prison for decades. He agonizes and cogitates and doesn't say a word to anyone. Not to Captain Delgado, Hard's punctilious second in command, ten years his junior and with an eye on the chief's job, or to Detective Sergeant Spooner, the man in charge of assignments and a protégé. Their daily meeting goes without a hitch and the two men leave Hard's office with no sense anything is amiss. But its all Hard can do to keep from punching the wall when Dr. Foyle calls to tell him the toxology report she ran on Bane reveals that he probably died of a Valium overdose.

Hard is seated at his desk staring out over the parking lot to the arid hills in the distance and mumbling, almost chanting *Crazy bitch murdered Bane, crazy bitch murdered Bane* as if the words had the power to bestow shape and form on the incomprehensible. *Crazy bitch murdered Bane . . .*

"Chief?" Detective Arnaldo Escovedo is trying to get

Hard's attention. Says his name again. This time Hard whirls around in his swivel chair.

"I need you to sign some paperwork."

Hard stares at Arnaldo with as black a look as the veteran detective has seen, and in a tone that sounds as if it is emanating from a crypt says, "And I need you to not stand there looking like a dumb fuckin worthless piece of shit Mexican and get the fuck out of my office."

When Arnaldo retreats, Hard turns to face the portrait of General George S. Patton on the wall behind him. This is something he will do in moments of consternation, in the hope that he will be able to draw strength from beholding the visage of the war hero. The town of Desert Hot Springs is not where Hard wants to end up. Lost in the foothills of the Little San Bernardino Mountains, no one outside the desert has ever heard of it. Why couldn't Hard have become the Police Chief of Palm Springs, a glamorous place known the world over? Why is he stuck in this sun-baked ordinariness surrounded by trailer parks stuffed with retirees? Why must he work with idiots? He is usually able to keep these feelings repressed, but when someone kills your dog, they can start to seep out.

Before returning to his work, Hard takes a last look at General Patton and shakes his head in dismay. He's glad the General is unable to see Harding Marvin. He knows the great warrior would not be impressed. It is Hard's urgent intention to change that.

CHAPTER SIXTEEN

Fake 'n' Bake is a clean, well-lighted place. Wheat-colored industrial carpet covers the floor and the walls are painted lavender. Toward the back of the room are five tanning booths, two vertical and three horizontal. Shelves are lined with moisteners, tanning creams, and exfoliation unguents. Canned ukulele music embroiders the room.

Nadine hates the ukulele. She would have preferred something more aggressive but Krystle, the owner, refuses to play anything else. The woman recently returned from a Hawaiian cruise to celebrate her third divorce and in the last week has installed several potted palms and hung a large framed map of the Hawaiian Islands behind the reception desk. As she and Nadine were vacuuming out the tanning beds, she announced that Fake 'n' Bake would be rebranded with a tropical motif to make it stand out from the local competition. A sign with the words *Hawaiian Heaven* is on order.

In a Hawaiian shirt and baggy flowered shorts, Nadine sits alone behind the glass counter. Her flip-flops are on the floor next to her. She can't decide which is more annoying: the ukulele music or the outfit her job requires. Earlier she had put on a CD by a goddess of hip-hop. There is a woman: an African-American-Amazon songstress who takes no shit from men. Nadine admires that, wants to channel some of that hip-hop deity attitude and use it in her own life. Would the goddess have approved of how she had attacked Hard? Tough to say. In the light of day Nadine worries that drugging the dog was a little overboard, but she believes the singer would have loved the way she stuck Hard with the salad fork.

Unfortunately, Nadine had to rein in the musical mojo an hour ago when Krystle, a large, extremely tan woman in a tropical print muu-muu, stopped by and heard the gynocentric hip-hop. She had said not only do I hate that shit but the next time I walk in here and don't hear a ukulele playing you're fired. Nadine would have liked to quit on the spot and is still in a bad mood about not being in a financial position to walk away.

Other than Krystle's unscheduled drop-in, it has been a quiet morning at Fake 'n' Bake. A local podiatrist stopped by for his weekly bronzing, and a single woman who had moved to the desert from Kansas has just begun a twenty-minute session in booth #2. Nadine has straightened up, finished her coffee, and is on the Internet researching the city of Seattle. She has to get away from the desert, from Hard Marvin. If she stays here things will only get worse.

The bells on the door announce a visitor and Nadine looks up from a photograph of Puget Sound. A thin, blonde man dressed in a dark suit glances around. She forces herself to smile.

"Are you interested in tanning?" She hates to ask this question. If he was interested in fruits and vegetables or shoes would he be in Fake 'n' Bake? But Krystle insists on it and for all Nadine knows she sent this guy to check on whether her employee is sticking to the script. "We have two intense UVB beds and three browning UVB beds. Would you be interested in an individual session or a membership?"

He walks silently across the carpet, peers around the place.

"We offer a starter session for five dollars," she recites. "One week is twenty-five, two weeks is thirty, one month is forty. Payable cash, check, or credit card."

Now he is standing directly across the counter from her. Whoever this person is, Nadine doesn't like him. Why won't he say anything? She notices that he is squeezing a tennis ball in his left hand.

"How are you, Nadine?"

His voice is quiet, sinuous, almost a purr. How does he know her name? She hopes he doesn't work for the bank that owns the mortgage on her house. What's the punishment for squatting?

"I'm good." Suspicious. Has be been here before? No, she would have remembered. "Are you here for tanning?"

This guy is giving her the creeps. It's a bright day outside and they're in a mini-mall just off Route 111. It's not like anything can happen. Still, she wishes Krystle had installed some kind of panic button. The man gives her a look—is that sympathy?—and puts his hands on the counter. Nadine notices a ring with a blue stone on his left hand. He leans toward her. "You need to play within your game, Nadine."

"Sir, are you here for tanning?"

"A good player doesn't want to take unnecessary risks."

She ceases to notice the ukulele music wafting through the room. Out of a pale face now devoid of expression—where has the sympathy gone?—his intense blue eyes stare through her.

"You can serve and volley, but if you underestimate your opponent, if you make the slightest tactical error . . . " and here he pauses, as if he is daring her to say something. When she remains silent, he continues, "Your opponent will hit a winner."

Nadine isn't sure what he is talking about but senses it's some kind of threat. Did Hard send this guy? He doesn't seem like a cop, but how can you tell? She doesn't like to be threatened. Hard had provoked her and look what she'd done to him. It was only a matter of time before she and Krystle crossed swords. But this guy? This pale, thin, weak-looking reed? Who is he to come in here and try to intimidate her? Rising from her stool, she places her hands on her hips.

"Know what I did yesterday? I jammed a fork into my boyfriend's neck and he's a way scarier dude than you."

"Really?" Flat. Giving her nothing.

"Yeah, *really*," she says, trying to keep her voice from trembling. "Now, if you don't get your ass out of here, I'm gonna call the police."

"You were always an amateur, weren't you?" he asks, apparently unmoved by her bluster. His steely affect is starting to unnerve her. "The game is different on the amateur level," he says. "You never played professionally."

The slight man with the thinning blond hair regards Nadine dispassionately. The slender vein that runs along his right temple appears to quiver slightly. She tries to stare him down. The space they share seems to shrink to nothing more than the distance between them. She is conscious only of his presence. Suddenly, she has the urge to urinate. That her mouth is dry and her breath shallow is something of which she is not aware. Then he reaches into his pocket and Nadine realizes she's about to be shot. Her mind flashes to her father and a trip they took to an ocean pier when she was six. At sunset they rode a Ferris wheel and Nadine remembers the way the indigo horizon seemed to elongate as if toward infinity. When the Ferris wheel reached it apex for the first time, her hands flew into the air. Which is where they are right now. The man sees this and his thin lips twist upward. He's holding a tennis ball. A yellow tennis ball. Nadine exhales. She lowers her hands. He tosses the ball toward her and she reflexively grabs it. If a raptor could smile it would look like the man in front of her. He says: "Next time you won't see it coming."

She has no idea what makes her say this but the words "Try me!" come flying out of her mouth. Instantly, she would like to bring them back, to snatch them out of the ether, deposit them once again on her tongue and from there transport the two words back to their place of origin in the dark recesses of her brain but of course this is something she is unable to do. The man's laugh is dry and brittle.

When he turns and strides toward the door, his oxblood loafers are silent on the carpet. She watches as he walks past the plate glass window and disappears. The tropical music is playing again. Traffic glides past on the road. Life, which had stopped moving, resumes. Should she report this? After what she had done, would Hard even allow the police to help her?

A perfectly restored burgundy 1966 Oldsmobile Toronado is parked outside an empty storefront. Maxon sits in the driver's seat watching the door of the tanning salon. After a moment, he opens the glove compartment, removes his Smith and Wesson .38 and checks the load. The gun was purchased from an unlicensed dealer at a gun show in Riverside and is untraceable. Right now, he regrets not showing it to Nadine. Perhaps that might have had the desired effect. This woman was impossible to get a read on. That she was nervous he was certain. But there was something in the way they had interacted that makes him believe she might be a little unstable. Stabbing her boyfriend with a fork was obviously a lie, but the story itself concerned him. If this was how her mind worked, she could be a problem. Actually, she already is a problem, which is why Maxon is here. His task in going to see her was to determine the degree to which this problem could metastasize. The prognosis: not good.

He takes a last look at Fake 'n' Bake. Nadine is still inside. Maxon thinks about his father, who lives outside of Washington, D.C. with a woman who is not Maxon's mother. He knows the man to be ruthless, someone who never lets sentiment get in the way of achieving what he wants. Maxon has often wondered whether he possesses his father's gene for ruthlessness, to leave no wounded on the battlefield. He thinks perhaps he does. But now he places the gun back in the glove compartment, starts the engine, pulls out of the parking lot and calculates the wisdom of doing nothing.

CHAPTER SEVENTEEN

T he District Attorney's Indio branch office is on the top floor of the four-story glass and sandstone County of Riverside Administrative Center on Highway 111 a few miles south of where the road becomes the Deputy Bruce Lee Memorial Highway. The Investigators' office is in the basement of the building. An entire subterranean hallway is lined floor to ceiling with boxes of case files, crimes, tragedies, lives rendered in ink and slowly decomposing paper, stacked, filed, crammed, forgotten. Jimmy is standing with Senior Investigator Oz Spengler who is showing him around. Around forty, and gym-toned, his dark hair is buzz cut. He holds ceramic coffee cup advertising a local casino. Oz gestures toward the mountains of legal records.

"We're putting the files into digital format. There must be a million." Jimmy nods, trying to look interested. It's his first day on the new job and he wants to make a good impression, figures if they like him they're more inclined to leave him to his own devices. "There were this many when I got here. Pile's no smaller now. What you need to understand is it's not gonna be any smaller when you leave. So don't drive yourself nuts over anything."

Jimmy assures him that he won't.

Oz moves down the hallway. Jimmy is now one of ten investigators working out of this office. Oz is his immediate boss, the man he will be reporting to and Jimmy likes him well enough. They push through the double doors leading to the investigators' bullpen. The room is about sixty feet long and thirty feet wide. There are ten cubicles, several of which are occupied by investigators talking on the phone, doing paperwork, writing checks to their divorce lawyers. The offices of the higher-ups in the Investigations Department, the guys who would rate windows and doors if they weren't in a basement, surround the room.

"Every Monday morning," Oz tells him, "Five new felony files land on your desk. So what you need to do is allocate your time." Pointing to an empty cubicle in the middle of the room where a desktop computer sits on a work surface bare but for several manila files, Oz says, "That's your space. Do with it what you want but keep it neat."

Jimmy thanks him for the tour. Oz says he'd like to grab a burger with him soon so they can shoot the shit, get to know one another. Then he disappears. Jimmy spots a couple of confederates, Danny Stringer, ex-cop from Riverside, and Miguel Sandoval, a guy with whom he's worked several homicides, goes over and says hello. They're glad to see him.

Jimmy talks with them for a couple of minutes but doesn't say why he's working here now. Then settles into his cubicle and glances at the files on his desk. It's the usual array of check kiters, drug dealers, domestic abusers, deadbeat dads, armed robbers, rapists, child molesters, and kidnappers. None are high profile, so none are anyone's priority save for the victim's.

Investigators for the District Attorney's office are given wide leeway in what they choose to pursue. Their evaluations rest on how many successful prosecutions they contribute to so, with this in mind, Jimmy sets about looking for cases he thinks can lead to convictions without too much effort on his part. The plan: maintain a low profile, avoid trouble, and clock hours toward a pension.

The files he was given contain a hundred cases. Jimmy breaks them down into five groups of twenty each. He will rank the cases in each group. Using this system, he intends to come up with five cases he can begin exploring more deeply tomorrow.

After forty-five minutes of strained diligence, it becomes hard for Jimmy to disguise exactly how much he does not enjoy sitting in an office. He is cogitating on this and trying to stay awake when a cell phone ring spackles his brain.

"Jimmy, it's Maxon Brae."

"Yeah?" Skipping the pleasantries.

"Your brother needs a favor." Silence. It isn't enough he made the pilgrimage to Mecca to look in on Dale. If Maxon is waiting for him to ask what can I do, he's not going to give him the pleasure. "Randall's going to give a speech at the first annual Riverside County Purity Ball and he thinks it'd be a good thing if you introduced him. We booked Jay Leno but he canceled."

"What's a Purity Ball?"

"It's a campaign event."

"And I'm replacing Jay Leno?"

"No one can replace Jay Leno, Jimmy. Jay's an institution. But he had a conflict."

He figures Maxon is lying. "Kenny Chesney's playing somewhere local tomorrow night, isn't he?"

"Kenny Chesney doesn't like your brother. Asked him for a campaign favor one time. He was kind of an A-hole about it."

"What do you want me to say?"

"Just talk a little about working in law enforcement and what it means to have a brother like Randall."

"You mean someone who can hook me up at the D.A.'s office after I resign from the police force?"

"Frankly, he looks pretty good in that story. And he'd like it if you wore your uniform."

"We don't wear those at the DA's office, Maxon."

"Your *police* uniform."

"That would be illegal since I'm not a cop."

"Since when do you worry about what's illegal and what's not?" Maxon knows what ended Jimmy's tenure on the Desert Hot Springs police force, so there's an uneasy silence while Jimmy decides whether to let the comment slide. "Randall wants it, okay? There won't be a problem."

Jimmy does not want to make any speeches on Randall's behalf. He is not interested in politics. But Randall had gone to bat for him and now he is calling in the favor. *Quid pro quo.* It isn't like his brother can ask Dale. He tells Maxon to give him the time and the place, he'll be there. When he hangs up he briefly considers calling Cali to ask if she wants to go as his date, the evening a potential source of shared mirth. But then he realizes he doesn't know her well enough to trust that she will be able to parse the ironies certain to be on display and decides their next evening together should not involve any of his family members.

CHAPTER EIGHTEEN

G rowing up middle class in the broad agricultural fields of Modesto, Maxon Brae was not the only boy without a father. But only Maxon's had a reputation extending beyond Stanislaus County. In the late 1970s his mother had been a graduate student getting a masters degree in history at Berkeley. Maxon was the result of a brief affair with a pony-tailed former sixties radical who was a visiting professor at the university. When this man met bright-eyed, young Anita Brae, daughter of a school teacher in Eugene, Oregon, he was in the process of undergoing a conversion common to certain types of strident, slightly hysterical leftists who, having discovered flaws in liberal dogma, don't simply reject their former comrades but treat them as if they have plague, and transmogrify into equally annoying conservatives. He cut his hair, traded his sandals for wingtips and founded a neo-conservative magazine called the *New Clarion*. All of this occurred in the years following the one time he had sex with Maxon's mother.

Subsequently, this man married an heir to a timber fortune (it was her money that funded the *New Clarion*) and fathered two sons, one of whom graduated from Princeton and serves on the staff of a United States Senator, the other a Georgetown graduate employed as the youngest speechwriter for a prominent cabinet member. The father periodically turns up on various cable news shout-fests opining on the issues of the day. They are Maxon's shadow family and it would be inaccurate to report that he does not think of them often.

When Maxon was born Anita Brae wrote to his father—teaching at the University of Chicago by then—who took a few moments away from the composition of his magnum opus, *The Liberal Attack on America*, to politely write back requesting that she not contact him again. This she acceded to, in the belief that someone who had turned out, in her view, entirely soulless, would have an influence on Maxon that could only be baleful. When the boy was ten, his mother—she had made a life as a high school teacher, never marrying—told him whom his father was but Maxon did not ask to meet him. And he has still never met the man, although he has always known he will introduce himself in time.

After graduating from an obscure state school in central California, Maxon began working as a legislative aide in Sacramento. The zeitgeist was blowing toward Jesus and Maxon was betting Christians to win. So while his Sunday devotions mainly revolved around visiting flea markets in search of mid-century modern collectibles, Maxon joined a mega-church that would allow him to remain anonymous while still claiming membership in a religious congregation.

Maxon Brae adheres to no religious dogma. Zealots are suckers who believe in the malleability of reality, that it can be changed through prayer. History has taught him that none of it has to do with prayer. It's all about power. People can be sold anything, at least for a time. They might wise up eventually, but then they'll be sold something else. He sees this in his own deluded father who first swallowed the cant of the left before rejecting it to make room for the comforting shibboleths of the other side. This knowledge simplifies life for him.

Although Maxon is not a believer in a traditional deity, he worships at the altar of Harmony, particularly the kind that finds aesthetic expression, and so he will occasionally dip into a museum when he finds himself in need of a quiet place to reflect. Today is one of those days. After his encounter with

Nadine, he drives a few miles west to the Palm Springs Museum of Art. The museum is currently exhibiting a show of Bauhaus architecture. It is his hope that the cool, clean elegance will help settle his mind. If Maxon has a core belief, it is reflected in the beauty and order of the Bauhaus school.

The exhibit is divided into three galleries, the first showing architectural models, the second arts and crafts, and the third interior design. Maxon walks past black and white photographic portraits of Walter Gropius and Ludwig Mies Van der Rohe, two of his heroes, flanking the door leading to the galleries. Gazing at a model of an apartment building, he removes the tennis ball from his jacket pocket. He begins to work it in his fingers while he considers what to do about Nadine. What was it she had shouted at him? *Try me?* That did not bode well. This woman can, with the stroke of a computer key, destroy Randall Duke's political viability and with it deliver a serious blow to Maxon's own plans. How do you recover if the throne behind which you have chosen to stand becomes radioactive? One either takes a long sabbatical and waits for the stench to dissipate, or finds another line of work. Neither of these alternatives is attractive.

As he considers his options, a distinguished-looking elderly male docent with a full head of white hair and tasteful eye makeup leads a tour group of senior citizens past on their way to the next gallery. Maxon has already ruled out trying to pay the woman to go away. Not having a solution immediately at hand is the kind of thing that ordinarily makes Maxon uncomfortable. But the clean Bauhaus lines soothe him. He holds to the idea that everything will meet in a pleasing way and all will be put right. How this will happen, he is not sure.

The heap of case files in front of Jimmy seems to have grown in the hours he has been at his desk although he knows this is not so. On his lunch break, he distractedly eats an apple he brought with him then goes to his car and turns on the air conditioner. But he does not put the car in gear and drive anywhere. Instead, he places his hands palms up on his knees and attempts to meditate. Rather than the elusive sense of calm he seeks, he finds himself lurching through the thicket of Randall and the Purity Ball—What do I owe Randall? What will he owe me if I do this?—and these thoughts crowd out everything else except the memory of his time with Cali. Although that evening was the high point of his past year, Jimmy is not sure he needs anyone else in his life right now. What would it mean other than more obligations? And how can he dock with someone else when he is sorting out his own way of being in the world? Hadn't that been his problem with Darleen? Not to minimize her cheating and his drinking.

When he asks himself why, exactly, did he return to the work force with such alacrity he is not sure of the answer. His expenses are relatively low and he has no dependents. A long restorative vacation was an option. And yet here he is sitting in a pickup truck in the broiling Indio parking lot. He checks his watch and sees he has been at it for fifteen minutes, an eternity for him and more than enough in the current circumstances. He returns to his office and, keen to make sense of his tangled thoughts, logs on to his computer.

His on-line dharma coach Bodhi Colletti, whose computer image Jimmy has spent the past several Sunday mornings staring at, has let it be known that she is available for individual consultation. Bodhi does not respond when he first tries to contact her, but half an hour later his second attempt bears fruit.

AIM IM with DharmaGirl@gmail.com10.31 3:09 P.M.
Jimmy Duke
My bigshot brother wants me to do something inappropriate on his behalf. I feel like I owe him because he helped me get

a new job. Is there a way I can do this while practicing the dharma?

Jimmy Duke

I should have asked if this is a good time to talk. Is it?

DharmaGirl@gmail.com

Jimmy, it's always great to see your icon—but a little relational tip . . . in the future you might want to start by saying hi, asking me how I'm doing, and whether I have a moment to go over something with you.

Jimmy Duke

Sorry. So do you?

DharmaGirl@gmail.com

We were going to start with you just saying hi and asking me how I'm doing.

Jimmy Duke

How are you doing?

DharmaGirl@gmail.com

good, thanks for asking, how about you?

Jimmy Duke

Not great. Like I said, Randall wants me to introduce him at an event (he actually requested I wear my old uniform which is a crime) and I'm feeling a lot of anger toward him.

DharmaGirl@gmail.com

yes, there's a lot wrapped up into that one sentence—your brother wants you to introduce him—he's asking you a favor—what he's asking you to do is a crime apparently even though it seems like a small thing—and you're having feelings around all of it.

DharmaGirl@gmail.com

So let's try to slow it down a bit and feel what's happening in your mind and body right now.

Jimmy Duke

yeah, you could say I'm having feelings. Like I want to rip his heart out.

DharmaGirl@gmail.com
is that a feeling?

Jimmy Duke
That's what's happening in my mind. Is it a feeling? I don't know.
I think it's a fantasy that I'm having because I'm pissed off.

DharmaGirl@gmail.com
what's going on in your body?

Jimmy Duke
I'm tense.

DharmaGirl@gmail.com
Where?

Jimmy Duke
Head, neck, back.

DharmaGirl@gmail.com
Kalu Rinpoche said "We will never again have a chance to
be born into a body like this one." You need to take care of
it. now take a sec, breathe a bit, and see what area of your
body stands out as the least comfortable.

Jimmy Duke
Listen, I can go to a chiropractor for that, ok? I need some
help with my thoughts.

DharmaGirl@gmail.com
your mind and your body and your muscles aren't separate
though, they're related to each other, soften the body and
your thoughts may soften too.

Jimmy Duke
I went to look in on my other brother. He just got let out of jail.
I think he's going to have a hard time staying out of trouble.
I feel like I'm responsible for him somehow even though I'm
not and that's making me tenser.

DharmaGirl@gmail.com
ok so let's back up a bit,

Jimmy Duke
Ok.

Jimmy Duke

You're the boss.

DharmaGirl@gmail.com

take a second, breathe a little bit, and see if you can feel a space in the eye of the storm of thoughts in your head right how—here's a hint—to access the doorway into that space may well require you to feel your way into it rather than think your way into it.

DharmaGirl@gmail.com

And Jimmy . . . . I'm not the boss. You are.

Jimmy Duke

I'm breathing better now. So how can I stop thinking about my brothers when I try and meditate?

DharmaGirl@gmail.com

Jimmy, you're doing great—the idea here isn't to stop thinking about your brothers or anything else when you meditate, it's to become aware of the thoughts (that you're thinking about your brothers) but not to engage in them.

Jimmy Duke

How do I not engage in them?

DharmaGirl@gmail.com

The heart of Buddhist practice is something called beginner's mind which means looking at something with no judgements or expectations, just with pure openness. Think of it this way—you're watching a movie—the movie is about two guys who look a lot like your brothers, you're interested in the movie, it may even stir some emotions in you, but you're not going to write the dialogue yourself, you're listening, watching, waiting to see what's going to happen next, you're participating in the movie to the extent you're curious about it but the movie isn't you—it's just a movie—so with beginner's mind try to keep a little healthy emotional distance from it right now then see what happens to your feelings—do they change?

Jimmy Duke
I'd like to walk out of this movie.
DharmaGirl@gmail.com
That's okay, too.

The earnestness with which Bodhi Colletti relates to the world is not something Jimmy ordinarily responds to, but he cannot argue with her general point. When he logs off and goes back to his case files, he is still vexed about Randall but he feels better equipped to get to the end of the day without sticking his head out the window and screaming. Before he leaves work he will sit at his desk and sip a cup of warm tea. He will experience the liquid as it rolls over his tongue, down this throat and into his stomach. He will pay attention as his lungs expand and contract. He will sense the cool air of the office on his skin. But while he will find all of this relaxing he will still be unable to walk out of the movie.

Dale Duke is not a man known for his sense of responsibility and Maxon can't be sure that the freshly sprung ex-con will keep his rendezvous with the dentist. So he has taken it upon himself to get him there.

"How's the new place working out?"

"All right"

Maxon thinking: You pissant ingrate, after living in a state prison for three years, inmates howling like wolves all night long, worried about getting shanked, bad food, locked in a cell and the most you can say is all right? It might as well be the Four Seasons your brother put you in yesterday. But Maxon doesn't want to lecture Dale, so what he says is: "Randall really stepped up for you."

"Want me to write him a thank-you card? Take me to Wal-Mart and I'll get one."

As they drive past the adobe walls of a popular resort

Maxon thinks about the people currently booked into the rooms and suites. On the golf course, in the pool and at the tennis complex, they are oblivious to Maxon's struggles. He knows they must remain that way. It will be a catastrophe if a day from now his problem is what they are chattering about over their fajitas and margaritas.

Maxon glances over at Dale in a black tee shirt with the words *My Tongue Still Works* emblazoned across the front. He had been wearing it under the polo shirt the RV dealership owner insists on, which he peeled off the second they left the lot. How does Dale get his hands on something like that so quickly? He is resourceful, no doubt. Maxon will have to make sure no enterprising photographer takes his picture in it before the campaign is over. That kind of sartorial display could cost votes. For all of Billy Carter's watch-me-urinate-by-the-side-of-the-road, regular guy charm, no one could reasonably argue that it helped his brother. Dale's narrative is meant to be redemptive. Advertisements for cunnilingus will have to wait.

As far as bending Dale to his will, Maxon has a fundamental problem: he senses Dale does not respect him. As a householder and a taxpayer, he is the embodiment of everything the former inmate holds in contempt. And he senses Dale views him as Randall's errand boy. Ordinarily, he would not care but right now he needs the ex-con to stay out of trouble.

"What kind of guys do you know up in prison, some pretty rough customers?"

"What the fuck you think?"

Maxon does not pretend to have any insight into the criminal mind but he truly doesn't get Dale. Why the prime-cut attitude? Being a paraplegic is an endless raw deal but all paraplegics aren't pricks. Maxon never knew Dale when he could walk so couldn't do the before and after comparison, although he would have bet his vintage Toronado Dale was no angel before the motorcycle accident that severed his spinal cord. He only knows Dale Duke has a personality that can shave glass. Maxon thinks about it because this is the first time the two have ever been alone. He never thought much about Dale before, Randall's brother always background, the low hum of a future calamity everyone is expecting.

A ringing cell phone intrudes on these thoughts: Randall. Maxon reports that the visit to Nadine did not go as well as he would have liked but in his opinion they should wait and see what she does next. Randall pushes back and tells Maxon waiting does not represent the kind of proactive plan he was looking for. Maxon's voice has lost it's Bauhaus-induced cool and takes on a strained edge as he talks. He does not care that Dale is listening. If anything he wants his passenger to hear him stand up to Randall, to show the cantankerous criminal that while he may have not done time on the prison yard, neither is he made of jelly. Not bothering to hide his irritation, Maxon repeats his thought about not doing anything for the time being in more forceful language. Randall emphasizes his lack of enthusiasm for that idea and hangs up.

"Everything okay?" Dale asks. Is that a smirk on his face?

"No need to trouble yourself."

Calmly, Maxon reaches into his jacket pocket. Dale's eyes dart with the movement but he relaxes when Maxon produces a tennis ball. He rolls the ball on his palm, pressing his fingertips into the fuzzy yellow surface.

"What's my brother hot about?"

Maxon quickly summarizes the recent events, leaving out the more lurid details of Kendra's predicament. When Dale asks about the woman who is causing the problem, Maxon tells him what he knows, working the tennis ball the whole time. Dale listens, nodding his head. When Maxon has finished Dale asks what they plan to do.

"You have any ideas?' Maxon says. His tone is fake jocular, but he'd like to know.

"Ain't that what you get paid for, to clean up the mess?"

They ride in silence the rest of the way, Maxon continuing to mull the situation. It is a modern truism that the scandalous secrets of people in public life are nearly always exposed and usually in the most embarrassing manner. Perhaps they should just brace themselves and try to ride out the storm. A cheating spouse is hardly a reason for the electorate to turn on a candidate. He worries that they have allowed themselves to get agitated over something that might just blow over.

After the appointment with the dentist, Dale turns down Maxon's offer of a ride back to work, telling him he prefers to take a cab. Dale tells the driver to take him to the Wells Fargo Bank branch in Borrego Springs. There, an overweight female teller in a turquoise pants suit leads him to his safety deposit box where he is reunited with the money he had stashed before going to prison.

http://WWW.DESERT-MACHIAVELLI.COM
10.31 – 9:14 P.M.

When it comes to winning no one can argue that certain political types are above practicing dirty tricks. Least of all the
Machiavelli. Not to point fingers, but your humble correspondent is going to tell you that in the race here in the desert
between Randall and the Stewardess, it is the Stewardess
who's having sex with Satan, and I don't mean her husband.
No one will say this for attribution but the fearless Machiavelli
hears that the Swain campaign is spreading vicious rumors
about Duke and his wife Kendra. There have been stories cir-
culating for years that the Honorable Member is not one to
keep the banana in its peel. Frankly, the Machiavelli doesn't
care what Randall screws, as long as it's not his constituents.
But the whispers emanating like swamp gas from the
cesspool that is the Stewardess's camp have sunk to a different low—they are about Randall Duke's wife. Why should we,
as responsible voters, as people who care deeply about democracy, worry about what his wife has done? I need not remind
you that it was the wife of a former President who founded the
Betty Ford Center. I don't care if she's drinking a quart of
vodka a day. Okay, the Betty Ford Center doesn't treat people
for extra-marital affairs . . . oops, did I spill the beans? I am
not here to cast aspersions on the Duke marriage, about
which I have no opinion other than if those two can get married, why can't any two people who share a deep and abiding
bank account? I am only here to report the rumors and innu-
endoes the traditional media, constrained as is it by anti-
quated notions of taste, will not tell you about. Is it gossip? Of
course. Is in unsubstantiated? Ditto. But don't you Blogheads
want to know about it anyway? I do. And so does someone
from the Stewardess's campaign, whose name I would love to
disclose. Forgive me if I don't. The Machiavelli needs to protect his most unscrupulous sources.

Stay tuned for a revelation about the Stewardess. She's got four beautiful Caucasian children she's always parading around but word is there's a fifth kid, an older one, and he or she is black. Just a rumor, but so was the guy who shot Biggie Smalls until the bullets started flying.

THURSDAY, NOVEMBER 1

T he kitchen window is open but no breeze ruffles the worn curtains. It's just after seven in the morning and Vonda Jean can already feel the heat of the day. She is still wiping the sleep from her eyes when she pulls the orange juice container from the refrigerator. It feels light, not even enough for a glass. Dammit, how many times does she have to tell Hard to buy more when it's nearly done? He's still in the bedroom. She'll tell him when he walks in to get his coffee. Sees her reflection in the kitchen window. The loose plaid nightdress hangs on her like a potato sack. Glances down at the furry pink slippers on her feet. If she was trying to look alluring she might be worried but right now she doesn't care if Hard finds her attractive. The slippers are comfortable and that's what matters. Hard likes younger women anyway. Vonda Jean has a sense that there was something going on between him and that woman who showed up at the house the other night. She could tell he was lying about her but didn't have the vigor to press the matter. Or the interest. Vonda Jean has been thinking about fleeing the marriage and doesn't want to waste any more energy fighting.

Bread in the toaster and the coffee on, she heads to the garage looking for a carton of frozen orange juice. The Marvins have a horizontal freezer there that Hard uses to store meat from his hunting trips. Every autumn he drives to the Sierra Nevada range and roams the woods for several days stalking deer and elk. Vonda Jean used to accompany him.

They would sit in a tree, rifles at the ready, not saying a word for hours as they waited for game to appear. It was bliss for Hard, being in the woods with an attractive woman with whom he didn't have to make inane conversation while he cradled a high-powered weapon. Vonda Jean didn't particularly like to hunt, but at that time in the marriage she enjoyed being with her husband. She had stopped going with him when her sons grew old enough. Then the boys developed other interests and the last few years Hard has made the trip alone. Usually he'd get a kill and the freezer in the garage would be stuffed with venison steaks the family would eat throughout the winter. This past hunting season had ended a month earlier and it had not been a good one. Despite tracking an eight point buck five miles through the woods, Hard never got a clean shot and drove home empty-handed. There was an unanticipated upside to this, however, since it left room in the freezer for Bane, something Hard had neglected to mention to Vonda Jean.

Hard is in the bedroom pulling on his boxers when he hears Vonda Jean's scream. Figures she must have just opened the freezer. He could have warned her about the dog but imagines it would have led to an argument. He's had enough of those lately. Hard continues getting dressed, taking his time, and when he walks into the kitchen he sees his wife seated at the table sipping her coffee.

"G'morning," Hard says.

"For you, maybe."

Hard opens a cabinet, takes out a box of cornflakes and pours them in a bowl. Removing the milk from the refrigerator, he drowns his cereal. Then he takes a spoon from a drawer and joins Vonda Jean at the table.

"Sleep well?" Hard says.

"I nearly had a seizure," Vonda Jean informs him. "You want to tell me what that animal is doing in the freezer?"

Hard chews his cornflakes, swallows. Looks her in the eye: "I'm gonna have him stuffed."

"What, and put him in the living room?" Her tone suggests he has a greater chance of doing that with her.

"Something like that."

"The hell you are."

"This is why I didn't tell you he was there."

"I thought I was gonna have a heart attack, Harding. You probably would've enjoyed it."

"No, I don't want to kill you, Vonda Jean. Not like that, anyway."

She doesn't laugh at his remarkably tone deaf attempt at humor. Vonda Jean is sick of Hard, hates him right now, wishes he would just get out of her life. But she knows if she plays it wrong, she could get screwed in the settlement. And Hard has nearly twenty years on the force. His pension, a subject that comes up regularly during their frequent fights, won't be small change.

"I want that dog gone."

"The nearest taxidermist's in Apple Valley. I'll take him up there my next day off."

"That's not how it's working, Harding. You're gonna get rid of that dog pronto. And I don't want him back here as a living room decoration either."

"What do you want me to do?"

"Pretend you're normal. Bury him."

"Just stick him in the ground?"

"Cremate him if you want. Bury the ashes. Just get that dog out of my goddamn freezer." Hard eats his cereal in silence. "I'm not fooling."

"Or what?"

"I'll toss his carcass on the side of the road."

Hard desperately wants to wrap himself in the cloak of self-justification that will come with telling Vonda Jean that Bane had been murdered. Of course he can't do that since it will open up a potentially incriminating line of questioning. Why, for instance, would anyone have wanted to harm Bane?

"Fine," he says. "Next day off, I'll bury him."

"If that dog isn't out of my freezer in twenty-four hours, this marriage is over."

"You think I'm worried about that?"

"Just remember I'm entitled to half your pension."

She stares at him with an expression as nurturing as an oil spill. Hard stares right back at her, the vein Nadine had nearly pierced with the salad fork pulsing like a strobe light.

CHAPTER TWENTY

N orth of the swank Coachella Valley with it's well-
tended golf course carpet is the considerably less swank
Morongo Valley and northwest of that, between the
Tehachapi and the San Gabriel Mountains is the still less grand
Antelope Valley where the meth labs outnumber the golfers
infinity to none. When Odin Brick told Princess he lived in the
Antelope Valley and wanted her to move in with him, she envisioned lush fruit trees in the shadows of cool mountains, not
the dried out furnace in which she found herself, with its blis-
tering winds and ruthless sun. Their home is a tiny bungalow
on a dusty road half a mile off a highway. In the back of the
house is an abandoned camper left there by the previous
owner. The surroundings are scrub, the nearest house half a
mile away and empty since the meth bust that sent the owners
to jail.

Princess is packing her yellow vinyl suitcase, which lies
open on the floor of the bedroom. A weak fan blows air in her
direction as beads of perspiration form on her soft upper lip.
She's a beautiful young woman, a little on the short side, but
built to move. Her long, dark hair is parted in the middle and
frames a tan face. She's wearing white short-shorts and a red
string-bikini top that shows off firm breasts. Princess gave
birth three years ago and takes pride in the way her body
recovered. Just short of her twenty-third birthday, she knows
she might need it if she has to start stripping again.

Folding a tiny blue tee shirt with a spray of rhinestones

across the front, she listens for her son Chance King who is napping in the living room. The toddler's ability to sleep in this heat amazes her. When she leans over to place the tee shirt in the suitcase, she hears the front door open. She isn't expecting anyone. She steps to the night table on her side of the bed and removes a .22 caliber handgun. A moment later her husband Odin is standing in door to the bedroom.

"You gonna shoot me?" He says this sweetly, like he's teasing, foreplay for the firearm set. In no mood for repartee, Princess puts the gun down, looks at Odin in work clothes, jeans and a dirty white tee shirt tight on his wiry frame. The tattoo on his right bicep is a red heart bisected by the letters P-R-I-N-C-E-S-S written in cursive. Odin is coiled, ready to spring, even when he's trying to project relaxation. Thick black hair is swept back from his pale face. His green eyes are a little too close together. A cross dangles from an earlobe and there is a streak of grease on his cheek. "Cause if you are, I should tell you, I took the bullets out of that gun last night while you were sleeping."

"Why are you home in the middle of the day?" Her voice is soft with a slight accent she has worked hard to lose.

"I forgot my meds." Odin notices the suitcase and looks at Princess. "You going on a trip?"

This is the moment Princess had been hoping to avoid by leaving while he was at work. "I got a phone call from my sister. Our mother is sick. I need to go to her."

"To the Philippines?"

"I need to leave today."

"How you gonna pay for your plane ticket? That's like a thousand bucks or something." Although Odin is still smiling, now there is a hint of suspicion in his voice. He and Princess have not been getting along, and he hit her last night. Only once, and with an open hand, but it was enough and she had told him so.

"I'm sorry about last night, okay?"

"My mother's very sick. Maybe dying."

"Hey, I know you're still pissed about last night but it won't happen again, I promise."

He leans against the doorjamb, gives her a repentant smile. It usually works. Odin whistles a few bars from a popular tune he heard her singing around the house the other day.

"You take me to bus station?"

"No, Princess, I will not take you to bus station. I think your mother's fine, okay? And if you go, you're not gonna hear my news."

"What news?"

"I'm gonna make ten grand this week."

"You bullshit."

"I no bullshit, baby. I'll be able to buy you that used truck you wanted. And if the job goes well, that's just the start."

"What kind of job?"

"Dude needs some help moving an oil rig. One time thing. Ten grand." Princess considers this intelligence. Odin was always talking about how he's going to make a huge score and they'll be living in a beautiful house on a hill with shade trees and a swimming pool. She wasn't sure how he was going to do this on what he was making at the auto body shop in Fontana, but he told her he had big plans and she should trust him.

The blast of a car horn rends the stifling air. Odin looks over his shoulder, then back at Princess. "You expecting someone?"

As she curses under her breath he turns and heads to the front door where he sees a taxicab parked in the street. He throws the door open and walks toward the cab, a white '94 Plymouth. A middle-aged Latino sits on a beaded seat cover. Sweat stains the armpits of his guayabera shirt.

"My wife don't need a taxi," Odin says. The Latino glowers at him then drives off without a word. Princess stands at the front door watching her escape plan depart. In the kitchen she pours herself a glass of lime Kool-Aid from a plastic pitcher. On the counter rests a foot high wood carving of Buddha that Odin brought back from his tour in Afghanistan. The light-toned Buddha is rotund and bald and his subtle smile comforts Princess. She wishes Odin would emulate the idol's peaceful aspect.

When she hears the screen door bang shut she says: "I can't take your bullshit no more, Odin."

He appears at the kitchen door. "I know, I know. I'm gonna start up with the meetings again. Going to one today, okay? Give it up to a higher power and all." Odin heads for the bathroom, just a few feet away. She hears him opening the medicine chest, reaching for his pills.

"You lie, man," she says.

From the bathroom, he says, "No, Princess, I'm true like Jesus, okay?" A moment later he is standing in the kitchen doorway. "I understand why you feel that way, so I'll try and do better. Can I have a sip of that Kool-Aid?"

She hands him the drink and watches as he places a pill on his tongue, takes a sip and swallows, before handing the glass back to her.

"Ten grand, little girl," he says. "That's a lot of *dinero*."

Could he possibly be telling the truth? Odin didn't actually lie that much, probably no more than most American guys. If it was true, they could pay all their overdue bills and she really could get that little Toyota pickup.

One of the best parts of fighting with Odin was the makeup sex. No matter how bad the altercation had been when the two of them finally reached the point where the conflict was exhausted they would invariably fall into each other hungrily and abuse the bedsprings, or the kitchen counter, or wherever they happened to find themselves at that moment if it provided a modicum of privacy. Today is no exception and after she and Odin tongue kiss, she allows him to pull her white short shorts down, bend her over the sink and thrust himself in from behind. As Odin is humping away, his white ass going up and down like the water pump in her rural village, Princess grips the chipped countertop, looks toward the distant stony brown mountains and reflects on what her idea of America was like when she was growing up in the Philippines. There would be large airy houses with vast green lawns. The people would be tall and blonde and they would have soft, golden skin. And this tall, blonde race of golden skinned gods would be welcoming, generous and kind. So it is with no small sense of disappointment that she finds herself living in the high desert with Odin and Chance King, and working forty hours a week as a sorter at the Fed-Ex Depot.

Odin is good at sex, though. That is a point she is happy to concede as he licks her neck with just the tip of his tongue and promises her that everything will change. He tells her he wants to please her, to make her happy, he'll do anything. She says yeah, oh, yeah, but what she's thinks is if you want to make me happy you could start by shutting up. When Odin climaxes in silence Princess takes this gap in the conversation as an opportunity to arrive at an orgasm herself.

CHAPTER TWENTY-ONE

I don't know what you're crying about," Randall says. "He's just some blogger. No one gives a flip what he says."

"He said I had an affair!"

"The guy wrote that Mary Swain might have an illegitimate black kid hidden somewhere."

"I don't care what he wrote about Mary Swain. I care what he wrote about me!" At this she dissolves into tears.

They are in the bedroom of their home and he is getting dressed for the Purity Ball. It's early evening but Kendra is under the covers, fully dressed in slacks, a blouse, and a sweater. She is able to do this because the air conditioning has cooled the house to the level of a meat locker.

"How do you even know it's a man? Can a man even be that bitchy?"

"I know a few," Randall says, adjusting his cummerbund. "Look, Kendy, politics are bloody. They're going to say all kinds of things about you. If you can't take the heat . . . "

"I know, I know, get out of the kitchen." She completes the cliché and reaches for the bedside tissues. After loudly blowing her nose, she asks, "Could you possibly say something that I haven't heard a thousand times?"

"You should stop reading the Internet."

"I wasn't. Maxon called to warn me. I still haven't looked at it." She reaches for another tissue, blows her nose again. "What happened with that other problem?" Kendra does not want to assign a proper name to it, for fear of making it more real.

"We're letting it ride right now."

"You seem awful calm about it."

Randall coolly regards his wife. The hours he spent training to defuse live ordnance when he was on the bomb squad in the Army are a deep well from which to draw in civilian life. When faced with problems that occur in a campaign, even ones as spiky as Nadine, nothing compares with the possibility that one crossed wire might result in an explosion that could literally separate your torso from your legs.

"I'm not that worried."

Randall takes a last glance in the mirror. In a tuxedo, he is a picture of elegant authority. Evaluating himself, he decides his mane is not quite rigid enough. Through the cloud of hairspray, he can hear Kendra sniffle on the bed behind him.

"I don't know what to do," she whines. "What should I do?" When Randall, who assumes the question is rhetorical, does not respond, she says, "I want you to ask Maxon to find out who this Machiavelli is, okay? Will you promise me?"

"You need to toughen up, soldier," Randall says. Then he leans over, kisses her on the head and retreats.

America is a God drunk nation and any politician who ignores this reality does so with the knowledge that it could cause his career to evaporate. The true believers don't have to worry about this since they are already in some kind of dialogue with the deity of their choice, but those with a more nuanced view of the universe and its sundry mysteries must navigate these shoals with precision. Although Randall Duke's father was a Pentecostal preacher, religion ceased to play an important role in his life once he left home. But with every election campaign, he has to pretend. For this reason, Randall is pleased to find himself surrounded by a news crew that has staked out the entrance to the Parker Palm Springs Hotel where the First Annual Riverside County Purity Ball is taking place.

The desert dowager has been smartly reinvented and is now a model of Palm Springs fabulous. A golf and tennis resort would have been the natural venue for this affair, but Maxon made the case that the contemporary quality of the Parker would provide a pleasing contrast to the traditional nature of the event. Near the giant bright orange front doors of the hotel, Randall holds forth for the camera with his daughter/prop Brittany standing at his side looking embarrassed. She is prettily attired in a powder blue satin gown with a bow on the back that Kendra had insisted on. Brittany's nod toward teenaged rebellion the absence of panties.

According to Maxon there was going to be more than one news crew at the event—are the others somewhere shooting footage of Mary Swain?—but Randall doesn't let disappointment dampen his enthusiasm.

"We need a new morality in America," Randall proclaims as several fathers and daughters who have gathered to listen nod in approval. Randall believes he looks particularly authoritative in a tuxedo. The trousers fit more snugly than he had recollected but he's generally pleased with his presentation. He needs to compliment Maxon for insisting the Ball be formal. "We've seen where having no values has led us. To Sodom and Gomorrah, and I don't mean that in a judgmental way, but I think we must teach positive values to our children and a good place to start is with our daughters since they will be the mothers of the next generation." *The mothers of the next generation?* The bloviating stops him in his cognitive tracks. Is that a phrase he can recycle, or does it make him sound like an idiot? Such a thin line. He'll ask Maxon. "We're going inside now. Don't forget to vote!"

Randall looks around for Jimmy, doesn't see him. Where the heck is he? Along with the fathers and daughters who witnessed this peroration, Brittany dutifully follows Congressman Randall Duke into the hotel.

The ballroom is in a free standing building at one side of the elaborate hotel gardens and tonight it looks as if John the Baptist was the design consultant. There are no extraneous decorations save for the large wooden cross at one end. Standing like a sentinel, it is a silent rebuke to any thoughts of frivolity. Randall's taste is livelier but he understands the metaphorical purpose of the decoration scheme. The last group to have held an event in the opulent room was the Transgendered Entertainers Association and other than the preponderance of tiaras on the girls, there is no hint of their many-splendored presence this evening. Again, he looks for Jimmy but there is no sign.

The marble walls imbedded with large rectangular mirrors make the tiny bar off the two story lobby of the hotel look like the inside of a jewel box. The legs of the six bar stools appear to be inspired by the horns of a delicately boned mammal found on the African veldt. In one sits a man dressed in a dark suit, white shirt and red patterned tie. He puts another peanut in his mouth and chases it with the last of his third non-alcoholic beer. Jimmy Duke: the respectable version. It's just after seven and the resort doesn't do a big bar business so the place is nearly empty. A blond surf kid in a black shirt and black pants stands behind the bar. The only other customers a couple in their forties. They're not talking so Jimmy makes them for married. It is moments like this, alone in a bar, that he regrets having quit drinking. The consumption of three non-alcoholic beers is an act that has no point. It's like going to a strip club to watch the cashier. Yet habit draws him toward the bar, the ambience, the bottle. He doesn't even like the taste, which is to say the lack of discernible taste, the weak-kneed imitation that non-alcoholic beer represents. He resents having received the call from Maxon requesting his presence here tonight. Resents that he didn't receive the call from Randall himself and resents that he was asked in the first place. But he knows he owes Randall and his brother is not shy about collecting. Randall trades favors like currency and generally Jimmy has a policy about staying out of his way. But this one was unavoidable so here is, a brooding barfly.

"Another near beer?" Surfer Joe says. Knows the kid doesn't mean it, but he feels like he's being mocked. Jimmy waves him off.

And what is he supposed to say to this roomful of virgins and their fathers? That Randall is a great guy? A terrific husband? A committed parent? Is he supposed to lie about a brother he doesn't particularly like? Sure, why the hell not? Jimmy doesn't mind prevaricating to an audience of strangers about something as unimportant as a Congressional election. What he knows about Mary Swain isn't particularly attractive—although he would definitely like to have sex with her—so if he is asked to perform a tiny part in the pageant of Randall's re-election campaign then he must.

"Jimmy!" He looks over and sees Maxon walking toward him, dressed in a tuxedo. Worry sears his bland features. "Where's the uniform?"

"In my truck. I was gonna change when I got here but I decided I'm not wearing it."

"The point of you doing this is that you're in a uniform."

"Yeah, well, like I said, forget it."

Jimmy turns back toward the bar and takes another sip of his drink. Maxon moves a little closer, leans in. With his voice lowered to just above a whisper, he says, "Randall got you the job with the D.A. after you stole that dog from the police department, didn't he?"

"I didn't steal that dog, Maxon. I pardoned him."

"Didn't he personally intervene so there were no charges? If I recall, this was after you had to resign because you threatened your boss."

"Randall's gonna take my job away if I don't wear a uniform?" Jimmy shakes his head, trying to tamp down the bitterness he feels at finding himself in this situation. The pink bubble appears and Jimmy places Maxon inside. It lifts off and carries the pasty operative up toward the ceiling, through the roof and into the night sky.

Breathe in one, two. Breathe out three, four.

"I'll introduce him," Jimmy says. "But forget the uniform."

Maxon pulls out his cell phone. Jimmy asks whom he is calling.

"Your brother." Maxon hesitates, waiting to see if this ploy has the desired effect. Jimmy turns his attention back to his drink. "Why are you making me bother him with this when you said you'd do it? It's one thing to take this kind of shit from Dale."

"Get Dale to introduce him."

Then, into the phone: "I need you to talk to Jimmy. He's having an issue." Maxon hands the phone over to Jimmy who reluctantly takes it and briefly explains how he feels. He listens for a moment, his expression darkening.

"That may be true, but . . . Randall, I know. Yeah, I said I know. And I appreciate it. Far as I'm concerned I'm here and now we're even."

Jimmy hands the phone to Maxon.

"Are you wearing the uniform?"

"Are you gonna blow me?"

Maxon pauses and appears to think about saying something. But if Randall is not able to persuade Jimmy to violate the law, it is beyond his powers as well.

"Here's your speech," Maxon says, shoving a typewritten page at him.

"I was gonna wing it."

"Not tonight." Jimmy looks at Maxon. Some men resemble James Bond when they put on a tuxedo. Maxon looks like a headwaiter. "Just read what's there."

Jimmy has always had a problem with authority and Maxon has strayed too far into the territory. It's not so much the words on the page that trouble him. What he does not respond to is the highhandedness of Maxon's manner, the implication that Jimmy is here to do his bidding. Never mind that this is exactly why Jimmy is here. He can't ascribe his words to drunkenness, as the three bottles of near beer bear witness, but to some deep contrarian strain that animates him, when he says, "I'm not a trained seal."

"You said you'd wear the uniform and you're not wearing it, which is duly noted. At least read the goddamn speech."

"Can't I . . . "

Cutting him off: "Read what's there."

"I don't appreciate the frontal assault, Maxon. You don't trust me or something?"

"Your brother would like you to read this paragraph. Put it in your own words if you want, but get the meaning across, that he's a family values kind of guy. That's all he wants you to say. Can you at least do that?"

Maxon's back makes an inviting target. Jimmy fights an urge to fling a bottle and crack the skull beneath the sparse blond hair, but restrains himself. The only thing he can think of that's even more pitiable than drinking non-alcoholic beer is braining someone with one of the bottles. He needs to settle down. Focus on the breath. Two counts in, four counts out. Jimmy knows this moment here in the precious little bar of the Parker Palm Springs Hotel with a ballroom full of family people waiting for him to introduce Randall is an excellent opportunity to practice the dharma: Maxon in a pink bubble. Jimmy lighting the pink bubble with a blowtorch. Maxon floating away, the pink bubble engulfed in flames.

No, that's not right.

He tries again. Breathes in. Breathes out. It's not working.

What he's thinking about: After he and Darleen had their

last fight, right before leaving the desert, she paid a visit to Randall. They had always gotten along well and no attractive woman ever escaped his eternally peeled eye. Darleen was from a modest background and having married the sibling of a United States Congressman was something of which she was unusually proud. Kendra was out of town at a tennis clinic with Brittany and Randall was home from Washington for the weekend. They had a couple of drinks and it was a warm evening so Randall asked if she wanted to go for a swim in the pool. She and Jimmy didn't have a pool and the proximity of her semi-famous, handsome brother-in-law, and the effects of the liquor made her keen to feel the cool water on her skin. Randall had lent her one of Kendra's bathing suits and it didn't stay on long.

Jimmy would never have discovered that his brother had "got nasty" with his wife if Darleen hadn't used that exact phrase in an email a few days later after he had warned her in a heated phone conversation not to think about touching him for alimony. Although this information did not come as a huge surprise it was nonetheless disappointing. Darleen and he may have no longer been together but Jimmy believed there were certain protocols siblings held to, a primary one being not to have sex with each other's spouses, ex or otherwise. In the year since this occurred he has chosen to never mention it for one simple reason: Jimmy is afraid he might kill his brother. Words devolve into emotions running red and then he's spending the rest of his life in prison. So why bring it up?

"Uncle Jimmy, I *have* to be here, but you?" Jimmy looks to his left where he sees Brittany with her hands on the back of a barstool. Jimmy tells her he's introducing her father to the gathering. "You couldn't dodge that assignment?" Jimmy assures her he could not. She asks him if he can believe this bullshit, indicating with a sweep of her arm the hotel, the event they are both about to attend, and a father/daughter pair that is walking past them toward the ballroom. "Maybe I'll unravel this cute bow on my butt and hang myself with it from one of the chandeliers," she remarks. "But that would imply that I cared about this crap, which I don't."

An unfamiliar feeling forms in Jimmy's chest and it rises to his throat and fills his cheeks before leaking out: laughter. He hasn't laughed in a while. Brittany smiles when she sees the effect she's having. "Why would anyone even want to be in Congress, much less go to some Purity Ball where they have to beg all these churchy people for their votes?"

"You got me there," Jimmy says, genuinely stumped. He's enjoying the conversation, though, won't mind if Brittany keeps talking. The kid's a pistol. Jimmy has no idea where it comes from, both of her parents nearly military in their embrace of conformity.

"I kind of wish the terrorists would just blow this place to smithereens but I'd probably feel bad about it if they did. I'm a softie, I guess."

"Just like me," Jimmy says.

"Hey, why don't we flee the premises, arm ourselves then come back and fight the power? Like revolutionaries. Shoot up the Purity Ball."

"You don't like things the way they are?"

"I should vote?"

"You could. When you turn eighteen. You're not eighteen yet, are you?"

"Next year. And I was kidding about going all Columbine in there."

"I know." Jimmy can't figure his niece out. Is she engaged? Disengaged? Does anything have meaning for her or is she one of those kids who float above everything, detached and superior? Is her ironic exterior just a rough blanket she uses to conceal a deeply romantic soul or is she truly someone who doesn't give any kind of a shit? Before he reaches a conclusion, Brittany opens her purse and produces a joint. "Want to blaze?" When Jimmy does nothing but widen his eyes, she says "Take it easy, Officer, I have medical card."

"Really?"

"Tennis elbow. Don't tell my parents, okay?"

Something over Jimmy's shoulder catches Brittany's eye and she quickly stuffs the joint back in the purse. Jimmy follows her nervous glance and sees Maxon striding toward them. He announces in a peevish voice that the Purity Ball is about to kick off and Randall would appreciate it if they joined the festivities.

It is genuinely difficult to generate a party hearty environment when the goal of the evening is to stop intercourse from occurring among people who are at the age where their sexuality is in the jungle cat phase. Thus the ballroom hums with nervous chatter. Doting fathers and abashed daughters ranging from pre-school to college age stand in embarrassed clumps as a string quartet plays a mixture of hymns and Carpenters' songs. The fathers are as tightly wound as a tuxedoed group of middle aged white men can be, which is to say rigor mortis would loosen them up. The daughters, all wearing ball gowns in different pastel hues, are more relaxed by virtue of their youth but their assigned roles for the evening serve as an effective cap on the teenaged excitement level. Most didn't want to come but there is solidarity to be had among their fellow prisoners.

Randall stands in a group of cheerfully chatting fathers, all of whom seem pleased to be in his presence. He continues to marvel at the personal response he inspires in his constituents. The antipathy most people profess toward politicians does not seem to extend to him. A tall investment counselor with a trim mustache says, "My daughter didn't want to come, but I told her God knows us by our actions." At this two of the other fathers chime in, "Amen." A burly systems analyst with a buzz

cut and a thick face says, "We need to set the example."
Everyone present nods. Randall has politely waited for all the
men in the group to say something. This allows him to maintain the illusion that he actually listens. The buzz cut man was
the last to speak. That is Randall's cue.

"Godlessness must be eradicated," Randall says, pausing
for effect. "Just not at the Indian casinos because that would
hurt the economy." Everyone hesitates a moment, then laughs.
It isn't that the joke is particularly amusing, since it is not. But
someone has the temerity to introduce a spark of levity on such
an august occasion, this gathering of the clan. These men, these
bastions of rectitude, have been silently hoping Randall would
take control of the conversation and relieve them of having to
say something they haven't already heard countless times. They
would all prefer discussing sports or business, but the weight-
iness of the evening's theme has made them want to elevate the
discourse.

That Randall Duke! What ease and humor! What command! The earnest, tuxedo-clad fathers have been slightly
intimidated by the seriousness of the event and he has light-
ened things with a gag. No wonder this man keeps getting
elected to office. Their relief is conspicuous and Randall can
feel it. "These Purity Balls are a good way to start but we each
need to pledge to take God into the world." More nodding at
this advice. "Mammon is a tempter, always lurking, ready to
seduce us with his smooth talk. If we give in, we can only
expect the same from our daughters. We have to tell them
they're beautiful, tell them we love them because if we don't
then they're going to look to hear it from some hip-hopping,
pants-around-his-ankles kid in a backwards baseball cap." A
few of the girls giggle in recognition, Randall having artfully
described several current boyfriends; the others all know a version of the predatory male invoked by the host. They are met
with what's-so-funny-about-that? stares from their escorts.

Randall spots Brittany with Maxon, hovering at the edge of the group. "Isn't that right, sweetie?" Maxon shoves the girl forward and she moves to her father's side where Randall puts his arm over her shoulder. "Everyone, this is my daughter, Brittany." Her anxious smile only conveys a fraction of the discomfort she feels at this moment.

When Randall had asked if he wanted to sit at his table as an honored guest Jimmy had demurred, telling his brother if it was all right with him he would just as soon deliver his introductory remarks then go home. He would have liked to talk more with Brittany but they can't have an honest conversation with Randall around. He feels for that girl, worries about how she's going to turn out. Now he scans the room from a doorway to the side of the podium. He doesn't care if Randall would prefer that he wear the uniform. As far as Jimmy's concerned, it's enough that he's wearing a tie.

There are a hundred and sixty-three guests, the odd number caused by a pair of thin, blonde twins in matching white chiffon, and they sit at sixteen round tables, father, daughter, father, daughter, circles of imagined, yearned for—*please God, tell me she didn't have sex with that imbecile in the Lakers jersey and the unlaced sneakers*—pristine goodness. They eat salad, and chicken, and after: a desert of apple pie, another masterful Maxon Brae touch.

Jimmy takes in the daughters, lovely in the glowing light of the ballroom, the severe cross at the head of the room, and the loud voices of the fathers as they struggle to keep conversations going. He thinks of his own father, the Reverend Donnie Duke. What would he have made of Randall hosting this event?

"Jimmy Duke is an Investigator for the Riverside County District Attorney." Too distracted by his own thoughts a moment earlier to notice that Maxon was at the podium, tentacles of discomfort now coil around Jimmy's stomach as he prepares to be introduced. "Please give a warm round of applause to the brother of the Congressman."

The crowd obeys and with a nod of his head Maxon indicates that it's showtime. Jimmy is thinking of his father as he steps to the lectern at the front of the room, how his father would have been proud of him for introducing his older brother. He pushes aside the thought that his father never knew this iteration of Randall and focuses on the task at hand.

"Good evening, folks. My name is Jimmy Duke," he says, then stops, caught by surprise as another smattering of applause breaks out. His career in law enforcement confers instant authority upon him, particularly with this crowd. When the applause subsides, he continues, getting comfortable, "My brother Randall is all about family. I don't know if you people know this, but our brother Dale has had some trouble with the law. That can be kind of hard to handle if you're in law enforcement." Jimmy pauses for the appreciative chuckles from the fathers. He knows the daughters are all tuning him out except his niece who gives him a little wave. And it's not an innocent wave either. There's something cagey about it, like she has a secret she wants to share but doesn't dare, at least not with her father around. He returns it with a smile and a nod. When the amused murmur passes, he continues, "Well, it can be real tough if you're in public office. But my brother Randall always puts family first. From his beautiful wife Kendra, to his daughter Brittany, to our brother Dale, and to me, Randall is a guy who comes through for his family. And he looks at his constituents as family, too. It's a pleasure to introduce your Congressman, my big brother, please give a round of applause to your member of the United States House of Representatives Randall Duke."

Jimmy steps away from the microphone and leads the clapping, relieved to have discharged his obligation. It worries him on some level that he can sling it so comfortably, but he knows it's not a bad skill to have at the ready.

With a grin and a wave Randall rises from his seat and walks to the lectern where he shakes hands with Jimmy. "I'd wish you'd worn the uniform," Randall says, the smile never flagging. Jimmy shakes his head and makes for the parking lot.

"My brother Jimmy Duke, everyone," Randall leads the cheers for Jimmy who waves at the crowd without looking at them before vanishing through a side door.

"I want to thank you all for coming tonight," he says to the bright faces. "Right now, I'd like all the daughters to stand up and be counted." Randall waits while, amid uneasy titters and scraping chairs, the virgins—and some for whom that ship has sailed—stand as one giant rebuke to the dominant culture. They fidget in their dresses, smiling nervously. "You girls are beautiful tonight, every last one of you. And your dads are so proud. I hope they tell you that at home. Dads, do you tell your daughters that they're beautiful?" Muffled waves of assent are offered. The men regard each other and smile, some a little guiltily. Randall continues: "I'm going to ask you to take a pledge tonight, and when you take it, please remember that you are not just making it to yourselves, but you're making it in the name of the Lord." He waits a moment for this to sink in. After a pause long enough to make sure those present absorb the import of what is about to occur, he raises his right hand and tells them to do the same. When all the girls have their right hands in the air Randall smiles and says, "I pledge to live a life of abstinence . . . repeat after me, please. I pledge . . . " The girls catch on and Randall continues, "I pledge to lead a life free of sin." They repeat the words. "And I pledge to walk in the path of the Lord Jesus Christ who will keep me pure until the day I marry." The young voices, some tentative and unsure, others ringing like church bells, intermingle and ascend in a chorus of renunciation (a considerable amount of it feigned), the fathers swell with pride shot through with a dash of confusion—these are not men wholly without sin both venial and mortal—and Randall Duke beams because votes are swimming into his net like he is St. James and the Purity Dads are campaign-check-writing fish. His coffers will get a sweet little bump the next day and he doesn't even have to ask for it.

Randall tells the girls to be seated and asks the fathers to stand. When the men are on their feet Randall informs them, "The world can be a scary place. There are temptations of the mind and of the flesh. Tonight I want you to redouble your efforts to be pure in your own hearts. We teach by example and there is no stronger example than our own behavior. Our daughters look to us for this. We are their rocks. The moms are important, too, but lets face it, we're the dads, right? We're the dads! Say it!"

"We're the dads!" arises the cry from the flock, low at first. The energy in the room is pent-up and Randall is offering release. He understands the power of the voice to free the soul and the man is throwing open the doors.

"Say it again!"

Louder: "WE'RE THE DADS!"

Some in the pink, yellow and blue sea of daughters try not to giggle, and their stern fathers attempt to ignore the suppressed merriment. Other girls watch with the intensity of St. Teresa of Avila, their expressions dialing into masks of devotion.

While the horde is being distracted by the exhortations of her father, Brittany has taken this opportunity to put her cell phone inside her dress where she is using it to take pictures of her vagina.

"One more time!"

Like a blast, horns in a parade, listen up You Endangered Girls: "WE'RE THE DADS!"

"That's right. We are the dads, and our precious daughters are confronted with a dark and dangerous world. They need us to shine a light, they need us to be a beacon, they need us to be a rock for them." If the litany of mixed metaphors bothers anyone present, they do not let it affect their enthusiasm for what Randall is saying. The audience is rapt. "The flames of hellfire are burning out there every day. They're burning in the cities, they're burning in the suburbs and they're burning right here in the desert. Our beautiful young daughters are confronted with levels of depravity we can hardly imagine on television, at the movies, and on the Internet. They are calling out for our help. Our daughters need us and it is our moral obligation to protect them." Randall pauses waiting for the results of his words to sink in. "Now if you would please turn your attention to the cross."

One hundred and sixty-three pairs of eyes swing around and behold two young Marine Corps members—thank you, Maxon Brae!—polished in formal dress stationed in front of the bare wooden cross. They face one another, each holding a gleaming sword upward at a forty-five degree angle, tips touching, to make an arch that glistens in the light of the chandeliers. The Marines are rigid, their expressions severe. If either has predatory designs on the assembly of virgins, it is impossible to discern.

"Dads, take your girls and walk beneath those swords. Then I want you to get down on your knees in front of that cross, fathers and daughters together, and take the purity vow. Say a prayer, share a few intimate words, walk in the light."

The string quartet begins to play "Are You Washed In The Blood" and attendees stand and form a quiet line. Two by two they proceed beneath the swords, past the stoic Marines and to the cross where they all kneel for a few moments. Some fathers whisper a few words to their daughters; some are silent, but all behave with a sense of purpose commensurate to the occasion.

Randall and Brittany are the last to go. Randall can feel the eyes of the room on him as they walk toward the Arc of Swords.

Truly, he reflects, this is an excellent way to get votes. As they kneel at the cross, Randall leans toward Brittany and whispers, "I will always be there for you, my darling." She rolls her eyes, but Randall does not see this since his own are closed as he concentrates on manufacturing devotion.

Father and daughter ride home in amiable silence. Randall is so pleased with how the evening went he fails to notice his daughter, slumped in the passenger seat and glued to her cell phone, is sending another labial trip-tych to her boyfriend.

His hope of getting to sleep without incident vanishes when he enters the bedroom and sees Kendra in a diaphanous white nightgown, propped up on a mound of pillows with a computer on her lap.

"Who *is* this Desert Machiavelli?" Randall tells her he doesn't know and asks what's wrong. "He outed me."

"What do you mean, he *outed* you? You're not gay."

"I swore I wouldn't read it but I broke down. He said someone working for that bitch Mary Swain told him I had an affair."

"With a woman?"

"No, but that doesn't matter. He said I had an affair, Randall! Read this," she says shoving the laptop over to him. Her voice has gone up several registers and as Randall glances through the blog he is concerned this might evolve into hysteria. She squeezes his arm, digging her nails into his skin. "The whole world's going to think I'm the sleaze!"

Sitting on the bed, Randall puts his arm around his wife's back and draws her close to him. She inclines her head on his shoulder. "If every politician who was suspected of having an affair had their career ended by it, I swear there'd be no one in Congress. You know that, right?" He sees her lower lip tremble and hears her sigh, but the expected waterworks do not arrive. "It's just a some dumbass blogger no one gives a flip about. Says more about the Swain campaign anyway."

Ten more minutes of reassurance and a large glass of wine do the trick and Kendra is finally calm enough to try and go to sleep. As for Randall, he makes a mental note to ask Maxon why he hasn't found out who this Desert Machiavelli character is and gotten him to knock it off. At least Nadine hasn't contacted the blogger because if she had they would certainly know about it. Another day gone by and still she has not surfaced. That can only be good.

http://WWW.DESERT-MACHIAVELLI.COM

11.1 – 11:52 P.M.

So Randall Duke hosted a Purity Ball tonight. Irony of ironies, this serial cocksman, this epic horndog, this priapic pol had the gall to stand in front of a roomful of teenage girls and tell them they should abstain from sex until they were married? The Machiavelli would like to know where he gets the gonads? At the Gonad Store for Forked Tongue Politicians? The Machiavelli had a spy there—a supporter of the Stewardess? You Blogheads be the judges—and he reported lots of upstanding family guys who took time off from cheating on their wives to escort their precious teenage vestals to this sham of an event. Does Randall think these people are going to forget his wife's love of the gays and vote for him anyway? Apparently, this is exactly what is going on. Randall knows a basic fact about political life right now—wave Jesus in front of a certain group and their brains get all mushy. The Machiavelli heard there was a whole lot of Randall love in that room. These dads (and they're the ones who matter since the virgins can't vote) are the kind of guys Mary Swain would love to have in her camp, but Randall jumped on the purity idea first. If I'm her I'm kicking my campaign manager's ass right about now.

On the other hand, all may not be smooth sailing in Dukeville. Sometimes the best news comes in at the end of the week and by best I mean most salacious, embarrassing or damaging. Now this is just a tip and I don't know how reliable it is. Safe to say, if I was the New York Times, I would not print it. But since I am a blogger without that professional baggage, I can report it as a rumor and let you make of it what you will. Someone whispered in my ear that there might, and the key word here is might, be some financial irregularities in the Duke campaign. Irregularities as in shenanigans, shenanigans as in illegal. Again, let me be

clear—this is a rumor. All I'm saying is people are saying.
Cynics out there—you know who you are—might be thinking these malevolent leaks are coming from the campaign
of the Stewardess. But you would be wrong. Let's just say
that my source is reliable and there could be an audit. The
Stewardess, on the other hand, would never have this problem because her husband can pay any bill and she does not
have to sully herself with the demeaning activity of
fundraising. She shakes that ass for free.

FRIDAY, NOVEMBER 2

Sporting designer knock-off shades, smoking a Camel and doing his best Johnny Depp, Odin is at the wheel of a dust-covered blue '98 Impala moving toward Cathedral City in the early afternoon. Man in the passenger seat: House Cat, ten years older, exudes the maleness familiar to rough trade aficionados everywhere. Relaxed fit jeans and a white tee shirt across a barbell chest. House Cat runs his hand over his salt and pepper crew cut, every finger a ring, coral on his pointer, amethyst on his middle, turquoise on his ring finger, and onyx on his pinky. A turquoise bracelet adorns his right wrist as he leafs through a design magazine called *California Interiors*. This is not reading material he would have been looking at in Calipatria where he had been doing three to five for burglary when Odin met him. He'd done over thirty successful jobs in the desert and as far west as the suburbs east of Los Angeles before being pinched, earning his nickname by dint of hard work. But now House Cat has his eye on a piece of property, an old California Victorian south of Barstow, built at the turn of the previous century. Knows it would make a great bed and breakfast. Figures he can re-wire it, update the plumbing, be open for business in a year. House Cat in the hospitality business. Who says you can't start over in life?

"You wouldn't believe what it costs to get a decent sofa."

"Just buy some shit down in Mexico and ship it up here."

"You don't have nice furniture, you don't get the good clientele."

"Long as their money's green, who cares?"

"It's not just the money, Odin. You want something with some taste and refinement."

"Fuck that."

"Where are you gonna get with that attitude?"

"To Vegas with a couple of hookers and a basket full of poker chips."

"What about your cute little wife?"

"Long as I buy her a cute little truck, she'll be all right."

"Think the two of you might want to work at the bed and breakfast?"

Odin's not sure if House Cat is kidding. Opening a bed and breakfast is the older man's dream, not his. Odin didn't even know what a bed and breakfast was until House Cat told him. And honestly, it sounds pretty damn gay. He doesn't want to tell that to House Cat, though. Where is the upside? Odin views himself as a practical man and there is nothing to be gained by pissing on his colleague's dream. If that's where the man wants to dump his money, it's fine by him. He notices House Cat is looking in his direction.

"Not the life for me," Odin tells him.

"Fine. Suit yourself." Turns his attention back to the magazine.

It's another sweltering afternoon and the Impala's air conditioning is balky so the windows are down. Odin's doing about seventy and a continuous rush of stifling air fills the car, gritty on their skin. Odin knows that House Cat wants to have sex with him, isn't put off by his frequent protestations that he's straight. But they have an understanding: the man so much as places a hand on his arm, Odin will get violent. House Cat tried it in a jokey way one time after a couple of sloe gins, got an elbow in his windpipe. It scared Odin that he had hit the old queen so hard, made him wonder exactly what was it he was reacting to so dramatically. When House Cat finally recovered the ability to speak, he told Odin he might want to think about what he'd done, one, because House Cat was his friend, and, two, because it could land him back in the joint on a parole violation, assault being frowned upon by those tasked with keeping tabs on ex-criminals. House Cat's circumspect, not to say kind, reaction nearly caused Odin to lose it again but he didn't have it in him to inflict further damage that day. He worries about his ability to feel sorry for someone like House Cat, makes him think he might be going soft. He'll have to make sure that doesn't happen. Show some belly and House Cat might take it the wrong way. Maybe he's on the far side of forty, but he is no punk. Guys didn't mess with him inside; the man could hold his own on the yard.

"We have to get the car washed," House Cat says.

"The fuck is wrong with my car?"

"It's filthy, Odin, easier to indentify. If it's clean it just looks like another car."

"So now it looks like another dirty car."

House Cat exhales through his nostrils. "I'm just saying we need to take precautions."

Odin doesn't like that his partner is frustrated with him, thinks maybe he should back off on the car wash, not worth a beef. "We'll get a car wash, all right? Don't have kittens."

Odin wants the job to go well. Princess and Chance King are bursting out of their little house and he has promised her something roomier, something he can't afford on a mechanic's salary. The money he's going to split with House Cat figures to be the biggest payday he's ever had, a lottery jackpot. He'd like to buy health insurance for his family. In prison, he developed agoraphobia and the pills he takes to control it cost him nearly two hundred dollars a month.

Odin was working at Papi's Auto Salvage in Fontana pulling the engine out of a '94 Le Sabre when his boss told him he had a phone call. He hadn't seen House Cat in a year, hadn't missed him either. Odin's parole required that he stay away from ex-cons, but curiosity said hello to financial anxiety and he agreed to a meet at Chavela's Bar on West Highland in San Bernardino. The drive from Fontana to San Bernardino lacked appeal but when House Cat told him he was coming down from Barstow, way up north—relatively speaking—he relented. Princess was working the night shift at the Fed Ex depot so he brought his son to the meet, dosing the kid with Benadryl to prevent a fuss.

Country music on the jukebox, a couple of drunks at the bar, a gang of bikers in the corner, and a waitress who looked like Clint Eastwood. The kid snoozed next to Odin in the booth while he listened to House Cat talk over a tequila sunrise. Someone needed a job done and House Cat figured two would work better than one, was he in? Odin took a sip from his longneck and nodded. Didn't even have to think about it. He'd just been discharged from the military when he got popped for a DUI. It should have gone down like milk, no more than a night in jail and some legal fees if he hadn't grabbed for the officer's gun. The judge sentenced him to three years, no mercy for a veteran. Served nearly eighteen months, time off for good behavior. Out six months now, working part time on dead cars for peanuts, looking to move into the next tax bracket, listening to House Cat tell him someone needs to take a short vacation.

Tough to get ahead with a prison record following you around like a hangover. Odin hears doors closing in his sleep now, only job he can get at the auto salvage where he's the one worker who speaks English and the air reeks of engine grease and oil. Will I do it? Shit, yeah, I'll do it, I'm a lean, mean government trained killing machine, your motherfuckin tax dollars at work he told House Cat, as he adjusted Chance King's bottle in his mouth. How much Benadryl can you put in a kid's milk anyway? Had he given the boy too much? How could you tell? Kids were like algebra, another thing Odin doesn't understand. But he loved his son. Could have done without the crying, goddamn that was annoying. And he wanted to provide, be a man. Odin ordered another beer and asked when the opportunity was going to avail itself. This was yesterday.

The five large he received in advance is safe in his house, the next five payable upon completion of the job. Too easy. He only hopes House Cat doesn't put a hand on his knee. He might kill him and no one is going to pay for that.

Odin reaches under his seat and pulls out a .38 caliber military-issue pistol. He brandishes it in front of House Cat.

"Say hi to Sweet Thing."

House Cat is not happy that his partner brought a gun along since he doesn't trust him not to use it.

"You gave your piece a name?"

"Marine special stole off a munitions depot."

"Why don't you put Sweet Thing away?"

"You're gonna be glad we have it," Odin says, shoving it back under the seat.

Times might have been tough recently, and Princess might have a foot out the door, but he knows the money from this job will make her give him another chance. There's still time to save his family. Odin hasn't felt a sense of purpose like this since he was hunting jihadis in the parched hills of Central Asia. And who knows, if this job works out, if he and House Cat turn out to be a good team, maybe it's just the beginning. Odin presses the accelerator, eases the Impala up to seventy-five, then eighty. He likes his future.

CHAPTER TWENTY-THREE

Vonda Jean is out teaching a jiu-jitsu class when Hard returns from work a little after seven in the evening. He knows she won't be home for a few more hours so he empties a can of chili into a bowl and puts it in the microwave. While it heats up he takes a bottle of beer out of the refrigerator and then he eats the chili and drinks the beer standing at the kitchen counter. It's been a day since Vonda Jean threatened to dump Bane on the side of the road but Hard knows her patience is limited. He finishes the dinner, puts the dishes in the sink and heads to the garage where he lifts the lid of the oblong freezer and gazes upon his friend. The folds of Bane's black muzzle are stiff and frost has formed on his eyelids. In his current condition he reminds Hard of a dog in one of the Yukon poems he loves so well. He only wishes Bane fell doing battle with a wolf pack instead of at the hands of an unhinged tanning technician.

Hard takes a red camp blanket from a shelf and spreads it on the floor of the garage. Grabs Bane by the front knees, hoists him out of the freezer and thuds him on to the blanket. The dog hits the floor with a force that makes Hard think for a second the corpse might crack in two, but Bane retains his structural integrity. Although Hard will not admit this to Vonda Jean, he is glad she insisted on not allowing Bane to be stuffed. Absent the spirit that animated him, Bane looks like nothing more than road kill. Hard upbraids himself for having been sentimental. Then he folds the blanket over his late companion and, heaving, grunting, muscles him toward the driveway and into the bed of his pickup next to a metal can that contains a gallon of gasoline.

Back in the house, he grabs an unopened pint bottle of bourbon and a Robert Service paperback. Tosses them on the front seat. Heads east from Twentynine Palms, then south on Gold Park Road and deep into the desert night. Hard turns on the radio to hear some music, but after a couple of seconds realizes music does not dovetail with the gloomy nature of his mission so he presses the off button and continues his journey in respectful silence.

Hard ruminates about funerals as the truck glides through the starry blackness. He did a little research on the Internet and now he knows a thing or two about how different cultures deal with the dead. He knows about Tibetan sky burials where the corpse is left on a rock in the Himalayas and birds dine on the remains until nothing is left but bleached bone. He read about Viking funerals where the dead warrior is placed on a boat that is then set aflame before being sent out to sea on the wind. And he learned about Egyptians who entombed their pharaohs in vast pyramids with gold and jewelry—and sometimes living slaves—to accompany them to the afterlife. Bane is deserving of a grand send off and Hard regrets not being able to provide one. He had thought briefly about doing the Viking version over at the Salton Sea and concluded that not only would procuring a small boat on short notice be challenging in the desert, but should anyone see him it would be difficult to explain what the police chief of Desert Hot Springs was doing there with a defrosting Rottweiler and a flaming dingy.

The road dead ends twenty minutes later and Hard pulls over. Throws a flashlight, the book and the bottle of bourbon into a knapsack, climbs out of the truck. Lashes the gallon of gasoline to the knapsack. Hard looks toward the mountains in the distance, their hulking silhouette rising from the desert floor.

He fills his lungs with the cool night air and picks a spot on the mountaintop. That will be his point of reference. Then he hoists the corpse over his back and bending under the weight sets off into the night.

Hard briefly investigated pet cemeteries but concluded there was something effeminate about them, something sappy and weak. Bane was a masculine dog, a burly canine and Hard doesn't want him to spend eternity in Pet Heaven Park next to Fritzie the Labradoodle. Where was the dignity in that?

A pale crescent moon hangs over the rocky Mojave landscape. Juniper and mesquite trees cast shadows along the desert plain. Hard trudges along, stumbling occasionally under his burden, but he remains on his feet. He's already miles away from any living human but he doesn't want to perform his task near the road. He's calculated that he will cover a mile of this terrain in about twenty minutes, even with the mass he's carrying. Five minutes into his walk he begins to sweat. Bane's body is not only heavy, but unwieldy and Hard has to keep shifting his weight to keep the dog on his shoulders. Hard is breathing heavily, panting at the exertion. This kind of weight is a lot for a young man to hump through the desert and Hard isn't exactly a spring flower. He thinks back to basic training, brutal hikes under searing sun, toting packs that weighed what he's carrying tonight. Pleased he hasn't keeled over. Imagines that headline: "Local Law Enforcement Official Collapses While Burying Dead Pet." Is he out of his mind to be doing this? Hard is brought back from contemplation of his potential humiliation by the strain in his lower back. Adjusts the weight again. Doesn't want to pull a muscle. Ten minutes more and he's sweated through his undershirt. Feels his heart drumbeating in his ribcage. Starts to worry that Bane could begin to thaw out before they reach the destination. What would *that* smell like? The breeze on his face reminds him of the coolness of the evening. He'd like to look up and see the stars but the weight of his cargo keeps his head canted forward. Maybe Canis Major is visible tonight, Hard's favorite constellation. To behold Sirius the Dog Star, brightest star in the sky and a stellar tribute to Bane.

Rivulets of sweat run down his shaved dome and down his face. Checks his watch. Twenty minutes of walking is a mile. Five minutes to go. Hard had told himself he'd walk a mile in to the desert and he'll be damned if he does anything less. He may ignore marital vows, laws even, but when he tells himself he's going to do something, he knows he'll do it.

Hard steps on a rock, loses his balance and recovers, hops lightly, a little dance, before straightening out with a grunt, re-orienting with the mountaintop. Deeper and deeper he walks, stumbling through the desiccated creosote bushes, the night breeze drying his moist face. Five minutes later Hard exhales through his mouth, gets down on his knee and with the aspect of Mary in the Pietà, lowers Bane to the ground. Takes a moment to catch his breath. Looks up at the sky, the stars. He spots Ursa Major, the bear. He's glad there's an animal up there. Likes the symmetry of it, the connection between stars and earth and it makes him feel less alone. Reflects on his good fortune at being born with a sense of direction or he might just wander off into the Nothing.

A little fortification is in order. Some consecration of the cir-cumstances. Hard takes the bourbon out of his knapsack and unscrews the top. Puts it to his lips, tilts his head back and swal-lows. Relishes the burn in his throat. By the third belt he's a lit-tle lightheaded. Realizes he had better get down to business.

Hard places the bourbon gently on the ground, screws the bottle into the dirt to make sure it doesn't tip over and detaches the gallon of gasoline from the knapsack. He stands over Bane for a moment, remembers the joy he shared with the dog. Shared wasn't the right word exactly, since he had no idea if Bane felt any joy, although he did wag his tail whenever it was just the two of them. What Hard will miss most about Bane is how he feels when they're together in the desert, or in the mountains, beneath the measureless sky, man and beast in the primordial world. It's always just the two of them, no one else there, and it is beautifully uncomplicated. It was easier than being with Nadine who has become a goddamn unguided missile. And it was sure as hell more pleasant than being with Vonda Jean. Hard plain and simple preferred Bane to humans and now the pleasure of his company would be denied him until the end of Time. He really could kill Nadine for doing this. Nadine. *Goddamn*, why did he talk to her that night in the convenience store? Why couldn't he have just walked away instead of falling right into the honey pot? The woman jams a *fork* into his neck, would have bled to death if she'd hit the carotid, and then she poisons the one living creature he interacted with on a daily basis and still cared about.

Now Hard grinds his knees on the desert floor, a supplicant. And he's here because of Nadine. If he isn't going to kill the woman, at least he can put the fear of God into her, create a sense of the acute spiritual discomfort he feels, the sense that something wrong is happening and can not be stopped.

Takes another swig of the bourbon. Pulls out his cell phone and dials. One, two, three, four rings, then that voice, the one that makes him grind his teeth tells him to leave a message.

"Nadine, you fuckin cunt." Hard turning on the charm. "I know what you did to Bane and I want you to know you're gonna spend the rest of your life looking over your pretty shoulder."

That feels good. Emboldened and exhilarated by the liquor, the delivery of this threat has irrationally buoyed him. If nothing else that should make her worry. It's not like she can report him for it either, since she killed his dog. Let her try to explain that one. His anger at Nadine is an animating force, coursing through him, making his cells howl in wordless grief. Hard is most alive when he hates something. Right now it's Nadine and what he is feeling for her is positively vivifying. But the rage slowly subsides like a tide washing out to sea, and he's left with the sadness of the dead dog at his feet. Realizes that, as much as he'd like to, staying in the desert all night is not an option. There's work in the morning, responsibilities.

Hard pours the gasoline over Bane soaking the fur from stem to stern. Although he is drunk, he is not so drunk that he doesn't know he should place the container several feet away from the drenched corpse. That would be embarrassing— How'd you blow yourself up, Hard? Lighting your dead dog on fire?—Then he returns to the body and gets down on one knee. Thinks about praying—*God bless the soul of this dog*— but Hard isn't big on religion and since the feeling is more reflexive than real it quickly dissipates.

He removes a book of matches from his pocket, strikes one and drops it on the animal's flank. Flames immediately engulf the body and in a few seconds the acrid stench of burning fur fills the air.

From the knapsack he retrieves the Robert Service paperback and the flashlight. His face lit by his flaming pet, Hard opens the book. Fumbles with the flashlight but gets it aimed at the page. Then he begins to read the poem *My Dog*. In a ringing voice that carries over the harsh desert plain toward the dark mountains, Hard intones:

My dog is dead. Though lone I be
I'll never have another;
For with his master-worship he. . .

By the time he reaches the end Hard is weeping desolate tears. He is not the kind of man who will display any emotion other than anger in public and sadness, which he is capable of feeling deeply, is something he will never reveal to an audience. But alone, here in the desert under the eternal night sky, he lets the melancholy course through him and as flames consume his friend and boon companion, Hard is wracked with heaving convulsive sobs. He cries for his lost youth, and his grown sons, and his dead marriage. He feels weak, pathetic even, but the bourbon has done its job and he doesn't care at all so he lets it flow and then he raises his arms to the heavens and roars a low sound, rough and resonant, that is beyond words and thoughts and is grief pure and deep coming from a bottomless well he hasn't drank from in years and he yells and rumbles, the demons running free, venting, purifying, and the fire consumes the flesh and the glow dances on Hard's face and the sounds drift into the still desert night mingling with the smell of the fire and then Hard is suddenly exhausted and he sinks down near the pyre, his dead companion partially consumed now and he puts the bourbon to his lips and swallows deeply, feels the lightning down his throat and all the way to his heart which throbs in quick sorrow.

CHAPTER TWENTY-FOUR

The white room is bright against the deep darkness of the night. Diablo sits on the bed, head canted to one side as he watches Nadine stuff her belongings into a pair of duffel bags. She wears a skin-tight short white tennis dress that she had chosen in the hope it would put her in better mood, moving never any fun and it's always worse when you're doing it because plans haven't worked out. Nadine wants to get back to the tennis world, wants to be optimistic about the chances of her life improving, so two minutes after the packing session started she found herself removing the tennis dress from the drawer and, rather than placing it in a duffel bag, decided to wear it. After squeezing into the sausage like casing of the dress, she pulled her hair back into a ponytail with a scrunchie. Her racquets were stacked against the wall. She would pack them last, placing them in the front seat next to her, charms to invoke blessings for a new life.

All of the windows are open but the house still retains the heat of the day. Nadine is looking forward to cooler nights. The thank-you note to the man from the bank that allowed her to occupy the foreclosed property she is now vacating sits on the bureau. She will track down his mailing address when she gets to Seattle and send it from there. Once she arrives in Seattle she will look for a tennis instructor job. A country club, a municipal court, she does not care. Right now she does not want to think about how difficult that will be, Seattle not being any kind of tennis capital. It is the cold and the rain that beckon her, and the vast ocean. Nadine wants to learn how to sail. She will have to meet a guy with a boat, but does not think that will be a problem if she puts an ad on a dating site. The pictures of the Pacific Northwest she has checked out on-line have captivated her with their nordic beauty. Gloomy weather and rolling, forested topography make it the un-desert, and for Nadine, who is looking to forget as much of the past two years as she possibly can, that is a major selling point. Her plan is to drive to San Francisco, spend the night, then power straight through to Seattle the next morning. She has mapped it out and figures the journey to be about twenty hours. She isn't thrilled to be doing it alone but she will have Diablo for company.

She zips the duffel bag shut and turns toward the laptop sitting on her desk against a white wall bleached from the sun. The house felt like a microwave oven for much of the six months Nadine has lived here and she will be glad to see the last of it. She settles into the flimsy desk chair and turns the computer on. As it boots up, she ponders her options. One: send the emails Hard wrote to several media outlets. Two: send a note along with a picture of her manga kitten tattoo and an admonition the reporters or bloggers ask Kendra about the matching one she has.

She tries to remember if Hard and Kendra know each other. Can't recall. And isn't Hard backing Kendra's husband's opponent? The two of them can't possibly like one another so it would certainly be amusing to see them yoked together in this situation.

Gazing into her laptop, smiling to herself, she creates a file stuffed with enough incriminating material to give a tabloid editor heart palpitations. If it isn't enough to ruin lives, it is certainly of a level to cause serious career problems. She is determined to bury Hard Marvin and whatever public future he has envisioned in that big gleaming head.

But what does she have against Kendra? When she asks

herself that question and considers the answer, here's what comes back: Nothing, really. An affair that didn't work out is hardly news and it isn't as if she'd been driven cheetah wild with love. They had been sexually attracted, had acted on it, and then it had ended, just like the countless other American relationships that rose and fell simultaneously in this era of readily available sex that comes without warning, stays for the evening, and departs without consequence. And how many of those people are considering providing innuendo about their ex-lovers to the news media? Not many, Nadine guesses. Why is she even considering implicating Kendra? She hadn't intended to threaten her until they were seated across from each other at Melvyn's. That had not been the plan at all. The threat emerged as a result of Kendra's understandably upset reaction to Nadine's attempt to draw her into the scheme. The woman has done nothing to Nadine and Congressman Randall Duke is barely on her radar. The prevaricating brute of a police chief dishonoring his marriage vows is of interest to the media since he is in the middle of an election campaign and exposing his misbehavior can be morally justified in Nadine's mind, but the allegations about a Congressman's wife in a bawdy romp that rest on the skimpy evidence of matching tattoos on their respective nether regions? Kendra is a private citizen, so Nadine is already operating in a morally hazy area (that she is constantly operating in this area is not something that occurs to her). There is no doubt Hard deserves the veritable soufflé of indignity he will be forced to devour. But not Kendra. The ambivalence Nadine has been feeling comes into sharper focus now. Her loathing of Hard, complicated by her continuing sexual attraction to him, has dashed brain inhibitors designed to control extreme behavior. She has been on the verge of striking out indiscriminately at anyone within her range, and knows that violates one of her few deeply held principles. Nadine is well aware that she is not a particularly good person.

But neither does she think she is the kind of black-heart who would try to obliterate someone purely from spite. In her view, Hard deserves it. He will reap the whirlwind, but Kendra will be spared.

She thinks about Hard: the trysts, the shooting guns in the desert, the assurances. Baby, I'll be like a bad dream to you, Nadine promises as she types an address. She slides the cursor to the document file and attaches the Hard Marvin file to the email. Images of the day in the desert with Hard flood back, the feel of the gun in her hand, Hard pressing against her, the sun burning into her skin. Her sense memory of the Glock's powerful recoil is disrupted by a high-pitched buzz.

The doorbell.

Cleaved from her daydream, she has enough presence of mind to hope it isn't someone from the bank that owns the mortgage on the house. She briefly thinks about not answering but knows her presence has already been revealed by the houselights. Quickly she checks her reflection in the mirror. Thinks the tennis dress, which she has not worn in months, makes her ass look big so she slips a pair of jeans on under it and zips them up. Nadine opens the door and sees a young man holding a pizza and a check.

"You order the pepperoni?" Diablo is at her feet, lunatic barks tearing through his tiny throat.

"I didn't order any pizza." She shushes the dog, smiles apologetically. The pizza smells good.

The man looks at the check, then back at Nadine. "This is your address, right?" He shows the check to Nadine, who keeps the yapping Chihuahua at bay with her foot as she examines it.

"Yeah, but I didn't order this."

"You sure?"

"I'd remember. I didn't order a pepperoni pizza." Nadine

says she's sorry he had to come out here for nothing, shakes her head sympathetically. But this motion is arrested by the abrupt arrival of a hand over her mouth and what feel like rings clinking against her teeth. Jerked back, neck twisting, she flashes that it is Hard, and feels a perverse gladness for a moment—he's paying attention!—then remembers Hard does not wear rings. Nadine is dragged into the house. The pizza man follows, yanks the door shut behind him. Adrenaline fires madly and a powerful survival instinct kicks in. A writhing alligator, she digs an elbow in the abdomen of her unseen assailant and reflexively bites the hand covering her mouth and she hears him curse. The pizza man drives a fist into her stomach and she gasps for air as the man with the rings grunts and throws her to the floor. She kicks at him, connects with a knee. A yell of raw pain. Another loud curse as Diablo clamps his jaw on exposed flesh. The dog yelps at the kick he receives and Nadine can hear him whimper as if from another dimension. Unable to breathe she claws violently. Tackled, flipped on her stomach, panicking. She catches a glimpse of the ring man. Middle aged, with short, graying hair, his eyes flare as he rolls her. Palms on the floor, she pushes up, but her wrist is yanked away and the dead weight of the man's body on her back causes her to crash to the floor, her face grinding the carpet. She's suffocating now, can't draw breath. A knee jams into her spine. Then both men are on her and there is a stabbing pain as shoulders wrench sharply, hands yanked behind. A piece of duct tape seals her mouth. She can taste her own blood. Wrists bound, then legs. Another piece of duct tape ends Diablo's contribution to the noise level. Her cheek pressed against the floor, Nadine can see the pizza man toss the apoplectic dog into a drawer and boot it shut. A pillowcase slips over her head eradicating the room. With superhuman effort she forces a gasp of oxygen into her lungs. Nadine bucks and kicks until something blunt smashes into her head and she lies still. Throbbing, she again hears the sibilant hiss of duct tape being ripped from its spool and then it's wrapped around her neck, affixing the pillowcase. For a moment she thinks they're going to choke her with the tape and is relieved when she is able to resume breathing.

CHAPTER TWENTY-FIVE

H ouse Cat has no experience as a kidnapper, but in the new economy a person needs to adapt. Take work where you can get it, punch the clock and don't ask questions. When he got the call, he contacted Odin because he knew the man was a stone killer, U.S. government trained. House Cat had done time for breaking and entering but he'd never snatched a human being. Didn't want to, either. It wasn't like he had qualms, just a weak stomach.

The plan: secure the target in the trunk, drive the target back to Odin's place, stow the target blindfolded in the abandoned camper in the backyard until the middle of the following week. Feed her. Give her water. Let her go.

Catch and release.

The lights are off and the place is dark. House Cat stands at the front window looking out over the street. Odin sits on the couch, having helped himself to a bag of potato chips. Nadine lies on the floor, hands tied behind her with rope, feet bound, a pillow over her head and electrical tape sealing her mouth. Diablo's muffled barks escape intermittently from the drawer into which he has been stuffed. House Cat figures he'll let the dog live. Doesn't want to shoot it and breaking its neck too risky, the little rat-catcher obviously borderline feral. In the glow of the streetlights, the nearby houses look like a stage set with their empty front yards, their dark windows. The neighborhood is middle class and the tan stucco single story homes are well kept. The one notable detail is the absence of vehicles in the immediate area. This is because several homes on the street are in foreclosure, so they are empty.

The men have been waiting nearly an hour. They want to make sure the place is completely quiet before they relocate Nadine.

House Cat heads into the bedroom and removes a thin blanket. Returning to the living room, he lays it on the floor next to Nadine. Odin puts the bag of potato chips down and grabs Nadine's ankles. House Cat takes her shoulders and they roll her on to the blanket and quickly wrap her up. Then House Cat rips two pieces of duct tape, each about a yard long. He hands one to Odin who seals the blanket at Nadine's feet. House Cat does the same at the head. Their parcel ready, House Cat takes a last look out the front window. The street is deserted. Grabbing one end of the rolled blanket, he signals Odin to take the other. The two of them lift Nadine. She pitches and bucks but Odin thumps a fist into her head. There's a groan from within the blanket and she goes limp. When they carry her out of the house the cooler air hits them. Arriving at the car, they lay the wrapped blanket on the driveway. Odin opens the trunk and the two of them bend to pick her up. Nadine rolls but they quickly arrest her movement, lift her and toss her in the trunk. House Cat slams it shut. He looks up and down the street. No signs of life.

Odin is behind the wheel and they cut north, toward Route 62. He stares straight ahead. House Cat wonders if he's nervous. He's strangely calm himself, everything having gone easy after the initial struggle. The Sonny Bono Highway is behind them and the desert spreads out on both sides. To the west a forest of giant steel windmills, arms whirling crazily in the moonlight. They climb into the hills, neither man talking. Houses dot the hillsides, a business strip up ahead with a Korean restaurant, a Pentecostal storefront church, a unisex hair salon and a service station. They drive by a couple of walled developments, only the roofs visible. The Bonnie Dunes trailer park, hookups available, drifts past the windshield. House Cat thinking about the down payment on the bed and breakfast.

The road is a sweet dream as they climb into the hills, smooth and easy. The high headlights of a truck are bearing down on them now, beams shining into their eyes. The snatch went without a hitch and this has House Cat pondering a little improvisation. He looks at Odin, staring straight ahead, gripping the wheel. Knows Odin is the right man for the job, his military background excellent training for this kind of hardcore stunt. Figures he might be amenable to upping the ante. The open-backed truck whooshes past, its piled-high cargo of quarry rock visible for a blink. The slipstream causes a barely discernible shudder in the car. Deeper into the hills the road curves and heads west.

"I was thinking," House Cat says. "Maybe we find out a little more about this girl we got in the trunk, find out who her people are."

"Then what?"

"Hold her for ransom."

Odin nods. Sounds like a pretty good plan. Rolls down the window to let some air in the car. House Cat peers into the distance, sees the glow of a night business up ahead. Probably a convenience store. There was nothing to drink at Nadine's, House Cat thinking he might like some liquid refreshment. Better to stop out here. There could be Sheriff's deputies on Route 62 so best make straight for Antelope Valley once they hit the highway.

"Feel like a beer?"

Then the car swerves wildly, House Cat's stomach reels as he jerks his head to the side, sees Odin twisting the wheel, looks out the window and registers rocks the size of cinderblocks scattered across the road, then feels a sickening thump and hears what sounds like a gloved fist hitting a speed bag as the car lurches and shudders to a stop. Flat tire. Shit. "Rocks must have fallen off that fuckin truck," Odin says. "Yeah." From House Cat, like understanding the provenance of their misfortune makes it easier to deal with.

House Cat asks if there's a spare and Odin tells him it's in the trunk. The two of them get out and head to the back of the car. The stillness of the desert at night is unearthly. House Cat breathes deeply, gazes up at the sky, takes in the immensity, the quiet, clean air filling his chest, the man feeling nearly spiritual as he thinks about the boundless future so he's not prepared for the jagged scream he hears a moment after his partner opens the trunk. Grunts of pain and to his left Odin is imploding, collapsing, there's a blur then House Cat feels like he's been shot as Nadine is pressing a piece of metal into his side and the 75,000 volts liquefy his spine, the pain radiating like a demonic pin wheel, urine running down his leg, bowels loosening. House Cat has heard of neuromuscular incapacitation, but to experience it is something else altogether. Lungs immobilized, excruciating, can't inhale or exhale. Drops to the ground, smacks the pavement, the dull blow a relief compared to the sensation he just experienced. On his back now, neck stiff, eyes wide in shock, palms flat against the gritty roadway. Slowly, muscular control asserts itself. He can hear the other man's staggering footsteps and his curses. House Cat rolls on to his side and pushes himself to a standing position. Sees Nadine running, her dress a white smudge, toward the lights in the distance, tennis trained legs carrying her swiftly toward the store, it's yellowish lights, it's perceived safety. House Cat quickly realizes they did not tie her tightly enough and had they bothered to look through her pockets they might have found the Taser, thus forestalling the events with which they are now dealing. Berates himself for not remembering this simple procedure. Nadine, meanwhile, jackrabbits down the highway, her shapely form shrinking in the bright headlights. Odin pulls the stolen military pistol from under the seat. Nadine further away now, Odin giving chase on unsteady legs. House Cat follows at a slow trot, his muscles not having entirely recovered from the shock.

The convenience store looms in the distance like a Mars station, a lone single story structure glowing in a vast nightscape. Nadine dashes beneath a plastic sign mounted on a metal pole reading Super #1 Store. Her breathing ragged, she doesn't look over her shoulder. If she did she would see Odin closing the distance between them, hurtling through the dark, backlit by headlights, arms pumping, a gun gripped in his right hand.

The place is long and narrow, a refrigerator case packed with beer and soft drinks to the right and a counter to the left, two aisles of groceries perpendicular to the door. The wall behind the counter is stocked with liquor bottles. The place smells of disinfectant. The lone counterman a Latino in his forties. Seated on a high stool, overweight and tired looking, a birthmark the size of a nickel on his left cheek. Glances up from the copy of *Hustler* he's reading and stares at Nadine heaving, pulling a cell phone from her pocket. She tries to open it, hands shaking so violently it drops to the floor and skitters down an aisle then she's screaming in a voice like thumbtacks for the clerk to call the police. Yanked from his torpor, the man rises to his feet, shouts what's going on? *Call the police someone wants to kill me!* Nadine whirls and locks the door behind her. The counterman pulls out his phone, and is dialing 911 when the first bullet shatters the glass, catches Nadine just below her collarbone, sends her reeling toward the twilight. The counterman ducks out of sight as Odin's hand reaches through the broken pane, and *click* unlocks the door. Pushes it open, steps into the store, out of breath, raging. Nadine lies on the floor, a red stain spreading on her tennis dress, blood pooling around her, gurgling in her throat. Odin eases up when he sees the results of his first shot. He casually walks over and pumps two bullets into her chest. Then reflexively looks for surveillance cameras. Sees one mounted above the liquor wall pointed at the door. Knows he's going to have to destroy whatever it's feeding to, but figures he might as well blow out the lens, too. He's getting a bead on it with his gun when the counterman pops up like a jack-in-the-box with a sawed-off, *boom*, sonic, ear shattering through the store and Odin grunts in pain as the buckshot tears flesh off his left arm, neck and the side of his face. Glass splinters in the refrigerator case, beer, soda, gingko-infused iced tea shoot out of the perforated cans bathing the floor. Odin pivots toward the cash register, squeezing the trigger and puts two bullets into the counterman, one in the head, one in the neck, blood spurting backward baptizing the whiskey bottles red. The counterman drops like a bag of laundry. Odin looks at Nadine's prostrate form. Her right leg twitches and then she is still.

"This was not the fuckin plan." House Cat surveys the damage from the door. His voice has sawdust in it now, the anxiety coursing through his body dropping the register as he tries to remain cool. Wheezing from the run. Eyes riveted on Nadine's body, he looks up, gasps when he sees Odin, the left side of his face like hamburger.

Blood drips to the just mopped floor where it shines brightly in the fluorescent glow. House Cat staring at Odin, not moving. Odin staring at House Cat.

"Whore fuckin tased me," Odin says in a strangled voice, the shock having driven his register up an octave.

"She have a gun, too?"

"There's a dead guy behind the counter with a sawed-off." House Cat peering over the counter, groaning, calculates the years a second dead body could add to a prison sentence. House Cat's future: a three-time loser looking at life. Wrong! It was death this time, lethal injection. A Niagara of curses pours forth. Odin receives them like an indictment. He rubs his bleeding arm, says, "What the fuck you expect me to do? Motherfucker's blasting like it's the road to fuckin Kandahar."

"Clean the wound," House Cat says, aggravated at the whole situation. Grabs a water bottle from the refrigerator, twists the top off, hands it to Odin who tilts his face and pours it over the torn skin.

"They got band-aids in here?" Odin asks.

"Band-aids won't do squat."

"Ain't going to no hospital."

House Cat pulls a bulky package off a shelf, throws it at Odin, who catches it with both hands. It's the size of a small suitcase.

"Diapers?"

"Put one on your head."

"You want me to put a fuckin diaper on my head?"

For a moment, House Cat thinks if Odin has a problem with the suggestion he might just blow the dumb shit's head off, let the cops sort that one out. Nadine, the counterman, and Odin with his prison record, shotgun wounds and a bullet in his head. Good luck figuring out what happened. But Odin says nothing, just wipes blood from his eye with the heel of his hand. He jams the revolver into his belt.

"Half your face is torn off," House Cat says. "It'll stop the bleeding."

Odin is considering this when a pair of headlights slices through the night. Both men stop talking and stare at the road until the car moves past and disappears into the darkness. Then Odin rips open the package, pulls out a diaper and, after examining it from several angles, places it over his head with the crotch at the crown. He resembles a bloody Q-tip, but the soft absorbency of the diaper, snug against his leaking face, arrests the profusion of blood.

After a brief debate about whether or not to remove Nadine's body and dump it where they had originally planned, House Cat steps over the recumbent corpse of the counterman, averts his eyes from the lifeless face, and opens the cash register. Grabs the bills and shoves them in his pockets. Tells Odin they need to make it look like a robbery. Odin demands half the money now. Exasperated, but not wanting to create additional problems, House Cat counts it, singles, fives, tens, twenties, and hands a wad to his bandaged partner. Tells him they need to clear out before another customer shows up. Odin shoves the bills into his pockets. Steps behind the counter, spots a VCR. Presses 'eject' and removes the tape. Then he aims the gun at the security camera and fires. As pieces of the obliterated camera rain to the floor, he grabs a fifth of Southern Comfort from behind the counter and they're out the shattered door.

The headlights of the Impala throw off a long glow creating stretched shadows as House Cat and Odin make for the car. House Cat asking Odin if he's going to be all right and Odin, the blood-soaked diaper clinging to his head, swigging from the Southern Comfort, tells him to shut the fuck up and not worry about it. House Cat takes the vinegar as a positive sign.

Because the headlights are shining in their eyes, it takes a moment for the pair to realize someone is standing next to the car.

The man is gaunt and appears to be around sixty. He's wearing greasy jeans and a green windbreaker with U.S.M.C. stitched in white across the left breast. An unfiltered cigarette sticks out of a week's worth of gray beard that looks like someone has been chewing on it.

"Flat tire?" the man says.

"Yeah." From House Cat. "Got a spare in the trunk."

The man staring at Odin. "That a diaper on your head?"

"Bandage." Odin all sensitive.

"Looks like you been wrestling a bobcat," the man says.

"Cut himself shaving," House Cat says. The man nods, like this might have actually been what happened. Odin and House

Cat stare knives at the interloper, willing him to move along. He doesn't take the hint but instead stands there as if they're all waiting for an elevator. Odin places his hand on the unseen gun jammed into his waistband. House Cat sees the movement and barely perceptibly shakes his head side to side.

"Need a hand with the tire?" Both men mumble no and House Cat reaches into the trunk. He pulls at something but it's stuck. The man moves toward the trunk, turning his back to Odin. Odin pulls out the gun, points it at the back of the man's head. The man is bent over the trunk now, trying to help House Cat.

"I said I got it," House Cat says, turning from the trunk with a jack in his hand. The man is still fumbling in the trunk. House Cat violently motions for Odin to put the gun away. Odin jams the gun back in his pants as the man turns around holding a flashlight. He flips it on as House Cat hands the jack to Odin. The man shifts the beam from Odin to House Cat, their faces horror show puppets in the lurid glare.

"Turn the fuckin light off!" Odin says. House Cat grabs the flashlight from the man, turns it off and tosses it back in the trunk.

The man says, "Can I have it?"

"No, you can't fuckin have it," Odin says.

The man shrugs and watches as Odin places the jack under the car while House Cat digs the spare out from under a dirty blanket. It's a donut, about half the size of a regular tire. "Can't drive more than forty miles an hour with that thing."

They ignore him. The man doesn't move, just stands there smoking his cigarette. Odin pumps the jack and the car rises several inches. He goes to the trunk and removes a tire iron. House Cat hopes he doesn't smash it over the man's skull and is relieved when his partner kneels next to the jack. Odin spins the lugnuts one by one and removes the flat, replacing it with the spare. All this is done in silence.

"I'm out here all the time," the man says. "Looking for aliens."

"Lot of beaners out this way?" House Cat asks.

"Extraterrestrials," the man says. Odin and House Cat look at each other. Whatever perceived danger this apparition represented just dissipated. "Buy me a cup of coffee?"

"Maybe some other time," House Cat says.

"I could be dead tomorrow," the man says.

"You could be dead tonight," Odin says, tossing the flat in the trunk and slamming it shut. If the man takes offence at the perceived threat he does not show it. Odin notices the letters on the windbreaker. "You in the Corps?"

"Khe Sanh, 1968. Got a purple heart."

"No shit," Odin says, impressed.

"You?"

"Operation Enduring Freedom," Odin reports. "Two tours in Ass-Crack-istan."

This information is received in a way that takes the exchange in a salutary direction. Now it's a band of brothers out here on the desert highway in the middle of the California night. "Looks like they're open," the man says, peering up the road. Odin and House Cat follow his gaze to the Super #1 Store, glowing against the vastness of the dark sky.

"They're closed," House Cat says.

"Ain't closed," the man says. "Lights on."

"We just tried," House Cat says, looks at Odin, *do something.* Odin reaches into his pocket, pulls out the wad of bills, peels off a twenty and hands it to the man.

"You buy yourself a cup of coffee, Pops. Just not there."

The man holds the bill in both hands, stares at it then folds it in half and sticks it in the pocket of his dirty jeans. "You really in the Corps?"

"Fuck, yeah," Odin says. "2nd Battalion, 14th Marine Regiment, Delta Battery."

The man nods, absorbing Odin's C.V. Takes a long drag on his cigarette and exhales. "Well, whatever you two done . . . I ain't telling."

"Semper Fi," Odin says.

Ten minutes later Guillermo Robles, a fifty-four year old short haul truck driver from Clovis who is on his way back from delivering a load of apples in Palm Springs pulls into the parking lot at Super #1. He notices the shattered glass in the doors, looks inside and sees the dead bodies. In the age of Reagan, Guillermo Robles served on a *Contra* death squad in Nicaragua, so although he is surprised at the grisly scene, it does not shock him. He dials 911 from his cell phone and reports the carnage. Then he calmly waits in the cab of his truck until the police arrive.

Chapter Twenty-six

Princess lies in bed wearing a thin, gold nylon nightgown trying to get back to sleep. The bedroom is right off the living room. Her son Chance King's tiny room is off the kitchen. Still, he's only about twenty-five feet away. Straining to hear, she concludes that he has finally drifted off. The boy has been having night terrors. Nerves jangled and spent from lack of rest, she tosses in the bed trying to find a comfortable position. There was no chance to shower today and her hair is dirty but she doesn't want to take one now because the water pressure is bad. She exhales in frustration, stares at the ceiling. She wants to talk to Odin about moving to a place where she can take a shower that doesn't require her to spend half the morning to get clean. If she wanted bad plumbing, she could have stayed in the Philippines. Forty hours a week sorting packages at the Fed Ex depot, sometimes more with the overtime they needed in order to survive, this would have to change. Odin's job at the auto salvage place is only part time. He has promised to look for new work but told her it might take a while since people are not keen to hire ex-convicts, particularly in a down economy.

There were lots of guys who came on to her at the strip club in Redlands where they had met, some of them with nice cars and good jobs with benefits. She was making a few hundred dollars a night in tips as a dancer and most of the guys who bought her ten dollar glasses of fake champagne at the long bar had hit on her hard, offered to buy her gifts, take her on trips, marry her. Dressed in a teddy, her back aching from the five-inch heels she had to wear, she'd listen as they talked about their work, or their guns, or their trucks. The ones who didn't stare at her breasts while they talked were rare as snow at home, but one night it finally happened. A handsome Marine chatted her up and he bought her a few drinks and told her his uncle had been stationed at the United States Naval base in Subic Bay and he'd always wanted to visit the Philippines. He was polite and respectful and she agreed to see him away from the club. A month later she was pregnant then Odin was in Afghanistan and didn't make it back for Chance King's birth. He was only out of the service a month before the incident with the police that landed him in prison. Lately she's been thinking about quitting the Fed Ex job and going back to dancing where she could make a lot more money, but that would probably lead to a fight with Odin who had told her he didn't want his woman strutting around shaking her nakedness in front of strangers every night. She was going to have to do something, though. They were cutting people's hours at work and she couldn't depend on Odin to make up what she was going to be losing in wages. Why didn't she escape the other day like she had planned? If he comes back with the money he talked about maybe she'd give him another chance.

The front door opens and she hears footsteps. Princess doesn't want to deal with any of this in the middle of the night, so she rolls over and pretends to be asleep. She hopes he won't try to wake her to have sex. Is that another set of footsteps? Whoever is with Odin, she prays the two of them haven't been drinking.

"Princess, wake up."

Odin's voice has strained quality that alarms her. She sits up in bed and sees him silhouetted in the doorway. Something's wrong. Backlit by the dull glow of the 40 watt bulb in the living room ceiling, he looks deformed, as if his head has swollen. She asks what's going on. He tells her get dressed and get in the kitchen. Is that a liquor bottle he's holding?

Pulling on a robe, Princess squints in the kitchen light and quickly realizes Odin's Elephant Man-like deformity is being caused by the diaper on his head. Her eyes swing to the visitor, a thick set man with close cropped hair and a lot of rings on his fingers. He grunts at her. It takes her a moment to notice that Odin is bare-chested and his handsome face is bleeding through the tee shirt he is pressing against it. She stares at him, bewildered.

"Hunting accident," Odin tells her. Takes a swig from the bottle.

"I thought you were moving an oil rig."

"We stopped to do a little hunting."

"At night?"

"It was a bad decision."

From the other room Chance King starts to cry. Odin fills a glass with two fingers of Southern Comfort and hands it to Princess.

"Put this in his bottle with some milk. Can't listen to the boy crying right now."

Then he tells Princess to get some tweezers. When she returns a moment later—she ignored his instruction to give the boy liquor, hid the glass where he won't see it—Odin has removed the diaper from his head. His face looks ghastly. Princess stares, frozen. Odin is seated in a chair with his head tilted back, the man examining him.

"Give me the tweezers," the man says. She doesn't move. When he barks "Hey!" she snaps out of her trance and hands them to him. Wonders where Odin met this guy since he doesn't look like the ex-servicemen he usually pals around with. Hopes he's not a prison buddy but no one's making introductions. The crying continues and Odin yells at her to make sure the kid drinks the booze and then the man resumes his ministrations.

The curses that rain from Odin's mouth as the man begins removing what look like tiny metal pellets from his bloody cheek, are a lot even for Princess who is no prude when it comes to provocative language. She stands and watches and hopes her son goes back to sleep. The man concentrates over Odin's face, his thick forearms tensing with the effort. Neither of the men says a word. Odin grabs the carved wood Buddha on the kitchen counter, his souvenir from Afghanistan, and squeezes its smiling face to distract from the pain. Princess wonders what really happened but doesn't want to ask, not now anyway. Glances toward the sink and notices the blood-soaked diaper lying there like a dead animal. Gingerly, she picks it up between two fingers and drops it in the plastic trash can under the sink.

After nearly ten minutes, the man says, "I got all I could. A doc can do the rest." Princess takes a sponge from the counter and starts cleaning the blood from the floor. She once saw someone get stabbed back home and he didn't bleed as much as Odin is bleeding right now.

"I can't go to no hospital, man," Odin says. "Gun shot wounds show up in an E.R., the docs have to call the cops."

"Tell them you were cleaning your gun and it went off," the man says.

"Like I'm a moron?" Odin says.

The man is rinsing his hands off in the sink. He dries them with a dirty dishtowel. Princess stands at the sink now, wringing out the sponge, Odin's blood running through her fingers and down the drain.

"You got a better idea?" the man says.

"Princess," Odin barks. Turning to face him, she crosses her brown arms over her small breasts. Why did she ever have a child with this man? "You're gonna say you accidentally shot me."

CHAPTER TWENTY-SEVEN

He takes a last look at the Salton Sea, it's splendid isolation, its fragile beauty, and the Harley accelerates, screeching, leaving a pungent rubber trail. Dale guns the motor and swings the machine around and he's headed straight for the water and then he's bouncing along the beach fishtailing on the sand and he rolls the bike and the bike crushes his legs but it doesn't matter because they're dead already and he crawls along the sand, his hands grabbing fistfuls, then he feels the water on his fingers, on his forearms, his chest and shoulders and he is hauling his lifeless legs behind him and he is swimming beneath the crystalline desert sky, muscles straining under taut skin, he's filling his lungs with the clean desert air, pulling himself through the cool healing water to the far shore where he emerges and he walks, yes, he walks through the desert, and he climbs up the mountains and lifts off into the star-dappled sky, and he shivers as if the cold emptiness has just now taken solid form. There is something metallic pressed against his neck.

"Get up," a voice says.

Through gritty eyes there's House Cat two feet from his face, smiling down at him in the darkness. He's seated on the bed holding a gun and smoking a cigarette. Close enough that Dale can smell his sour breath.

For a moment he thinks the gun's current direction is an indication of his visitor's carelessness with firearms but a quick check of House Cat's expression brings home the point: that gun is meant to be aimed at him. This realization makes Dale exceedingly uncomfortable. He blinks, has the thought that he should reach for the ten-inch knife under his pillow, the one with the serrated edge.

Clears his throat, mumbles, "What're you doing here?"

"Came to get paid, Dale. The second half."

"Said you'd get paid when the job got done." Collecting himself, Dale is awake now and not happy. Propped up on his elbow, he says, "Fuck, man, you broke into my house? And lose the gun."

House Cat keeps it pointed at him. "Job's done."

"Where's the girl?"

"She's with Jesus, Dale."

"What do you mean she's with Jesus?"

"Shit got a little crazy and Odin shot her."

The oxygen in the room seems to vanish, because Dale suddenly has trouble breathing. His head tilts back and he closes his eyes. For a moment, he is consumed with the fear that he is going to have a seizure. He knows they can be brought on by stress. Dale waits in silence for the telltale signs, the stiffening of muscles, the narrowing of vision. House Cat stares at him.

"You still owe us the money."

"You weren't supposed to *kill* her!"

"I know that Dale but no use crying over spilt milk. Odin took some incoming, too."

"I told you to put the fuckin gun away."

House Cat clears his throat and thrusts the pistol into his waistband, having made his point. Dale leans over and turns on the bedside lamp. Sees blood on House Cat's jeans. "We need the second half of the money," House Cat says, this time more insistently.

"What happened?"

"Odin nearly got his head blown off is what happened."

"To the girl!"

"Fuck the girl! And if you think my buddy's got health insurance, you're wrong."

"I don't have the money yet," he says. House Cat's face growls. "I'm getting it as soon as I tell the guy the job got done. Then he pays me and I pay you."

"We're gonna be wanting a little bonus to pay for Odin's medical, you understand."

"I'll try. Fuck! You didn't have to kill her."

"How's ten grand sound?"

"On top of what you got coming? Where am I supposed to get that?"

"The fuck should I know?"

"Let me talk to my guy."

"You talk to your guy all you want, Dale. But you don't come across with it, man." House Cat shakes his head. He doesn't need to finish the threat.

At this point, Dale wouldn't mind having a seizure. As hugely unpleasant as they are, it would be an improvement over the conversation with his sub-contractor.

"At least give me until after the election."

"What election? What's that have to do with this?"

"Nothing. I'm doing some work for my brother is all."

"This have something to do with your brother?"

"No."

"Dale, tell Daddy the truth." House Cat sticks the muzzle of the gun against Dale's neck. The cold of the metal pricks him like a needle.

"The election's Tuesday."

"Tell you what. Since I'm a patriot, you got til Election Day."

Given that a moment ago Dale had thought he was about to be killed in his own bed, this seems like a fair compromise. House Cat rises, places his hands on Dale's motorized wheelchair. Although he's only had the chair for a couple of days, Dale has already created a bond with it, the kind of bond you can have with an inanimate object such as a car or a piece of jewelry. He doesn't understand this, but nonetheless feels it deeply.

"I like this gizmo, Dale. You could take it out on the freeway."

"It's a good one, yeah."

House Cat sits in the chair, settles into the seat. He asks Dale how to turn it on and Dale tells him. The engine hums to life and House Cat rides the chair out of the room. Dale stares after him in alarm, not believing House Cat's move. From the living room comes House Cat's voice: "I'm taking it as collateral."

"The fuck you are!"

"Just want to make sure we get paid," Dale hears him say. "You'll get it back. And if you don't come up with the money in two days, it's going on e-Bay."

"Motherfucker!"

"Don't take it personally," House Cat says. He's standing in the doorway now. "I support handicapped rights and shit. I'll tell Odin you asked how he was doing." House Cat winks and then he's gone.

Marooned in bed with no wheelchair, Dale is overcome with an all-encompassing sense of futility. He hears the front door of his apartment open and close.

Dale had planned on presenting Nadine's kidnapping as a fait accompli. He'd instructed the men to hold her until after Election Day and then turn her loose. With the problem addressed so boldly, he believed that Maxon would be happy to pay the rest of the money he had guaranteed House Cat. The new situation was considerably more problematic.

Briefly, he considers calling Randall. But what could his brother do now? Better to get this sorted out without his knowledge. It isn't like Randall doesn't have enough on his mind. He picks up his phone. Maxon answers on the third ring.

"Dude, we got a serious problem."

Awakened in the middle of the night, it takes Maxon a

moment to realize who has called him. And when he does, he has no idea what Dale is talking about. The elliptical explanation Dale offers is cut short when what has occurred becomes clear. During the gap in the conversation, Dale yearns for a magical way out but he fears the only solution to this problem may be a time machine. When Maxon finally speaks it is to inform him that any further communication should not be held on the telephone. Then he hangs up.

In the ensuing silence Dale contemplates what he has wrought. All he had wanted was to prove his worth to his brother. This is all he has wanted for his entire life. He had seen the look of forbearance in Randall's eyes on his infrequent visits to the prison. How Randall had pitied him. How Randall had wished he had made better choices. Dale knows he will have to make this right but has absolutely no idea how.

Lying in his prison bed Dale would spend nights fantasizing about how he could get back on a motorcycle. He would dream of scientific breakthroughs that would once again allow him the use of his legs. He so desperately wanted to prove his worth but that did not seem within the realm of possibility so he lived in frivolous daydreams. That the opportunity to do something for Randall would ever arrive seemed hopeless. And yet it had. And catastrophe ensued. It is unbearable.

His notebook is on the night table next to his bed. Reaching for a pen, he opens it and begins to write:

Randall, Randall, I'm a burning candle, fame and shame will be my game . . .

http://WWW.DESERT-MACHIAVELLI.COM
11.2 – 10:21 P.M.

When disaster occurs in politics or in life, you have to be light on your feet. Well-laid plans can go seriously awry, but what separates the survivors from the whiny bitches is the ability to turn a setback to an advantage. It is a little known piece of information that before the Flight Attendant was serving drinks on the Gulfstream jet of her future husband and benefactor, before she became a baby factory and political candidate, she was a student sportscaster at one of the many institutions of higher learning she attended. This school—which I don't want to name but is a public institution in Arizona—has a fine football program. While she was slutting around the sidelines in a short skirt, filing in-depth reports and shaking her bodalicious booty for the school's student-run cable channel rumor has it she attracted the attention of a certain wide receiver named LaMarcus Abdul-Rahim. They "dated" for a while and the Machiavelli hears that she got herself in the family way. Being a right-to-lifer, she dropped out of school and had the baby who was then put up for adoption. The Stewardess is nothing if not highly attractive and a quick Internet search will tell you that LaMarcus Abdul-Rahim is a fine hunk of dark meat, so there is one good-looking bi-racial teenager out there somewhere. At least that's the rumor. So if this starts to unfold, who knows what it would do to her electoral chances. The bi-racial aspect is nothing these days and we as Americans are all grateful for that. But the out-of-wedlock birth is still a bad career move for someone who claims to walk the godly path as she aspires to elective office.

SATURDAY, NOVEMBER 3

CHAPTER TWENTY-EIGHT

There is a right way to break bad news and a wrong way. He knows the wrong way: come right out and say it. And what good has that ever done? The brutal truth leads to shock, keening, rending of garments. As for the right way, he isn't even sure what that looks like. But he's going to have to tell Kendra about Nadine.

Randall had been standing in his kitchen dressed in his pajamas drinking coffee just after seven in the morning when Maxon called to tell him to look at the web site of the *Desert News*. Randall had seen the item about the carnage at the convenience store and after a chasm of silence and dread managed to croak the following words: "Don't tell me this was your solution."

"I mentioned our predicament to Dale."

"To my brother? Why, Maxon?"

"Because you were reaming me out and I was frustrated."

"Dale's in a wheelchair. How's he supposed to be involved in this rat's nest?"

"The boy has friends, Randall. Serious bad guys."

There is another silence during which Randall tries to determine the most efficient course of action. His mind ratchets to the first time he had to disarm a live explosive device on his own. Not for a moment did he believe anything would go wrong. He knows how to perform under the kind of pressure that transforms a grain of sand into a pearl.

"Have you talked to him today?"

"Hell no. You want me to call him?"

"Leave it. Just hold tight."

A few minutes have passed. Randall is extraordinarily displeased with Maxon, but cannot deliver the dressing down he deserves until after the election. And he is frustrated with himself for having brought the problem to Maxon in the first place. He has no intention of telling Kendra until he knows exactly what to say but when she staggers in from the bedroom hollow-eyed and clutching her own handheld device, it is clear she already knows.

Barely choking the words out, she says something that sounds like *oh my god* but he can't be sure because it could also be *I'm going to die*. Kendra is wearing a flimsy white cotton nightgown with a red and blue fleur de lys pattern she had purchased when accompanying Randall on a junket to Paris and her form seems to deflate as he envelops her in his arms. He squeezes her close and strokes her hair, still flat and tangled from sleep. She heaves and sobs until she is unable to catch her breath. Then she chokes, wheezes and subsides into a whimper.

Brittany is standing in the kitchen in a tiny tee shirt and plaid short-shorts. It is the kind of ensemble with which she could make a tidy living selling used to Japanese businessmen on the Internet.

"What's wrong with Mom?"

"She just heard some upsetting news."

Brittany places an uncertain hand on her mother's back and rubs it with the passion of a gay man handling a female breast.

"Mom, do you have cancer or something?"

Kendra manages to discharge "No," before lapsing back into convulsive sobs. Brittany looks at her father who shakes his head and shrugs, as if to say one day you'll understand.

Brittany nods and goes to the refrigerator where she takes out the non-fat milk and pours a glass for herself.

Over his wife's quaking back, Randall addresses their daughter: "Your mom's going to be okay."

Randall isn't sure what Kendra says as she runs out of the room but thinks it sounds like *no I won't*. Brittany drains the milk, tells her father she's going to her boyfriend's house for the day and scampers off to get dressed. Her discomfort at having been exposed to this frightening world of adult emotion escapes Randall whose mind is elsewhere.

Maxon did not offer any details over the phone but Randall assumes whatever the plan was, a grisly bloodbath in a convenience store was not the intended outcome. Draining the rest of his coffee, he sits at the kitchen table. The morning sun shines like a joyful invitation. A full day of campaigning awaits, stops at shopping centers, a church fair, and a grip-and-grin is scheduled for the middle of the afternoon in the heart of the downtown Palm Springs business district. Kendra had said she would accompany him. The election is less than seventy-two hours away and every waking moment is supposed to be spent campaigning. In twenty minutes, he will be late for his first event of the day, a stroll through the clubhouse of a golf course in Palm Desert.

How had this happened? How had she gone from a Congressman's wife to an accomplice to what had somehow become a double homicide? Kendra lays under the covers curled in a fetal position, a pale green, six hundred-thread count Egyptian cotton sheet clutched in both hands and pulled over her stinging eyes. Thoughts careen through her mind at a pace so breakneck she can't parse them.

In high school she only wanted to lead the band on to the football field at halftime, her baton arcing through the western sky all the way to the University of Southern California where she remembers herself dressed in spangles, boots and a tall hat in front of crowds at football games each one of her four undergraduate years. And then she's standing in front of a microphone, and a fleeting image of the singing career she pursued upon graduation provides a second of relief, before marriage and motherhood plant their stake, and she takes brief refuge in the solid means of identity all of this had provided until a few minutes ago.

Now everything has come crashing down like the contents of a poisoned piñata. The last she could recall, before her mind had taken leave of its moorings, was that Randall had said he would take care of it. She had assumed that to mean that someone would have a word with—Kendra doesn't even want to think of the name, but it bursts through the still permeable wall of denial—NADINE! Good Lord! Dead!

Someone was going to talk to her. They were going to talk to her and take care of it. Did that not work? Had that not happened? Whose idea was *this*, this epic blunder, this abomination, this tragedy that had occurred a short distance from Kendra's home while she had slept and for which she believes herself responsible. Will it be possible for her to ever again be anything other than a fraud, that as far as pretending to be an ordinary human is concerned she will forever be an imposter since now, at her essence, she is a murderess.

Murderess? She's no murderess! She is a baton twirler. And a singer. Whose karaoke version of "Dancing Queen", belted out at an early Duke fundraiser, will be forever cherished by the desert's gay legion.

Through the black fog of her confusion, regret, terror, and incipient grief—yes, *grief*, because no matter how irate Nadine's behavior made her, she had never denied the woman's essential humanity—Kendra knows that in the annals of overreaction this massacre will vie for a blue ribbon. Snot and tears stain the sheet. Her breathing is ragged. A massive headache blooms, it's iron tendrils extending from the crown of her head toward her temples, squeezing. This is misery so profound it cannot be quantified. Then she feels a hand on her shoulder and nearly jumps out of the bed.

Randall's voice: "Are you all right?"

"Nooohhh." The sound comes from an uncharted place somewhere deep within her viscera. She can feel him sit next to her. His proximity causes her to curl into a tighter ball. "Kendy, look," she can hear him say. It is warm under the sheet and she can feel perspiration begin to collect in her armpits and under her breasts. It's suddenly too warm. Isn't the air conditioning on high? The back of her neck begins to itch.

Randall rubs her arm. She wishes he would stop. She wishes he would get out of the bedroom, the house, her life. She wishes she had never met him, married him, or had a family. She is seized with the desire to run out of the house, get into her car, drive to the police station and throw herself on the mercy of the law because everyone will instantly know who is responsible for the carnage so what is the point of resisting the inevitable and prolonging the torture of her guilt? That brain hemorrhage of a thought passes in a nanosecond and she thinks about swallowing a bottle of pills and the sweet oblivion that would bring, and that thought vanishes and she is back to contemplating the bleak futility of their situation.

Randall's voice: "Do you want to talk about it?"

She thrusts the sheet away and from her fetal position stares at him. By his reaction, she can only imagine what her face looks like. She's going to have to avoid mirrors for the rest of her life.

She manages to say, "What is there to talk about?"

"It obviously got out of hand."

"Was this someone's plan?"

"We didn't have anything to do with it."

"Don't tell me what happened. I don't want to know."

"Maxon talked to her. That was all."

"I told you not to tell me!"

"Everything will be okay."

Okay? Has he lost his mind, too? How is everything going

to be okay? Everything is not going to be okay. If they fail to come clean immediately they will be pursued, and caught, and tried and convicted and after all their appeals are exhausted they will be the first American couple executed since the Rosenbergs only they will be more reviled than the Rosenbergs since the Rosenbergs never actually had anyone killed. A soon-to-be-former Congressman and his ex-twirler wife. She could write a book about their ordeal during the appeals process. *From the Rose Bowl to Death Row, Confessions of a Drum Majorette.*

"You better take the day off," he says.

"Thank-you, I think I will." She grabs a wad of bedside tissue and violently blows her nose. The pressure makes her ears pop.

"Just don't talk to anyone, all right?"

"Who the *fuck* am I going to talk to?"

She throws the obscenity in his face like acid. Ordinarily, Randall would upbraid her for using profanity. He tries not to curse and he prefers that she not use bad language either. But today he gives her a pass. Instead, he suggests she take a few aspirin, get some rest and says he'll call later. She can't bear seeing his face anymore, with it's combination of terror and doubt forced into a grotesque simulacrum of equanimity. When he leaves the room she pulls the covers over her head again, blacking out the world.

On the drive to the day's first event, a visit to a senior center, Randall considers calling Dale. But he quickly discards that idea. What good would that possibly do? The less contact he has with Dale at this point, the better it will be. He will tell Maxon to get his brother out of town as soon as the election is over.

CHAPTER TWENTY-NINE

An overweight woman in her fifties with a coarse blonde bob and wearing a pink tracksuit is talking to Maxon. She holds a red tee shirt with the logo **RE-ELECT RANDALL** across the front and **I'M A DUKIE** printed on the back in white lettering.

"You know 'dukie' means turd."

Maxon sighs, tries not to show either his exasperation or exhaustion. "It's a play on Randall's name." He would like to snatch the tee shirt out of her pudgy hand and wrap it around her sagging neck but this is belied by an expression of amused forbearance. He sips a non-fat latte and throttles a tennis ball with his free hand.

"My son told me," she says, shoving her cell phone at Maxon. "It's youth slang. He's on the phone, you can talk to him."

Ignoring the phone, Maxon tells her, "Randall's name is Duke, that's what people are going to think. Please don't worry about it, okay?"

"Do you want to ask my son?" she says, waving the phone. "His name is Kirk."

"No, thank-you."

The woman shrugs and walks away. Maxon can't believe that with his plan having blown up in his face, this is what he's dealing with right now. It's just after eight in the morning at Duke Headquarters and the storefront is filled with volunteers milling around drinking coffee and nibbling on pastries laid out in boxes of flimsy cardboard. There is a phone bank in the back where ten campaign workers are calling potential voters.

He steals a glance at the small crowd of people who have assembled. A desert cross-section of seniors and gays, League of Women Voter types and a handful of fresh-faced college interns, they are clad as ordered in comfortable shoes and campaign tee shirts. Maxon's twenty-three year old aide de camp Tyson Griggs stands nearby checking names on a clipboard. A tall, skinny kid with a shock of hair that makes him look like Bob's Big Boy, he catches Maxon's eye, holds his wrist up and points at his watch. They've got to get the first wave of Dukies on the streets.

Maxon's sleep was shattered by the phone call from Dale and he's been jittery for the last three hours. The morning has been an orgy of self-recrimination. He's been cursing himself for discussing the situation with the poetical ex-con. But it's over and all he can do is wait. It had been embarrassing to have to report what had happened to Randall. *Should* he have even told him? Has he compromised the deniability he had been so concerned about? Someone taps him on his shoulder.

"Maxon, are you okay?"

He looks up and sees Tyson.

"I'm fine."

The words are steel filings.

Maxon claps his hands to get everyone's attention. The din of conversation dies down and the crowd faces him. In their campaign tee shirts, they're a giant red blob, a faceless mass of hope and energy. It always amazes him that people volunteer for political campaigns. That they think they have a voice in the process, that the fix is not in. Which candidate ultimately wins will not matter in a larger sense since Maxon hews to the view that elections might be framed in the context of ideas but what they are truly about is who controls the flow of dollars to the entities that fund the elections. Whether it is Mary

Swain or Randall Duke, the post office will deliver the mail and the borders will be defended. Ordinarily, it would be touching to him that these people are here this morning in their comfortable shoes and their silly tee shirts. But not today. He girds himself to give a short talk about the value of democracy.

"Thank-you for coming," he says. "What you're doing is incredibly important because this election is about you, the people."

They applaud this sentiment and he smiles.

At this moment, Maxon notices the door to the street open but no one seems to be there. Then he shifts his perspective and realizes the reason no one appeared to be there is that the man in the doorway is only four feet tall. He would be just under six feet were he to stand but he is seated in a wheelchair. As if summoned by a malevolent sprite, Dale has arrived.

Maxon can see him saying excuse me to several of the volunteers as he maneuvers his manually operated chair toward the front of the crowd. The dodgy teeth flash when he smiles at the volunteers who make way. From their reaction, Maxon can tell that many of them know the identity of this late arrival. At the front of the room, Dale stops the chair and grins. Maxon nods hello, swallows.

"You all know Dale, everyone," Maxon says. "The Congressman's brother."

Dale waves like he's the one running for office. There is mild, uneasy applause, then the volunteers turn their attention back to Maxon who finishes giving instructions to the workers. When he is done he tells the group to ask Tyson if they need clarification about their assignments for the day.

"What the hell are you doing here?"

Maxon and Dale are in the back room of the headquarters. Campaign literature is stacked on shelves and various cardboard signs with messages like *Be a Dukie* and *Randall Again!* are arrayed against the walls.

"I'm not staying in that apartment no more. Had to call the fire department. Those boys got me a wheelchair, and I'll tell you what, it's a piece of shit." Maxon takes a moment to consider what to do with Dale. He clearly cannot send him on his way. "Want me to answer phones?"

"God, no!"

"Then get someone to take me to Randall's house, cause that's where I'm staying until this gets fixed."

"You can't stay at Randall's house." As Maxon says this he feels his throat constricting. What to do with this misfit? He can't trust him in a hotel.

"Why not?"

"You can't be seen with him and you can't call him." Maxon catches himself as his voice begins to rise. He can't be observed screaming at Dale. More quietly: "You haven't called him, have you?"

"No."

"Don't. And don't ask me to explain."

"Maxon, you know you got to take care of me, right?"

This hangs between them for a moment. Both men are aware that Dale could blow the doors and windows off the edifice with one phone call that could land everyone in jail for the rest of their lives. Maxon might not have ordered Dale to put his plan in motion, but who knows what song Dale would sing should he wind up on trial. Where can he possibly stow him for the next few days?

"You can stay with me." Maxon says. "You'll be looked after."

Hard lies in bed in his boxers. He feels the weight of his head, never a good sign. There is a dull ache at the base of his skull and it is radiating upward, valiantly attempting to join forces at the top of his throbbing head with the sharp pain

pushing up from his temples. Adding to this, something per-
cussive is going on behind his eyes. There is no sense of his
body below the neck except for his bile-filled stomach. And he
hasn't opened his eyes yet. He has no recollection of going to
sleep, doesn't even remember driving home. Steels himself for
the onslaught of daylight and the havoc that will ensue as his
cornea sends a terrified message to his weakly pulsing brain
receptors—*Danger, sunlight!*—that in turn will alert the pain
center to hit the panic button. He opens his right eye a crack.
The predictable sensation of hot knives being inserted is mitigated by the realization that Vonda Jean is no longer in the
bed. Already things are looking up.

Hard rolls on his side and waits for his stomach to settle.
This takes a moment as the various internal ducts recalibrate
and determine whether or not to send the contents of the
Marvin stomach pouring out. The bourbon-drenched volcano
rumbles, threatens, sloshes it's sour lava, but mercifully fails to
erupt. Hard places a tentative foot on the floor. The brain
seems preoccupied with it's own horrifying situation and the
pressure of the floor against the pad of his foot does not provoke an unmanageable reaction. This leads Hard to place his
other foot down. Collects himself for the task at hand: standing. Takes a deep breath and tries to ignore the sensation that
a preternaturally strong and malevolent chimpanzee is man-
handling his cerebral cortex. One, two, three: pushes his hands
against the sheets and—there, he's standing. Wobbles. The
stomach again, riled. Hard waits a moment for the seas to
calm. He lurches toward the bathroom.

He throws some water on his face. Opens the medicine
chest sees a bottle of eye drops. He puts them in and blinks.
He gargles mouthwash and spits it out. Looks at his stubbly
face and considers shaving for a moment but decides that is
entirely too ambitious a plan. He opens a bottle of extra-
strength Tylenol and swallows four.

"Any coffee left?"

Vonda Jean cooking eggs at the kitchen stove. She is wearing workout clothes, her hair pulled back with a clip. She tells Hard to help himself. Hard dressed in a robe now, still unsteady, takes a ceramic cup from the pressed wood cabinet and fills it with coffee.

"You go for a run?"

"It's a beautiful day," she says. "Where'd you go last night?" Her voice sounds like broken glass.

"You asked me to get rid of Bane, so I did." His own voice sounds to him as if it is coming from someone else, someplace far away.

Hard takes the coffee and goes to the living room. He does not want to engage with Vonda Jean any further right now. He sits in his recliner and sips the coffee. He's supposed to do some campaigning for Mary Swain today, and he doesn't want to leave the house feeling like this. Through the picture window in the living room he looks east over Twentynine Palms. The town has grown into a little metropolis since the Marvins settled here over twenty years ago, the population closing in on thirty thousand now. There's a big new hotel being built and retirees, artists, and students at the new community college are all moving in because of the good land values. And all that's not even counting the upwards of five thousand Marines at the combat training base just outside of town. Hard considers the place well on it's way to being a redneck Palm Springs and he likes the idea of being mayor. Doesn't just like it, but puffs up at the thought. In Los Angeles, two former Chiefs of Police had run for Mayor and been elected. One of them had even been a black guy and that was before black guys were getting elected to anything. It's as good a starting point for a political career as any and Hard intends to find out how soon he can file papers for the next election.

The knock at the door is as welcome as shingles. Vonda

Jean has girlfriends in the neighborhood and they sometimes stop by unannounced to visit. Hard has requested she tell her friends to call before dropping by but the women either don't care or, more likely, Vonda Jean hasn't bothered to relay his instructions.

Vonda Jean's voice from the next room: "Harding, can you get the door? I'm still eating breakfast."

He does not like this at all. It's bad enough they drop by without calling, now he has to drag himself across the room and pretend to be nice to one of Vonda Jean's friends when the mere thought of human company makes him more ill than he already is. He takes another sip of his coffee before placing the mug on an end table. Then he rises and ties his robe. Pads toward the door, fighting the Mexican Revolution in his gut. When Hard opens the door and sees Detectives Arnaldo Escovedo and Cali Pasco, his bloodshot eyes narrow and his head tilts slightly to one side.

"Sorry to bother you, Chief," Detective Escovedo says

"What are you doing here?" Hard trying to keep any sense of doom out of his voice. Right now he regrets cursing out Escovedo the other day. Had he filed a grievance?

Detective Escovedo produces an official-looking piece of paper. Pasco is looking directly into his eyes. For a moment he thinks Vonda Jean is going to accuse him of having an affair with her. He hopes she stays in the kitchen.

"Chief, we have a warrant to search your house," Escovedo says.

Hard's mind rockets back to last night: the desert, the dog, the fire. The fire! Was he supposed to get a permit for the fire? Who could have seen him in the wash of scrub? He is certain there was no one around for miles. And even if it is illegal, and yes, it probably is, this is the jurisdiction of the Sherriff's Department, not the Desert Hot Springs Police Department. What are his own people doing here asking to search his house, no, not asking but telling him they are going to rifle his home? Reflexively, Hard grabs the piece of paper out of Detective Escovedo's hand and stares at it. Rendered in bold print at the top of the page are the words Search Warrant. At the bottom of the page is the signature of Judge Allan Diemer, a magistrate Hard knows to be rigid. Now Hard is desperately hoping this is some kind of horrible practical joke that will be revealed to him in a moment, people jumping out with video cameras, shouting happy birthday or April Fools, but he does a quick survey of his logy mind and remembers it's not his birthday and it's November, and no one jumps out yelling anything, the only sounds the cars rolling by on the long highway below. Until Vonda Jean pipes up from the next room.

"Harding, who is it?"

"Some people from the force."

Vonda Jean appears in the doorway. "Howdy," she says. "Should I put more coffee on?"

"They're here to search the house." No one says anything for a moment. Arnaldo and Cali look at Hard. Vonda Jean does, too. Hard looks out the door toward the desert. A shaft of sunlight falling through the picture window illuminates a river of dust motes that refract the light as they loop and twist in a chaotic ballet. Cali and Arnaldo exchange an uncomfortable glance.

"This house?" Vonda Jean says. Her voice rises slightly at the end of the second word. "What for?"

Cali tells her that someone Hard knew was murdered and before she can say another word, Vonda Jean asks, "So why are you here?"

Arnaldo says, "M'am, would you mind stepping out of the house, please? Chief, I'll need you to do the same thing."

At this moment, two Sherriff's Deputies reveal themselves, young men in their thirties, ex-Marines. Hard knows them both, nods hello as he and Vonda Jean walk past them and on to their scrubby lawn. The Deputies greet them neutrally. There won't be any fraternization this morning.

The Marvins are standing on the street looking toward their house. The sun is still low in the sky but it's not as hot as it was yesterday. Hard sees a red-tailed hawk soaring overhead, searching for prey. He can feel Vonda Jean looking at him.

"You want to tell me what the hell this is about?"

The District Attorney's Indio office is usually empty on Saturdays but Jimmy comes in to start getting caught up. He is seated in his basement office sifting through the files when Oz Spengler appears at his desk and wants to know if he would like to get something to eat. Although Jimmy is not hungry, Oz is his new boss and he has vowed that he is going make more of an effort to get along with his superiors so he says he'd be happy to take a break.

To make conversation on the drive to the restaurant in Oz's Ford Taurus, Jimmy asks if he's got a wife and kids. When Oz answers in the affirmative, Jimmy asks if the family owns a dog. "Hairball," Oz says. "A rescue." A smile creases Jimmy's lips and he tells Oz about *The Book of Dogs*. Oz says his young sons would like to see it. This is encouraging to Jimmy who allows himself to think, however briefly, that they might actually connect on a human level.

Now the two men are seated across from each other at Cactus Jack's, a desert chain restaurant just down Highway 111, Oz saying "I believe in second chances, all right?" Jimmy would have preferred if Oz had not mentioned the circumstances of his arrival at the District Attorney's office but he was determined to make it to his pension without further turbulence so he let it slide.

The place is half-filled in the middle of the afternoon, families and workers getting off hotel shifts. The two of them seated in a rear booth. Jimmy chewing his jalapeno burger when Oz asks him what went wrong up in Desert Hot Springs.

"It's all in the record," Jimmy says. Wishes Oz would just let it go.

"I read the record. I know what's in there. Prior to the incident did you and Chief Marvin have a personal beef?"

Jimmy takes another bite of the jalapeno burger, chews, swallows. Oz not one of those guys that have to fill a silence with the sound of his own chatter. Jimmy likes that. But he feels the first inkling of temper. Takes a sip of his soda. Remember to breathe, one count in, two counts out.

"I don't have personal beefs with anyone. People might have them with me. If they do, I can't control it. It's their problem."

"Chief Marvin wrote some stuff in your record, something about a dog."

Jimmy tells Oz the story and his new boss says makes sympathetic noises. Jimmy doesn't want to continue the conversation at this point, just wants to finish his lunch, go back to the office and resume working his way through the files.

Breathe in, one, two. Breathe out, three, four. Starts to worry he looks like a balloon losing air, wonders if Oz notices.

"You freed him down in the Anza-Borrego Desert?"

Looks directly at Oz, unblinking: "That's right."

"What about bailing out of the anger management. The report said they mandated ten sessions, you went to three."

"I got out of it what I needed to."

"Sure about that?"

"I seem angry to you?"

"Average for a cop."

Jimmy had thought he had a lid on this but all the talk about Hard and the dog lit his fuse. The breathing is not getting the job done, because while he's hiding his roiling interior, it's a sandstorm in there. He drains the rest of his soda, cracks the ice cubes with his teeth.

"Can you do your job on an even keel?"

The anger again rises but Jimmy, relying on the techniques he's been practicing, observes it for a moment, watches it crash like an ocean wave against the shore and then recede. "You can put me on anything."

"Yeah, well, this conversation's about what I'm not gonna put you on." Jimmy looks at him quizzically. In all of his years in law enforcement, no one had ever taken him aside for the express purpose of informing him about a case to which he wasn't going to be assigned.

What Oz tells him: "They caught a double on your old stomping grounds. Male convenience store clerk and a female were killed last night. The coroner put the deaths at around 11:00 P.M. There's a hinky detail turned up, so someone from our office has to check it out. You might want to work it, and I have to tell you, that's not gonna happen. I'm assigning Glenn Korver." Korver had been the DA's investigator on some of Jimmy's cases. A guy with ten years at the DA's office. Thorough. By the book. Jimmy doesn't like him. Korver, in Jimmy's view, too careful about what he thinks will stand up in court.

"Is this cause Hard Marvin might have a problem with me?"

"Not exactly."

"What's that mean?"

"They're calling him a person of interest."

Jimmy looks at Oz as if he had suddenly begun speaking Farsi. "Harding Marvin?" The granite-like expression on his new boss's face lets Jimmy know that, ludicrous as it sounds, this is not a joke. His mind ranges back over the ten years he's known Hard. The man loves guns, loves to shoot, but a double murder where one of the victims is a clerk in a convenience store doesn't hit the right notes. And it's not only that he can't place Hard in the scene. The whole idea of Hard having anything to do with it seems crazy.

"They tossed his house this morning and he's been put on administrative leave." Jimmy asks what else he knows and Oz tells him it looks like the female victim might have been Hard's girlfriend. This information causes a surge in Jimmy's adrenal glands that continues for the next hour. After lunch he tries to concentrate on his new files but this proves impossible. Because the more he considers the events at the convenience store and the more he thinks back over the years he's known Hard Marvin, the more he is willing to entertain the possibility that Hard might be the shooter. For starters, the man is turpentine in human form, abrasive and toxic. And as a man who wrestled with anger, Jimmy is acute when it comes to observing the problems it can cause.

Princess drove Odin to Our Lady of Lourdes Hospital in San Bernardino. They arrived in the middle of the night and it took the emergency room team three hours to treat Odin. They shot him full of painkillers then cleaned the wound, pulling out several pieces of buckshot that House Cat had been unable to remove, and told him he was lucky he hadn't lost an eye. Princess spent the time in the waiting room filling out forms and tending to Chance King. She dutifully reported that she had accidentally shot Odin while cleaning the gun and her signature was on the paperwork the hospital was required to file with the police. She didn't bother asking Odin what happened to the "hunting accident."

"You put our real address down?" Odin incredulous.

"They ask to see my drivers license."

Princess and Odin are standing in their kitchen. Chance King sits in front of the television in the next room watching cartoons. Odin dressed in nothing but bikini briefs. The shredded half of his face is covered with a bandage. He takes one of his agoraphobia pills and chases it with a glass of water.

"That wasn't real smart."

"I lie like you want me to."

"They could still send someone around to talk to us."

"I'm sorry, Odin. I don't know what to do, you come home all shot up."

"Was out working for us."

"I know."

"Come here."

She moves toward him and he drives a fist into her face, snapping her head back and knocking her to the floor. Lying there, hand to her cheek, she can hear the high-pitched voices of the cartoon her son is watching. Odin stands over her, the visible side of his face going red.

"I risk my life for you and you're leading the cops right here." He waits for her to respond, but she says nothing. The pure hatred she feels for him, for their life in this stain of a town, for everything in the world but her son is overwhelming. She only wants to leave the house alive.

When he determines she is not going to fight back, Odin turns away. Princess remains on the floor. She glances at the drawer that contains the kitchen knives, thinks for a moment she might get up and go for one, let Odin try and stop her. But she knows there are better options available. The survival instinct that led her to leave the Philippines, to strip when she had to, to get a job working for Fed-Ex because of the benefits, tells her to remain where she is.

There will be time.

She watches Odin take two painkillers and without saying another word to her he lumbers into the bedroom. Didn't he just dose himself half an hour ago? Another ten minutes pass before she gets up from the floor. She takes a hand mirror out of her purse and checks her reflection. There is already swelling around her left eye. Chance King enters the kitchen wearing *Sponge-Bob* pajamas and she gives him small bowl of potato chips. With no sense anything is amiss, he wanders back to the television.

Odin is lying on his back snoring when Princess enters the bedroom. The grubby plastic shades are drawn and the room is in shadow. The painkillers should keep him out for a while. She starts by looking in his drawers. Rifles his underwear, his socks, his tee shirts. Nothing. She goes into the closet and takes out the cardboard boxes on the floor. The boxes have been there since she and Odin moved into the place and she had never wondered what they held. Now she sees: Odin's baseball card collection, some military papers she quickly leafs through and determines are of no interest, and pornography. Odin mumbles something and she turns around, expecting him to get up from the bed. Relief washes over her when she realizes he is talking in his sleep. Back in the closet, she peers into two pairs of beat-up leather sneakers, a pair of military issue combat boots, and a pair of scuffed black loafers.

Chance King doesn't look away from the television when Princess ransacks the living room, searching under the cushions of the stained brown couch, even checking to see if the cheap carpet had been lifted and something hidden beneath. There is only dust.

Frustrated, she walks through the kitchen and out into the backyard. She can see the distant mountains and would like nothing more than to fly above them and away from this place, but she knows that will happen soon enough so returns to the task at hand. Odin had built a small plywood playhouse for Chance King and Princess sticks her head in there. She sees nothing inside but a plastic chair and a toy gun.

Two garbage cans stand against the side of the house. Princess opens them and looks in. People here cart their refuse to a landfill so this would be an excellent hiding place. She lifts one lid, then the next, sees nothing there but bagged trash. She moves each can, and looks beneath. Empty ground.

The only place left to search is Odin's car. The Impala is parked in the driveway and Princess glances at the house as she walks toward it, wanting to make sure Odin doesn't catch her by surprise. Placing her hand on the door handle she pulls and realizes the car is locked. She had driven it last, but Odin had asked for the keys when they returned home. They were probably in his pants pocket.

In the bedroom Odin has rolled on to his side but still appears to be asleep. Princess sees his blood-spattered jeans lying in a pile of dirty clothes on the floor. Crouching down, she thrusts her hand into the front pocket. The floor creaks as she tiptoes out of the room. She freezes, looks over at Odin. His mouth hangs open and saliva dribbles to the pillow.

Princess lets herself into the car and immediately opens the glove compartment: a pair of sunglasses, two maps, a flashlight, the registration and the insurance card. She looks under the driver's seat and the passenger seat and sees a few empty beer bottles, a Homer Simpson toy Chance King liked to play with and a broken pencil. In the backseat are more bottles and a couple of car parts.

Her last hope is the trunk. Again she glances at the house. If Odin is watching her from the window, she will say she is looking for something that belongs to their son. The sunlight illuminates a perforated tire, some old newspapers, a wrench and a fire extinguisher. She is about to lower the trunk lid when she remembers there is a compartment for the spare tire. And the spare tire wasn't in it since it is currently in use. Quickly she lifts the grease stained carpet that lines the bottom of the trunk and then the lid of the spare tire compartment.

It's empty.

Princess is overcome with a familiar sense of desolation. The sun is climbing into the sky and the day will be hot again. In a few hours Odin will awaken and she doesn't want to deal with him. Her mind goes to the knife drawer in the kitchen. Then she remembers the abandoned camper, lying in the backyard weeds. The camper is a sleeping unit that fits on the back of a pickup. Odin occasionally talks about fixing it up and taking them on camping trips, Odin, Chance King, and Princess in the mountains, fishing, swimming, being a family.

She opens the door to the camper and peers inside. The place reeks of mold. There are two bunks and a cabinet with three drawers and it doesn't appear as if anyone has been inside here in years. Her heart sinks but she knows she has to keep looking.

More nothing.

Princess walks back into the house where her son is waiting for her.

"Hungry," he says.

The two of them are in the kitchen now. She reaches into the refrigerator and hands the boy a jar of peanut butter. Normally, she would make him a sandwich but she is feeling too discouraged. She notices the Buddha statue smiling enigmatically on the kitchen counter. On a whim, Princess lifts the Buddha and examines the bottom to see if there is a hidden cavity. She runs her fingertips along its solid wood base and up its back. There is no hidden compartment. Dejected, she returns the statue to its place on the counter and tries to decide what to do next.

Chance King is struggling with the top of the peanut butter jar. She watches him grow increasingly frustrated. Unable to open it, the boy hands it to his mother who tells him to wait a moment. Turning her attention back to the Buddha, she tries to unscrew the head. Nothing happens. Chance King again tries to give her the peanut butter jar. She tells him to wait. With the palm of her hand smothering the wooden idol's serene face, she tenses the muscles in her wrists and arms and exerts the maximum amount of pressure she is capable of summoning. After several seconds the Buddha's head twists off like a bottle cap. The torso is hollow and stuffed inside is a thick wad of cash. Her joyful yelp startles Chance King and Princess quickly makes him a peanut butter and jelly on white bread. He devours it while she hurriedly counts the money.

If Odin hadn't smacked her, Princess would have left some for him. Five thousand dollars. She and Chance King can get back to the Philippines.

CHAPTER THIRTY

The lonesome Bakersfield twang of Merle Haggard fills the truck's cab as Jimmy considers Hard and fate and murder. There is genuine hope in his breast that Hard isn't guilty. As much as he considers his former boss an enemy, he is trying to evolve into someone for whom the concept of enemies is anathema. And even at Jimmy's current nascent level of spiritual development, the rooms of his heart are still not dark enough to wish the fate of a convicted killer on him, Hard in a San Quentin cell, appeals exhausted, waiting for the needle and oblivion.

Desert Hot Springs police headquarters looks just like it did the day he departed nearly two months ago. It's old home week when he gets buzzed pass the security doors, everyone how are you, how's the new job, hello stranger. In the bullpen he sees Arnaldo talking to Glenn Korver who is taking notes on a legal pad. Arnaldo and Jimmy clasp hands, Arnaldo shaking his head, can you believe this? Hard Marvin? Glenn Korver stands and says hello. A short guy in his forties, he's got a widow's peak and a weightlifter's build. He's wearing chinos and a green golf shirt with an eagle on the breast. They greet each other with a firm handshake and blank expressions. Korver ex-military and Jimmy always thought Korver didn't like him because he never served.

Arnaldo tells Jimmy everyone is on the fresh double at the convenience store. Jimmy nods, goes to the coffee pot in the corner, takes a Styrofoam cup and serves himself. Then he pulls a chair up to Arnaldo's desk, sits next to Korver, says: "So?"

Korver taps him on the shoulder. Jimmy looks at him. Korver stands and motions that Jimmy should join him in a sidebar. The two men step away from Arnaldo who pretends nothing unusual is going on.

Korver whispers, "This is my case."

"I know that, Glenn. I'm just visiting with my friends. Not here to step on your toes." Glenn Korver thinks about this, but does not seem placated. "The circumstances make me curious."

Jimmy places himself in the chair next to Arnaldo's desk. Magnanimously indicates Korver should join them. Senses Korver does not appreciate Jimmy's magnanimity, but the man takes the seat next to him. Now Cali approaches, pulls up a chair, sits next to Jimmy, says, "This is gonna blow your doors off," like nothing happened between them the other night. Jimmy likes the way she's playing it. Cali and Glenn nod to each other. Jimmy makes introductions. He likes that Glenn is not enjoying Jimmy's familiarity with the people and the place. Then he upbraids himself for liking it. This is attachment. Let it go. There is freedom from suffering.

Breathe in, one, two. Breathe out, three, four.

Arnaldo's voice interrupts his self-excoriation: "I get a call around midnight last night. Get up to the #1 Convenience Store on Valley View. Two dead bodies. Hispanic male clerk and a Caucasian female customer, multiple gunshot wounds, both of them, it's a horror show, blood, broken glass, total mess. There's a cell phone on the floor so we open it and right on the screen's a picture of Hard."

Although Jimmy knows there was a relationship between Hard and the female victim, when he hears this his head jerks back. Arnaldo moves his computer mouse and clicks. Hard's image appears.

"He left her a phone message last night," Arnaldo says. He moves the cursor to another icon and clicks the mouse. Jimmy listens, trying to sort through the cacophony in his head as

Hard's rough, bourbon-fuelled voice can be heard saying *Nadine, you fuckin cunt, I know what you did to Bane and I want you to know you're going to spend the rest of your life looking over your pretty shoulder.*

Cali breaks the silence, says, "He has a way with the ladies." Korver remains stone-faced but the mordant joke gets an appreciative chuckle from Jimmy and Arnaldo.

"The female's name is Nadine Never," Cali says. "We did a little recon, found out she worked at a tanning salon called Fake 'n' Bake. The owner told us she was living illegally in a foreclosure in Cathedral City." Jimmy asks if they've been to the house. "Tossed it a couple of hours ago," Cali says. "She had a laptop. We're downloading everything now. And there was a dog in a drawer."

"Really?" Jimmy says with no more than professional interest. "What kind?"

"Yappy little Chihuahua tried to take a piece out of my hand," Arnaldo says. "Animal control came and got it."

When Jimmy requests copies of all the files on the victim's computer, Korver interrupts. "I know you got an interest in this, and I respect that," he says. "But this is my case, Jimmy. I don't want anything going toes up because the judge finds out you had a beef with Hard."

"I already told you, Glenn." Jimmy trying to keep the cactus out of his voice. "Wanted to stop by say hi to my friends here at the department." Korver shrugs, tells him not to worry about it and Jimmy says he definitely won't. To Cali and Arnaldo: "What about the store clerk? This wasn't a drug thing?"

Cali reads off her notes, "Carlos Salinas, forty-five years old, married, four kids, no record. Guy was in the wrong place at the wrong time."

No point sticking around any longer. Jimmy says goodbye to Cali and Arnaldo, wishes Glenn Korver good luck. While he still has trouble believing Hard is the shooter, his doubts are quickly dissipating. On the way back to Indio he dials Cali. She picks up and Jimmy says I was going to call you today. Sure you were, she says. He asks if she feels like going out again sometime and she tells him she'll have to think about it but he can tell she's joking because a couple of seconds later she suggests tonight. Just before Jimmy hangs up he asks her if she thinks Hard could have completely lost control of himself and shot up the convenience store. She says hell yeah, I do.

After his shift, Jimmy goes home, feeds Bruno, showers and changes into jeans, a black tee shirt and a lightweight sports coat. Then he meets Cali at a Korean restaurant in Desert Hot Springs. She's dressed in jeans and a fitted red blouse that hugs her athletic form. There are three silver bangles on her left wrist and her earrings are little gold hoops with a pearl on each one. Jimmy doesn't remember whether he's ever seen her wear jewelry before, or maybe he hasn't bothered to notice. She puts her chin in her left hand when she talks to him, and the bangles find the soft light. Her hair is loose and falls past her shoulders and Jimmy catches himself thinking there might be something going on between them. They eat kimchi and have tofu bowls with beef, Cali takes hers medium, Jimmy spicy. Cali tells him about enlisting in the Army to make some money to pay for college and a brief first marriage to a guy back in Texas. Jimmy tells her about Darleen and how whatever went wrong with that relationship was at least fifty per cent his fault. An hour passes before they find themselves talking about the convenience store killings and for the first time Cali clues him in about her own history with the chief. This doesn't surprise Jimmy who says he's heard these kinds of rumors for years.

"My boss over at the D.A.'s office made a point of telling me not to go near Hard's case."

"Yeah, well, the dust-up you and him had went public, didn't it?"

"I admire your self control. Didn't file a grievance. Just nearly broke his jaw." Jimmy laughing now.

"What good would a filing a grievance have done? Then I'm a bitch no other cop wants to work with."

After dinner they see a movie in Palm Springs, a science fiction story in which a virus sweeps the planet and Bruce Willis has to lead everyone to another solar system, and when that's over Cali asks Jimmy if he wants to come back to her place in Yucaipa, west of the desert.

She lives in a condo on a hill overlooking the freeway, but with the windows closed the place is quiet and the headlights speeding east and west below have a hypnotic effect. The place is a simply decorated one bedroom. There's a table with a glass top that seats four just off the kitchen. The living room has a white sectional couch arranged in front of a television and a bamboo and glass bookshelf that holds decorative plates and vases, a few large books of photographs, a small stereo and a row of CDs. Cali puts on some Sade and pours a cognac for herself, asks Jimmy if he wants one. Then she's embarrassed to have forgotten he quit drinking. He tells her not to worry about it and twirls her around the living room to the music, pulling her close, kissing her neck, inhaling her perfume that smells like night blooming jasmine.

They make love in the bedroom and after her second orgasm Cali shoves her cognac-coated tongue deep into Jimmy's throat, says she could get accustomed to this, then curls up next to him and falls asleep.

He didn't intend to go into Cali's computer but when he couldn't sleep after lying in bed for twenty minutes he got up and walked into the living room. He didn't want to turn the television on because the sound might wake her so he thought he would fool around on the Internet until he was tired enough to go back to bed and drift off. Cali's laptop is on the table just off the kitchen. Jimmy turns it on and waits for it to boot up.

He spends some time on the American Kennel Club site, researching different breeds then visits a German shepherd chat room where he reads some comments but doesn't post anything. He begins to feel fatigued and exits the Internet. When the screensaver, a panoramic shot of the Colorado River in Austin, Texas, returns, Jimmy's eyes drift lazily over the icons. There are thumbnail-sized photographs, several software programs, including ones for taxes and Internet poker, and a folder marked Current Case Files. This would normally present an ethical quandary and Jimmy doesn't like to think of himself as a snoop when he's off duty, but given that he has been summarily blocked from participating in what might have been the biggest case of his career, his curiosity eats like battery acid against the membrane of his self-control. What the hell, he figures Cali would do the same thing. He checks that she is sleeping soundly then opens the file.

It does not take him long to figure out that Cali has downloaded the contents of Nadine Never's hard drive on to her laptop. Jimmy begins scrolling. There are credit card bills that show restaurants, nail salons, waxing treatments, supermarkets, pet stores, and pharmacies. There are several PDF files of bank statements, the most recent one indicating that Nadine had a little over two thousand dollars in a savings account at the time of her death.

He scans through files of Nadine's, sees she's bookmarked several tennis sites. There are pictures, snapshots of Nadine with friends by the beach, in the hills above San Diego with the Pacific Ocean in the background. There are pictures of her playing tennis. There are countless pictures of a little dog that Jimmy recognizes as a Chihuahua. He finds a file of an on-line application to a reality show, and several files about sailing and the Pacific Northwest. She was not a user of social networking sites, which was too bad for Hard since they might have been a fecund source of suspects. He is almost ready to go back to bed when he sees a file marked Travel. Jimmy clicks it open and sees there are some video tours of resorts far above Nadine's financial means in places like Bali, the kind that feature bungalows suspended over sparkling azure waters and cost thousands of dollars for a single night. There is a bill for a weekend at a budget hotel in Las Vegas. There is a boarding pass for a flight to San Francisco. There are two more boarding passes, both for Cabo San Lucas. One of them is for Nadine Never, the other for Kendra Duke: Delta Airlines, flight #4753, Seats 14A and 14B, from LAX.

Jimmy assumes Cali knows the contents of Nadine's computer and has chosen not to share that knowledge. He doesn't blame her, but still, he doesn't like it. Indeed, this information in Jimmy's hands represents a slight conflict of interest. He knows departing after sex is not good form but he needs to figure out what to do and lying awake the entire night at her condo is not conducive to clear thought.

He glances around the room. There is a portable printer on a bookshelf. Again he checks on Cali. Satisfied she is still sleeping soundly Jimmy makes a copy of the boarding pass with his sister-in-law's name on it. The moment before he is about to turn the computer off, it occurs to him that there might be another emerald to be discovered in the mine of Nadine's computer and this thought puts him back in the chair. Another half hour of rummaging through the files turns up nothing of interest, but when he discovers a file of photographs taken during the Mexican holiday he is buoyed. There is his sister-in-law on the beach in a bikini. There she is holding a tennis racquet and standing to the side of a court, palm trees in the background. There she is in a restaurant wearing sunglasses and drinking a margarita. There she is in front of a Mexican tattoo parlor. There she is in a hotel room with her yellow pastel skirt hiked, finger pointing to a tattoo of a cartoon kitten rendered on the canvas of her naked ass. And there she in standing next to

Nadine. Both women have their backs to the camera. Both women are wearing nothing but thongs. He notices they are kissing before he sees that Nadine has the same cartoon kitten tattooed in the exact same place. He wonders if Randall knows about this. And considers whether or not to tell him. It would be awkward. And awkward would really be the least of it. Jimmy knows this picture could put his brother in Mary Swain's crosshairs and she won't let go of the trigger until the fusillade kills him twice. Then there are the legal ramifications. A woman with whom Randall's wife appeared to be sexually involved turns up dead right before an election. At the very least, should this get out, people are going to ask uncomfortable questions. Jimmy knows one thing: the karmic wheel is bearing down on Randall Duke.

"Cali." Jimmy kneels by the side of the bed, a gentle hand on her soft shoulder. "I can't sleep. I'm gonna drive back to my place."

"Mmmm," she says, eyes closed. "Okay."

When he leans in to kiss her on the mouth she turns away and his lips brush her cheek. He tells her he'll call tomorrow but she's already asleep.

http://WWW.DESERT-MACHIAVELLI.COM
11.3 – 11:58 P.M.

In my darkest, most cynical moments, I never would have thought Hard Marvin had it in him to murder his girlfriend. The Chief always looked like the kind of guy who could go off like a bottle rocket, fast, cheap and out of control. But not like this. And not with such remarkably bad timing. As a visible presence in the Mary Swain campaign, this is not going to help the Stewardess get elected. Not that I know much about murder, but an investigator looks at who benefits. If a wife dies, first person you look at is the husband. Sue me. It's that kind of world. Well, who benefits here? Chief Marvin you could say, since he gets rid of his girlfriend who (assuming he was the guy who killed her) he presumably found highly annoying.

Addendum: The Machiavelli received a slew of angry emails from the Swain campaign denying the rumors of an illegitimate bi-racial child. I also received an email from a political reporter who writes for the local dead tree daily. In tomorrow's edition you can read her story detailing my unsubstantiated report and the Flight Attendant's denial. I'll say this for her opponent: Randall may be another in a long line of snake oil slinging shit peddlers, but at least there's a brain in his head and no out-of-wedlock bi-racial child in his past. And let me be clear—the Machiavelli has nothing against bi-racial children, only when they occur without the benefit of wedlock in the background of a saint like Mary Swain.

See you in church.

SUNDAY, NOVEMBER 4

Randall's church attendance ramps up exponentially whenever an election looms and he looks to buff his spiritual credentials. This is the fourth week in a row he has been present at the Church of the Desert, a non-denominational Palm Springs house of worship that he joined in hopes of alienating the fewest constituents. This Sunday morning he is seated in the front row on the center aisle. Kendra is next to him, her sunglasses masking a catatonic expression, and to her right is Brittany. In the aisle to Randall's left, Dale is slumped in his replacement wheelchair. It is Randall's intention to get the maximum juice out of his brother's release and where to better show off this broken trophy, this reflection of Randall's generosity, forbearance, and forgiveness than at Sunday services? As for Dale's disastrous attempt to help the campaign, they have not discussed it. Randall has no intention of ever discussing it.

Kendra ordinarily does not like to attend church services but in the wake of Nadine's death, she is clinging to some tiny hope of redemption. As for Brittany, she spends most of the time sending surreptitious text messages to friends who have evaded this obligation. But Randall knows the only thing better for a politician than an intact family is an intact family that attends religious services. That his wife and daughter are disengaged from their surroundings does not matter. What matters: they are next to him. Randall would have liked Jimmy to be here. The three brothers have not been together since Dale's release and a photograph of all of them would convey a comforting message to the electorate. But as Randall listens to the minister intone about how the Lord desires a personal and loving relationship with us, and the choir raises their voices in shimmering song, he tunes out his family long enough to be infused with a sense that the election will go well and this difficult period will soon pass.

Dale has let it be known that he does not want his non-motorized chair pushed by anyone so when the service ends he does a quick-wheeled pirouette and is rolling toward the door under his own power. Kendra and Brittany trail behind and Randall brings up the rear, shaking hands with parishioners as he does. A young couple with two sons ask Randall if he'd mind posing for a picture with the boys and he happily obliges, throwing an arm over the shoulder of each one as their mother snaps away with her cell phone. From the smiles and handshakes Randall receives parading up the aisle, he is certain few of these people will vote for Mary Swain on Tuesday.

At the rear of the church Maxon is standing with Kendra and Brittany. Randall greets him and Maxon says, "I got a photographer from the *Desert Sun* here to get a family shot."

Jimmy parks his truck a block from the Church of the Desert. He didn't get a lot of sleep and is buzzing from three cups of dark Sumatra. He wants to talk to Randall and find out what he knows before anyone from the force sticks their nose in. Nadine Never's death couldn't have had anything to do with his brother in Jimmy's view, but he wants to get a sense of her relationship to Randall's family if only to satisfy his own curiosity. Arnaldo, Cali and the rest of the department will be digging around. Since Randall had managed to save Jimmy's career, the least he could do is give a warning.

A short middle-aged woman dressed in a black tunic and leggings and with two 35mm cameras slung around her neck is arranging Randall, Kendra, Brittany and Dale into a tableau in front of the church as a small crowd of parishioners watches, some taking their own snapshots of the Duke family. When Randall spots Jimmy a broad smile breaks out.

"Jimmy Ray, get in here!"

Jimmy glances at Dale, who is stone-faced, and Kendra who appears to be staring at the firebrick red-hued mountains in the distance. His niece is in her default setting of ennui.

"Come on, man! For Mom and Dad!" Randall says. Then, to the photographer: "Don't take another picture until all three Duke brothers are in the shot."

Jimmy looks at Dale but his younger brother will not meet his gaze. Nor will his sister-in-law, whom he is now regarding with fresh eyes after seeing the photograph of the backside tattoo. Randall energetically gestures him over. Jimmy realizes the more diffident he is, the longer this will take, and reluctantly steps into the picture. Randall throws an arm around him, lays a palm on Dale's shoulder. Jimmy has already made up his mind that whatever debt he owes Randall will be discharged by a combination of his speech at the Purity Ball and his appearance in this photograph. He looks over at Randall who is tickling Brittany in an attempt to make her smile. He wonders what Kendra is thinking, how she would react if she knew why he was here. And why is she wearing those sunglasses for the picture? When the photographer finishes, Jimmy asks Randall if he can have a word.

Standing on the sidewalk beyond the church plaza Jimmy informs his brother that he has reason to suspect Kendra and a murder victim named Nadine Never knew each other well and that they flew to Mexico together. When Randall knits his brow, Jimmy again wonders how much of this his brother already knows.

"How'd you find this out?"

"Both their names are on boarding passes, sitting next to

each other. I wasn't sure, I wouldn't have bothered you. But it was in the victim's computer. So Kendra knew this woman?" Jimmy has to ask, rhetorical questions part of the job.

"Yeah, she knew her."

"They were friends?"

"She taught Brittany tennis."

"I'm wondering why you didn't give me a heads up Kendra knew the woman, Randall, her being a murder victim. It's weird. She got killed Friday night, now it's Sunday. You still read the local papers, right? News was right on the front page."

"What's this got to do with me?"

"She and Kendra on a vacation together? This'll look strange, it comes out. I'm wondering what's going on here."

"Nothing going on, Jimmy."

"And I'm trying to figure out why you didn't mention any of this until I found a copy of a boarding pass on a computer."

"Because I'm in the middle of a tough campaign and while I feel nothing but pain for this poor woman and her family, and that poor clerk and his family, I have other things on my mind."

"I can understand that, but you don't think this is gonna land at your door?"

"I'm supposed to stop everything and call, tell you my wife knows a murder victim?"

Two parishioners walk past, a middle-aged couple. He's wearing a cowboy hat and a western-cut suit, she's in a floral print dress.

"Good luck on Tuesday!" The man says.

Randall thanks them and waits until they're out of earshot.

"What happens now?"

This is a source of great discomfort since Randall is on the fringe of a murder investigation and Jimmy has enough family loyalty to not want him gratuitously ruined. He briefly debates whether to tell his brother that he believes the women were sexually involved but concludes nothing beneficial will come of passing that information along today.

"The detectives investigating the case will want to talk to Kendra."

"Should she get a lawyer?"

"You tell me."

"Any suspects?"

When Jimmy tells him about the situation with Hard, he notices a subtle transition in Randall's reaction, from disbelief through a barely discernable hint of elation to outrage that an official could so betray the public trust. "I can't get into particulars," Jimmy says, "since the investigation is ongoing, but it doesn't look good for Chief Marvin right now."

"Will Kendra have to come to the station to talk to the detectives?"

"They make house calls."

Around the corner from the church, worshippers are walking to their cars. On the sidewalk next to a pair of towering palm trees Dale is staring up at Maxon who is holding both his hands up in a placating gesture. The tendon on the left side of Dale's neck is as taut as a guitar string.

"You got to get it for me somehow."

"Look, I told you, it's just not that easy to put my hands on ten thousand dollars in cash. Campaigns get audited sometimes." Maxon holds his hands together in front of him, fingers intertwined. He doesn't want to give Dale the money, and is starting to wonder whether he should just leave him to his own devices. "I thought these guys were your friends."

"I got rough friends."

"You didn't tell them anything, did you?"

"Shit, no. They could kill me, understand? That's gonna be on you."

Maxon removes a tennis ball from his pocket and starts

worrying it in the fingers of his left hand. If only he could depend on Dale's colleagues to do what he says they will.

When Jimmy is done talking to Randall, he searches for Dale. He hasn't seen him since the day of his release and is feeling slightly guilty about it. Looking through the dwindling flock he spots Dale talking animatedly to Maxon on the sidewalk next to the church. He can see Dale moving in his chair as he gestures. The two of them stop conversing when Jimmy approaches.

"Sorry you missed the sermon," Maxon says.

"Bet you are," Jimmy says. Then, to Dale: "Where's your tricked out wheelchair?"

"Repair shop," Dale says, a little too quickly.

"So soon?"

"Korean piece of shit," Dale says with another smile. Jimmy wishes his brother would stop smiling. The bad teeth make him look like the career criminal he is and Jimmy is tired of seeing him that way.

"You want a lift back to Mecca? Give us a chance to talk."

"Not going back down there," Dale says.

"He's working on the campaign," Maxon says.

"Oh, yeah? What do they have you doing?"

"You know," Dale says. "This and that."

"How about we get some dinner tomorrow night?" Jimmy says.

"That's the night before the election," Maxon says.

"Guess you're pretty valuable to the re-election effort, Dale."

There is an uncomfortable pause, during which Dale looks away from his brother. Jimmy notices that Maxon is staring at him with a slightly strained expression. Sees Maxon is squeezing a tennis ball with his left hand.

"How about Wednesday," Dale says.

"Sure, yeah. That's good. I'll give you a lift down to Mecca after." Turning to Maxon, Jimmy says, "What's the tennis ball for? Got a game later?"

"Great way to relieve tension," Maxon says.

"You should try meditation," Jimmy says.

"I'm a Christian," Maxon says.

Jimmy walks away wondering what he has just witnessed. They had appeared to be arguing when he came upon them then stopped immediately when they sensed his presence. What could those two possibly have to argue about? Jimmy plans to ask Dale when he next sees him.

CHAPTER THIRTY-TWO

Only ministers and priests like to work on a Sunday morning, but this is an unusual situation. While Cali examines Nadine Never's computer files at headquarters, Arnaldo sips coffee from a Styrofoam cup and briefs her on the chilling checklist of Chief Harding Marvin's depredations. Along with the cell phone photograph, there is a threatening text message from Hard to the victim, a threatening voice mail from Hard to the victim, and a theory develops—based on Arnaldo's recollection of overhearing Chief Marvin saying "Crazy bitch murdered Bane," prior to cursing him out and ejecting him from the office—that the victim may have killed Hard's dog, thus providing a motive for the crime.

All of this is on Cali's mind an hour later as she sits across from Hard and his lawyer in the interrogation room at Desert Hot Springs Police Headquarters. She is working the double homicide now, along with every detective on the force. The plan, outlined earlier this morning in a meeting with Captain Delgado, Hard's former second-in-command and now the acting chief, is for her to do the initial interrogation of Hard, just annoy him mostly, before Arnaldo and other senior detectives take over.

Cali knows if she had mentioned her history with Hard to Delgado, she would have been asked to stake out another meth lab. That Hard had used his position as a means to have sex with her, and that their encounter had ended violently, is something she believes can be overlooked. Whether or not Hard believes this is immaterial to her. He won't be bringing it up.

Jolene Ryder is short and feisty and slightly overweight. A barrette keeps her blunt cut hair off a wide forehead. She has narrow gray eyes and her complexion is slightly mottled. She wears a print dress and Birkenstocks. Her only jewelry is a wristwatch on a thin metal band. A briefcase sits next to her on the floor. Jolene's father was a cop and she has defended a lot of police officers accused of crimes committed in the line of duty. Hard is dressed in khakis and a white button-front shirt. When the Desert Hot Springs Town Supervisor temporarily removed him from active duty he was forbidden to wear his uniform until further notice, a terrific indignity for a man who has worn one his entire adult life.

In a black slacks, flats and a black linen blouse, Cali has dressed for the occasion. They've been there for an hour and Hard has spent the entire time explaining to Cali that he had nothing to do with the terrible fate that has befallen Nadine.

"You can tell me you were in the desert lighting your dog on fire all you want, Chief, and we can have a forensic guy determine when the fire was burning, but it won't be accurate enough for an alibi."

It would be incorrect to report that Cali did not derive a slight degree of sadistic pleasure from watching Hard squirm. She believes he has wanted to get rid of her for years and resisted the temptation because of a potential employment lawsuit. That their most recent encounter had been adversarial in nature and had revolved around her request to work a homicide was an irony lost on neither of them. It does not surprise Cali that she is enjoying the unaccustomed role of being in the position of power with Hard. What does surprise her, though, is that she does not feel hatred for Hard, the philanderer, sexual predator and now the accused murderer. What she feels is something like sympathy.

Jolene checks her watch. "Are we done? The Chief is here of his own volition and I think an hour of his valuable time on a Sunday morning is enough." Cali believes Hard is in considerably deeper trouble than his attorney wants to acknowledge so she doesn't bother to answer. "And now that we've established that Chief Marvin didn't have anything to do with this, we're done."

Cali and Jolene go back. The lawyer represented a suspect in a fraud case she was working and got the guy off. Cali knew her client was guilty. Doesn't like the woman, but knows her to be a formidable adversary.

"Chief, I'm touched by the story about your dog," Cali says, unable to resist baiting Hard. "But you're gonna have to come up with something better."

Hard chews his tongue to keep from spitting something back at Cali.

"Chief Marvin doesn't need an alibi. Until you charge him. And there's not a single piece of forensic evidence tying him to the crime scene," Jolene says. "This is a deeply unfortunate coincidence. The chief's record is spotless and the female victim is not going to be sympathetic to a jury."

"Chief Marvin, we have you threatening to kill Nadine Never on tape. She winds up dead. You might want to think about making a deal. This is a death penalty case."

Hard does not react to this, but instead looks at Jolene.

"If you file charges we're going to move to dismiss immediately," she says. Then, turning to Hard, "We're leaving." Hard pushes away from the table, rises from the chair and walks out of the room without looking at Cali. She takes a moment to marvel how quickly fate can reverse. Hard in the car trying to fuck her, Cali working in the shadow of their sordid secret too scared to report it, and now the karma wheel poised to grind Hard to a fine powder. What was it Jimmy had told her? Something about if you sit on a riverbank on and wait long enough, you will see the body of your enemy float by.

Of the thousands of times Hard has passed through the portals of the Desert Hot Springs police headquarters and into the parking lot, this is the first time he has done it as a person of interest in a murder investigation. He glances over his shoulder at the K-9 vehicle parked in the lot. Wonders if somehow this is all connected to the way things went down with that police dog, the one Jimmy Duke claimed to have released in the desert. He should have been more empathic, should have recognized Jimmy's feelings for that dog. This is particularly difficult for Hard to grapple with in the wake of Bane's demise. Had he gone through that grief prior to being confronted with Bruno's malfeasance, Hard believes he would have acted different.

A deepening sense of his lack of popularity gnaws at Hard as he walks toward his truck. It wasn't that he was expecting a banner strung along the front of the station reading *WE SUPPORT YOU, CHIEF* but he finds the response of his erstwhile minions infuriating. Hard knows the officers are professionals and have to be objective but he is not feeling much in the way of love, no subtle winks, no sympathetic pats on the back—not a single *We're with you, sir!*—and some of these people he has worked with for a decade. It makes him question humanity.

So what if the troops aren't rallying around him in any discernible way. He'd be suspicious, too, if one of his people were hauled in under the same circumstances. Hard isn't going to judge. The facts will come out and all will be back to normal in short order. There may be a murder indictment hanging over him, but he knows he didn't do it, and believes, no he's *certain,* he can recover from what he views as nothing more than character assassination.

As he climbs into his truck and jams the key in the ignition, he realizes there is one person who can stand up for him, who can guarantee the public sees him for the man he really is, an heroic figure, a paragon of the law enforcement community who is on the verge of being railroaded by the system he has gallantly served: Mary Swain. Hard knows he has to talk to her as soon as he possibly can. Given that he is in extremis at the moment, he's surprised he has not heard from her.

To anyone familiar with the world of politics, Mary Swain's lack of contact with Hard would seem ordinary. Why should a rising political candidate, someone already getting national attention before she's even won a local contest, reach out to any supporter—much less a government employee—who has found himself in the middle of an imbroglio that smells like this one? But Hard does not understand. He spoke forcefully on her behalf just a few days earlier, blessed the Mary Swain rally with the power of his uniform. Is she a woman of honor, he wonders, or just another hack, albeit a more attractive one. A sympathetic phone call should have come his way by now.

Mary Swain had scribbled her cell phone number on a torn piece of paper and given it to him a few weeks earlier. Rather than transcribing it in his own writing, or programming it into his cell phone, he had folded the paper and placed it in his wallet, the paper scrap imbued by Hard with talismanic significance by virtue of it's source. He takes it out now and dials the number. Gets the message, a computer-generated voice. Hard disappointed, would have liked to experience the comfort of hearing Mary Swain right now, even the recorded version.

There are several gated communities in the Coachella Valley but Casa Sereno is the one to which the residents of all the others aspire. Not because the streets are more pristine, the homes more exquisitely designed, or the residents more beautiful. But like people who are famous for being famous, the neighborhood's exclusivity is Platonic. Casa Sereno is the most sought after simply because that is how this collection of homes and lanes and landscaping is perceived. This is where Mary Swain told her husband she would like to live. Their house, one of four homes they own, is a five bedroom Spanish modern with a soaring entrance hall, huge living and dining rooms, a landscaped back yard, and a four car garage occupied by a Mercedes sedan, a Land Rover, a Bentley convertible and a Mini. That they could afford something far more impressive is a given, since among their other homes is a Fifth Avenue apartment in New York and a pied a terre near Hyde Park in London, but Mary Swain has what in the Palm Springs area passes for the common touch and this place was purchased only a few years ago with her political ambitions in mind.

Hard knows from an internal campaign memo that Mary has some down time this afternoon, which she plans to spend at home, and as he drives toward her house, he thinks about the couple of hours he and Vonda Jean spent there one evening last Spring. It was a fundraiser and when they walked in Hard had been immediately struck by two things: he was the only person there who worked for a salary and he had never in his life been around this much concentrated wealth.

After Hard heard Mary Swain was running for office he had written her a note volunteering his services and was surprised when she answered him with a personal note of her own. Yes, she would be thrilled to have the Desert Hot Springs Chief of Police work on her campaign. In fact, she was having a fundraiser at her home and would he like to attend? Hard waved that letter in front of Vonda Jean like it was Lincoln's own copy of the Gettysburg Address.

He savors the visit to her house, remembers it like a favorite film, one that has unspooled in his mind many times. It had been a warm evening in late April. At the front door of Mary Swain's home a silent young Mexican man in a white coat had greeted them and looked quizzically at the dress blue police uniform Hard was wearing. When he proudly displayed his invitation the man obsequiously gestured toward the backyard, where the event was taking place around the pool. The air in the house was cool and as Hard and Vonda Jean passed through he noticed the art on the walls, local scenes of desert landscapes and skies, modern furniture, variations in metal, leather and rich, dark wood that appeared to be daring people to use it.

A group of men surrounded a beautiful woman, listening as if the words from her lips revealed heretofore inaccessible secrets, the knowledge of which would allow those who possessed them to pass into celestial realms and Hard realized he was gazing at Mary Swain in the flesh. In a moment, she was gliding toward Hard, a vision in a white sleeveless dress that showed off her toned body, perfect hair swept to the top of her head. She introduced herself to Hard and Vonda Jean in a voice that held hidden promises and had she asked him, Hard would have run off with her that night. There were thanks for coming, and offers of drinks, and suggestions to mingle and then she was gone, flitting around the party like a faerie, dispensing her magic wherever she deigned to alight. That night Hard thought Mary Swain whispered of possibility, of hope. It made him want to be around her for the rest of his life, but since that was not possible, he knew he would throw himself into her campaign.

Hard remembers standing to the side of the shimmering pool, its limpid surface reflecting the white paper lanterns that had been hung for the party, remembers recognizing the owners of several local companies, two casinos, and a golf resort. And he knew the woman across the water whose beauty appeared to him otherworldly was a movie star because he had seen her in a romantic comedy Vonda Jean had wanted to watch on cable just a few weeks earlier.

That evening Vonda Jean had been wearing a simple green cotton dress, belted at the waist. Hard had sensed without asking that she felt underdressed and overmatched. She drank her wine like she was quenching a thirst and after a few glasses informed Hard what she thought of this collection of swells. There is no money in Vonda Jean's family and on the drive home Hard had accused her of resenting those who have it. As for him, he had felt no class resentment, his attitude where do I sign up? The business world was not attractive to Hard, the man no great lover of lucre. But he liked the idea of power and was only too happy to labor on behalf of Mary Swain if it got him closer to the throne.

The next day he had phoned her office and was immediately invited to attend several functions with her and would he please be sure to wear his uniform. Hard is not much of a conversationalist, prefers to work the strong, silent side of the street and leave the yammering to the pencil-necks, so he and Mary Swain didn't do much in the way of talking. During the campaign events where they were together Hard mostly basked in her glowing rays. Ever gracious, Mary Swain expressed her appreciation for Hard whenever he was with her, and Hard was seduced by her ability to look into someone's eyes and make them forget anyone else was within miles. He never invited Vonda Jean to any of the events and she didn't seem particularly interested which was fine with him. The relationship between Hard and Mary Swain found its apotheosis when he was asked to introduce her at the outdoor rally in the SaveMart Parking Lot the week before the election.

All of this is racing though his mind as he pulls up to the guardhouse at the gates of Casa Sereno. Hard recognizes the uniformed man at the gate. Rolls down the window of his truck and identifies himself the way a celebrity would introduce himself to a fan, we both know you know who I am but I'm doing this to be polite. The man greets Hard and then looks over his head, like he doesn't want to make eye contact.

"Ms. Swain's not there, Chief."

"Her campaign schedule says she's home with the kids today." The man nods his head. Laconic. He'll wait. "You see her leave?"

"Don't know where she is."

"Maybe you want to call the house and check?" Hard grips the steering wheel a little tighter. In the rearview mirror he sees a BMW 750i pull up behind him. The driver is a woman who appears to be in her sixties. Her lacquered hair rises in a pompadour several inches above her head.

"Do you have an appointment?"

"No I don't have an appointment." The security guard holds up his index finger to the driver of the BMW, indicating that she should be patient. Hard fixes his stare on the security guard. "Pick up the phone and call her." The man hesitates, then dials. Tells whoever it is on the other end that he has Chief Marvin here and he would like to stop by. After a pause, he hangs up and tells Hard that Mary Swain can't see him right now.

"Did you talk to her?"

Now the security guard looks Hard directly in the eye and says, "I talked to *Mr.* Swain," invoking the male territorial prerogative for which he is the proxy and suggesting by his tone that Hard should have the good sense to infer their conversation is now officially over. But Hard did not get to be a leader of men by hanging back, and he is not going to let this wage slave who couldn't get hired as a real cop determine how this scrape in which Hard finds himself will play out. So he steps on the gas and rolls past the gate and into Casa Sereno.

The guard must have called reinforcements immediately because in less than thirty seconds Hard notices a security vehicle in his rearview mirror. Exhausted from lack of sleep and psychologically disoriented from finding himself in the unfamiliar role of suspect, Hard desperately tries to remember the way to Mary Swain's home but the palm lined streets all look alike and he realizes he has no idea where he's going. When the distorted and magnified voice blares, "You in the truck, pull over!" there is a brief internal debate during which he weighs the pros and cons of having a roadside conversation with the rent-a-cop on his tail, or just turning around and try-

ing to get out of there with a scrap of dignity. In no mood to
talk, he executes a three-point turn and heads in the direction
he thinks will lead him out of Casa Sereno. The guard in the
patrol car sticks to him and in the rearview Hard can see the
man talking into the dashboard-mounted microphone, probably relaying Hard's whereabouts to the guard at the gate who
is going to be calling the Palm Springs Police Department if he
hasn't already. If only he could take back this entire day, Hard
thinks, no, the week, the month, the year, if only he could go
back to the night he met Nadine and walk right past her. Then
he would not be desperately searching for a way out of this
gated community, stage set for his mad dash to the girl of his
heart, the perfect woman and now he aches at the situation in
which he finds himself, his political future in jeopardy—his
political future? His life!—the private patrol car right behind
him now "Pull over," but Hard knows if he does the police will
arrive in moments so when he rounds a corner and sees he's
headed back to the gate, he guns the truck and hopes the security guard on his tail won't follow him on to public property.

When Kendra returns from church, she changes out of her
dress and into a cotton nightgown. Then she pulls the shades
in the bedroom shutting out the relentless desert light and
crawls back into bed. The morning has been an ordeal. To
have to sit in church between Randall and Brittany and act as
if nothing was wrong had seriously taxed her capacity to cope.
For an hour, she had stared at the cross that was mounted on
the wall behind the pulpit so she wouldn't have to look at
another human being. It struck her as a miracle on the order
of the loaves and fishes that she was able to maintain her com-
posure.

Her daughter is at a friend's house and Randall is campaigning. She did not even bother to ask where he would be.
Kendra has taken a sedative and is hoping this will allow her to

drift off to sleep. She is alone in the house. Which is why she is surprised to hear footsteps outside her bedroom. And then someone's voice calling her name. Kendra climbs out of bed and throws the door open.

"I didn't want to walk into the bedroom," Jimmy says. He's standing in the hall, ten feet from the bedroom door.

"Who let you in, Jimmy Ray?" Kendra says. Despite the sedative, she notices one of her legs is shaking.

"I rang the bell but no one answered, so I went around back. You should lock your doors before you lie down."

Kendra leans against the doorjamb, head tilted back. Tries to steady her leg. The door to the bedroom remains open and she becomes conscious of the unmade bed and the intimacy of the nightgown, the top two buttons of which are undone. She's not wearing panties or a bra. Whether because of her nervousness or the air conditioning the outlines of her nipples are visible against the flimsy cotton. Kendra briefly recalls flying home a day early from a weekend holiday after catching her husband with a chambermaid. The drive to Jimmy's condo, the bottle of vodka. Was that the last time she had been alone with her brother-in-law?

"Randall's not here. I'll tell him you stopped by." Her voice is granite.

"I don't want to talk to Randall."

"I don't feel well. I was trying to take a nap."

"Take it later. I want to talk to you."

"What about?"

"All right if we sit in the living room?"

"I said I wasn't feeling well."

"This won't take long." His tone says it's all business, that he doesn't want to trade in forgotten intimacies.

In the living room Kendra and Jimmy sit in adjoining chairs overlooking the backyard and the mountains. She has put a bathrobe on. Kendra is glad she took the tranquilizer before Jimmy arrived. She feigned surprise when he brings up the subject of the murders at the Super #1 Convenience Store. What could this possibly have to do with her, she asks. Then he describes the evidence found in Nadine Never's computer, the matching tattoos, the women kissing. Despite the tranquilizer, Kendra's mind is a Catherine wheel. Exactly how much does Jimmy know? Has he somehow already figured out what happened? Is he here to toy with her? Does he have some kind of plan to make her expose her complicity in this distasteful mess?

"The police will want to talk to you."

"I knew her and she was killed. What else is there to talk about?"

"Probably not much." He leans back in his chair. His body language is relaxed.

If he knew anything, wouldn't he be bearing down on her? Or is he feinting, waiting for her to stumble? "Were you still friends?"

"Sure."

"Doesn't sound like you're convinced."

"We didn't see much of each other."

"But you went on a vacation together?"

"Jimmy Ray, in what capacity are you here?"

"As your brother-in-law," he says, momentarily dropping the all-business affect. "This kind of thing gets out, people could misinterpret it. Believe me, I'm doing you a favor."

"Do the police know we're talking?"

"They wouldn't like it if they knew so you probably shouldn't mention it. I want you to be ready if they start leaning on you."

"Why are you telling me this?"

"They already have someone they think did it. But they have to cover all their bases. Don't want you to get caught by surprise is all."

"Is that it?"

"Yeah, that's it."

But that isn't it. Since they were kids, Jimmy has always known Randall to have his eye on the main chance, to be a man who would not let small things like other people get in the way of his grab for whatever glittering prize he had his eye on. The way Randall served Dale into the meat grinder back in law school, the way he rationalized it by saying Dale was a juvenile and *I have a lot more to lose*. He has seen Randall run his first campaign for the House of Representatives, the way in which his organization shamelessly slimed the opposition candidate. When Randall was through with the woman you would have thought she was a personal friend of Osama bin Laden's. Jimmy couldn't claim with certainty that Randall knew anything about the murders, but one of the victims was a potential threat to his political career and this is a coincidence that, given what Jimmy knows about his brother, must be explored. Never mind that Jimmy has been instructed to stay away from this case because of the history with Hard. He needs to know for his own peace of mind. Maybe he'd like it if Hard were guilty. It would make things easier on him. But he sees the outline of Randall's hand. And he doesn't like being lied to.

The tension in the back of Kendra's neck has hardened into a peach pit. Reaching behind her head, she kneads the muscle with the fingers of her right hand. She sees Jimmy looking at her, waiting. She knows a good interviewer will just listen and bet the person from whom he is trying to elicit information will find the quiet so intolerable they will be impelled to fill it with words. Jimmy continues to wait. Is he an ally to be trusted or an enemy whom she must evade? The toast Jimmy gave at her wedding is a resonant memory, his sincerity that long ago afternoon never in doubt. And she believes their connection remained when she visited his condo the night she first thought about leaving Randall. She suspects he would have taken her to bed if he had liked her less.

"I'd offer you a drink or something, but as I said, I'm kind of under the weather. I'll tell Randall we spoke. He'll appreciate it."

"Who killed those people at the convenience store?" The turn in Jimmy's manner is so abrupt that it penetrates the fog in her frontal cortex. He's leaning forward now, staring into her eyes. "Do you know?"

This is the moment Kendra hikes her nightgown over her knees, places her head between her legs and vomits on the floor. It is an involuntary action that could not have been better timed. She moans as a rope of saliva descends from her mouth. Jimmy goes into the kitchen and returns with two dishtowels that he uses to clean up the mess. Kendra is reclining in the chair, her head thrown back when he returns from the laundry room where he has deposited the soiled towels.

"Do you know anyone who had a grudge against Nadine?"

"Aren't we done?"

"Almost."

"No, I don't."

She looks right at him. The eruption from her stomach had a relaxing effect and the stress is gone from her body. It enables her to convey a sense of fatigue and shocked innocence. Still, she is not certain that Jimmy does not know everything already. When the silence lasts for a minute she asks him if he would mind if she didn't see him to the door.

After he departs she returns to bed and calls Randall. She leaves a message telling him that Jimmy just broke into their house and did an unofficial police interview with her. Then she falls into a thick sleep.

CHAPTER THIRTY-THREE

Hard hits the Twentynine Palms Highway and the tension drains away. He castigates himself for acting so impulsively. The Sunday traffic is light as he drives home. Thinks about stopping to pick up a sandwich but doesn't want to chance running into anyone he might know. Vonda Jean is at the dojo, so when he gets home he makes himself a ham sandwich and falls into an uneasy nap. The two hours of sleep he gets barely rejuvenates him and the shower he takes when he wakes up doesn't do much good either. Toweling off, he goes to check his email then remembers the Desert Hot Springs Police Department has seized his computer.

Hard hasn't barbecued since the heat arrived back in May but he wants to buy a little good will with Vonda Jean—the woman of his dreams having let him know he is not welcome in her world—so he goes to the garage and takes two thick venison steaks out of the freezer. Then he gets in his truck and heads for the supermarket where he buys a couple of baking potatoes, some greens with which to make a salad and a six pack of beer. Standing at the grill he seasons the venison with salt and pepper and contemplates his day, the face off with Cali Pasco, the run to Mary Swain. What had made him drive to her home other than an unacknowledged weakness he had better take some time to examine? Why did he think Mary Swain, a woman with whom he is barely acquainted, an aspiring politician who, for all he knew, would say absolutely anything to get elected, could be depended upon to speak on his behalf? At least the rent-a-cops had not pursued him out of the gated community and on to the public roads. He should be thankful for professional courtesy. The way things were going he might find himself asking them for a job.

The woman with whom he had shared his life for over twenty years was a much better bet than Mary Swain and it was to Vonda Jean that Hard realizes he should have gone for succor today. They may have had their ups and downs but she is the mother of his sons and has been a rock for nearly half his life. He puts Mary Swain squarely in the past and thinks about his wife, their future together. He congratulates himself for defrosting the venison steaks and preparing this meal for her tonight. A husband should periodically show his appreciation for his wife and Hard vows to do this on a more regular basis. He nervously glances at the clock, as if he's waiting for a date to arrive. Has the brief thought that he should have called Vonda Jean but reassures himself she will appreciate the surprise, Hard not one for romantic gestures the last few years and he thinks this will buy him some much-needed good will.

He places the grilled steaks on a plate beneath an upside down metal bowl so they'll retain their heat then parks himself in the recliner where he waits for his wife to return home, which she does around six thirty. When Vonda Jean walks in Hard says he wants to do something special tonight as thanks for her being understanding of the difficult circumstances in which he finds himself. She's wearing a turquoise tracksuit with dark red piping and her hair is tied back with a rubber band. The ease with which she carries her body looks particularly good to Hard right now, her athlete's gait a familiar comfort to him. He considers kissing her hello but given the thorny nature of their recent relations decides not to try his luck, doesn't want to go for lips and find himself being offered cheek. Vonda Jean is teaching a night class in an hour and had just planned on resting until she had to go back to the dojo so she seems happy when Hard informs her he's made dinner.

Seated at the table in the kitchen, Hard tells her about Mary Swain, how he tried to get a little face time today, how she let him down. Vonda Jean listens sympathetically, says she never particularly liked that woman and is not surprised at her behavior. She asks him how the interrogation went and he tells her not to worry, it's all under control. Hard is famished and devours his steak, washing it down with a couple of beers. He looks up at Vonda Jean who is picking desultorily at her plate. When he asks her how she likes the food she tells him it's good and thanks him for cooking it but something in her voice makes Hard think all is not well. Tonight he doesn't want to push it, just wants to have dinner with his wife and maybe watch a little television together before she goes back to the dojo. He won't even argue if she chooses a program he doesn't like. He's bought ice cream and chocolate sauce and Hard makes her a sundae that she seems to enjoy although the conversation, which tapered off during dinner, does not improve with dessert. Hard clears the dishes and when he asks Vonda Jean if she'd like coffee, she tells him she intends to move out.

"You were with that girl who showed up at our house, weren't you?" Vonda Jean is still seated at the table. Hard has done the dishes and wiped the counters. Now he leans against the sink. "And if you deny it and I find out it's true . . . "

Hard has thought about this, weighed the pros and cons of further lying and decided if he expects Vonda Jean to stand by her man, her man better come clean.

"I made a mistake."

"I'd say you did, yeah."

"You know I didn't kill her right? Didn't have anything to do with it."

"I want to believe that."

"I want you to stay."

"I need to think about the rest of my life, Harding. And I don't want you around when I'm thinking about it."

The ray of hope she presents, the suggestion that he might be given a second chance, makes him generously offer to be the one to move out, but Vonda Jean tells him she's going to be the one to leave. As she packs, he sits in the living room pretending to read a hunting magazine. Until now, it has not occurred to Hard that what he feels for his wife, despite the way the years have worn the two of them down, made them less tolerant of one another's foibles, less patient and understanding of the strain the burdens of simple existence cause in the other, is something like love. After what seems like a short time, he looks up to see her holding a suitcase.

"I'll be at the Best Western," she says. "You can call me if there's an emergency."

"If there's an emergency?" Trying to keep his panic at bay. "Like if things get worse?"

Hard gets out of his chair and walks toward her. She looks down as if examining something on the rug and when he goes to kiss her she offers him her cheek. There is the hint of a smile, one that feels wrung out of her, and then she is gone, the only evidence of her presence a hint of perfume in the air. Had she been wearing that when she came in? Or had she put it on to go teach the evening karate class? He tries to remember if she has worn perfume to class before but quickly realizes that is not a productive line of thought.

Hard collapses into his recliner and stares straight ahead. Vonda Jean leaving is not something he had anticipated and he silently berates himself for not seeing it coming. He takes comfort in the notion that she has left the door open, however slightly, to a reconciliation. Settling back into his chair, he reaches for the remote control and clicks on the local news. The first story is about a group of Marines from the Twentynine Palms base who are preparing to deploy. It is not without a certain degree of envy that Hard watches the young warriors, torqued and ready to rock. Sips his beer, wishes he were accompanying them. Enough of this pansy civilian bullshit. The second story is about the upcoming Congressional election. Randall Duke and Mary Swain are all smiles and great hair as they assess their chances the next day.

The face of Lacey Pall, a young correspondent Hard likes appears on screen. "There's been a new development in the Convenience Store Murders in Desert Hot Springs," Lacey intones. Hard leans forward in the chair, grips the beer can tighter. "Sources in the Desert Hot Springs Police Department have informed me that suspended Police Chief Harding Marvin is now a person of interest in the case." The dissemination of his personal situation was not something Hard thought he would be dealing with quite this quickly. He has assumed the investigation would take several more days before anything definitive occurred, at least that is what Jolene Ryder has assured him. But this development seizes him by the throat and yanks him directly toward where he had hoped he would not go. A *person of interest* is not something anyone ever wants to be. Hard does not hear the rest of Lacey Pall's report. The program has moved on to a story about a local artists' collective that has painted a mural of George H.W. Bush's life when the telephone rings the first time. Before three minutes go by, there have been five more callers. Hard does not check caller ID. After the fifth caller, he turns off the ringer.

Hard gets another beer and drains it standing at the refrigerator. He belches loudly then notices a piece of stray dog kibble on the floor. Silently berates Vonda Jean for not keeping a cleaner home then remembers Bane is dead and that a few minutes earlier he had been desperately wishing his wife were here. A wave of impotent sadness washes over him and he vows that he will treat Vonda Jean more kindly should she decide to forgive him and return. This thought is interrupted by the doorbell.

A bulky white guy in a uniform is standing there: Don Crenshaw, someone Hard knows from the Highway Patrol. Out of respect, he's got his hat under his arm. Ordinarily, Hard is happy to see a uniform, but he knows *ordinarily* is over. His first thought is that something has happened to Vonda Jean and he feels a quick tightening in his chest. When he sees Crenshaw is holding a piece of paper, he adjusts his thinking.

"You're not here to search the house, are you?"

"It's a restraining order, Chief. From Mary Swain."

Hard grabs the paper out of Crenshaw's hand and quickly scans it.

The Honorable Judge Alma Meserve has signed the order.

If someone had asked Don Crenshaw whether Hard seemed bothered to be on the receiving end of a restraining order, the patrolman would have said that the man took it entirely in stride, thanked him and said goodnight. This is because Hard was able to hide the hot shame that ran riot through his body, burning his tendons, his blood and his bones.

http://WWW.DESERT-MACHIAVELLI.COM

11.4 – 6:12 P.M.

I was looking at some poll numbers and it seemed to the Machiavelli that the Stewardess was coming on strong. I had her picked to win, but right now they're saying it's still too close to call. Late this afternoon she spoke to news crews and attacked the elites, the media, and those who want to make America weak. If she loses, the Machiavelli senses she's going to cultivate her sense of grievance and resentment, then take another crack at getting Randall's seat. Actually, it may not be his seat at that point. I'm hearing rumors that he's going to make a run for the United States Senate. That election's in two years and he would have to declare relatively soon so he could start shaking cash from the trees. But that's not even the biggest piece of local news today, readers. What's the over/under on Hard Marvin being arrested? When you're pulling the lever, you Blogheads should remember that he was campaigning with the Stewardess only a few days ago and now he's suspected of a double murder. The Machiavelli isn't saying she has bad judgment. But if this is the kind of person she associates with while she's campaigning, try to imagine the kind of person she'll associate with in Washington. Can Randall Duke, the former Army bomb technician, defuse the ordnance that is Mary Swain?

CHAPTER THIRTY-FOUR

The master bath is Kendra's domain and she regards it from the large white sunken tub inlaid with Spanish tiles. Six massage jets shoot powerful streams of water toward her submerged body as she gazes at the twin porcelain sinks with brushed steel fixtures, the large shower with steam capacity, and the bidet she had insisted on. Here, she has whiled away relaxed hours. But she is hardly relaxed right now, despite the dependably therapeutic effects of the warm water thrusting toward her beneath the surface of the bath and the George Winston music wafting out of the iPod dock she has parked on the toilet lid. Were it not for the Ativan she ingested half an hour earlier, Kendra would be thrumming like a jet engine.

Unofficial though it may have been, the prickly law enforcement reality of Jimmy's visit further unsettled her. Although she eventually arrived at the conclusion that he knew nothing, this did little to ameliorate her anxiety since a female police detective called a few hours later and scheduled an interview for tomorrow.

The area of second thoughts is a bad neighborhood into which Kendra is unwilling to voluntarily venture, so she is trying to stop ruminating on Nadine's fate. The effort is not going well. Nadine had slipped into that fourth dimension occupied by ex-lovers who might have played a central role in her life at one time but were now consigned to a dim corner of the memory bank. That she has burst forth with all the subtly of a Mardi

Gras float is becoming an ongoing source of consternation. So as Kendra lies in the bath, she tries to stuff Nadine back into the place she occupied prior to the meeting at Melvyn's. But she refuses to go back there. While Nadine herself has become a void, this does nothing to vitiate the power of her memory, or her spirit, or whatever it is that is causing the disquiet Kendra is experiencing.

Soaping her arms for the third time, Kendra assures herself that the United States House of Representatives needs Randall. If Nadine had the poor judgment to threaten his position, why should Kendra worry about it? Guilt is as pointless as the Pope in Tel Aviv. She will move on. Eventually. She's not sure how. But she will. This is what Kendra is thinking as she climbs out of the tub and dries herself with a thick towel.

The bathroom scale. As forbidding as Dracula's castle. Unerringly accurate, it beckons her, dares her to get on and confront the ramifications of her body mass. Pushing thoughts of Nadine away she considers her ass. The relationship Kendra has to her weight is fraught and has only become more complicated since she began suspecting her daughter might have an eating disorder. She doesn't want to set a bad example by being weight-obsessed, but worse than a bad example is being fat. Now she steps on to the digital scale and stares at the numbers as they scramble and then come to rest. It is with a combination of satisfaction laced with deep unease that she realizes she's dropped three pounds since yesterday. She suspects this precipitous weight loss is attributable to stress she is feeling as a result of the series of events her actions have set in motion. She considers the possibility that regret might be infecting her system and it might flower into something far more discomfiting at a later date.

The windows of Randall and Kendra's ground floor bedroom are open and a dry breeze rustles the diaphanous white curtains. Randall, dressed in loose, cotton pajamas is propped up on a pile of pillows, half glasses on the end of his nose, eyes focused on a personal reading device. The soft glow of a bedside lamp creates a nimbus of light around him. He does not look up when Kendra enters, her face shiny from skin cream, hair slick with moisture. She has put on a matching pink satin camisole and sleeping shorts. Kendra arranges the pillows, lays back, stares at the ceiling and waits for Randall to say something. After a few seconds go by, she looks over and sees him scrolling down.

Finally, Randall says: "I'd pay to find out who this Desert Machiavelli guy is,"

"Maxon couldn't find out?"

"No flippin idea. The other day he called me another in a long line of snake oil slinging shit peddlers." Kendra isn't sure how to respond to that so she asks him how it went on the campaign trail today. Randall tells her Maxon showed him the latest poll numbers and the election is too close to call.

She assures him he will win but he does not respond, just continues to read. Lowering her voice to where it is little more than a rattle in her throat, Kendra says, "Tell me no one is going to jail."

"Unlikely."

"Have you talked to Jimmy since he was here?"

"Me hassling him about coming to see you will only make him wonder what we've got going on."

Again, she waits for him to say something, to reassure her, to quiet the racket in her head that has been building since she climbed out of the bath ten minutes earlier.

Again, he is no help.

"Doesn't this affect you at all?"

"I compartmentalize."

"Could you at least put down what you're reading for a second and talk to me?"

Making a show of placing the reading device aside, Randall

focuses on his wife's cream-smeared face. "Maybe the situation didn't go exactly the way we wanted it to but nothing's going to happen. I promise."

"How am I supposed to sleep?"

"Are we out of Ativan?"

"I already took four today. And I almost drank an entire bottle of wine tonight. Is that safe?"

"I think a horse tranquilizer's safe for you tonight."

"But the police . . . "

"You're a person who went on a Mexican vacation with someone who was killed in a random act of violence. There's nothing to connect you to what happened to that poor girl. Nothing at all. Be yourself. They'll love you. And don't forget to ask the detectives if they're voting for me."

Tired of lying on his side staring at the wall, Jimmy gets out of bed a few minutes before midnight and turns on his computer. Over the past few days he's photographed a Cocker Spaniel, a Labrador Retriever, and several mixed breeds and he uploads their pictures from his cell phone into his laptop, prints them out and places them in the Book of Dogs as Bruno watches from the corner. The work calms him down but it doesn't make him any sleepier. He draws a glass of water from the tap and sits on the couch. Thinks about turning on the television, but decides against it. Drops his face into his hands and rubs his temples. Feels the day's growth of stubble against his soft palms. Maybe he'll grow a beard. The Desert Hot Springs Police Department has regulations against that but he doesn't think the D.A.'s office does. He'll have to ask Oz Spengler. Wonders why he's thinking about beards, never been a beard guy before. Is it a disguise, a yearning for a new identity? Or is he just too lazy to shave? No, it's not that. He's not lazy, he tells himself. He may have a lot of faults, but sloth isn't one of them.

He needs to get away. He could quit his job, leave the desert, get out of California and start somewhere new. It looks to Jimmy like Hard Marvin isn't going to get that chance. Jimmy knows Hard to be the human equivalent of a cactus but doesn't think he has murder in him. Why would Hard, the man in law enforcement for over twenty years, have left a trail of breadcrumbs to his door? Hard no nuclear physicist, probably can't fill out a Soduku puzzle as far as Jimmy can tell. But, still. Yes, revenge is a plausible motive here, Hard on the warpath over his dead dog. But to kill that woman? And the clerk?

The path from Hard leads to Randall, the only other person who could possibly benefit from the crime scene at the Super #1. Jimmy did not believe Randall to be a moral paragon, but neither did he think him capable of engineering what had occurred that night. It is nonetheless curious that Kendra's friend was found dead right before an election. The encounter with Kendra only piqued his curiosity. She looked terrible, drawn and jittery. Was this a normal reaction to the death of an ex-friend? And how close were the two women?

Jimmy bears no love for Hard, yet his essential sense of fairness gives him a rooting interest in seeing that justice is done. If meditation is supposed to bring about clarity then it's done the job. When it comes to Hard, Jimmy clearly sees one thing: he despises the man. And he takes a certain pleasure in envisioning Hard's confinement in a max prison. The tough guy would probably spend the rest of his life in protective custody for fear of being simultaneously disemboweled and raped by a massive shank-wielding fiend already serving consecutive life terms for butchering his relatives with an axe. Unless his lawyer could prove he didn't do it, a difficult task given that he had more or less told Nadine he was going to kill her a day before she turned up dead. It would be so easy to sit back and let the train pull out of the station with Hard on board, so easy.

Although it is now the middle of the night, Jimmy has the urge to communicate with Bodhi Colletti. He logs on to his computer. Behind tired eyes, in the frontal cortex of his brain fireworks of gratitude quietly explode when he realizes she is on-line.

AIM IM with DharmaGirl@gmail.com11.4 – 11:58 P.M.

Jimmy Duke

Hi Bodhi. Is this a good time to chat? How are you?

DharmaGirl@gmail.com

Thanks for asking—I'm ok and am happy to chat with you.

Jimmy Duke

So here's my question—there was a double murder that happened here over the weekend. It's not my case but I can't stop thinking about it. When I try to meditate, that's all I think about. How can I stop this?

DharmaGirl@gmail.com

We've talked about this before—meditation isn't about getting rid of things—trying to get rid of a thought, an emotion, a physical sensation that isn't the point. The point is to bring a gentle awareness to what's happening in your mind and body, if you're able to do that then a few very interesting and important things start to happen

Jimmy Duke

Is it good or bad that I care about this situation? And how can I stop from caring?

DharmaGirl@gmail.com

I wish that I had a simple answer for you—did you ever read The Angry Buddhist?

Jimmy Duke

What's that?

DharmaGirl@gmail.com

It's a book that was written by a guy a lot like you. The author was westerner, a divorced guy, problems with his family, nothing had any meaning for him and this made him frustrated and angry. He looked everywhere, tried every religion and spiritual practice he never got any closer to sorting it out and this made him more and more angry. But he didn't give up. He found teacher after teacher and he always asked the same question and none of the answers were satisfactory. It took him years but he finally met this one Buddhist teacher and when he asked this guy the question, the teacher said Googolplex. What the teacher was trying to convey was that there is an infinite number of answers to this question, and that the answer that the angry guy wanted could be found inside of him, and not inside of any teacher because the answer is different for everyone.

Jimmy Duke

So the answer is a non-answer?

DharmaGirl@gmail.com

The answer is a process it's not an absolute—

Jimmy Duke

Okay, riddle me this: how is it possible to practice non-attachment if you have a moral perspective on the world? How do you not attach to what you think is good?

DharmaGirl@gmail.com

The answer lies in a way of being in the world where you see the connections between everything, you see that we're not separate, you see the whole. Non-attachment doesn't mean that you don't have discernment—that you can't tell whether one action is more or less wholesome than another.

Jimmy Duke

What is the way of the dharma when you think someone close to you might be involved in a serious crime?

DharmaGirl@gmail.com

Only you know that. The answer is already here right inside of you—you just need to clear your perspective a bit to find it.

Jimmy Duke

That kind of sounds like a cheesy movie line.

DharmaGirl@gmail.com

Profundity can be found in the strangest places. Everyone makes fun of fortune cookies. I don't know why.

Jimmy Duke

Last question: What would Buddha do?

DharmaGirl@gmail.com

Buddha would practice beginner's mind. Remember when I told you about that? Buddha would take off his shoes and socks, put on a pair of sweatpants, and sit in a quiet place with as few distractions as possible—always mindful he would breathe in, always mindful he would breathe out and that process would take him—did take him—wherever it was he had to go and bring him into a direct experience with all his demons, with all his strengths and with the answers to all of his questions.

Jimmy Duke

You make it sound easy. I'll meditate on that.

DharmaGirl@gmail.com

Try to rest in a moment of emptiness with nothing but curiosity and compassion to guide you.

Jimmy logs off and thinks about his conversation with Bodhi for a few minutes. Then he gets the best night's sleep he has had in months. When he wakes up he's not sure this represents the end of suffering to which the Second Noble Truth refers.

But it's a start.

MONDAY, NOVEMBER 5

T he day before the polls open and Maxon can barely contain himself. Election Day is like a massive shot of heroin for a junkie. He wakes at dawn and dressed in his pajamas and a green silk robe puts a pot of coffee on. At his kitchen table he checks the Internet while he waits for it to brew. The first thing he reads is the Machiavelli's blog where the speculation about Hard Marvin's arrest gets his hopes up. Then he breezes through the political news on the websites of the big dailies and quickly checks his stocks.

The sun is barely over the horizon and the light from the louvered windows creates a pleasingly geometric play of soft shadows on the kitchen wall. He goes to the refrigerator and takes a carton of eggs out. He'll scramble a couple and make some toast when he's had his first cup of coffee. The last polls showed Randall with a slight lead, but fell within the margin of error. Maxon briefly entertains the idea that his man could lose. It would be surprising but not unprecedented. Mary Swain is an unusual opponent. She has something ineffable, something Maxon deeply admires: her ability to connect with ordinary people. Randall has it too, but he's been distracted lately. Maxon could hardly blame him, though. Things popped up that you couldn't anticipate. How well a politician dealt with the unexpected; that was what prolonged a career. One survives turning up in a hooker's black book, another gets re-elected after a car accident kills a woman with whom he was returning from a tryst. Yet padding the office budget and siphoning the excess end the career of a less deft official. You have to be light on your feet.

Maxon is about to crack an egg when the doorbell rings. When he opens the front door, Jimmy Duke asks if he can spare a moment. Maxon notes what he's wearing, dark slacks, coat and tie. This is a work call.

Jimmy apologizes for stopping by so early in the morning. Maxon tells him not to worry about it, offers a cup of coffee. Jimmy accepts and the two of them sit at the kitchen table. Maxon hits the sleep button on his laptop, inclines the screen at a forty-five degree angle to the keyboard and smiles at Jimmy, who says nothing. He doesn't touch his coffee either. A full thirty seconds pass. Maxon feels Jimmy's eyes on him and knows he cannot look away since the other man might think he is not able to meet his gaze. He could pretend to be distracted—this is, after all, the day before the election and there are countless details to be dealt with—but whatever it is Jimmy wants, it is better that he address it right now.

Finally, Maxon says: "I'd love to sit here all day."

His relief is palpable when the visitor begins speaking.

"I don't want to lean on Randall right now but I need to tell you something." Jimmy pauses here, makes sure he has Maxon's full attention. "I know he wouldn't blow his nose without running it by you."

"You flatter me. Your brother's his own man."

"Yeah, well, I'm not saying he was involved in the Nadine Never business, but having her dead didn't hurt him, did it?" Jimmy can't possibly know anything, can he? Has he gotten something out of Dale? The thought occurs to Maxon that he should have shipped the youngest Duke brother out of town the moment the plan went off the rails. "And I'd appreciate you don't play dumb since I know Randall and you most likely already discussed it."

"Did you really just say that?"

"I'm saying Randall is lucky, he's always been lucky, and he probably thinks his luck's gonna hold."

"Jimmy, it's nice having this visit, but I'm not really sure why you're here."

"If you know anything about what happened to Nadine Never, you ought to think about telling me now." Maxon looks at Jimmy as if he's lost his mind. Although he has attempted to convey the idea that this line of inquiry is completely out of bounds Jimmy presses on. "If there's any kind of . . . I don't want to say conspiracy, you understand, because that's kind of a heavy word, but if you know anything and we find that out . . . " He doesn't bother to finish the thought.

Maxon stares at him. His gaze is steady. He feels his heart rate increase. The residual taste of coffee in his mouth is bitter. Then he quietly says: "Your brother saved your ass once already. He is a member of the United States Congress. That police chief killed those people, Jimmy. Is there something wrong with you?"

"We already know Nadine Never communicated with Kendra in the past week."

Maxon looks away from Jimmy, shakes his head. His eyes pan the kitchen, the neat counters, the gleaming appliances, everything in perfect order.

"So you think there was a conspiracy to murder the woman? Jimmy, that is so ridiculous I don't know what to say."

Maxon notices the way the light from the louvered windows is rendered as bars on the kitchen table. Jimmy's coffee sits in front of him, untouched. Maxon senses that Jimmy is waiting to see if he will elaborate. He chooses not to. Why protest too much?

"You don't have to say anything. You can take your chances. The police like Marvin for the murders. He threatens the victim, she turns up dead, circumstantial evidence wrapped around his neck like a damn noose."

"But you don't think he did it?"

"No one's that thick."

"You think that's going to be Marvin's defense?"

"I don't know what strategy his lawyer's going to pursue. I'm telling you for your own edification." Maxon nods. He's waiting for Jimmy to bring this to a close. He'd like to throw him out, but that would likely be taken the wrong way. "Let me ask you a question."

"Go right ahead."

"Do you think anyone could be that stupid?"

"Anything's possible."

"The detectives are gonna take Kendra's temperature. We'll see how she does."

"Jimmy, this is ludicrous." Again, Jimmy just stares at Maxon, waiting. "I have a lot to do today, so unless there's something else to discuss . . . "

"When you talk to Randall, I want you to keep one thing in mind: he'll kick you to the curb in a second. I'm not saying Randall's involved, and I'm not saying there's a conspiracy. I'm just giving you the benefit of my professional advice."

Maxon walks Jimmy to the door, opens it for him. The smile he delivers is practiced and empty. "The victory party's at the Cahuilla Casino. Come celebrate."

Jimmy emits a hollow laugh as Maxon closes the door behind him. In the kitchen he opens a bottle of water and takes four quick gulps. Then he showers and gets dressed. He skips breakfast since his appetite has vanished.

As Maxon is leaving, he hears a voice behind him, calling his name. It's Dale. He has rolled himself out of the guest bedroom. Seated in his chair in his underwear, he regards Maxon suspiciously. "You leaving without saying goodbye?"

"I was about to stick my head in your room. I thought you liked privacy. You missed Jimmy."

"What you think, I'd come out here and say hello? No need to talk to him right now." Dale sounds no more bitter than usual. Maxon braces himself for whatever it is he plans to ask for next. "How am I supposed to get to work?"

"I think you better take the next couple of days off, maybe just hang around here and watch television. You can call in sick. There's food in the refrigerator."

"And the money?"

"We're going to have to wait until the election's over, okay?"

It is almost impossible for Maxon to comprehend that after what Dale has engineered, he has the audacity to hound Maxon for money to bail himself out of his self-created mess. Maxon supposes that he would have to bring this financial matter to Randall eventually, but not for a few days yet. In the meantime, he needs Dale to remain scarce. The delaying tactic works and Dale agrees to tell his boss at the RV dealership the campaign needs him today. When Maxon leaves, Dale is seated in front of the television in the living room, a bowl of cereal on his lap.

Early afternoon and Kendra is in the powder room near the front door of her house checking her makeup. With a practiced hand she has applied foundation, berry stain lipstick, and a touch of blue-gray eye shadow. She reaches into her makeup bag for a mascara pencil and deftly applies it. If she is able to cry, the mascara will run. She is counting on that.

The yellow sundress she wears has been selected to convey respectful cooperation without too much formality. Her delicately painted maroon toenails are set off against gold thong sandals that she hopes are not too flashy. Her hair is arranged in a chignon. She weighed herself again this morning and has dropped another pound. It is with no small degree of satisfaction that she imagines herself looking thinner in Randall's victory pictures.

Kendra is fixing a tiny smear on her cheek when the doorbell rings. Randall had told her it would look less suspicious to a couple of police detectives if she did not have a lawyer present during their visit, so she is alone in the house when she opens the door for Detectives Cali Pasco and Arnaldo Escovedo. Detective Pasco had called her a day earlier and asked if she and her partner might drop by after lunch. Kendra had inquired whether the detective could tell her what this was about and was informed that there was an ongoing murder investigation and they hoped she could shed some light on the victim. After feigning what she hopes is the correct degree of concern, Kendra tells her visitors she will do whatever she can to help.

Now she leads them to the living room. As the detectives admire the view of the San Jacinto Mountains Kendra asks if they'd like some iced tea but the offer is declined. She excuses herself to go to the kitchen and pours a glass for herself. Upon her return she gestures to the steel and vinyl sofa, and the detectives take seats next to one another. Kendra sits on an Eames chair perpendicular to them. She leans back crossing one thigh over the other, her elbow resting on the back of the chair. The picture of relaxation she paints is attributable more to the two large glasses of Zinfandel with which she fortified herself prior to the detectives' arrival, than any actual sense of ease.

They make small talk for what feels to Kendra like half an hour but isn't more than a minute, how long have you lived here, isn't the desert beautiful this time of year. Three chatty people. She nods when Detective Escovedo apologizes for dragging her into what he calls "this nasty business."

Jimmy was right. He had done her a favor by visiting. It had been a dress rehearsal.

"Detective Pasco told you about the situation at the convenience store," Detective Escovedo says. Kendra nods, affects what she hopes is the correct level of sympathetic, non-neurotic concern.

"How well did you know Nadine Never?"

Kendra inhales through her nostrils. She spent some time considering how to play this question, too. She could be honest. That would help. Her lines would be easier to remember.

"Nadine was my daughter's tennis coach for a few months."

"Was she a good coach?" Detective Escovedo asks.

Kendra says yes, she was. "I didn't know her that long." Kendra entwines her fingers and places her linked hands on her lap. She hopes she is conveying the reticence appropriate to the wife of a Congressman, the exact degree of degradation and chagrin congruent with being involved in something as sordid as a murder investigation, and a sincere desire to perform her civic duty, however painful that might be at this difficult juncture.

"When did you two meet?" Detective Pasco asks.

"Nearly two years ago," she says.

"Did you have a falling out?" Detective Pasco asks.

"No, nothing like that," Kendra says.

"At the time of her death were you still friends?" Pasco again.

"Not really."

"Mind if I ask why not?" Pasco once more.

"We didn't have that much in common."

"But you went to Mexico together," Pasco says.

Kendra wonders if they are expecting a reaction to this revelation. She does not give them one. Instead, she says, "Didn't you ever have a friend and after a while you just kind of stopped being friends?"

"It happens," Detective Escovedo says.

"I have to ask you a personal question," Detective Pasco says, "So I hope you don't get offended."

"I'm a big girl."

"Were you lovers?"

Kendra takes a moment before answering. This is intended to suggest modesty, discretion and most of all embarrassment.

A long pause, then: "Yes." Unsure if they were expecting

her to lie, she had discussed it with Randall and he had advised her to not hide this since they might be able to figure it out anyway and if they caught her in a lie it could indicate a pattern of lying that would not help the cause. "Briefly. I ended it. But I certainly didn't wish anything bad on her."

"Your husband know?" Escovedo.

Kendra allows another lacuna to occur in the conversation, during which she tries to silently convey the ongoing pain in her marriage and the valiant effort she is making to deal with it. From the sympathetic look on the male detective's face, she surmises that this is a good performance.

"That was not a fun conversation."

The detectives pause in their questioning for a moment. Kendra senses they're embarrassed on her behalf. She hopes that will make them more sympathetic to her plight.

"How did the relationship end?" Detective Pasco asks.

"It wasn't a big thing," Kendra says. "We fooled around a few times, went down to Mexico, kind of a mistake."

"Why?" From Escovedo.

"My husband and I were trying to work on our marriage. I deeply regret my conduct."

"And there you are in a murder victim's computer." Escovedo again.

"I guess I'm just lucky," Kendra deadpans. Her voice does not waver. She delivers the line off-handedly, as if rehearsed. Which it is. She knows the detectives are going to establish the parameters of the discussion early and several responses have been readied. The one she delivered is the most tossed-off. She does not want to project an uncaring mien—two people, after all, have been murdered—but insouciance strikes her as the strongest tactical position to take. The two detectives exchange a glance without moving their heads.

"The whole thing only lasted a month."

"And you never saw her again?" Pasco.

Kendra has given some thought to denying the recent meeting had taken place but knows there are witnesses and telephone records. She composes herself, lets them know this is painful but she is forging ahead in the interests of justice.

"Nadine called me on October 30th. I know because I checked my cell phone to make sure," and although Kendra wants to add *I'm sure you did, too* she restrains the impulse. "We met for a drink at Melvyn's. She told me she had some kind of incriminating emails from the police chief in Desert Hot Springs, Chief Marvin, and did I want to show them to my husband so he could use them in his campaign."

"Why did she think that could help your husband?" Detective Escovedo asks.

"He was working for Mary Swain and I guess Nadine thought something like that might embarrass her."

"What did you say?" Detective Pasco asks.

"That Randall wouldn't be interested."

"Did she tell you anything else?" Escovedo.

Kendra hopes they think she's deciding whether or not to come clean but she's already made the decision. This is just stage management. "She told me . . . and I couldn't believe this . . . that she might try to embarrass Chief Marvin in public."

"Did she threaten you in any way?" Escovedo again.

"Absolutely not. She had nothing against Randall or me. She was angry with the police chief. She told me they had an affair."

"What did you do then?" Detective Pasco asks.

"I left the restaurant and drove home."

"Did she contact you again?" Detective Escovedo asks.

"She sent me a video of her dancing naked. It was mortifying. My daughter could have seen it."

"Do you think she was implying anything?" Detective Pasco asks.

"Honestly, I have no idea what that was about. Nadine was a pretty unhappy woman. She seemed kind of unbalanced."

Detective Escovedo asks: "Did you tell your husband?"

"Immediately."

"And what did he say?"

"He said it's not a threat so . . . "

"It was a threat," Detective Pasco says.

"He thought maybe she just wanted to start seeing me again."

The detectives look at each other. Kendra takes a sip of her iced tea. She clinks the ice cubes in the tall glass.

"Is that what you thought?" Detective Pasco asks.

"I was just completely weirded out by it."

"Why didn't you report it?" Detective Escovedo asks.

"Honestly?"

"We'd like that," Detective Escovedo says.

The icy plunge: "It's nearly Election Day and this was not going to help my husband. I don't know if you've heard but he's in a tight race."

The pair is silent for a moment. Kendra hopes this is caused by shock at her forthrightness. It's remarkable, she reflects, what a powerful weapon the truth can be, as long as it is used sparingly.

"But when someone is making veiled threats," Detective Pasco says "It's always good to notify the police."

"You're right," Kendra says. "We probably should have. But it's impossible to control leaks. I don't mean to imply you two . . . " Detective Escovedo shakes his head, of course not! "But there are people who'd probably like to embarrass my husband. You understand."

Now the tears arrive exactly on schedule, and not off a specific revelation, but as a result of the accumulated indignities and general stress, tears announcing that this woman, this baton twirler, singer of pop tunes and chirpy political wife has taken all she can take from these messengers from a far shadier world than the one in which she dwells. The detectives pause.

They're accustomed to waterworks. Detective Pasco reaches for a packet of tissues she keeps in her pants pocket for these occasions and hands it to Kendra who removes one and dabs her eyes, careful to allow her mascara to run a little. Between sniffles she says, "When I learned it was Nadine, I flipped out."

They wait to see if Kendra will pick up the thread but the only thing forthcoming at this moment is sniffles. Detective Escovedo presses ahead: "Did you have any contact after she sent you the video?" Kendra shakes her head no.

"Nadine was a good person," she manages to choke out. "Just confused."

"She didn't deserve what she got," Detective Pasco says, "And neither did that poor clerk."

Kendra collects herself, blows her nose. "Do you have any idea who might have done it?" It doesn't bother her that she's heard that line in a hundred television shows. She expects the detectives have heard it, too.

Detective Pasco informs her they have a few leads. Kendra tells her interlocutors she'd like to help them any way she can and they should not hesitate to call. Detective Pasco tells her they'll be in touch. As they stand to leave, Detective Escovedo asks: "Do you have any idea who killed those two people?"

Kendra quickly responds "Of course not." Wonders if she should have played it differently, been quiet for a moment as if stunned by the question. But her voice remains strong and her gaze sure. "Why would I?"

"You never know," Detective Pasco says

Kendra smiles as if to say I know you're just doing your job and all of us want to catch whatever monster did this. After showing her visitors out and gently closing the door behind them Kendra pours a third glass of Zinfandel and sits at the kitchen table. She reflects on her performance and concludes it went well. For not a single moment did she feel compromised in any way. The house is quiet. Her pulse rate feels normal. Realizing she does not actually need the wine, Kendra pours the contents of the glass back in the bottle and places the bottle in the refrigerator.

Driving to school to pick up Brittany, she examines her reflection in the rearview mirror and after daubing her eye makeup with a tissue, concludes she is holding up relatively well. Then the gossamer membrane that barely restrains her roiling emotions bursts and she begins to sob with such force she has to pull to the side of the road. She thinks about Nadine: whether she had a family—they'd never talked about it—whether a death notice would appear in the paper to recount her life as something other than a murder victim, who would claim the body and if there would be a funeral. If there were some way to find out she would. And send money to defray the expenses. It was the least she could do.

At school Brittany asks why she's late and Kendra says a friend of hers had a problem and she was helping her deal with it. Brittany spends the entire ride banging away on her computer and doesn't look up. For once, Kendra is happy her daughter does not want to talk.

CHAPTER THIRTY-SIX

S eated in the window of Palm Springs Koffe on North Palm Canyon Drive, Jimmy waits for Cali and Arnaldo. As a personal favor, they've agreed to brief him on the investigation. He's got several work files he needs to review, drops in the stream of endless domestic complaints. Jimmy thinks there would be a lot fewer failed marriages if a visit to the District Attorney's office were mandated for all couples considering the nuptial state. They could see the sheer volume of former spouses gunning for each other and perhaps reconsider their own decisions. But he knows that won't happen. People are going to do what they're going to do.

While he waits, he checks his phone messages. There's one from his landlord asking him whether he wants to extend his lease on the trailer and another from a robocall service reminding him to vote. The third message is from Coral, the woman who works at the animal control center in Indio. No idea what she wants, that's a call he can return later. He's on his second iced coffee when his colleagues arrive. Cali sits with Jimmy while Arnaldo orders their coffees at the counter.

"Did you know your sister-in-law knew one of the victims?"

"She told me." He doesn't mention his visit with Kendra.

"We talked to her," Cali says. "She's a piece of work."

Arnaldo joins them, placing Cali's coffee in front of her.

"Butter wouldn't melt in her mouth," Arnaldo says, settling into a chair. "This is turning into the case of the century. Congressman's wife and chief of police both banging a murder victim? Someone should write a book about it."

"I want Anne Hathaway to play me in the movie," Cali says. She and Arnaldo laugh. Jimmy doesn't find any of this amusing. Maybe if he was being allowed to work the case he would.

"I like Hard for this," Arnaldo says.

Jimmy nods, looks at Cali. Pushes aside his resentment for a moment and remembers the other night, the way she moved the strand of hair out of her eyes when she was looking at the *Book of Dogs*.

"Is that what you think?"

"I'm with Arnaldo."

"Glenn Korver's with us," Arnaldo says. Jimmy looks at Cali. She nods. And now it starts, the tightening of the muscles in the neck and upper back, the shallowness of breath, the pressure in his head. Why does he care? Why is he still attached? Where is the freedom from the craving to matter in the world?

Breathe in one, two. Breathe out, three, four.

"Sorry you couldn't work the case with us," Arnaldo says.

Cali says nothing. She offers a what-can-I-do arch of the eyebrows.

Jimmy rises, nods and walks out. Arnaldo calls after him in a bantering tone but Jimmy does not turn around. He's not even tempted. On his way to the truck, he passes a blonde cocker spaniel, a miniature dachshund, and a pair of black standard poodles. He does not ask for permission to photograph any of them. He will regret this as soon as his emotions are back under control.

Although the motor of the pickup is running and the air conditioner is on the vehicle is still parked in a lot just off of North Palm Canyon Drive. Jimmy had thrown his meditation cushion in the back seat today on the off chance he would have some time to try sitting in the desert. Instead, he had spent his first five minutes back in the front seat pounding it with his fist like a punching bag. When he was through channeling his copious frustration, he leaned back, breathed deeply with his eyes closed. He had tried to access the state of beginner's mind Bodhi had told him about but found it to be a territory into which he could not cross. Meditation is fine, but when it comes to taking the edge off, there is nothing like beating the shit out of something. He has been visualizing Arnaldo and Cali floating away in a pink bubble and the image is a balm to his scabrous feelings.

But what had he logically expected them to conclude? Was he meant to have made a plea on behalf of his brother's culpability? They would have looked at him as if he were insane, as if he were discharging some age-old fraternal pathology. And on what had he based his conclusion? It's based on what he knows of his brother and how he operates and maybe this is an extreme version but it is the logical conclusion of the Randall Duke no prisoners ethos. All of this would have been impossible for Jimmy to credibly convey. And he still isn't certain he believes it himself. But he knows it's a possibility and as long as he believes this to be so, he will not sign on to the prosecution of his former boss.

Jimmy's in no mood to drive to the office. He still can't get his mind around Hard Marvin as the shooter but with nothing to tie anyone else to the crime there isn't a lot he can do except keep his eyes open for dogs to photograph. With this in mind, he decides to stop by the animal control center and see what Coral wants.

The sounds of muffled barking greet him when he steps into the cool air of the low cinderblock building. A short young Latina with a nose ring in her left nostril stands behind the counter in the reception area. Her curly hair is cut short and a gray smock fits snugly on her stocky frame. A nametag reads "Esmerelda." Jimmy asks if Coral is around and Esmerelda shouts toward the back of the building. A few seconds later, Coral emerges through a gray metal door drying her hands on a soiled white towel. She's short and stocky, too, like Esmerelda, and for all he knows they could be related.

"Just the man I was looking for," Coral says. Jimmy nods hello. "You still doing that book of dogs you told me about last time I saw you?" Jimmy says that he is. "You got a camera?" Jimmy tells her he does. "Then I got a good one for you." Coral excuses herself, says she'll be back in a minute. Jimmy turns around and leans against the counter, gazes toward the entrance. Like a pet grooming establishment, albeit one with a considerably less happy outcome for its denizens, the place exudes an animal funk, and it is not unpleasant to Jimmy.

"You writing a book about dogs?" Esmerelda asks.

Turning to face her, Jimmy says: "I take their pictures is all."

"Why you want to do that?"

Where to begin? The threat to Hard Marvin that got him thrown off the police force. The diminishment he experienced at the departure of his ex-wife. The insidious irritation that pervaded his life, that ate away at his ability to function and led to the mandating of anger management classes. But what he says is: "Helps me relax."

"I take pictures of all the dogs come here, wouldn't never look at them. Couldn't stop crying."

What do you say to that, Jimmy wonders. The woman works in a place where they put down a small city of dogs each year and she's emotional? A moment later the door leading to the back of the shelter opens and Coral returns holding a squirming, rodent-like creature the size of a large rabbit. A Chihuahua. "You got one of these in your book?" Jimmy shakes his head as the dog continues to writhe in Coral's arms. "Hate to do this one but that's way the cookie crumbles, right boy?" Coral addressing the dog. Then she pinches the fur on his neck like they're pals, never mind she's planning to kill him if he doesn't get rescued. Jimmy stares at the dog, and senses that the animal knows exactly what's going on. He reaches out to scratch the dog's head and the dog nips his finger. The curses that fly from Jimmy's mouth make both women laugh.

"Fella's got some personality, I'll tell you that," Coral says.

Jimmy pulls out his cell phone as Coral places the dog on the counter. The animal's nails click on the burnt-orange Formica surface in a mad tap dance as he tries to run over the side. Coral holds him in place by sticking a finger through his collar as Jimmy aims his camera-phone, centering the dog in the frame.

"You know that girl got murdered at the convenience store the other day?" Coral asks. "Little booger was hers."

This brings Jimmy up short. He takes the picture then turns to Coral. "Where'd they find him?"

"Stuffed in a drawer, I heard." Jimmy snaps another picture. "Cops brought him in. His dog tag says 'Diablo.'" Jimmy eyes the dog, still straining to leap off the counter. Diablo has no plans to go gently into that good night.

"Think anyone's gonna want him?" Jimmy asks.

"Adults are your hardest placements. I'd say this guy's six or seven years old, so his chances don't look so good."

"Tough luck," Jimmy says.

"No shit," says Esmeralda.

Coral says, "How about you, Jimmy?"

"How about me, what?"

"You know anyone might want this angry little son of a bitch?"

"Maybe for target practice," Jimmy says, taking a closer look at his finger, where a dot of blood has appeared.

TUESDAY, NOVEMBER 6
ELECTION DAY

Chapter Thirty-seven

Jimmy has just returned to the District Attorney's Indio office after having interviewed a complainant at the Whispering Sands trailer park whose husband owes her nearly twenty-three thousand dollars in spousal support and has not been heard from in six months. Perspiration dampens his short-sleeved plaid shirt and there's a two-inch high pile of paperwork in the in-box. He gets started on it but his mind keeps wandering to Hard, to Randall and Kendra, to Oz Spengler, to Glenn Korver, and to Cali and whether anything's going to happen between them. Jimmy's not sure he wants a girlfriend in his life right now. And after the way things went down with the investigation, he's not confident they can recreate whatever it was they had shared that evening anyway.

Jimmy drinks several cups of coffee. He reflects on his parents and the simple faith they shared. Truly, he wishes he had that to cling to. Then, seated at his office desk, he has the following IM exchange with Bodhi Colletti.

Jimmy Duke
Is the dharma something to believe in, like a religion?
DharmaGirl@gmail.com
it's something you experience, and once you get a hint of the freedom inherent in the experience, you become motivated to practice more to develop the capacity to extend the experience for longer periods, even during difficult times in your life.

At first he is disappointed with Bodhi Colletti's answer. He wishes the dharma were something in which he could believe for the simple reason that belief is easy. If he could believe in something it would solve so many of his problems. If the dharma can be for someone who believes in nothing, it could be exactly what he is looking for. It's not that he believes in nothing. At the very least, he has an abiding belief in Jimmy Ray Duke. He is not sure how this squares with the Buddhist concept of no-self that he has recently discovered. At some point in the future, he will have to ask

In the waiting area an eye-catching woman is talking to the receptionist. She's wearing white short-shorts, red pumps and a clinging sleeveless black top with a scooped neckline that shows off several inches of tanned cleavage. Her long dark hair is parted in the middle and she wears large black-rimmed, designer knock-off sunglasses. He immediately makes her for an exotic dancer.

The receptionist, a middle-aged Latina with short dark hair and large gold hoop earrings turns to Jimmy, who is on his way to the bathroom. "This lady says she has information on the murders at the convenience store. That's Glenn Korver's case, right?"

"That's right," Jimmy says.

"Mr. Korver's not here right now," the receptionist tells the woman.

Jimmy introduces himself and extends his hand to the woman. "Mr. Korver's one of my colleagues." Her handshake is light, airy, like a cloud. He notices her French manicure.

"I'm Princess," she says. He asks her what she wants to talk to his colleague about and tells him she has information germane to the investigation. Because Jimmy can't face more paperwork, and because he would like to have sex with Princess despite how unethical that would be, and most of all because he wants to be working on this case, he suggests they go around the corner for coffee, his treat.

As they walk to the coffee shop Jimmy notices the outline of the red thong she's wearing through the fabric stretched across her perfect bottom. It's impossible to place her barely discernible accent but he wants to go there and lie on the beach under the shade of a palm tree while Princess, wearing exactly what she has on now, lovingly performs a cornucopia of sex acts on him. In the midst of this reverie he wonders if the Buddha ever had to deal with someone like Princess.

The coffee shop is a chain. Princess has taken a table in the back and she smiles at Jimmy in a practiced way as he places a coffee with cream and two sugars on the table in front of her. Her teeth are large and white. They are seated in the back and at mid-morning, the place is empty. A slightly overweight girl with an inch of dark roots in her lank blonde hair wipes the counter with a rag.

Princess looks around the coffee shop. When Jimmy catches her in profile he clocks the bruise surrounding her left eye. She says: "Can there be a reward in a case where someone got accused but now there's information saying someone else did the crime?"

"Why do you ask?" Wonders what exactly she's talking about and hopes it's not something dull and domestic.

"Do you have a tree in your backyard that grows money?" Jimmy shakes his head no, says he wishes he did. "Me neither. So how do you find out if there's rewards?"

"You can research this on-line, you know," Jimmy hoping she gets to the point. Despite his attraction, the man has his limits.

"You know that case where they say maybe some police chief did two murders?" Jimmy's ears prick up like a Doberman's. He is no longer thinking of sex with Princess.

"Yeah?"

"That police chief, he didn't kill those people."

"Really?"

She takes a sip of her coffee. Jimmy looks away, not wanting to pressure her. A pair of retirees, a husband and wife, is now seated quietly at a window table. Princess dips her head and lowers her voice. "A couple of days ago, those two people at the convenience store? That was Odin and another guy."

"Who's Odin?"

"My husband," she says.

The scenario where the aggrieved female looking for revenge lays something on the male's doorstep is one with which Jimmy is familiar so he looks directly into her eyes and says: "He knock you around?"

"You a social worker?"

"Just trying to figure out what's going on."

"His name is Odin Brick, and you need to arrest him."

"Someone's already being charged in that crime."

Princess returns his gaze without blinking. "I'm telling you, they got the wrong guy."

"How come you didn't notify anyone sooner?"

"What, like yesterday? This thing only happened a couple of days ago." Rising, she smoothes her shorts over the inch of her thighs they cover. "I can go to the cops . . . "

"No, no, no . . . wait" he says, grabbing her wrist. "Don't." She bites her lip, hesitates, then she sits back down. Jimmy asks her why she didn't go to the cops in the first place.

"You work for the D.A., right?" Jimmy nods. "I like to watch my cop shows on TV. Don't the cops have to bring it to the D.A, before anything can happen?"

Jimmy tells her that's true. He asks her about Odin, and why she thinks he was involved in the murders, and the story she tells makes him think maybe she's more than an unhappy wife. But when she says this: "The other night he walks in and his face has been shot up. First he tells me it's a hunting accident, like I'm slow. I had to go to the hospital in San Bernardino and say I accidentally shot him"—that's when Jimmy is convinced.

"It wasn't you who shot him?" he says, testing her.

Princess glares across the table. "I should have gone to the cops."

"Easy, Tiger."

Taking out a pen and pad, Jimmy gets Princess to give all of Odin's particulars, full name, address, where he works, who his friends are, what kind of hours he keeps and whether he's armed. When Jimmy asks her if she and Odin are still cohabitating, she says she's at a motel. She's left her son with a friend and she'd like to go get him. This hangs between them for a moment. Jimmy thinks about inviting her to stay in his trailer. Realizes it might not look good. He takes his wallet out and counts six twenties, cleans himself out in the process.

"This should help you out."

"I don't need money."

Impressed, he folds the cash and places it back in his pocket. He assumed she would try to hustle him. "One more thing. What hospital did you say you took him to?"

"Our Lady of Lourdes in San Bernardino."

He asks for her cell phone number and jots it down. Hands her his card, tells her he'll be in touch. Jimmy says goodbye to Princess in front of the coffee shop. As soon as she rounds the corner, he phones Our Lady of Lourdes Hospital to see if her story checks out. When he hears that a man came in with buckshot in his face and a wife who claimed to be the marksman he doesn't bother returning to the office. Jimmy punches a search into his hand held device. The results come up instantly. Odin Brick: Afghanistan vet, busted for assaulting a police officer, sentenced to three years in Calipatria, time off for good behavior. It does not escape his notice that Odin's dates at the prison overlap those of his brother.

As a teenager, Jimmy had gone to the Fontana Speedway a few times to watch the races and even then sensed there was something ridiculous about it, testosterone-choked men driving in circles like they had some kind of obsessive-compulsive disorder. He hasn't been to Fontana in years. The town is an unsightly sprawl of mini-malls and cheaply built houses. Papi's Auto Salvage is on an industrial road a couple of miles from the Speedway. As Jimmy parks his truck, two young Latinos in green jumpsuits and baseball caps are removing an engine from a Chevy four door sedan that has been totaled. They ignore him when he gets out and heads for the office.

The first thing Jimmy notices is an old Pit Bull resting on a filthy pillow. The wall is a collage of naked women taken from girly magazines, a multi-ethnic forest of breasts, shaved pudenda, and perfectly formed derrieres so profuse as to almost be abstract. A wiry Latino with a gray ponytail that flops over a work shirt, greasy jeans and black boots looks up from a ledger.

"Can I help you?" The man's tone is friendly.

Jimmy holds off on badging him. "Does a guy called Odin Brick work here?"

"He owe you money or something?"

"Nothing like that."

"Ain't seen him since last week."

"He quit?"

"Ain't showed up for work, ain't called in sick. Ain't got a job no more, you know? I got a business to run." The man smiles, but he's done talking. Jimmy senses the man wants him gone.

"What kind of guy is he?"

"You a cop?"

"Used to be. Now I work with the District Attorney's office."

"What he do?"

"We're not sure yet, but I want to talk to him."

Jimmy takes out a pad, folds it open and asks the man's name. The man says, "You first," so Jimmy introduces himself and the man tells him his name is Roberto Ayala, but everyone calls him Papi. "I hired Odin 'cause he said he been to Afghanistan to fight with the Marines. Support the troops, right?"

"Any of his friends ever come around?"

"Never saw no one."

Jimmy ponders this as he glances around the office. He focuses on a woman in the collage whose face reminds him of Darleen's. Briefly, his mind flits to his ex-wife and he realizes he doesn't even know where she's living. He turns to the sleeping Pit Bull.

"One last thing. What's the dog's name?"

"That's Gasoline."

"Mind if I take his picture?"

"No problem."

As Jimmy pulls out his cell phone to photograph the dog, he hears a boy yelling "Papi, check this out." Looking over he sees a young Latino kid, maybe twelve, popping a wheelie on a motorized bicycle with high, motorcycle-style handlebars. The engine on the bike is bright red and when the kid pulls up outside the door of the office Jimmy can see it's new.

"Nice bike," Jimmy says to the kid. "Where'd you get it?" Papi glances at Jimmy. Where's this going?

"My uncle gave it to me," the kid says, looking at Papi.

"I used to have one just like it," Jimmy says. "Put the engine in myself." He sees Papi relax a little. "Where'd you get the engine?"

"e-Bay," Papi says. "Stuff they got is amazing."

"Sure is," Jimmy says, nodding. The kid looks at Papi, wondering if he did anything wrong. Papi stares at Jimmy. The Pit Bull stretches but doesn't get up, and Jimmy takes his picture.

"You got a receipt from the e-Bay purchase?" Jimmy says, casual.

"Threw it out," Papi says.

Jimmy nods. "Of course you did." Then, to the kid: "Enjoy the bike."

He returns to his truck, marveling at a world where an auto body business in Fontana can be a chop shop for stolen wheelchairs.

http://WWW.DESERT-MACHIAVELLI.COM
11.6 – 2:17 P.M.

Every November the Machiavelli has his faith in our system restored. It may erode all other days of the year but
Election Day is always a new dawn. Year after year the voters may send the same parade of lying pimps and crooked
whores back to Congress but the beauty of democracy is
that there's always a chance things might improve.
Unfortunately, we in the desert don't have much of an
opportunity to raise the bar today. The incumbent is a hack
who reflects no glory on his constituents. But the challenger? She's not qualified to run a P.T.A meeting much less
walk the hallowed if slightly tainted halls of Congress. She
is a liar, a demagogue, and one of her major local supporters, suspended Desert Hot Springs Chief of Police Harding
Marvin, is in the middle of a murder investigation. I'm no
fan of Duke's, but compared to the Flight Attendant, he is
Nelson Mandela. Today, I will hold my nose and pull the
lever for him.

CHAPTER THIRTY-EIGHT

Odin and House Cat are in a motel room on Highway 16 just outside the town of Victorville at the north-western edge of the Mojave Desert. It's a run-down single story place with a battered sign out front that reads *Cable TV Swimming Pool Vacancy.* Twin beds are covered with musty patterned bedspreads. On the side of the room closest to the window is a table with two matching wood chairs. Littered with fast food wrappers and pizza boxes, the place exudes a locker room fug. The Venetian blinds are drawn, the dark drapes closed and only the flickering light of the television illuminates the shadows.

The previous Saturday Odin had awakened from his drug-induced slumber to discover Princess had abandoned him, taking their son and five thousand dollars in cash. In what he believed to be a particularly cruel gesture, she also absconded with his agoraphobia medication, which left had him scared to leave the house alone. Fearful the police would show up to question him about his treatment for gunshot wounds at the hospital, he immediately called House Cat who drove down in his dented blood red '98 Toyota Corolla to pick him up. Odin didn't want to leave the Impala behind since he thought Princess might come back and steal it, so he convinced his partner to leave the Corolla parked on a nearby street. When House Cat asked Odin why they couldn't just leave the Impala on a nearby street, Odin had replied: Because I think the bitch has superpowers and she'll track it down like a fuckin Indian, that's why.

For the last three days they have been holed up in this room, waiting for Dale to come up with the remainder of the money he owes. Odin lies on the bed sipping a can of soda. House Cat paces as he talks on a cell phone. Neatly dressed in dark pants and a checked shirt, he could be on his way to talk to a loan officer at a bank. Belying the circumstances, his voice is relaxed, even friendly. "This is the fourth message I'm leaving. Today's the day, buddy. I won't threaten you, cause I don't think I need to. You already know what we do." House Cat clicks the phone shut and runs his ringed fingers over his crew cut. Turning to Odin, he says, "Think Dale's gonna have the money?"

"Where's he gonna get it?"

"From whoever it was told him to hire us. Didn't need that lady out of the picture for himself, did he? We're sub-contractors."

"You gonna go down there and talk to him?"

"Am *I*?"

"I ain't leaving the motel room less you get me those meds."

"I'm not talking to Dale alone."

"What are you worried about? He's a damn cripple."

"Maybe he's got a gun. Maybe I walk up to him and he shoots me."

Odin finishes his soda, belches and tosses the empty on the floor. "Get me some Zoloft and I'm your wingman. Until then, I'll lie here and watch ESPN."

"Can't you treat this thing you got with homeopathy, some herbs or something?"

"What, like oregano? I got a diagnosed condition, dude." Odin's eyes steady on the football game. "I need some motherfuckin Zoloft."

Odin rises from the bed and lumbers to the bathroom in his socks, leaving the door open behind him. House Cat sits on one of the chairs, places his elbows on the table and rests his chin on his hands. He's not happy with Odin who is proving to be significantly higher maintenance than he had originally anticipated. There was the call to scoop him up from his home in the Antelope Valley—House Cat had found him curled in a ball on the living room floor—after his wife bolted with the kid and the money. Odin brought his own pillow, which House Cat found peculiar, even after it was explained that a prison psychiatrist had advised having certain familiar objects with him if he was going to be away from home for an extended period of time. On the drive to Victorville Odin had insisted on lying in the backseat covered with a ratty blanket because he claimed it was the only way he could stave off an attack. Then he suggested that since he had been the one to get shot, and now his wife had stolen his share, House Cat should split his own share so Odin wouldn't come out of this with nothing but a shredded face. House Cat is getting tired of dealing with Odin. He's starting to understand why Princess left. Whatever homoerotic attraction existed has dissipated significantly in the wake of three days in this motel room. And now House Cat is supposed to track down Zoloft just so the two of them could make the trip down to Mecca to put the screws to Dale? This is not working for him at all. Where, exactly, is he supposed to get his hands on Zoloft?

"The V.A. Hospital in Los Angeles," Odin says as he returns from the bathroom and once again reclines on the bed. "I'll give you my drivers' license and you tell them you're me."

"There's no resemblance, man." House Cat not bothering to look at him. "No one's gonna believe I'm you, especially if I'm trying to cop prescription drugs."

House Cat would just as soon abandon Odin right here. Too scared to leave, whomever it is that runs this dump would eventually call the police and that would be the end of him. But then House Cat would have to deal with Dale on his own.

Dale: he was wily, no mistake, and wouldn't allow himself to be surprised in his own bed again. No, House Cat would have to get his partner medicated so the two of them could go down to Mecca and collect.

CHAPTER THIRTY-NINE

As the daytime blue seeps from the sky and washes of yellowish pink and vermillion appear on the Eastern horizon Jimmy drives home where he feeds Bane and Diablo—yes, Diablo. The Chihuahua has moved into the trailer. He was not going to abandon the jumpy little bastard to Coral's tender mercies—and slices some garlic and lemon, breads two chicken cutlets, and cooks dinner for himself. When he glances at the clock over the kitchen sink, he sees it's just past eight. The polls close in a little under an hour. He briefly thinks about voting but decides against it.

Later in the evening, Jimmy turns on the news and sees that Randall Duke has been declared the winner, re-elected by less than five hundred votes. This comes as something of a surprise since he thought Mary Swain was going to win. So, apparently, did Mary Swain and she is demanding a recount. An urge arises to throw a hammer through the television screen but he recognizes the flash of anger—At his brothers? At Mary Swain? He doesn't even know—but he recognizes it for the temporary manifestation that it is and so waits for it to abate. In the meantime, he slips the fish tank DVD into the player, turns off the news and settles in to watch the various mollies, tetras, swordtails, and angelfish swim hypnotically back and forth across his television screen.

In the silent glow of the video fish tank, Jimmy reflects that with this election outcome the self-satisfaction level at which Randall exists will not decrease. Still, he finds himself wanting to muss Randall's spray-hard hair and this gets Jimmy wondering about why he can't seem to go two seconds without considering his brothers, and the way their lives resonate with his. It is as if part of him requires the upset they cause. Is he addicted to feeling angry? This had not previously occurred to him. And it strikes him as a serious insight. Never one to traffic in the language of addiction, Jimmy wonders if he is addicted to his own anger the way a smoker comes to depend on the nicotine buzz or the way runners can become addicted to endorphins. Is it actually something he uses as a motor to drive him in his work and life? It would go some of the way to explaining his marriage having gone south—not that Darleen didn't share the blame, but upon recollection, he did seem to be pissed off a lot when she was around—and it was directly related to the end of his tenure at the Desert Hot Springs Police Department. His violent behavior toward criminals had led to Hard mandating the anger management class, and Jimmy's failure to complete the course led to his raised tension with Hard, so when the business with Bruno occurred there was no reservoir of goodwill to fall back on and it had cost him his job. He concludes that, yes, there probably is some truth to this theory of anger addiction and that he is thinking about it is a hopeful sign since it means he is refining the ability to observe the darker thoughts from a distance and more effectively manage them.

He doesn't want to take Dale down, but this is how it goes. As for Randall, he deserves it. He has a moment where he fantasizes calling Randall and telling him it's over, but realizes the fleeting sense of satisfaction that would provide will only give Randall time to plan a countermove. Jimmy considers calling Cali and telling her what he has found out but thinks perhaps he will take the information directly to the District Attorney. Why tell Cali or Arnaldo, or Glenn Korver, or even Oz Spengler? This one is all his.

He thinks about logging on-line to talk to Bodhi Colletti. He wants to thank her for helping him to clarify his thoughts.

The phone rings. Jimmy debates whether or not to get up and answer it given that he is feeling calm now. But he thinks it might be Cali, so he picks up without checking caller ID. Maxon.

"Where are you, Jimmy?"

"What's it to you where I am?"

"I'd like it if you stopped by the victory party tonight."

When Jimmy hears this he stops breathing for a moment. Is he ready to go down there and speak to Randall at the celebration? Does he want to risk a scene? Taking note of his moist palms, he notices his mind is not as settled as he had thought. It occurs to Jimmy that there is a perfect place to put his insight about whether he is addicted to his anger to a real world test. He will talk to Maxon, he will see Randall, Dale will probably be there, too. He needs to do this, to challenge himself in this way, to stay calm and collected in the face of adverse stimuli because only when he masters this aspect of life can he turn his existence into something other than a daily trial. And tomorrow he will walk into the District Attorney's office.

CHAPTER FORTY

T he Cahuilla Casino is a sixteen story neon-trimmed curvilinear monolith that looms over the flat desert floor like a spaceship. It's just after ten o'clock when Jimmy pulls into the crowded parking lot. He's running through how he's going to play Dale. Jimmy won't mention Odin Brick at first. Instead, he'll just concentrate on what Dale has been doing since he's been out, who he's been talking to, what his plans are. Remembers Dale likes whiskey and Coke and plans to buy him a few. Get him loose, talkative, in a sharing mood. Dale likes to jabber and Jimmy knows if he's drunk enough, his tendency to brag is dependable.

A grand piano-sized faux-crystal chandelier illuminates the crowded lobby. Jimmy stands on the black marble floor and peers around. To his right, people drift in and out of the casino in a haze of dreamy avarice. Straight ahead is a curved stairwell that leads to the second floor where Randall's party is being held in the main ballroom. As Jimmy is moving in that direction, he sees Arnaldo and Cali. He's happy to see Cali, gives her a sideways smile, but she does not reciprocate. It makes him glad he didn't call her earlier. Was it going to be awkward between them now?

"Jimmy, can we talk to you outside?" Arnaldo says.

"Sure." Jimmy trying to process the ramifications of their presence. Then, lowers his voice: "What's up?"

Cali indicates the front door with a tilt of her chin and the three of them move toward it. Jimmy wonders if there's been some kind of break in the case, whether he's been beaten to the punch. If Cali and Arnaldo are here, he reasons, something around the campaign must have taken on a stink.

Outside in the warm evening, standing beneath the porte-cochere in the lurid light of the valet parking station, Jimmy turns to his colleagues.

"You're gonna tell me it's not Hard?"

"This is gonna seem kind of wrong to you," Arnaldo says.

"We don't like it either." From Cali.

"You got to be cool, okay?" Arnaldo again.

"Yeah, yeah, what?" Jimmy.

"You promise?" Cali once more. Now she smiles, but Jimmy senses it's forced. Cali and Arnaldo exchange a furtive glance but neither moves.

"I'm going back inside." Jimmy. Frustrated.

Arnaldo grabs his arm, says, "You can't do that."

"What are you talking about?" To Cali, "What's he talking about?"

"What he says, Jimmy. You can't go back inside."

"Because?"

"You're under arrest," Arnaldo says.

"Funny," Jimmy says.

He starts walking back into the casino but as soon as he does, Cali and Arnaldo grab him with enough force to let him know immediately this is not a joke and he only resists for the second it takes his conscious mind to control the part of his brain that reflexively prepares to fight. When they see he is not going to lash out, they let go. Jimmy's eyes challenge his former comrades to provide some kind of explanation for this absurd turn of events.

"We've got to take your gun," Cali says. The wrinkle of her lips suggests an aborted attempt at a sympathetic expression but her eyes are flint.

Arnaldo apologizes as he reaches inside Jimmy's sports

coat and removes his police-issue revolver. Checking the load, he takes the bullets out, puts them in his pocket then thrusts the gun into his belt. A crowd of revelers rolls past, not even glancing at the trio playing this surpassingly strange tune. Jimmy is thankful he doesn't know any of them.

"What are you arresting me for?"

"Grand larceny and falsifying a police report," Cali says.

Jimmy is dumbstruck, pole-axed, no idea what this is about.

Arnaldo informs him: "Someone tipped the Town Supervisor about you and the dog. Guy's so spooked about Hard everything has to be detergent clean."

The sag in Jimmy's shoulders is barely perceptible but it is the sign of defeat. This round is over and he is on the canvas, staring at the lights. Arnaldo and Cali seem almost embarrassed and genuinely regret having to do this. Jimmy nearly feels sorry for them. He nods like he understands, let's get on with it, perform the charade, then all go home. Out of respect, they will not put the bracelets on.

During the car ride Jimmy sits in the backseat cage usually reserved for the perp du jour. Cali riding shotgun while Arnaldo drives. Jimmy considers telling them about Princess and Odin Brick and Dale and the motor at Papi's but decides to let it lie. He wants to deal with it himself.

The sense of being outmaneuvered has begun to shift into something distinctly more recognizable. The techniques that had been showing such promise in controlling his anger are doing absolutely no good. He wants to scream and shout, to bellow until his throat is raw, to kick a hole in the seat. The fury renders him mute because there remains a still, quiet place where a small voice warns him that if he opens his mouth at this juncture what emerges will only reflect the rage-induced chaos in his head.

It's not as if he isn't guilty. Bruno is the property of the town of Desert Hot Springs and was not Jimmy's to take. But the timing of the complaint lets him know that he is being sent an unsubtle message. The job at the District Attorney's office is not going to survive this incident and with his job will go his pension.

"Jimmy, I'm feeling real bad about this," Cali says.

"Save it," Jimmy tells her.

Arnaldo says nothing, there being no point.

It is against policy to put a current or former employee of the Desert Hot Springs Police Department in a cell there so Jimmy is being ferried to the county lock-up in Indio. Since it is a Tuesday evening, he will appear in court tomorrow morning to answer the charges. And no one is on duty so he can't post bail until then. It does not please him to be spending his first night as a guest of the Riverside County District Attorney but he has made his peace with the situation and adhering to the proposition that what one cannot speak of one must pass over in silence he remains quiet for the remainder of the ride.

Jimmy is spared the intake paperwork, Arnaldo telling him they already know the information before going to take care of it. After Jimmy surrenders his wallet, watch, and belt, Cali asks for his house keys. When she pockets them, Jimmy looks at her. If this is flirty, he doesn't like the timing.

"Animal control is going out to your trailer first thing tomorrow."

"And you're gonna let them in?"

"I'm going tonight, dummy. The dog won't be there in the morning."

It is difficult for Jimmy to express the depth of his gratitude for his gesture, so he offers simple thanks. Cali says forget it and asks that he not mention it to Arnaldo. Then she escorts him through the metal door beyond which lie the three cells that make up the protective custody area. This is where Jimmy will be bunking since a law enforcement official that is under arrest will not be exposed to the general jail population. The cell nearest the door is empty, as is the one next to that, but the far cell is occupied by a large man reclining on his back. It is with a combination of disbelief, apprehension and chagrin that Jimmy realizes the man's identity.

CHAPTER FORTY-ONE

T he elevator door opens and Randall pushes Dale's wheelchair down the carpeted casino hallway toward the ballroom, Maxon trailing behind them talking to a journalist on his cell phone. "I want you to stay with me, Dale," Randall says. "I'll introduce you around."

"Whatever you want me to do, I'm here to spread the love for you."

"You can do all the rhyming you want tonight, baby brother."

Dale, clean-shaven, has on a red sweater over a white shirt and his hair has been washed and brushed. Maxon arranged for a taxi to pick him up and bring him to the casino and he is flattered to be a part of Randall's stagecraft. Neither of the brothers has mentioned what occurred at the Super #1 Convenience Store.

Kendra and Brittany are standing outside a doorway and Randall beams when he sees them. Dale notices that Kendra seems nervous, which surprises him since she's a performer. They all greet him perfunctorily. Kendra tells him she's glad he could come and he assumes she's lying. Ordinarily it's the kind of thing that would trouble him, but he's so pleased to be included in this event that he doesn't mind. It doesn't bother Dale that Randall's daughter barely looks in his direction. He isn't the kind who sends birthday cards, so he doesn't think twice about the snub. Maxon tells the assembled Dukes he's going to get up onstage and introduce them, then pushes through the doors leading to the party and disappears.

There is an awkward silence when Maxon leaves. The sounds of music, the volley of voices, the highly pitched din seeping in from the party can't alleviate it. Dale watches Randall spray breath freshener into his mouth. Kendra squeezes her husband's shoulder. Brittany runs her tongue along the inside of her upper pink-glossed lip. She was a kid when he went to prison. Her teenaged sex makes Dale twitchier than he'd like. He catches her staring at him but it's with the eye of a scientist examining a specimen. He's heard this girl is exceedingly bright but he's never had a chance to talk to her. And right now he doesn't have the inclination. He doesn't need some teenager to make him feel stupid.

The victory celebration for his brother the Congressman works on a vestigial aspect of Dale that still flickers inside of him, a memory of pledging allegiance to the flag, and the Founding Fathers and this country that was hewn from the wilderness, because although he is a criminal, that was not his intent in life and he clings to the thought that had things gone differently for him, had he been luckier, he wouldn't be in a wheelchair, wouldn't have *become* a criminal, and he would be here under an entirely more felicitous set of circumstances. The plot he had set in motion and that had veered so disastrously off course sprung from that more innocent place. Dale means well, believes his essential nature is good. If he can only escape from the forces that continually pull him to the ground, he will be able to live the rest of his life in an entirely new way. His atonement will begin tonight. After the party he will apologize to Randall.

A moment later he is being propelled into the packed ballroom, Randall behind him pushing the wheelchair, the crowd applauding and Dale waving like he's Miss America. What would have been a far more subdued event had a few hundred Duke supporters stayed away from the polls is now a raucous party. Bad rock music blares through a PA system flanking a bunting-bedecked stage and the cash bar is thronged. Randall is so pumped up from the win he magnanimously introduces Dale to every donor, campaign apparatchik and well-wisher in sight, Dale beaming like they're running mates, thanking people for giving Randall their vote, shaking hands and telling everyone how excellent it is to meet them. Not since he was speeding down the highway on his motorcycle, the road booming beneath him has Dale felt such a sense of unbridled exhilaration.

Randall has insisted he stay close—Dale doesn't know whether from generosity of spirit or fear that he would drain the entire contents of the cash bar—and he sticks by his brother's side for most of the evening. Upstanding citizens pump his hand all night, their sunny grins in no way redolent of the mild discomfort he knows most of them feel in the presence of a crippled criminal. As the celebration whirls around him he is briefly able to forget what he's done to Randall, to pretend it hasn't happened. When his sister-in-law gets up and sings a karaoke version of *I Will Survive* he joins in when the crowd chants along to the chorus. Then the music cuts out and Randall is on stage. He holds the microphone with two hands, as if in supplication, and gazes out at his supporters. At the beginning of the speech, after he thanks his wife and daughter and Maxon Brae, he thanks "My kid brother, Dale" right there in front of hundreds of people. *My kid brother Dale.* Dale is stunned. In his eyes, it is an entirely unexpected act of public forgiveness. He is so moved by the gesture he almost doesn't mind his failure to procure anything stronger than a ginger ale for the entire evening.

The only sour note occurs when Dale informs Maxon that he will need the ten thousand dollars immediately. It's after midnight and the party is winding down. *Don't Stop Thinking About Tomorrow* blares over the sound system. Several couples are on the dance floor, moving in the spasmodic manner of white people celebrating victory at a political event. Maxon stands next to Dale's chair at the side of the ballroom.

"We're talking the kind of shitbirds that steal a man's wheelchair."

"It might take a few weeks to sort out the money."

"Jimmy's already sniffing around."

"Don't worry about Jimmy."

"I'm the middleman here, know what I mean? I'll serve you up for breakfast."

Although Dale is the one in the chair, he believes Maxon can be intimidated by the prison stare. But after a few brief seconds, he has the curious thought that he might be underestimating him. A young couple on their way out stop to congratulate Maxon. He quickly thanks them, not bothering to introduce Dale.

When they depart, Dale says, "I need you to get me a gun."

"We're not going to talk about this here," Maxon says. "I got a surprise for you tomorrow morning."

"I don't want no more surprises." Dale beckons him closer. When Maxon leans in, Dale grabs the back of his head and yanks. He feels Maxon's neck straining, but he doesn't release him. Whispers: "I want that gun."

Dale eases his grip and Maxon straightens up, looks around to see if anyone has witnessed this. The clean up crew is working now. A few knots of people are in quiet conversation. No one appears to have noticed.

"This is the kind of surprise you'll like."

"The money?"

"Better than that."

"I got a surprise for you, bro. I'm staying at your house until you get it for me and I pay those guys the extra cash."

Maxon nods. This placates Dale. It's not like he can force Maxon to come across with the payment. At least he agreed to let Dale remain in his guestroom. He knows he'll get no slack from House Cat.

Dale asks where Randall is.

When Maxon says: "Gone for the night," Dale sinks a little in his chair. He did not have a chance to offer his sincere apology for the trouble he has caused.

In his time as a member of the Desert Hot Springs Police Department Jimmy escorted hundreds of criminals to the cells so it is disconcerting to find himself in the position of being led by his elbow to confinement. Compounding this sense of disorientation, his escort was his recent sex partner and winging it to a realm of weirdness so deep it can barely be fathomed is the identity of the other prisoner: Hard Marvin.

Jimmy looks at Cali, gestures toward the Chief. Cali shrugs tells Jimmy how sorry she is about this.

"This mean we're not going out tomorrow night?" Jimmy's idea of a joke, but the delivery is devoid of twinkly.

"Lets see if you make bail," she says, equally twinkle-free. Then she opens the cell nearest to the door and indicates he should step inside. There's a metal bed with no mattress. The Spartan space is lit by a fluorescent tube light on the ceiling encased in steel mesh intended to keep the inmates from fashioning it into a weapon or a means to commit a messy suicide. Cali asks if he wants a sandwich and he declines. She tells him to shout if he needs anything then leaves, the cell door clanging shut. Jimmy does not watch her retreat. He glances at Hard who is still lying on his back staring at the ceiling.

Jimmy wonders if Hard even realizes who just arrived but can't imagine it could have possibly escaped his attention. He lies down on the steel plank, tries to relax. Difficult to get comfortable on the metal. Meditation is a dim hope so he lies there and counts his breaths but he can't get past three before his mind starts to pinwheel. Ten minutes go by before he hears: "I hope this isn't some cocked up plan to get me to spill to you, because I got nothing to spill."

"It's no plan, Chief. Someone dropped a dime on me." He goes on to explain the charges that have placed him here leaving out the part about seeing Randall's hand in the evening's events. No point in sharing that with his former boss who does not seem interested in the details.

What he does say is: "You're fucked, Cowboy." The perfect stillness and recumbent position of Hard's body combine to give Jimmy the sense that the words are emanating from a cadaver.

"I know."

"But not as fucked as I am."

It doesn't take Jimmy long to realize Hard is right. Who knows how far Randall's reach extends? While Jimmy will probably be released on his own recognizance, due to the grizzly nature of the crime for which Hard has been arrested, bail will be set prohibitively high. The trial probably won't be for a year, time that will be spent behind bars. And if he's convicted, that year could stretch into the rest of his life.

Another half hour passes in silence before Hard picks up the conversation as if the gap was a couple of seconds.

"For the record, Duke, I had nothing to do with those murders. Maybe I was banging Nadine, but so what? I probably wasn't the only one. And yeah, she killed my dog, and yeah, I threatened her but Christ on the fuckin cross I didn't kill her and that guy."

"I believe you."

"Fuck you, Duke. You didn't believe me when it might've helped."

"I'm just saying."

"I'm firing my lawyer."

"Why?"

"Because she's a dimwit."

"Didn't she help you beat that manslaughter beef?"

"Let me tell you something about that, okay?" Hard's pauses

and his voice echoes off the tiled walls. Jimmy waits for him to continue. In all the years they worked together, he's never heard Hard's version. And he's not in the mood now to hear all about Hard killed some poor illegal alien. "The Mexican got killed that day? I never touched his greasy ass. Was one of the troopers, some old boy from Calexico. Whole bunch of us got investigated and anyone who asked I let them think it was me. You know how it is, you want folks scared of you. But was the guy from Calexico that did the killing. I was there and yeah maybe I could of stopped it but I was just an accessory. I'm no goddamn killer."

It's not easy for Jimmy to fathom how a law enforcement officer could think it was a good thing to be perceived as a killer but it was just another reason he never liked Hard.

"Maybe you can beat it."

"Look around, you ignorant sonofabitch. Where are we having this conversation?"

"I'd like to say we're at work, but we're on the wrong side of the cell doors."

"Keep fooling, Duke. Maybe you're here because you're a shit-for-brains wiseass who thought he could steal a dog but I'm here because my lawyer couldn't keep this from happening despite there being not one iota of evidence that isn't a hundred per cent bullshit."

Jimmy doesn't know if it is the fatigue he's feeling at the end of a perilously long and difficult day, or the utter impotence engendered by his current surroundings, or the cumulative effect of trying to quiet his mind over the last several months, but the hostility, anger and general dyspepsia he was experiencing moments ago begin to subside. Watching another person marinate in their own cosmic heartburn does wonders for your perspective, he reflects, glancing over at Hard. The vibrations of aggression and resentment emanating from the other man have a paradoxically calming effect on Jimmy, who is struck by the ridiculousness of Hard's behavior. That everything Hard said is true misses the larger point. While the former Chief can't change the circumstances in which he finds himself he is bereft of the insight that he can change the way in which he is responding to those circumstances. Jimmy knows that now is not the time to point this out.

"I saw you in a different way when my dog got murdered," Hard says.

"Saw me in a different way?"

"I was maybe too rough on you with what was his name?"

"Who?

"The dog?"

"Bruno?"

"I should have had a little more sympathy. Too little, too late, right? You said you freed him in the desert. Pack of coyotes probably ate him an hour later."

"I never freed him in the desert. I lied to you. That dog's in my trailer right now," Jimmy says with a degree of satisfaction he realizes his listener might not appreciate.

"No shit?"

"Yeah, no shit."

Jimmy waits for Hard's normal reaction to having his wishes contravened, the usual eruption and cursing rendered poignant by his current surroundings, but all the man says is: "Well, good for you."

"Nadine Never had a dog."

"Little fucker bit a hole in my ankle, deserved to die."

"Yeah, well, he's in my trailer, too."

"That ratdog escapes death, he's living the high life in your trailer while I'm locked up." Hard laughs drily. Then, "How's it feel, Duke?"

"How's what feel?"

"To lose your badge?"

For a moment Jimmy thinks that he might protest, tell Hard

he hasn't lost anything yet, that he'll get a lawyer, there will be hearings, he'll be allowed to defend himself, But he knows he is going to be out the door and spending a lot more time photographing dogs, his days as a crime buster over. So what he says is: "I should probably be in another line of work anyway."

"I never cared for you, Duke."

"You don't like anyone."

"People are worthless as a rule. But at least you had the balls to stand up for yourself. Pasco and Escovedo? Not those two. They just want to see me go down."

"It's not personal, Chief." These words are not said with a great deal of conviction.

"The hell it's not. You like anyone else for this?"

"I'm gonna be asked to resign from the law enforcement community tomorrow. What do you care who I like?" Jimmy wonders what would be served if he explicates his theory about his brothers' involvement in the killings. Then he says, "I got no idea."

"I know we've locked horns, but I always appreciated the quality of the work you did. Would of done yourself a favor if you could of kept a lid on your emotions a little more."

"I wish I hadn't threatened you, and I want to apologize for that."

"What's done is done. Point is, you get sprung tomorrow. And when you're walking around on the outside I got a favor."

"What's that?"

"I want you to think about me."

"That's all?"

"Finito."

Quiet minutes pass and then Jimmy hears snoring. Hard does not say another word for the rest of the night. The air is cool in the cells and the smell of disinfectant fills his nostrils. Jimmy does not sleep. As he lies there staring at the caged light he considers how the consequences of our behavior adhere to us as we move through life and concludes that if Hard is the author of his situation so Jimmy's destiny will be his own to seize. He knows his brother Randall has put him here. At least he thinks he's certain of that. Or is there a possibility that Randall is not behind Jimmy's current situation? He wonders if events occur that do not fit into a pattern, outliers that impede rational analysis? What happens when there is no sense to be made of a situation?

As Jimmy turns this over, he reflects that tonight might not be the worst time to be in a jail cell since it will keep him from doing something he might live to regret.

From his days burgling pharmacies for ingredients to sell to meth factories, House Cat knows independent businesses are easier to break into than chain stores since their burglar alarms are often less elaborate. For this reason, he is lying in the back seat of Odin's Impala in the parking lot behind Jojo's High Desert Pharmacy, a few miles outside of Victorville. The business is in a strip mall with a hardware store, a nail salon, a fried chicken restaurant, and an insurance broker. In the two hours he's been there a patrol car has driven by twice at forty-minute intervals. He's got burglar's tools with him and when the tail lights of the patrol car vanish down the highway a third time, he grabs them and walks across the parking lot to the back of the building.

It takes him about ten minutes to disable the system, then once he is inside another ten minutes to pry open the locked cabinets and locate enough anti-anxiety meds to treat a herd of neurotic elephants. By three in the morning he is back in the motel room where he hands them over to a grateful Odin.

http://WWW.DESERT-MACHIAVELLI.COM
11.6 – 11:53 P.M.
Election post-script. The Machiavelli is a little bleary-eyed
right now. I got back a little while ago from an incognito
appearance at the Duke victory celebration where I had a
few too many Singapore Slings. I'll get my thoughts
together when I wake up and post them when my hangover
wears off.

WEDNESDAY, NOVEMBER 7

K endra and Randall return to their house in Little Tuscany after one in the morning. When they are certain Brittany has gone to bed they share a nightcap in the kitchen. Still in the dress she wore to the party, Kendra has kicked off her pumps and put her feet on a chair at the kitchen table. Randall has taken off his jacket and loosened his tie. He is pouring them each a snifter of brandy. Holding the amber liquid up, Randall toasts his wife.

They clink glasses and sip the brandy. Having managed to suppress troublesome thoughts of Nadine so far this evening Kendra gazes over her snifter at her husband. Although he is exhausted, he shaved before the party and his helmet of political hair is perfect. He may have his faults as a spouse, she thinks, but when Nadine threatened to derail their plans, Congressman and Mrs. Randall Duke remained steady in the whirlwind.

"Does Harding Marvin being in jail bother you at all?"

"You know he killed an illegal, don't you?"

"I read that in the paper."

"So this is payback."

Kendra takes another sip of the brandy, feels the burn in her throat. "You ever think we might get payback sometime?"

Randall smiles, the corners of his mouth barely turning up. He takes the bottle and refills his glass. He takes a sip and swishes the brandy around in his mouth, feeling the fire on his tongue and gums. With the toe of one shoe he pushes down the heel of the other and kicks it off. He scratches the sole of his foot then removes his other shoe. Stretching both legs in front of him, he puts the snifter on the table, places his hands behind his head linking his fingers and leans back. "If I worried about payback," he says, "I couldn't get out of bed in the morning."

"He could get the death penalty."

"Better him than my brother."

"That's pretty cold."

"You want to succeed in this business, you can't worry about hurt feelings."

Kendra considers Randall's words. Life is a zero-sum game now and the world of politics exists as the unvarnished version of what Americans deal with each day. It's a nation of winners and losers and Kendra believes if you're not one, you're the other. Losers don't necessarily deserve to die, but Nadine's mistake had been to get in the way of a winner. The further her death recedes, the easier this is to believe.

As Kendra thinks about what has happened over the past week, the stress and the strain and the endless inner gyrations, she vows it will be the last time she will allow guilt to dominate the more rational part of her mind. What is the point in feeling guilty? She hasn't violated the rules. The way she sees it, she's playing by them.

She and Randall finish their drinks and, hand in hand, retreat to their bedroom. There they climb into bed and, believing a celebratory gesture is required, proceed to have sex for the first time in over a year.

Wallet, belt and cell phone returned, Jimmy sits with his fellow prisoners in an enclosed area to the side of the courtroom and listens as Judge Jaime Iglesias conducts examinations. His short gray hair is side-parted and horn-rimmed glasses lend him a professorial air. He moves swiftly through a drug deal, a burglary, shoplifting, and an assault. When Jimmy hears his name called he takes his place in front of the bench. He has appeared many times in front of the Judge in his capacity as a police detective. Iglesias raises his eyebrows when he sees him.

"Grand larceny and falsifying a police report?"

"I saved an innocent animal from a cruel fate, Judge."

The magistrate is unmoved by this explanation. Jimmy enters a plea of not guilty and is surprised when he is not remanded to his own custody but informed that bail will be ten thousand dollars. The judge explains that, despite the circumstances—which he promises to listen to in great detail at the trial—it is nonetheless a serious crime and it would not look kosher were he to be seen as going easy on a former police detective and current employee of the District Attorney's office. Jimmy is allowed a phone call that he uses to contact a bail bondsman he knows and is out in an hour. He doesn't bother going to the office, a call to Oz Spengler confirming his suspicions: suspended without pay, pending the adjudication of the State of California v. James Raymond Duke. A marshal he knows at the courthouse gives him a ride in an unmarked back to the Cahuilla Casino so he can pick up his truck.

Jimmy sits in the passenger seat pleased the marshal does not try to engage him in conversation. Driving north on Highway 111, he gazes up at the sky where a jet is flying west. In the plane the passengers are settling in for the short flight. The interior is hushed, the only sound the roar of the jet engines. In Row 12, Seat A, a woman looks out the window at the desert below, sees the granite mountains with their rough skin of scrub vegetation encircling the green oasis of Palm Springs, and all of it surrounded by the endless brown plain of the vast desert floor. To Princess the vista seems remarkably neat and ordered. Chance King has already drifted off to sleep in the seat next to her. Removing the bottle from his mouth, she places it on the boy's lap, then smoothes his hair. The trip to Los Angeles will take less than an hour. There they will change planes and board a flight to Manila. Princess knows she has seen the last of Odin. He will not follow them. And she will not return to the desert.

On a private airfield in the western Mojave, a striking woman in designer sunglasses and a red Armani suit stands with four children. A twelve-passenger Gulf Stream jet is parked nearby, the morning sun sparking off its windows. It is a more recent model than the one on which she served as a stewardess and she contentedly reflects on how far she has travelled. From the hangar, her husband emerges with the pilot. He puts his arm around his wife and they herd their family on to the jet. After calling Randall Duke to congratulate him on his victory, the Swains stayed up late talking and sipping wine. Mary was spoiling for a recount, but Shad talked her out of it, explaining that it would look unseemly in a House race and no one likes a sore loser. The two of them agreed that the reason she lost was she did not aim high enough. They toasted a former politician who failed in his first race for the House of Representatives, before being elected Governor and then President. It was decided that two years hence Mary Swain would run for Governor of California. In the meantime, she and Shad would establish the Greater Freedom Foundation for the purpose of funneling money to candidates of their political stripe.

An offer for a reality show had arrived—the producers want to show how a busy politician/mom runs her brood while swimming in the shark-infested waters of electoral politics—and there is a book deal on the table. And she had lost! Imagine what will be hers when she is victorious. All of this confirms Mary Swain's belief that the nation wants more of what she's selling and that she, not the Randall Dukes of the world, represents tomorrow: a glamorous, child-bearing woman who can run with the lions.

The jet taxis down the runway and rises into the autumn sky. The Swain family is heading for Hawaii. There, the four children will gambol in tropical waters under the watchful eyes of a nanny (who signed a non-disclosure agreement when she took the job) while their parents take long walks on the white sands and plan for the coming days. In the evening, with a cool drink in her manicured hand, Mary Swain will stand on the beach and gaze east toward the star spangled shores of her future.

A restless night spent on an aqua-colored vinyl day bed in Maxon's guestroom does not leave Dale in a good mood. Maxon scrambles some eggs for breakfast, then tells Dale to make himself comfortable in front of the television while he goes and runs a quick errand. Once more Dale asks about getting a gun for protection and Maxon tells him they will deal with that later.

Dale wheels himself into the bathroom to wash up. Having spent the previous three years in a state prison, he still can't get accustomed to the grooming products on display in Maxon's immaculate pink and white tiled bathroom. There is spiced pepper body wash, green tea under-eye ointment, skin-balance toning lotion, anti-aging cream, moisturizer, cleanser, and high-performance shaving gel. As Dale examines this panoply of self-indulgence he tries to envision Maxon on the yard in Calipatria and the incongruity of the image almost makes him laugh.

When Maxon returns he informs Dale they're going for a ride.

"There's a surprise for you," Maxon says.

"I don't need any more surprises," Dale says.

"You're going to like this one."

"I can always give these guys your address, Maxon. You need to remember that."

"We're on the same side here, my friend. You'll thank me when you see what's coming."

Maxon loads Dale's substitute wheelchair in the backseat of the Toronado and they drive toward Indio, Maxon's eyes hidden behind dark glasses. The car radio is tuned to a pop station and neither man talks. Dale thinks about Randall, how he needs to speak with him, to explain what has occurred, how he wanted to help and how he is collapsing inside now, how he feels that he has gone back to prison but the prison he's in today is one from which he can never escape or be paroled. And he wants to receive absolution. These thoughts are interrupted when Maxon pulls on to a car lot, Lucky Bob's Chevy, Dale looking around wondering what they're doing here.

Maxon walks into the office as Dale gazes admiringly at the rows of clean, new sedans, four wheel drive vehicles, trucks and vans. Calculates once again how much he's going to need for a down payment on something of his own.

Lying on his bed in prison, one of his most persistent fantasies involved an endless motorcycle ride, nothing but the sun, the wind and the eternal road. He has made his peace with his bad legs, and settled for the idea of movement. But the craving is as desperate as any he's known and being on the lot of this auto dealership is stoking it this morning.

Maxon returns a minute later, opens the trunk, pulls Dale's wheelchair out, rolls it to the passenger side and tells him to get in, he wants to show him something. Whether because of the beautiful morning or the aimlessness of a day that has allowed him to temporarily shove his troubles aside, Dale is in a more accommodating mood than usual and slides into the chair. Maxon starts to push it but Dale tells him to take his hands off he'll do it himself. He rolls alongside Maxon until they're standing in front of a brand new black Chevy sport utility vehicle.

"You like it?" Dale tells him he likes it fine. "Well, its yours."

Dale stares at the vehicle for a moment, not sure if what he's hearing is true. He says: "I'm not taking this."

"What do you mean you're not taking it? We got it fitted out with hand controls and everything."

"Serious?"

"You can drive it right off the lot. Lucky Bob's a friend of the campaign. The man believes in redemption, Dale. He wants you to have the vehicle."

Dale looks from Maxon to the SUV, then back to Maxon. "Forget the damn vehicle. I need the money to pay those motherfuckers."

"We can get you the money in a day or two. In the meantime, lets take it for a drive. You want to earn the money yourself, we'll work out some kind of payment plan with Lucky Bob."

"Cause he's a friend of Randall?"

"You know the drill."

Dale is too tempted by the proximity of wheels that have been personally kitted out for him to resist and finally agrees to take the SUV for a drive. The exquisite sense of joy that suffuses him as he steers off the lot is unlike anything he has known since the accident. He tests the hand brake a few times and twists the grip that controls the accelerator.

Now they're headed down Highway 111 toward the Salton Sea. The sun is high enough that the light on the mountains has flattened out. A few wispy clouds drift overhead in the piercing blue sky. Dale straightens his back, sits up as tall as he can. The traffic is moving, the hand controls easy to use. The highway, the desert air and the speed all improve his mood immensely. They ride in companionable quietude.

"You have a good time at the party last night?" Maxon asks.

"Okay, I guess."

"People seemed to like meeting you." Dale eyes Maxon, tries to decide if he's kidding. "You keep your nose clean, there's no reason you can't work in Randall's office in Palm Springs if you want."

"Already told you I didn't want no more charity from Randall."

"I'm just saying, your brother has faith in you."

Dale turns the radio on. It's a Spanish language station. Dale has no idea what the announcer is saying, but the man has a deep, mellifluous voice and he figures that maybe now he won't have to hear any more about Randall.

Maxon says, "Why don't we stop at the Date Oasis, get a shake?"

"Serious?"

"Didn't you want to do that the day you got released? You said that place has the best date shakes in the world."

The Medjool Date Oasis has been on this stretch of highway just north of the Salton Sea since 1921. On the edge of a dense grove of date palms imported years ago from the Middle East, the well-maintained one-story building is the kind of roadside attraction now usually seen only on kitschy postcards.

Dale and Maxon sip their date shakes at a picnic table to the side of the building. Two older couples, golf shirts and floppy hats on the men, loose skirts and baggy tee shirts on the women, sit at a nearby picnic table enjoying the lazy morning.

"Look at those people," Maxon says. "No worries at all. Imagine that."

Dale nods. It's difficult for him to conjure a state of mind devoid of worry and he doesn't bother to try. But the shakes are so thick Dale is eating his with a spoon, and today that will suffice.

"I grew up in raisin country," Maxon says. "Flat, agricultural land, bore you to death. It amazes me sometimes how far I've come, working with Randall." Maxon gazes at a pickup truck gliding south on the highway. Dale doesn't step into the silence. "I'm thinking about the consulting business now, other people's campaigns."

"Yeah?" Dale says, wishing Maxon would just shut up.

"Have to build up my own war chest, can't just be a one-trick pony, but my heart will always be with your brother."

"Mine, too." Dale thinks that must be what Maxon wants to hear.

"When he runs for higher office, I'll be there." This time Dale just nods. Figures if he stops responding, maybe Maxon will just let the conversation die out. The older couples ramble toward their RV. Dale and Maxon sit in silence for a full minute during which time only an eighteen-wheeler owned by a giant supermarket chain rumbles past on the highway.

"Why don't we take a look at Bombay Beach?" Maxon says.

"What for?"

"Heard you didn't like Mecca."

"It's a shithole."

"I made a few calls, think we can swing you a place down near the water."

Dale looks over at Maxon in disbelief. Could this be possible? Whatever he thinks of Randall, he is a man of his word. Now the risk he has taken on his brother's behalf seems once again more understandable. He'll get the money to pay Odin and House Cat and before long be in Bombay Beach with a view of the Salton Sea and his own hand-controlled SUV. A week after being paroled, it is as good a situation as he could reasonably hope for.

They're driving south on Highway 111 again, Maxon telling Dale about the architectural history of the area. "Back in the fifties," Maxon says, "After the war, a lot of people thought this could be a fancy resort."

"Oh, yeah?" Dale trying to pretend he cares.

"A man named Albert Frey, an Austrian immigrant, was an important figure in the mid-century modern movement and he was hired to design the North Shore Yacht Club. They let it fall apart but this organization I'm on the board of, the Palm Springs Preservation Society, we had it on our radar and we got the county to step up and do a restoration."

Dale nods affably. It's hard to feign interest in Maxon's chattering, but they're on the way to Bombay Beach, so he'll indulge him. Maxon continues to wax poetic about the avatars of mid-century modern architecture, how the school emerged in the late forties, flowered in the fifties and was spent by the end of the sixties and how an army of new residents armed with nothing more than reserves of will and their exquisite taste have turned the area into an international magnet for design aficionados. Dale nods and grunts and in a few minutes the Salton Sea comes mercifully into view on the right. Although it's late morning now, the fog on the far shore has not entirely burned off and the sun creates a thin line of dazzling light that stretches across the southern horizon like an illuminated portal to another world. It is radiant and calm and for a moment Dale is able to forget House Cat and Odin and he breathes the sea air and feels the sun on his skin as he pilots his new SUV along the sandy shoreline. Maxon keeps prattling and in a couple of minutes the North Shore Yacht Club comes into view on their right. It's a long low building with a curved upper section lined with four duct-like windows meant to suggest portholes. The whimsically seafaring quality it evokes is all that remains of the fun that occurred there years earlier. The renovation is nearly complete but the restored structure appears deserted today.

"Turn in here," Maxon says. "I want to take a few pictures."

In temporary thrall to Maxon's largesse, Dale guides the SUV off the empty highway toward the seaside building. The SUV judders over the rocky parking lot. "Just like it must have looked fifty years ago," Maxon says, gazing out toward the low-slung building.

They jounce slowly along over the uneven surface and then Dale notices a familiar blurring of his eyesight. His neck begins to stiffen and his molars grind. Frustration and fear rise like bile in his throat. In the excitement of the election and the party and the anxiety in the aftermath of House Cat's visit he neglected to take his medication this morning. His vision begins to narrow. In the brief window during which he can still control his body he brings the SUV to a halt as his eyes roll back in his head and his heart thuds like a fist pounding the wall in his chest. His spine stiffens and flexes backward as he feels his tongue go slack. Then his entire body begins to jerk spasmodically. Dale is unable to look left or right so at first he doesn't know why he can't breathe but just before he slips out of consciousness he feels strange fingers pinching his nose and a warm palm over his mouth. There is pressure on his chest. Dimly he returns to consciousness—a few seconds later? He can't be sure—the fingers and hand still in his face impeding the flow of oxygen and his body jerks wildly struggling for air then his lungs collapse and consciousness cedes to black and oblivion.

When Maxon is sure Dale is gone he looks over his shoulder toward the deserted highway. Then he releases the hand brake and gently guides the vehicle toward the water. The SUV rumbles over the hardpack, breaches the retaining wall and rolls nose down into the Salton Sea. The impact causes the airbags deploy, pinning them back and the water pours through the open windows filling the bright new vehicle as it sinks. The temperature of the water is surprisingly cold and Maxon can feel the muscles of his upper body contract as it rises to his chest and his throat and then there is a salty taste in his mouth. He slithers out through an open window and wades to shore, losing his sunglasses in the process. He suppresses the urge to go back and look for them. Over his shoulder he sees the entire front end of the SUV submerged. Maxon had not planned to kill Dale, but how could he not take advantage of the opportunity? It was impossible to know whether Dale could have kept his mouth shut, and now they would never have to worry.

Crouched in the shadow of the Albert Frey building, Maxon waits for several minutes. When only the roof of the SUV is visible on the sparkling blue surface of the water he walks to the highway and waits for a car to appear. He waves at the first three vehicles but no one stops. At last two landscapers in a pickup pull on to the shoulder and ask what's wrong. Maxon points and the men run toward the water.

CHAPTER FORTY-THREE

A fist pounding at his door awakens Jimmy. He had lay down to take a nap after being dropped off at his trailer and has no idea how long he's been asleep. He pulls on some boxers and looks out the window. There is an unmarked parked outside.

When he opens the door Cali and Arnaldo are standing there, grim-faced.

"You here to apologize?"

"No," Arnaldo says.

"So what do you want?" For all of his meditative equanimity he is not ready to let bygones be bygones.

Cali: "Your brother Dale is dead."

Jimmy waits a moment for the punch line. There is a barely perceptible weakening in his knees when he realizes none is coming. For several moments he forgets to breathe.

"I'm really sorry, man," Arnaldo says.

Jimmy looks past them up the mountain. It is almost as if the two detectives have ceased to exist. He thinks drugs, or alcohol, or suicide, some fitting endpoint to the futility of Dale's wasted life. "How did it happen?"

"The report says he drowned," Cali says.

"Drowned?" Jimmy isn't sure he's heard correctly.

"We wanted to come up and tell you ourselves," Arnaldo says.

"He drowned?"

"In the Salton Sea," Cali says.

"Was he with anybody?"

"Maxon Brae," Arnaldo says.

"With that prick? Were they swimming?" Incredulous.

"Your brother Dale just got a new vehicle," Cali says. "They're out driving it, Dale at the wheel, hand controls and everything. Story Brae's telling is Dale has a seizure, loses control of the vehicle, thing goes into the water and he can't pull your brother out. Claims he tried."

They all stand there, no one saying anything.

For years Jimmy has been anticipating the moment he would receive the news of his younger brother's untimely end. He didn't know if it would be a car wreck, a gunshot, or an overdose, but he had always known in his bones that Dale would not live to grow old. He will recall the strange sense of relief he experienced upon the realization that he would no longer have to uneasily anticipate the inexorable conclusion.

If Jimmy had been through a similar experience last year this is when he would have gone looking for a bar. And he would have kept drinking until either he crawled into his truck and passed out or called a cab to take him home so he could fight with his wife. He thinks about a drink. He watches the thought rise. He labels it. He waits for it to float away. It doesn't. He still wants a drink, but more out of habit. All pain comes from attachment.

"Tough break, man," Arnaldo says. Cali asks if he's going to be all right. Jimmy says he'll be fine. She asks him if there's anything they can do for him, and he tells them no, there is nothing for them to do. The condolences continue for few uncomfortable moments. The detectives tell Jimmy they'll be seeing him around and then they get in their car and drive away. Jimmy stands in the doorway and watches them disappear down the hill. He did not remember to ask where the dogs are or how they are doing.

CHAPTER FORTY-FOUR

M axon rode with the EMS workers who insisted on taking him to the Eisenhower Medical Center in Rancho Mirage. After he phones Randall from a landline to express his condolences, he calls his aide Tyson Griggs who is closing up the Duke storefront campaign head-quarters in Palm Springs. He asks Tyson to get some clean clothes for him, then drive to the hospital and give him a ride to the car lot so he can pick up his Toronado.

Maxon changes into slacks and a sports coat. On the ride, Tyson asks about what occurred and Maxon tells him that it is simply a tragedy and he would rather not talk about it right now.

Maxon slides behind the wheel of the Toronado and con-siders the day. He would like to check the messages on his BlackBerry but the waters of the Salton Sea have rendered it useless. When he sorts that out he knows there will be any number of calls from journalists and politicos wanting to express both their congratulations about the election and their concern for what he has been through this morning. But right now there is something more pressing he must attend to. He opens the glove compartment where an old pair of sunglasses is nestled next to his Smith and Wesson .38.

Maxon slides the key into the front door lock of Dale's apartment and lets himself in. The building is still unoccupied and with Dale gone there is no one in the immediate vicinity. It's important Maxon get here before the Imperial County

Sherriff's deputies in the event Dale has left something compromising around. Even though he lived there for only a week, the place is a mess. Maxon removes a tennis ball from his jacket pocket and starts to work it in his left hand.

The garbage can in the kitchen overflows and there are paper plates on the counters with half eaten sandwiches on them. Magazines litter the living room. Maxon is not sure what he's looking for. Perhaps Dale kept a journal. With the idiotic rhyming he was doing, he could have composed a notebook full of incriminating poetry. The kitchen drawers and cabinets reveal nothing but the rudimentary silverware and plates, two sets of each, with which they'd supplied him on his release along with a few pots and pans that appear to have not been used. There are three cans of beer in the otherwise empty refrigerator. A metal tin of breath mints is on the kitchen counter. Opening it, Maxon sees five tightly rolled joints. He'll leave them there.

A cursory examination of the living room is equally fruitless. Maxon lifts the cushions of the couch where the only thing that turns up is the remote control of the flat screen television the campaign had purchased.

The bathroom is located in the short hallway between the living room and bedroom. There are two dirty towels on the floor, a toothbrush, toothpaste, a deodorant stick, shaving gel, a razor and a hairbrush. The medicine chest is empty.

The bedroom. If anything is to be found, that's the place to look. The bureau contains an assortment of boxer shorts, tee shirts, and socks, all supplied by the Duke campaign. Maxon opens the closet. There is a pair of canvas sneakers on the floor and a small pile of dirty clothes. Maxon moves the clothes and looks to see if they're concealing anything. Again he comes up empty.

Dale's unmade bed beckons. Maxon lifts the pillow and exposes a high school notebook with a black and white marbled cover. Opening it, he sees Dale has only scribbled on the first few pages. Maxon can barely make out the scrawl but is able to discern the words *motorcycle, Calipatria* and what looks like *Salton Sea.* There is nothing to suggest anything other than casual jottings so he slips the notebook back under the pillow.

"You a friend of Dale's?"

Maxon starts at the sound and the tennis ball rolls out of his fingers, to the carpeted floor where it strikes his foot and caroms under the unmade bed. The voice is gruff, but not threatening. Maxon turns and sees two men standing in the doorway of the bedroom. One, lean with slicked back hair, wearing jeans and a tee shirt looks to be in his twenties. Half of his face is covered with a bandage. The other is dressed in slacks and a checked button-front long sleeved shirt. Muscular and crew cut, he appears at least a decade older than his associate. Maxon notices the rings on nearly every finger.

"No, I'm not his friend," Maxon says, keeping his voice steady. He consciously relaxes his shoulders. No one says anything for a moment. Maxon makes the wiry one for an ex-con. It does not take him long to realize who they are.

"So what are you doing here?" The young guy with the bandaged face. His tone is not as friendly as the older man's.

"I'm his parole officer," Maxon says. "Who are you?"

"Bullshit." Crew Cut says. His tone is less sociable now. Maxon looks from one man to the other. He can tell they don't believe him. The younger guy steps into the room, leaving the one with the rings blocking the doorway.

"What's your name?" the younger one asks, slowly moving toward him.

Maxon reaches into his pocket, pulls out his wallet. "Officer Brae."

The gold shield causes the younger man to freeze. Crew Cut tenses up. Maxon knows they're thinking the penalty for killing an officer of the court is not something they want raining down. Officiously, Maxon slaps the wallet shut and crams it back in his pocket.

"When you see, Dale," the older man says, backing up now, "Tell him his cousin stopped by."

"Hold on a minute," Maxon says. "No need for me to be a hard-on. Not going to cite you two for breaking in."

"That's good," the young guy. Nervous. Maxon sees him look at his partner, who avoids the bandaged man's eyes.

"Just want to ask you a couple of questions about Dale." With an upward tilt of his chin, Maxon indicates that the two men should leave the bedroom.

When the three of them are in the living room, he says, "Who did you two say you say you were?"

The two visitors look at each other as if to decide who should do the talking. The older guy opens his mouth but Maxon shoots him before he can say anything. The younger man looks at the bloodstain blooming on his partner's shirtfront and watches him crumple to the floor. Dumb with shock, he faces Maxon in time to take two in the chest. The gunshots resonate in the apartment but there are no neighbors to hear them.

Briefly, Maxon wonders whether his father would have had the balls to do what he has just done. He might have ruminated on what moral wounds were worth suffering in order to achieve one's goals in the wide brutal world. But could he have done what his illegitimate son has done here in the desert? Not a chance.

When Maxon leaves the apartment, there is no one in the street. The only cars in front of the building are Maxon's and a dusty blue Impala. As he eases the Toronado on to the highway that runs north from Mecca he gives silent thanks the dead men did not look closely at the badge and see that it reads *Honorary Sherriff's Deputy.*

Jimmy knows Dale writes things down and wants to look for anything that might shed some light on his state of mind over the past week. And he wants to have a look before anyone in law enforcement gets there. The Walther .38 he keeps for personal use is snug under a loose-fitting jacket. He pulls the truck in front of the empty complex and lets himself into Dale's condo. The living room is stifling and the air is still. He is not prepared for the dead welcoming committee splayed bloody on the floor. He quickly steps outside and glances around. Sun bakes the silent street. In the distance he can hear an eighteen-wheeler rolling south toward Mexico.

After determining no one is in the immediate vicinity, he walks around the back of the building and peers through the windows of the bathroom and bedroom to make sure no one is lurking in the unit. Satisfied the scene has been abandoned, he re-enters the condo and closes the door behind him.

Jimmy has been to enough crime scenes to know that these men have been dead for several hours. The wounds in their chests and heads have begun to congeal and flies are collecting in their nostrils and open eyes. When he sees one of the victims has a bandaged face, he immediately makes him for the husband of the woman who came to the office. Jimmy will call this in to the Sheriff's Department, but not before looking around. A quick search of the living room and kitchen turns up nothing of interest. He explores the bedroom. Under the pillow he finds the notebook. Several pages are filled with jottings that Jimmy glances through. As he is about to put the notebook down, he flips to the last page. There he sees, in Dale's handwriting, the words: *Randall, Randall, I'm a burning candle, fame and shame will be my game . . .*

And that is all. Nothing else. The beginning of a note? An explanation? Jimmy has no idea and he knows the larger mystery of this last rhyme will never be clear.

Disappointed, he drops to his knees to glance under the bed and his eyes go straight to a tennis ball.

Before he leaves, he takes another look at the dead men. Wonders about the bad road that led to where they are now, their torn flesh decaying on a condo floor. The cravings that ruled them, the striving in which they were engaged, are the earthbound qualities he has been trying to transcend. He wishes Dale were here to shed light on the horrific situation. A week ago the two brothers were in this room sharing sandwiches, and now one is dead. Standing in the middle of this gory crime scene, a deep sadness spreads through Jimmy and a sense of utter despair overwhelms him for a moment.

Light glints off metal. Kneeling down, Jimmy eyeballs the gun jammed in the belt of the man with the bandaged face. It occurs to him that this is could be the weapon used in the double murder. Jimmy goes to the kitchen and returns with a steak knife. He slips the blade under the barrel of the gun next to the trigger and lifts it from the dead man's belt. Then he drops it in a pillowcase he takes from the bed. It doesn't matter to him that he is disturbing a crime scene. There is no one he trusts to get this right. He will bring the gun to the District Attorney's office himself and let them know where he found it. Then he'll tell them about the dead men.

http://WWW.DESERT-MACHIAVELLI.COM
11.7 – 3:18 P.M.

Who would have thought that springing a criminal and using him to cynically manipulate an election might be a dangerous business? Not freshly re-elected Congressman Randall Duke, that's for sure. You can bring a hyena into your home, but you can't turn him into a pet and let him play with the kids. The Randall Duke Do Anything to Get Elected Freedom Experiment ended disastrously today. After being hailed from the stage at what I can personally report was a raucous victory celebration at the Cahuilla Casino, Randall's jailbird brother Dale was driving to a waterside community on the shores of the Salton Sea with Duke aide de camp and fixer par excellence Maxon Brae, whose role in this re-election campaign, one that it looked as if Randall would lose, deserves special mention. Truly, he is Randall Duke's brain, as anyone who has been following Randall's career will tell you. Dale, who had a history of drug and alcohol abuse, is said to have had a seizure of some kind and driven the vehicle into the water where he drowned. Brae claims he tried to extricate him from the submerged vehicle diving back into the water several times but was unable to do so. Maxon, if you're reading this, send me an email because I'd like to get your valiant attempts at rescue confirmed by you. Randall Duke won't comment.

CHAPTER FORTY-FIVE

Bombay Beach is laid out in a grid on the Eastern shore of the Salton Sea. Most of the homes are single story and some of them are trailers mounted on blocks. They are in varying states of disrepair and many appear forsaken. Some have been gutted by fire. Others collapsed from the weight of years and unremitting sunlight and neglect. Their yards, a mixture of gravel and sand, are strewn with bric-a-brac, rusted appliances, discarded tools, broken pottery. What surprises Jimmy is how many of the homes are fenced in, and the poignant implication that there is something inside these places worth protecting. Feral-looking dogs patrol nearly every yard and they growl at Jimmy as he walks past.

In the yard of a decrepit trailer an old man in overalls putters under the hood of a broken-down truck. His ancient wife wears a hair net and a floral housedress as she waters a row of clay pots. Neither acknowledges Jimmy as he drifts past. This is not how he remembers the town from when he was here nearly thirty years earlier with his two brothers and their father. The paint was fresh then, the people younger.

Because Dale wanted to come to Bombay Beach, Jimmy is here now. Could this be what his brother remembered when he talked about returning, this post-apocalyptic landscape of decay, ruin, and loss? Could this possibly have been what he recalled while he was locked away? Or did Dale remember the town as it was years before, the day they had all gone fishing here? Perhaps he just wanted to be someplace where he'd be left alone. But Jimmy notes with some irony that Dale would have been disappointed if he thought he was going to have a view of the water. Since the long-ago day the Duke family was here a high berm has been constructed around the western edge of the town to prevent flooding and it eliminated any view of the Salton Sea. Part of Bombay Beach can still be found beyond the great mound of earth but it's either under water or half-sunken in mud.

The sign reads *Beach Closed Keep Out* but Jimmy walks through the twenty-foot wide opening in the fortification. Beyond this point lies a parched plane of cracked mud stretching a few hundred yards to the shoreline. Jimmy thinks about the remarkable array of contingencies that have preceded this day. His preacher father who venerated a god in whom Jimmy could no longer believe. His brothers and their individual responses to their father's worldview; how one moved toward politics, one toward jail, both criminals. And how he, too, has joined them in the family business.

He thinks about the education he received, the books he read, the movies he saw and his exposure to the florid culture of modern America. The expectations he brought to work, to marriage, to life. Every experience he's had from his first tentative steps in his parents' house to his drive down here today. Every choice he's ever made, from getting up each morning to getting divorced to trying to do his job in an honest way. All of these things have combined to map the route that leads to now. This is what his teacher said: the past no longer exists, and the future is a chimera. There is only this moment and the act of inhabiting it fully, of being in it, not thinking, considering, reflecting, but simply *being*.

Jimmy doesn't buy all of that. He knows you can't shuck the past any more than you can say your family isn't your family. And the future is going to get here eventually if you just wait a few minutes. But he takes Bodhi Colletti's essential point: that he should try not to be beholden to the past or the future in a way that will distract him from the flock of white seabirds wheeling overhead, wings beating against the deepening blue of the desert sky.

Jimmy fills his lungs with air and he thinks about pride and striving and justice and the temporal nature of all of it and how none of these things contain any intrinsic meaning and how he has been defeated by attachment, whether to his family or his work, or his view of himself, and how he would dedicate whatever time he has left on this planet in the form that is Jimmy Duke to transcending his origins and conditioning and beginning anew, to freeing himself, to becoming a liberated being, one who has thrown off the shackles of the past and who will go forth in a new and openhearted way.

But if it were that easy, he already would have done it. Because no matter how much he concentrates on the exquisite desert nullity of his surroundings and absorbs their barren, fearsome beauty, no matter how much he strains to cast off the chains of the past and avoid prognosticating about the future in order to inhabit the eternal now, or how much he listens to his anger management teacher, or Bodhi Colletti, or spends times meditating over the *Book of Dogs,* no matter how much he does anything, the red rage that consumes him will not abate.

CHAPTER FORTY-SIX

The long-fingered rays of the sinking sun stream through the girl's bedroom. Barefoot in a baggy sweatshirt and shorts, Brittany Duke sits cross-legged on the bed with a laptop. In a few minutes she will eat dinner with her family who will remain oblivious of their chronicler, the gimlet-eyed teenaged observer of peccadilloes and portent who has been filing reports on the Internet. She reads what she has written one last time, changes a word; adjusts a punctuation mark. Here is the text:

http://WWW.DESERT-MACHIAVELLI.COM
11.7 – 5:12 P.M.
The Machiavelli is about to go on a much-needed vacation cruise but before he packs the sunscreen, sandals, and Speedo, some final thoughts about the epic contest we have just witnessed. Mary Swain will be back, of that you can bet your fancy boots. Whenever times are uncertain and people are fearful, there are those who are eager to exploit fear for personal gain. I'm surprised she didn't win on Tuesday. Like General MacArthur, she shall return and she'll look a lot better than he did. As for Randall, I wrote some nasty things about him, a few of which I might, after several vodka martinis, admit I regret. Because he is not that bad. There, I said it. No one is entirely governed by malevolence. And no one is entirely governed by virtue, either. That is the point you Blogheads, you fans of the food fight

American politics have become. We are flawed citizens, fallen creatures, trapped in the muck while reaching ineptly for the heavens. My fellow Americans, we are awful, really. Petty, shortsighted, greedy, foolish, and humorless. But we're beautiful, too: generous, kind, bright, hopeful and amusing. Yes, we occasionally invade the wrong country. But we also invented punk rock. I'll leave you to sort that out. So the next time you rant and rave about how you despise the worthless bastards in Washington, remember this: when you see their faces you are looking in a mirror.

The girl believes it to be a vivid and satisfying end to the story she has been telling. Perhaps one day it will all go in a book. A car door slams and Brittany glances toward the window. Her uncle is headed for the house.

Jimmy stands at the front door while the maid looks him over. A moment later Kendra appears behind her, drawn and wearing sunglasses. Her face is expressionless. The maid silently slips away.

"What are you doing here?" Kendra's voice is a rumor from the back of her throat. Her face remains immobile. Jimmy always made her for a second-rate performer, but now he sees she's not bad. Or maybe she's taking tranquilizers.

"You mean why am I not still locked up?"

She doesn't respond to this. He asks where Randall is and Kendra tells him to wait, he's on the phone. She indicates he should sit in the living room but he tells here he'll stand right here.

When Randall appears his shoulders sag as he moves toward Jimmy. His face is ashen, his eyes red-rimmed. They're so close he can smell Randall's aftershave, spicy with a hint of wintergreen. There is a brief moment where Jimmy sees himself bringing his hands to Randall's throat, pressing his thumbs into his larynx and squeezing until he drops to the floor.

Randall embraces Jimmy, whose arms remain at his sides.

"I was on the way to the airport when I heard the news," Randall says. "Turned around and came home."

"I'm glad you're here," Jimmy says, giving nothing.

"I feel terrible," Randall says. Jimmy lets this hang in the air. He begins to tremble. His chest expands as he closes his eyes and tries to rein himself in. When he opens his eyes again, Randall is saying, "Got him out, got him a job, an apartment." Then he releases Jimmy from his embrace and steps back. He looks at his younger brother as if he expects a pat on the back or a sympathetic nod, but Jimmy gave at the office. "I watched out for him all his life." At this Randall begins to sob, gently at first, but then he allows his feelings free reign and his body shakes with a representation of grief. Jimmy takes this in, waiting for the performance to play out. Whether it is real or manufactured doesn't matter. The mewling, the tear-streaked features, the familiar signposts of mourning must be performed for this audience of one.

Jimmy remains stoical. He feels a slight tremor in his right leg. It's difficult to remain composed while Randall enacts the role of grieving brother. Now Jimmy feels the red tide rising, the slow rage percolating, sending his blood coursing through his veins at a higher and higher velocity. His hands ball into fists. Several moments pass, during which the leaky politician makes a show of composing himself. There is no traffic behind them on the street. The sun is touching the mountains now. Indian summer is over, the heat gone until next year. Randall's sobs slowly abate then cease altogether, and he takes out a handkerchief and blows his nose. Jimmy would like to break that nose, drive the bone into his brother's soft brain. Randall's lips, barely moving, curl into a rueful smile and he says, "I did everything I could."

Jimmy has another urge: he wants to applaud but does not believe his brother would understand the meaning of the gesture. Instead, he gathers his roiling emotions, draws him close and whispers: "You're full of shit."

Randall reacts as if slapped, pretends to be stricken. He takes this moment to mutely express shock, outrage and deep hurt that this is what Jimmy has concluded. The brothers stare into each other eyes, neither breaking the stony gaze.

"At a time of such great sorrow, that's what you're thinking?"

"What I'm thinking is you should be the one laid out in a box."

"Don't turn a family tragedy into something it doesn't need to be," Randall says. His voice is no longer marinated in self-pity. The familial warmth is gone. "It's just us now, just you and me."

"That's right."

Randall's body stiffens when he feels the barrel of the gun in his ribs. This is not what he has been expecting. He opens his mouth but no sound emerges. Is he going to apologize, to unburden himself, to come clean before the avenger, flesh of his own flesh? The thought arises in Jimmy that now would be a good time to talk about what happened with Darleen, to finally get that out of the way, a last piece of business. But the idea quickly vanishes, swept away by wave of emotion equal parts anger and sadness and deep longing for a past he wishes were different, and a brother he wishes was someone else.

Please don't beg me not to do this, Jimmy thinks, because we are beyond everything we have already accomplished or left undone, beyond the parts we have enacted and the selves we thought we knew.

His mouth barely moving, Randall begins to speak in a dry whisper: "I didn't know what Dale was doing. You can accept that or not, I don't care." Randall's body is still. He makes no move to get away from the gun. There is no longer any fear. "I wasn't going to watch you take him down. It would have been wrong."

Breathe in, one, two.

Jimmy feels the crook of his finger on the trigger. An impulse to squeeze remains, but it is not as intense as he had imagined it would be at this moment because now he sees Randall floating into the desert sky and toward a bank of autumn clouds. Jimmy wants to wish him well, to be unburdened. His body relaxes, his heart rate settles, the tremors ease.

Breathe out, three, four.

He walks away from his brother, away from the bright house with the clean lines and the large windows overlooking the mountains. He hears the door close behind him and he is glad. In the gloaming, a breeze kicks up. It is cool on his face. He needs to make some phone calls before heading to the office where he will attempt to sort through this mess. Then, like a ragged refugee in flight from a burning village, he turns for a final look. Beside a drawn curtain and half in shadow he sees Brittany's uninflected young face. They regard each other impassively for a moment in silence and in stillness before Jimmy walks toward his truck. He wonders if she saw what just happened, wonders if she watched with the same non-attachment he is so assiduously slouching toward. He has no idea if the struggle ever ends, or if the end arrives when the struggle ceases.

Acknowledgments

I would like to thank my wife Susan, my first and best reader, for her patience, mindfulness and understanding of Buddhism. I lift a glass to my agents Henry Dunow and Sylvie Rabineau for their acumen and encouragement. And another to my editor Kent Carroll for his deft way with a red pen. Sylvie Mouches, my perspicacious French publisher, was remarkably helpful in bringing this project to fruition. I want to express deep gratitude to my friends Barry Blaustein, John Coles, Rae Dubow, Griffin Dunne, Sam Harper, Lindsey Lee Johnson, Tom Lutz, John Tomko and David Ulin for reading multiple drafts and offering valuable suggestions. My thanks to my brother Drew Greenland for his insights. To Dr. Ed Chung for his medical expertise. To Bruce Bauman and Steve Erickson for steering this novel toward Europa Editions. To Larry David for the great blurb. And finally, to Allegra Greenland and Gabriel Greenland, for all they so effortlessly provide.

About the Author

Seth Greenland is the author of the novels *The Bones* and *Shining City*. His first play, *Jungle Rot*, was the winner of the Kennedy Center/American Express Fund for New American Plays Award, the American Theater Critics Association Award and anthologized in Best American Plays. He was a writer-producer on the Emmy-nominated HBO series *Big Love* and one of the original bloggers on the *Huffington Post*. His work has appeared in the *Los Angeles Times* and the literary journal *Black Clock*. He lives in Los Angeles with his wife and two children.